SEA ✠ INTERLUDES

ROGUE ADVENTURE ON A TRAMP STEAMER CRUISE

By

Andreas Braddan

iUniverse, Inc.
New York   Bloomington

SEA INTERLUDES

Rogue Adventure On A Tramp Steamer Cruise

*This is a work of fiction. All of the characters, names, incidents,
organizations, and dialogue in this novel are either the products
of the author's imagination or are used fictitiously.*

iUniverse books may be ordered through booksellers or by contacting:

iUniverse
1663 Liberty Drive
Bloomington, IN 47403
www.iuniverse.com
1-800-Authors (1-800-288-4677)

ISBN: 978-0-595-52743-4 (pbk)
ISBN: 978-0-595-51619-3 (cloth)
ISBN: 978-0-595-62795-0 (ebk)

Printed in the United States of America

iUniverse rev. date: 12/23/08

WELCOME ABOARD!

Andreas Braddan's *Sea Interludes* is a delightfully fresh approach to a novel. It combines farce and allegory, humorously juxtaposing ideas both serious and sassy. On the surface, it is a collection of picaresque adventures, molded from the multi-cultural encounters of a young American bumming around the world working as a steward on a Norwegian tramp steamer. It is in many ways *The Odyssey* revisited, now set in America's Golden Age, the late 1950s.

With each port of call, with each new culture shock, with each shipboard or onshore relationship, with each unfolding international event, Andreas Braddan shapes not only the characters' involvement with history, but also a timeless human dynamic. In each episode, the steward and his fellow travelers find themselves caught in sometimes shocking, fantastic adventure. And in each, as many a "nauty" mariner knows, they narrowly extract themselves from the siren calls and quicksands of the cultures visited. Like Odysseus, they act boldly and take pleasure at will, only to escape back to the safety and sovereignty of their floating home.

Those of us sensitive to nostalgia do remember that glorious era. Life is sweet indeed, when one is young, and lusty, and carrying a then powerful greenback in one's pocket. Each new encounter, each strange culture, each day of the journey is greeted as a sumptuous feast, rich in flavor and thrilling to every of one's senses. Ah, to be young, and American, and abroad!

But *Sea Interludes* is about more than the madcap awakenings of youth. It is about life. As each new episode relates with the others, a provoking, ageless message evolves. In spite of customs, prides, passions, traditions and idiosyncrasies that give each person and culture individuality, some grander design, some ultimate force carries us all through the expanse of time. Mankind's fanciful exterior trappings and zealous proclamations are swallowed up by some unfathomable wisdom of the universe. The past is but prologue, yet once again.

INTERLUDE:

a. Short farcical entertainment performed between the acts of a medieval mystery or morality play.

b. A short musical piece inserted between the parts of a grander composition.

S.S. TALABOT — LOG ENTRIES

PASSENGER MANIFEST

Stateroom #1: Mr. Bullock S. Brububber
              Mrs. Belle Brububber
              Pedo Grande, Florida, USA

Stateroom #2   Mr. Bill Bob Lovelake
              Mrs. Pammy Sue Lovelake
              Pissant Ranch, Texas, USA

Stateroom #3   Mr. Byron Boost
              Mrs. Shelly Boost
              Great Butte, Montana, USA

Stateroom #4   Mr. Michael P. O'Rouark
              Mrs. Louise O'Rouark
              Mumzerton, Oregon, USA

Stateroom #5   Mr. Anthony Potter-Smythe
              Mrs. Drucilla Potter-Smythe
              Teatlick on Sotley, Surrey, UK

Stateroom #6   Mr. Herman Landgrave
              Mrs. Fiona Landgrave
              Kasekopf, Wisconsin, USA

—SEA INTERLUDES—

Odysseus is smiling somewhere…
You are about to embark on the world cruise of a lifetime.

—MANILA—

"Splat."

The bottle smacked the water bottom down, its fall carrying it below the surface for a few seconds. Then it bobbed up, struggling to keep its frothing neck above the ripples.

Slightly above, motion of winged flight interrupted the light. A flapping, more shadow than shape, strobed its way down out of the sunglare... flapping and fluttering and circling down, until it landed in a belly plop right upon the bobbing miniature life ring... alas, which promptly sank out from under it with a final foamy bloop. Then, flopping about in embarrassed spasms, the mysterious Ariel succumbed as the surface tension of the water overcame the full expanse of its wings.

"Deep six one thirsty butterfly," he muttered without emotion, still quietly lamenting his accidental drop of a half-filled Carlsberg.

He had been standing on the port rail for nearly an hour now, smoking an occasional Maryland, reflecting, and watching the sun settle seductively into Manila Bay. Lights flickered on across the harbour as the city struggled through its evening metamorphosis. He leaned casually on the top line with his hands, with one foot pushing the lower line into a wide taut "v" between the stanchions, fascinated at the small spectacle of impending death before him. The reddening light of approaching dusk played frivolously on tiny

1

ripples that skeeted by, stroked by the soft breezes that now carried the butterfly along the ship.

"What have you done with your life, butterfly? All that flitting around from flower to flower... island to island... and this is how you end up? On a beer bottle in the bay... What've you got to show for it all? That you're fish food after all is said and done?"

The feckless butterfly sputtered and flapped its pathetic little dance a few more times, belly down in the water's salty clutches, but seemingly energized in response to his interest. He stood about 25 feet up, on the deck of the old Norwegian freighter waiting at anchor far out in the vast harbour. But he could see his infelicitous new friend quite clearly, maybe four or so yards out from the ship, as nothing else was near on the bay... Just lengthening sunbeams... sending shimmering shards of light dashing about on random play, highlighting the details of the butterfly. It appeared to be about the size of the palm of his hand, rather large for a butterfly, and it didn't have the same shape or markings of any butterfly he knew. It looked more like a translucent flying wing, the kind of exaggerated technology airplane he used to draw when he was a kid.

"Humh...Strange design for a butterfly, boy. No tail sections, no fancy camouflage. How do you fly?.." he chuckled. "Obviously you need landing practice."

He leaned over the rail, cudding up a sufficient wad. "You may fire when you are ready, Gridley..." he mused, and then spit in the butterfly's direction, falling far short of the mark. Splat. He chewed for a bit, and spit once more. Splat again, nearer, but still way off. "Better put you out of your misery before some grouper snaps you up..." he thought with a hint of sympathy mixed in with his boyish desire to bomb the flopping flying wing with spit.

He scanned the harbour. Nature had its way of creating magical moments, and dusk was one of them. "Things seem to simplify as the sun falls closer to the horizon," he pondered. "May be the different wave lengths... Cuts through the haze of day and lets a person focus on things more profound... like a butterfly floundering in the bay."

He stared out into the blinding mirror before him, shielding his eyes from pain. Shifting light... A swell... Swell again... Then blinding glare.... Swallowed up by a shadowed swell... Shifting... Hypnotic... Always shifting... Always flaring, then dying... Riding the sighs and heaves of some slumbering giant beneath the surface... He startled, as the butterfly seemed to call out to him.

> *"O Freunde, nicht diese Tone!*
>
> *Sondern lasst uns angenehmere anstimmen, und freudenvollere."*

In perfect sympathy, the clarion plea of Beethoven's Ninth Symphony called out into the evening air from the captain's stateroom. He smiled. His trance now broken, he thought back to those primordial hours of shipboard silence... to that day he had noticed the captain storming about in frustrated attempts to utilize his record collection. LP's had become the rage now, throughout the world. The captain too was hooked, obviously having started his collection years before, when the first hi-fidelity RCA's hit the market. His shelves now boasted over two hundred jackets.

But the problem from the start had been how to play them aboard a ship. Few seagoing souls besides this captain had ever entertained such a volume venture into folly. Occasionally when pierside in port, or on the stillest of waters at anchor, the delicately balanced diamond needle would stay in the groove. But with the slightest roll, off track it would go with an expensive nerve grinding SCRAAATTCCCHHHH! Soon after they had left Genoa, he had by chance passed by the captain's stateroom, and had found him cursing and throwing records about, shouting, "*Fi faen i helvete!* How the devil can I play these goddamn records on a goddamn rolling ship!" And ZING! Another 33 would sail out the porthole and into a great sound sump of a sea.

After watching momentarily in horror and dismay, and realizing his own craving for music, he had put his head to task. Within a short time, and after the captain was well into his early cocktail hour, the joyous collaboration of Beethoven and Schiller had come blasting out of the portholes of the stateroom...

"Freude, schoner Gotterfunken, Tochter aus Elysium,

Wir betreten feuer-trunken, Himmlische, dein Heiligtum!

Deine Zauber binden weider, Was die Mode streng geteilt;

Alle Menschen werden Bruder, Wo dein sanfter Flugel weilt."

The captain had appeared breathless and wide-eyed in the hatchway, mouth agape. "How'd you do it? How?"

There, spinning away, stylus happily in the groove, suspended from an overhead beam by four cords like a potted plant, hung the new RCA Victor record player, with its electrical cord airily lofted as well to equalize any offsetting pull it might have on the pendular swings.

"Learned it from Isaac Newton..." he had grinned back.

"Fucking genius..." the captain had mumbled in awe.

"I couldn't just stand and watch you sling the musical heritage of the Western World over the side, one by one..." he had replied.

The captain had beamed with pleasure. "You know, Steward... This could be the beginning of a beautiful friendship..."

The harbour this evening carried with it its own quiet joy, a pleasant relief from the craze of freighters and tankers and tugs and patrol boats vying for position after the big blow two day's before. The wind, rather testy earlier, had subsided to a gentle, steady lean that swung the old freighter off to the Southeast on its anchorage. Calm after a storm indeed makes one glad to be alive. And in dry clothes. And listening to Ludwig.

The sun ricocheted off the water, highlighting the hull below. The old freighter was home for the time being. "In fair shape, considering its hard-use history through the war..." he mused, looking fore and aft. "S.S. Talabot. Tryggvasson Lines. Oslo." Painted in blue across the stern.

"Not a bad idea," he mused to himself. "Every person should be tattooed across the stern at birth... name, date and home port. Much better than passports. Just shout 'Identify yourself!' and hundreds of people would drop their shorts and moon the source. Fat asses lined up on the left, skinny asses on the right. Mama Nature's simple ordering of mankind... No if's, no and's. Just five billion butts."

The shifting light flared up again into his eyes, blinding his view of the cityscape beyond. Only a handful of crew had remained aboard the Talabot. The captain and the twelve passengers were ashore in Manila for the day and evening, seeing the awesome aftermath of the typhoon and getting potted on land for a change.

"Steward's night off..." he muttered to himself as he watched another flip flap from his little friend on the water's surface. " And aboard ship for once..."

Yesterday had been one hell of a day, and his head still ached. He pulled a crumpled pack of Players out of his shirt pocket and flipped one into his lips. "Here's a life raft for you, butterfly..." he mumbled as he lit up, then tossed the match in a smoking arc down toward his floating friend.

The glare made him squint for a moment, shielding him from the present. His thoughts spun back over the past 48 hours.

Yesterday he had had the day off in Manila. He had returned just after dawn, to serve breakfast to the captain and the pampered twelve "First Class" passengers who were "tramping" their way around the world, freighter style, and having quite a trip so far.

The ship was actually hanging around Manila at least one day longer than its usual one day in port, because of the typhoon. Port traffic was all backed up, while the locals repaired the piers and cranes and dragged ships off the mud flats. The Talabot was lucky. She had been 150 miles West when the typhoon hit the islands.

A few earlier images flashed into his thoughts...

Not a fun place to be - in a typhoon - either at sea or in port. He had charted its path with great interest and a good deal of fear, considering his previous experiences with the big winds. The radio reports were lousy in the South China Sea. Serious contact with the owner's office was only possible in port, as the radiotelephone seldom seemed to work. Ever since Malacca, sea faring information had been sketchy, almost non-existent, except for the good old Aussies who chattered constantly on air about everything concerning sea lanes, sex and smugglers. Seems they admire the audacity of the illegal shipping and smuggling throughout the China Sea, but still manage to keep the junks and dhows off their dear old *Terra Australis Incognita.*

A puff of wind sent golden sparkles scurrying off into the West. The sky above tossed about lilac and rose-tinted cotton wads, each fleeting cloud carrying the after moisture of the day before. "Never know a typhoon had been up there..." he pondered, watching the sky. "Nature sure knows how to vacuum up..."

He remembered the playful patter on the short wave earlier. A few scattered Aussies had let the world know more than any other maritime aid or radio service where old Mary was going. That is, if one could understand their accent. "Steer clear of Bloody Miry, mite. She's on a Northwesterly track about 500 due North of Timor. Comin' fast up the Molucca Passage. Nasty liedy, mite. She'll give you what for. Saw two junks swimmin' ass up this morning. No monks in sight. Bie the wie, if you got any beer on board, let us know when and where you're going to flounder. We don't care if you fuck up your ship, mite. Just don't fuck up the beer. Moorsby out. Laughter... crackle... wheeze... whistle..." and the radio faded out into a static haze.

He chuckled at the Aussies' practical nature, as he reflected on how fortunate the Talabot had been. Mary had clobbered the Philippines thirty-six hours ago. While the eye and its big winds had just missed Manila, the big rains had surely found it. He scanned the shoreline once again. A real mess, everywhere flooding, wrecked villages, downed power lines... Reports kept coming in that Mary was the worst in 50 years, no, in 150 years. Shipping caught at sea was devastated. Small ships caught in the harbour were badly bashed about. Two island tankers had sunk outside Boca Grande. Local sails and powerboats lay scattered all over the beach. And all around the islands, fishermen by the score never returned. Coastal villages had been flattened. Fate and Mama Nature had joined in a cruel contract, surprising thousands of simple folk without the faintest clue that Bloody Mary was hell bent on giving them what for.

With each new glare fracturing off the water's surface, images of the events before continued to flash in his thoughts...

It had been a long night. Steadily up past Borneo and Brunei, up past Balabac and Palawan, then the Calamians, up past Mindoro and Lubang, uneasy but undaunted the Talabot had pressed on through the night. The seas were restless but not stormy. Bloody Mary had apparently trekked off to the North after her night of howling island revelry. But a sleepless steward had kept his ear to the radio and his eye on the lightening horizon off East, regardless.

By the time that the Talabot had inched cautiously into Manila Bay, around 0700, up past El Fraile and into the South Channel through Boca Grande, an eerie peace hung over the scene. The sun had come up cheery bright, not in the least bit guilty over its lack of appearance the day before. Clumps of frisky cumulus scrambled across a crisp blue sky, betraying the speedy winds still following in the wake of Mary. Ships and junks from many nations, spotted all across the 30-mile wide harbour, swung in awkward parallel about their moorings. Here and there, small patrol craft made their way from ship to ship, stopping to hail the storm's survivors, take off injured, then venture on to others. Those still afloat and with anchors or moorings intact were the lucky ones. But numerous others lay beached or capsized or battered beyond comprehension, their crews in disarray.

"Welcome to the ultimate officers' mess..." he had punned out loud, surveying the harbour panorama. Then, as the old Talabot maneuvered into its anchorage, he took a deep breath, savoring the pungent tropical air, and exhaling with relief at their being intact.

The captain, who had been lounging in his bridge chair, had overheard, and had answered, "Look about you, Steward. You could have stayed at home and watched travelogues... But oh, no...You have to go sailing off into the great unknown..."

7

"Me? Live a vicarious life? TV can't compare with the real thing, Captain... It leaves out the smells."

Off on the shoreline some half-mile away, the storm's wrath still visibly fresh, both humans and animals had begun digging out of their soggy hovels and mucking about in the scatter and mess, looking for possessions and anything to eat.

He looked up to the clearing sky above, a sharp contrast to the littered shore. Seagulls joyously soared the winds and dropped hungrily to the wave tops. "I always wondered what happened to the birds..." he had said to the captain. "How do they survive such a storm?"

"They are much smarter mariners than we are," the captain had replied. "They know when a blow is coming, they feel the low pressure in their tail feathers, and they fly across the wind, which carries them around the back of the storm on the weak side. They know there is no place to hide, so they fly like sons of bitches out of its way. We should be so smart... But no, the owners tell us to stick to our schedule and hold our course. It is all about luck. Look at these poor bastards. This is what happens! *Faen i vold!* This mess is their luck... It is all fish shit!"

"It's a wonder anything's still alive after..." he had added.

"I can assure you, Steward... There is something always very much alive after the storm..." the captain had cut him off, while surveying the destruction around them. "That is the profound joy of it all..."

"Sir?"

"The sea!... The sea is still very much alive!"

It had been one of Einar Eiriksson's more sober and lucid moments. When he cared to reveal it, he had real depth and wisdom for a 43-year old alcoholic sea captain, his once orange hair and beard now sun bleached and wizened, making him look older than Ahab. Throughout the voyage so far, only for about three hours a day had the captain's reasonings actually been fathomable. The rest of the time he floated in his own merry fog of OH radicals, with his deeper thoughts well hidden.

The steward thought about this amazing hulk of a Viking, and smiled to himself.

Eiriksson's daily schedule was to rise at noon, or rather this giant Viking with ashen skin and snow white hair and shaggy beard would stagger forth, holding his temples, shielding red bulging eyes from the glare of day, his posture revealing the afterrath of excessive pillage and spoil the night before. Further plunder out of question for the moment, a wobbly Eiriksson would carefully pace himself into the ship's galley, grabbing the doorways and cutting counter for stability. Once there he would gulp down a half dozen pieces of chilled raw herring set out for him by the trusty steward from his prized personal kegs, which lay faithfully iced under lock and key in the cold locker. Then, after a slow uncertain series of ruminations followed by a peptic gag, he would pour down a tumbler of *akvavit* that had been kept on ice, near to freezing. Shudder... and shudder again. The water of life. And out of yesterday's ashes the miracle would repeat itself... A strange warming glow would come over him, starting at his heart and working its way visibly outward to his extremities. His eyes would retract into their sockets, his ears would regain a fleshy pink, and beneath a relieved sigh the hint of a smile would pry its way out through the craggy stubble. While nowhere to be found in the *St. James Bible* as a means of resurrection, this pagan ritual steadied the captain's course, at least for the next four hour watch, day after day after day. A Viking's miracle elixir... raw herring and a good slug of *akvavit*.

Each morning was pure Wagnerian theater. All eyes were fixed as each new ingestion of raw protein coursed through and reconstituted his system... Until... Once again, transfiguration would occur! Once again, joyous relief would sweep through the galley, as the great Norse deity made mortal would reenter the lesser world of the Walsungs, working there in Valhalla aft.

Finally, after a few deep belches punctuated by a fart, Eiriksson would ask where the ship was, its course and speed, and the time. After it all seemed to register, off he would go to his cabin where he would sit his morning constitutional for half an hour, mumbling and cursing (praying would have phrased such litany more graciously). Then he would shower and shave around his beard, and, amazingly fresh and alert, he would appear again from his lofty lair.

Ceremoniously about 1300 Eiricsson would enter the dining room where the twelve passengers were just finishing up their luncheon smorgasbord. After appropriate greetings to all, he would select his usual sampling of rich brown *gjeit ost*, boiled shrimp and iced caviar, so artfully prepared by the ever vigilant steward, poke at it in a feigned attempt to eat with pleasure, and then in a hearty voice encourage all his passengers to join him in an after luncheon toast of French champagne dedicated to whatever subject seemed to have been well hashed out by the time feasting was finished.

The passengers clearly loved him. To say that Eiriksson was imposing was gross understatement. He was overwhelming. Einar Eiriksson was a huge 6 foot 6 inches and 270 pounds, certainly oversized for a Norwegian, and he exuded a commanding air that just dazzled his retinue of retired American and British couples whose only mistake so far in life was, in a fit of romantic whimsy and thirst for adventure, to have opted for a world cruise, not on a luxury liner, but on a tramp steamer.

The captain's laugh was infectious - a bellowing base Ho Ho Har Har!! - and he used it frequently, usually after telling his captive *innocenti* one of his many off-color jokes. He in fact truly liked people, respected the sea, and loved any and all kinds of alcohol. He prided himself a fair man, taking great care to ridicule all races and ethnic groups equally. Yet in spite of his powerful personality, he was quite diplomatic, holding his true views as closely guarded secrets. Seldom to any of the passengers did he ever come to profess profound opinions on the most ardently debated subjects of politics, religion or marriage beyond concluding, "Haahhh! Fishshit! It is all fishshit!! That is why I go to sea!"

As consummate foil in the daily heated discussions of touchy topics, Eiriksson would take it upon himself to confound any and all proponents of reason, then fall into an arm-waving, coughing, roaring fit of laughter, only to buy everyone another drink out of the captain's private stock. He would then drink on through the afternoon with gusto, on through the cocktail hour, through dinner, and far on into the night.

Early on, it was quite obvious that no one aboard, including crew, could keep up in the captain's drinking marathon. Seldom at dinner were more than nine of the twelve passengers present. The more or less fortunate others the captain had corralled after lunch were face down, either in their bunks or in the head. Capacity for alcohol, it seemed, was a prerequisite for command in the Norwegian merchant marine.

And somehow, after all the initial grousing was said and done, after all the personal inconveniences and the daily overindulgences, the passengers themselves went through their own metamorphosis. The pressures and problems of their recent pasts faded back into the horizon as the endless routine of a steamer cruise, in slow circumnavigation of the earth, became their universe. Increasingly they came to realize they were the chosen ones. At this point in their lives, they had somehow been afforded the privileged, lofty perspective of "first class" travel. The rest of the world was struggling with life, not lounging imperiously in a cane deck chair with drink in hand. The rest of the world therefore could be damned and dissected with impunity. Religious, cultural and political folly became topics of the day, fueled by each new port of call. Solutions to an infinite number of world problems were found deep within each new drink. Organized Labor was unanimously seen as the core of everything wrong. Non-Caucasians were, by universal agreement, surly underclass, lacking in proper respect, and increasingly ungovernable. Lesser ethnic groups were castigated and put into proper place. Anglo-American culture was judged infinitely more advanced, and deservedly ruled the globe. Ultimately, in their isolation at sea, all passengers came to appreciate the old S.S. Talabot as the favored ark of what remained of civilized mankind.

In point of fact, freighterboard life was not all that bad. During the long day hours, novels were read by the shelfful. Card games flourished. During mealtimes, lobster and caviar and shrimp were consumed by the barrel, but only after the cook and steward had first fingersnacked on the choicest morsels. A sumptuous smorgasbord appeared at breakfast, lunch and dinner, only to be melded together with all one could eat and drink in between. On any real or invented occasion, French champagne, Chivas and V.S.O.P. flowed in abundance. For playtime hours, an above deck, circular swimming pool, about 12 feet wide, served as a communal cool tub during the heat of the day. Drinks miraculously appeared to those hanging on to its canvas sides. Secret skinnydips after dark entertained those more frolicsome. Yes, even long forgotten sexplay re-emerged in timeworn marriages. Ahhh, yes...life aboard a Norwegian freighter was near paradise - for about three days. But, then... alas...any initial bliss was swallowed up by unrelenting tedium, interrupted only by wild drinking fests fostered by the captain's sense of duty and personal love of booze.

The steward stood alone for the moment at the rail, savoring the solitude. The night air was fresh and relaxing. The ship swung slowly on its anchor, sung to by the constant murrrrr of untaxed motors and gyros blending with Beethoven.

The shifting glare kept up its strange hypnotic effect. He thought more about the past few days and weeks. "Strange..." he mused to himself. "There's no accounting for time at sea. Time loses all dimension... Now becomes then... Today, yesterday..."

The swells came in a series, each one lifting the ship ever so subtly, altering the glare and shadows below. Shifting... then shimmering... then shifting again... The swells kept coming, softly but with certainty, in from the South.

"Some days fly by...some drag on..." he spoke to the swells. "Day after day, nothing happens at sea, but day after day, everything seems to happen... all at once... then not at all..."

His thoughts danced amidst the glares and shadows, once again back into the past.

The image of a cool, bright spring day in Genoa harbour flashed into his mind, the first time he had seen the ship. By pure chance he had signed on board. The Talabot had been alongside the wharf, offloading. And one crew member short. He had considered himself lucky to find cheap passage to the Orient.

"Bumming around the world," he had hailed up to the captain from the wharf. "Need any hands? I work cheap. Just food."

"We need a steward," Eiriksson had yelled back. "Want the job? Come on aboard," Eiriksson had confirmed after giving him a visual once over. But after inspecting his American passport with occupation as Lieutenant, U. S. Navy, the captain had given him a knowing smile, and somehow impressed him into broader duties without saying a word.

Somehow? He thought more on it. Somehow? The first mate was usually drunk in his bunk, or somebody's bunk. Thereafter, uneven links of less able bodied seamen followed down the chain of command - young and old men, all sun-bleached, bored out of their minds, all of them drinking heavily to pass the time and dull the screaming monotony of life at sea. Some were still able to stand their duties on deck and at the helm, but never sober. The captain himself set the standards for the crew. Seldom was he on the bridge, and rarely ever did he plot the position or direct the course of the ship. Rather, he played and sang and drank and laughed with the passengers, leaving control of the Talabot to subordinates. Or more correctly, to any subordinates still functioning. Which now fell down through this wobbly chain of command... to the ship's steward? Led by the hand of providence that first day to the bridge, the steward had discovered no one manning the helm. Thereafter, and for the remainder of the transit, it was quite apparent that, on this cruise, he was unlikely to get much sleep.

And so it came to pass that, aboard the Talabot, it fell to the vigilance of the steward to insure the safety of the steamship... through the Strait of Messina, with traffic as schizophrenic as the streets of Rome... or through that gash in the desert, the Suez Canal, where one could only lock the rudder amidships and pray to Mecca that the local stevedores would not steal the compass...

or down through the Strait of Malacca swarming with an armada of smugglers' craft as far as one could see. Yes, it fell to the lowly steward to guide the Talabot in and out of port, to plot her bearings, to chart her course, to keep her out of ever-present harm's way.

Sophisticated Loran positioning? Radar eyes? The Talabot had these. So why? Because the steward had seen from his first day aboard that the rest of the crew was chronically blitzed, lessening any ability to guide the ship in critical situations. Out at sea, with miles of ocean, where one seldom sees another ship, he could usually sleep. Not much traffic trouble far out at sea. But when nearing port, or navigating channels and straits, hundreds of other ships, thousands of reefs and hazards by the score would appear, with potential to sink a ship in seconds. At these times, the steward had assumed unauthorized bridge command. He simply wanted to stay alive.

So once again, there had been the steward, on the bridge that night, assuming without orders the control of the ship. The crewmembers were happily all sleeping and virtually incapable of making trouble, including, he had thought, the captain. But some sense of a new presence had caused the steward to look up from his calculations across the nightlight gloom in the charthouse, and there he was. Silent. Steely-eyed. Watching. Listening. And, of all things... surprisingly sober.

Eiriksson had spoken quietly. "What have you heard?"

The steward had straightened up from the chart and strained into gloom to find the captain's eyes. "Probably she will miss us. Seems to be going straight at Manila. Winds 145. Should hit about 1700 and then head off to Northwest. E.T.A. Manila is dawn the next day."

The captain had passed by the helm, glancing at the compass course, then stepped out of the bridge house to the starboard wing, and stared at the eastern horizon. The sky was clear and the moon almost full... It had been a calm night, with not even the smallest hint of an impending typhoon some 500 miles off to the Southeast.

Like any one of a myriad of beautiful evenings at sea, with God relaxed in his bunk and the world at peace.

After a few moments, without looking back, Eiriksson had mumbled something like "Thank you, Steward." And then he was gone as silently and quickly as he had appeared.

———————————

The butterfly gave a shiver and flapped its wings a few beats, causing golden sparkles around it. The steward snapped back from his reflections and noted his little waterbound friend. "You still alive?" he pondered as the butterfly drifted slowly downwind along the side of the ship. "How'd you make it through Mary's fury?"

As if in response, the butterfly sort of shrugged its shoulders and, with a certain lack of flair, sunk below the surface about an inch. "Go with Neptune, little friend..." he whispered sadly, and once again he spit over the side.

Yet something was not right. He squinted into the scattering shards of sunlight to see his target better. It wasn't sinking. It was moving about under the water. It was... swimming.

The butterfly was swimming about, in jerking, flapping movements, like a ray. It circled around in a 10 foot area, diving down to about a foot, and then working its way back to just under the surface of the water, only to dive down again. It was swimming, not drowning.

"Incredible..." he said to himself, fascinated. "You're the strangest butterfly I ever saw, boy. Or are you just taking a few laps before going down for the third time?" The butterfly amazingly seemed none the worse for its predicament, and paddled around more vigorously. It was sort of a spasmed flapstroke, about one tenth the speed of the airborne version it used just before it had made its unfortunate crash landing in the bay. He tried to mimic the stroke with his shoulders, flapping his elbows as wings.

"You shouldn't drink gin," a voice called down from the bridge.

"What?" he looked up to see who spoke.

"Gin. It affects the nerve endings. Makes people twitch and flap about the day after." Bjarni Herjolfsson, the first mate, smiled as he leaned his forearms on the metal bulwark that shielded the flying wing on the side of the bridge. He needed a shave, but otherwise he looked well pressed and comfortable in khaki shorts and summer white uniform shirt. He always wore leather sandals with his standard uniform, which gave him the look more of a resort guest rather than the second most senior officer. He had a shock of coarse yellow hair that stood two inches straight up, and a healthy tan that added balance to his close-cropped, dirty yellow goatee. All this was accented by the soft brown eyes of a stag deer that belied his Norwegian heritage.

"You might be right," the steward added, "If I liked gin. But you drank it all."

He smiled at the mate, partially in jest and partly in sympathy, as he considered what a steady diet of gin could do to a man. The first mate was about 45 and a husky 5 foot 7, with a devilish personality, one who liked to make pranks on passengers and crew alike, when he was sober enough. He promoted himself as the serious shipboard lover, saving forgotten spouses from pubic atrophy. He tried to create the impression that he was frequently invited into the cabins of sex-starved wives for a *cinc-a-sept*, while their husbands were doing liquid battle with the captain. But the real truth, as the steward was best able to account for the first mate's time and capacity for self-destruction, was that he drank almost as much as the captain but was cycled forward about four hours, so that he awoke about 0500 and passed out at about 1900 in the evening, just as the wives were dressing for dinner and the captain was roaring into full gear. Whether Bjarni ever actually got any swooning dowager in a bliss grip before passing out, was still undocumented.

"Look out there, Bjarni..." The steward pointed to the water five or so yards out from where he was standing. "See that thing swimming? Near the surface?" He looked back up at the mate, who casually moved his eyes over to the target area. He seemed reasonably sober this evening, even though nearing his bunktime.

"It's a mermaid," Bjarni stated without emotion.

"No, really. There. About five yards out from me. See that butterfly swimming?"

"It's the gin. We all see things sometimes," Bjarni muttered.

"Right there." He hocked up some spit and fired a salvo that landed almost smack on top of the little submersible. "What do you see?"

"Spit..." Bjarni Herolfsson scoffed and went into the charthouse.

The steward cursed the first mate under his breath, and looked back at the ringlets emanating from his frothy missal. "Damned if I didn't bomb it good, though..." he thought. But there it was, whatever it was, still swimming around a few inches under the surface, oblivious to his aerial attack.

He shifted his gaze off to the North, where the city's lights were popping on amidst the blue wash of impending dusk. Visual sirens began hawking their wares, "Come to me... Come to me..." Silent voices... calling in neon's of anxious ambers and sugary pinks and bilious greens... singing of unknown certainties... of sensual pleasures... of exploitation... Lights that promised excitement and adventure... a slowly expanding, slowly heating dance of more and more neon, drawing one's attention to the sensuous pockets of nightlife activity in Manila.

But oddly, what finally held the steward's eyes was apart, high up on a hill above the artificial neon glow unfolding over the city. One white light stood bright and clear, a watchful counterpoint to the pulsing, confusing aura below that signaled of humanity.

The sun was making its final statement of the day now, firing shafts of brilliance into lingering fluffs, painting their wispy outer-reaches with blues and corals. The water across the bay had flattened in the quieting evening, assuming playful plains of gold and crimson and black, fracturing and splintering into tiny explosions of sundust as the swells rose and fell to equilibrium. Sunset... In this mystical moment, a mystical thing happened.

The butterfly/ray floated to the surface of the water. There it rested a few seconds, only to shed its watery mantle and burst forth, in a shower of shimmering droplets, flapping in stuttered spasms out of the clutches of the bay and into the air.

"Now I believe it's the gin," said the steward to himself. "It flies again. What kind of beastie are ye? From air to surface to sea to air again. A snorkling butterfly?.. A flying stingray?.. A trifibian?.." He watched as the butterfly flapped and flitted about in the air, crisscrossing his line of vision to a sun of molten steel, casting haunting shadows on the shimmering sea below it, then moving out towards Manila's glow across the bay.

"Bjarni..." he shouted toward the bridge. "Hey, Bjarni? Did you see him? Right out there. He took off again! Right out of the water. He changed back into a butterfly."

"Who did?" a sleepy voice drifted out of the charthouse.

"Proteus..." he replied out to the sea.

"Flipped."

"That best describes it", he thought. Everywhere he looked, the world was flipped. Trees upside down. Houses upside down. Cars upside down. Signs dangling upside down. Utility wires on the ground, shattered poles lofting their splintered bases in the air. Everything inanimate seemed now to be standing, lying, or probing out in a direction 180 degrees opposite to its normal structural bearing. Typhoon Mary had flipped Manila upside down.

As he motored closer to shore on the harbour patrol launch he had hailed from the ship, the steward started to sense the awesome power of the storm that had roared through Manila the previous evening. Any structure not built of steel and concrete was badly battered, if not torn open. Water was everywhere. Behind him was the bay - and as far as he could see inland past the shore were puddles and ponds and pools of water left by the angry sea and skies. And mud. Everywhere mud.

As he drew closer, he started to count people. There they were, many of them, digging out, bailing out, emptying out their belongings. A surprising sense of calm prevailed in their efforts.

No screams, no frantic crowds, no blinking emergency lights. Just a strange relief, a silent joy. Here and there tired wet human beings picked slowly through the mud and puddles, awed by their loss of property yet heartened by their good fortune of being alive. Even an encouraging sun in a crisp sky smiled down between scattered cumulus, happy to help in the drying out as well.

The motor launch crunched its starboard side against the pier, and a skinny Philippino boy about 15 leapt over with the bowline. He wore a grime-streaked T-shirt and black shorts and high top Keds. He struggled with the pull of the launch against the pier, and failed to keep it from splintering more than a few timbers as it lurched up and down in the choppy bay swells. The skipper, a stocky Philippino with a collared, short sleeved white shirt with oversized epaulets, cursed profusely at the boy in some local dialect of Tagalog, but every third word sounded something like "fucking" with a island accent, an affectation surely to show that he was a seasoned sailor, and to hide the fact that he didn't bring the launch alongside the pier on its lee side. After noting a shrug from the boy followed by an impassioned plea with his eyes, the steward timed a three-foot leap to the pier and landed like a feather, as the sea swell sent the launch in the opposite direction. The skipper, jockeying gear and throttle while watching his landing, resumed his invective a full tone higher. Seasoned sailor indeed.

The boy made a half-hearted push on the bow, then scampered aboard, only to watch more splintering on the side of the pier. Amidst loud curses and gunning the engine and a frantic shifting of gears, the skipper succeeded in bringing the bow into the waves and sputtered off in a cloud of blue-gray smoke, back to his appointed rounds. Disregard of the steward's final wave indicated he had been more than happy to risk his craft for this blue eyes's pleasure.

The steward looked around to get his bearings. "Manila..." he spoke to himself. "Or what's still above water."

Spying a few tall buildings that had been indicated on his charts of the harbour, the steward started in down the pier to the loading yards and gates beyond, intent on exploring the city or seeing if he could help after the storm. The captain had given him the day off from his duties, as the Talabot had been instructed to stay at anchorage until the harbour got itself functioning again. The passengers were either sick from weathering the sea swells following the typhoon on the way in to Manila, or were passionately balking against coming ashore in the face of certain typhoid epidemics, rape and pillaging. After all, where could they possibly eat? While the captain surely felt like living up to his traditions a little spoil and pillaging, his sense of duty to the ship's owners and the passengers prevailed. So the steward was ordered to take the day ashore, scout the area, and report back by dinnertime on what creature comforts still survived.

One of those amazing balances of nature is that wherever there is a wayfarer, there will be a highwayman. In modern symbiosis, wherever there is a tourist, there will be a guide, intent on siphoning off a few of the tourist's dollars as a commission for fulfilling pleasures of the day. Even after the worst typhoon in recent history. And there he was. Standing on his seat in his Jeepney, a tiny, wiry Philippino who looked to be in his mid-twenties, waving his hands as the steward strode inland down the pier. "Hey! Hey, buddy! You need a ride? You want to see Manila? You want a virgin?" A case study of survival of the fittest, his was the first, and only, Jeepney at the gate. Today was to be good business.

The steward smiled at the beaming Philippino, who was sporting a clean, open neck shirt emblazoned with wild oranges and yellow bananas and pineapples and passion fruit, blended around the subtle greeting 'Aloha'. "Not your quintessential pressed-white, pleated-front Luzono," the steward noted to himself.

"Hello. *Hola.* My name is Riccardito Cebuano. Call me Ricky. I speak English, German, French, and Spanish," shouted the eager Philippino, eyeing the young man approaching in open collared white shirt and khaki shorts. "What are you? *Was sind sie?*"

"Just a simple steward," he shouted back, "Washed ashore in search of garlic and rice."

The Philippino looked heartsick. The one survivor of the world's biggest typhoon, and he has to be a poor slob of a ship's steward. He hurriedly scanned the bay for other launch movement toward the pier, and after finding none, looked back at the steward who was approaching quite near now. Then, sizing up the lump in the steward's shirt pocket, and still standing on the seat of his dented, fanciful, open-top Jeepney, he broke into a big, toothy smile, and said, "Garlic and rice it is. I have a cousin who makes the best."

Ricky was a tour guide. Or Jeepney driver. Or commissioned salesman. Or pimp. Certainly he was an entrepreneur of the first order. Life was to him a daily succession of marks, pleading to be exploited and relieved of their burdensome cash. Riccardito Cebuano prided himself as Manila's finest Jeepney driver.

Yet there was an instant rapport between the two, starting with garlic and rice. Ricky sensed the steward probably cared little about eating - if he was a typical steward he had already gorged himself on the finest delicacies aboard ship. Yet here was this young blue-eyes with a tall, healthy physique and a ready grin, quipping about garlic and rice. Strange humor, these foreigners. Making jokes about food. Garlic to a Phillipino, to much of the world for that matter, is the zest of life, a gift from the gods. But Ricky laughed anyway, for here was the last surviving sucker in the universe, waiting for his grand tour of the city. Still, there was more to this young stranger than met the eyes. Ricky invited him into the Jeepney with a dramatic wave of his hand.

"I know where they serve <u>virgin</u> garlic and rice," he laughed. "That interest you?"

"Your cousin's place?" the steward retorted, as he swung into the right front seat along side the Jeepney driver, knees up to his chin.

The WWII surplus jeep was typical Jeepney - reconditioned with a fringed surrey bar overhead, but with the canvas roof missing. The Jeepney was custom-painted in a wild fantasy of reds and yellows and greens and turquoise and corals and pinks, all splashed together in some kind of palm trees and flowers motif. Two individual front seats were newer and covered with plush purple fabric, obviously expropriated from some later model car, and somehow stuffed functionally in to the front.

He noted that the back seat was loaded with a variety of gas cans, bottles, and a case of Heineken's. "You buying or selling?" the steward asked casually.

"Some of both, wherever I can," chirped Ricky. "It is a land of opportunity. I learned that in Hawaii. Want a cold beer? Just one dollar."

"I see Harry Truman sold you his last shirt," quipped the steward as he grabbed a bottle and popped the cap on a door handle.

Oh, Ho ho ho he he," laughed Ricky. "I knew you were American, not European. You walked different."

"How's that?" he mumbled through his first swill of the day.

"Like a *vaquero*. You Americans are all bowlegged."

The steward pondered this remark, thinking that his legs were rather long and straight. But then he put this remark in perspective, as he noted that Ricky, like all Philippinos, looked like the evolutionary link between man and spider monkey. Beauty, and flaw, are in the eyes of the biased beholder.

"What'll it be, Cowboy?" Ricky urged. "Want to see what was once Manila?"

"Exactly that," the steward replied. "Show me the sights, Little Richard. Hit the afternoon bars, point out the evening hot spots, but get me to a virgin. Fast."

Ricky laughed and nodded vigorously. "O.K. But it is not going to be easy. The roads are all blocked and flooded. I don't think I can get down to the center of town at all."

The steward shifted into a more serious tack. "How are your people? Lots of injuries? I've got the afternoon to spend here. Anything I can do to help?"

"Probably not," Ricky replied. "Most of what I've seen is flooding and building damage. I've seen very few rescue trucks or military. I guess they can't get around or the people got through it fairly well. Radio station is out, so I only know what I see."

"Well, let's take a ride. You have a cowboy on your hands for the rest of the day," nodded the steward as he sat back and smiled.

Being somewhat experienced in the likes of Ricky, he added, "How much for the trip? Up to 6 in the evening."

Ricky started to posture himself for a serious negotiation, but the cowboy pre-empted him by popping open another Heineken and shoving it at Ricky. "You need a day off, Rick. Let's go see this mess called Manila. There may be some virgins still out there in need of our help." He put one foot up on the dashboard, and leaned back, quite at home.

"O.K., *Vaquero*," confirmed Ricky. "You buy the drinks and the ride is free. Deal?"

"Deal." They both took long swigs on their bottles, and Ricky snapped the Jeepney into first and roared out through the pier gates, intentionally imparting a small lake of stagnated water onto the guard who dozed by his hut.

Very soon it became quite clear that they were not going to be able to roar very far at all. The Jeepney abruptly came to a halt as it smacked into a deep puddle in the middle of the road, a mere 50 yards outside the gate. Flooding and mud seemed everywhere in sight. Standing up in the seat like Magellenes himself, the steward scanned the horizon for dry land, pointed dramatically off to the West and high ground, and lofted his beer bottle to the sky. "In search of the sacred virgins!" he bellowed. Then he bounced unceremoniously off the windscreen and fell back into the Jeepney as Rick floored it in reverse to exit the flooded street.

For about a half hour, they zigged through Manila, dodged fallen poles and trees, skirted flooded streets, changed directions in a maze of water-clogged wreckage and confusion. But people on the street seemed all right. They were engaged in digging out, and hanging out their belongings on ropes and wires and boards to dry in the well-appreciated sunlight. The locals were actually happy to see such occasional signs of traffic splashing through their moats of isolation. They waved and smiled as the Jeepney passed by, particularly the children, at the tall, blond blue-eye foreigner hanging on along side the wiry little driver. And they broke into curls of laughter when the dubious duo would return shortly from a flooded dead end, with the cowboy standing, holding on to the surrey frame, dramatically pointing the new course in the reverse direction with his bottle of Heineken. Manila, or certainly its resilient people, had somehow survived typhoon Mary.

"I know this one place in the hills, up in Elysio, if we can get to it," Ricky said as he downstripped the gears into first to plow through a pond. "Only for local rich guys. No foreigners ever get taken there. Prima ladies. Not the typical nightclub. Really first class. All virgins." He looked over with a smile of anticipation.

"Onward, coxswain, to the hidden daughters of Elysio!" pointed the steward dramatically with his bottle.

They wove their way for another ten minutes through dead ends and downed wires to a point where Ricky pulled the Jeepney up to a large lake of muddy water and stopped. "It's out there, about three blocks into this mess. See that sign on the roof? I can't get us any closer," he lamented with a disappointed gaze into the distance.

"Keep the faith," said the steward. Then he stood up on the seat and spied out into the fresh brown lake, about two hundred yards away, where children were laughing and playing on some section of a broken utility pole. They straddled it like floating log and paddled with their hands and a couple of boards. One held up a shirt for a sail. Their craft was slow but sturdy, and its progress along the street punctuated with splashes and peals of laughter.

"Hello! Ahoy! Hey kids!" he called across the pond. "Come on over here. Paddle over here." A flurry of strokes and splashes turned the jolly craft in their direction, and ever so slowly it churned its way over to the Jeepney.

The children ranged from about 10 down to 5, both boys and girls. They all had huge grins on their faces as they paddled forth, proud of newly acquired nautical skills. Flushed with the thrill of accomplishment, they edged the log up to the edge of the pond right by the Jeepney.

"Want ride?" hailed an older lad in the bow. "Only one dollar."

Centuries of exploitation by first the Spanish and then the Americans had left its mark, even on the young at heart.

"Entrepreneurship runs in the blood," thought the steward. "What is your name?" he called.

"Juan Sebastian d'Elcano, Senior," saluted the oldest boy.

"Can you take us to the end of this great sea, *Almirante?*" the steward called.

"Oh yes, Sir. For two dollars," replied the boy quite seriously.

"You have a deal," he hailed back, and he and Ricky waded out to the waiting paddleboat and climbed aboard, straddling the log and grabbing a piece of board that floated nearby.

"Take us to Paradise!" Ricky laughed, and pointed down the flooded street. The children seemed to know exactly where this destination was located, and in a flurry of arms and boards, churned off in its direction.

The water level seemed to be about 5 to 7 feet deep in most places, judging by the height of poles and car roofs and houses that dotted above their *lago nuevo*. Perfect calm lay over the lake, except for the ripples and swirls left by the children's paddling. An ideal day for a cruise. The water seemed rather clear, even though it was surely going to get polluted in time by local refuse and mud. But for the time being, after the storm, in the bright sunshine and warm, pleasant weather, the water-swollen street made a perfect playground for the young. The children were so happy that their faces all looked the same - all laughing teeth and sparkling brown eyes.

A strange throbbing floated on the air, something almost sensed rather than heard, amidst the wail of an occasional siren in the distance. A few hundred yards along their merry trip, Ricky pointed to a large white stucco building with elaborately barred windows, rising like an island out of the sea. A wide bulb-studded sign with a crooked letter P capped a tiled roof. *CLUB PARAISO* appeared to be in a world all by itself, standing proudly on a slight rise, but still half submerged in water. The throbbing grew increasingly palpable, now even varying in its tone. The steward and Ricky watched and strained their ears for signs of life. The pulsing sound transformed to their surprise into music, pounding its way out of the open front door that was framed in a grand, pillared archway, interlaced with red, purple and orange Bougainvillea.

"Rock and Roll!" cheered Ricky, taking up the beat to urge the excited miniature crew on to its destination.

The boy at the stern, a richly tanned nine-year old named Enrique de Molucca, turned the craft to starboard and took a beeline right at the front arch. "All ahead full," hailed the steward.

And with powerful strokes stoked by the beat of the music, the good ship utility pole steamed right through the arch, passed the double front doors without a scratch, churned across a large foyer and right into a spacious room where it ran smack into the shiny pier of wood just above the water level - a long mahogany bar.

The upbeat sounds of Chuck Berry hammered their ears...

> *"Well Ah looked at mah watch an' it wuz 10:05,*
>
> *Man, Ah didn't know if Ah wuz dead or alive..."*

Squeals of laughter and cheers cut their way above the booming from a colorful, bubbling-light, round-top Wurlitzer perched high and dry on top of the bar:

> *"Reelin' an' a rockin'...*
>
> *We wuz reelin' an' a rockin'...*
>
> *Rollin' 'til the break of dawn!..."*

Just inches above the water that lapped at its feet, an extension cord giving it life draped up to the roof rafters, then off to the muffled chug of a diesel generator somewhere out back.

Behind the bar was a Philippino teenager about 18, standing waist deep in water and howling with laughter. "Our best customers!" he bellowed. "Welcome to *Paraiso!*"

Across the room near the windows, with the sun beaming in through the barred windows like mottled spotlights, the steward noticed what at first looked like a three-dimensional Cézanne still life. Displayed like colorful ripe spices over chairs and pillows carefully stacked on top of tables, all just above the water level, lounged six stunning young women. They all seemed in their late teens or early twenties, and were dressed in a variety of clothing from shorts to lounging saris to silk pajamas to T-shirts. Their origins seemed varied, but they appeared to be islanders, not Malay or Indochine. These daughters of paradise somehow had remained high and dry, and amazingly still fragrantly decorated with their finest make-up and jewelry. Initial looks of shock and surprise broke into beams of warmth and compassion for the children crew, and joyous cheers and smiles for the steward and Ricky.

An assertive, happy faced little nymph with a Sampaguita flower behind her ear, dressed in a simple white T-shirt and red sarong, jumped down into the inland sea up to her waist, squealing as she hit the chill of the water, and came skipping her way over to the log and tried to climb aboard. It almost tipped, and amid cries of fear and joy, she slipped off and under the water. Then, she broke the surface with a splashy leap and landed on her back, only to float, sputtering and laughing, hair drawn back like a sleek pelt to drain, to the cheers and chantey of underage sailors.

The steward surveyed the water near the bar, and with an equally dramatic move, swung his legs over and off the log, and on to a submerged bar stool, where he rose like some figure of heroic importance, almost walking on water.

Everybody cheered, and the steward waved his arms and shouted above the din, "To all you fortunate denizens of this island Paradise... Drinks are on me! Barman, rum for my mates! Tonight we sail!"

With that, all the girls jumped down into the water and sloshed and giggled their way over to the child-laden log and music bar. The barman beamed his biggest smile yet and reached down into the depths of the water under the bar, and with his neck strained to keep his chin above the waves, started coming up with whiskey bottles in both hands, spiriting more cheering.

Someone turned up the juke box even louder, and as Bill Haley took over the party, two of the girls pulled Ricky off the log and the three started to dance, high waist deep in the water...

"When chimes ring five, six and seven...

27

> *We'll be right in seventh heaven...*
>
> *We're gonna rock around the clock tonight,*
>
> *We're gonna rock rock rock 'till broad daylight,*
>
> *We're gonna rock, gonna rock, around the clock tonight!"*

One of the girls found a small refrigerator, disconnected and temporarily set on a high ledge against the wall behind the bar, and opened it to find still frosty beers and bottles of soft drinks. More cheers filled the air, particularly from the admiral and his crew.

Two laughing naiads sided up to the steward and pulled him down on the bar stool, so he sat chest high in the water. Everybody was dancing and singing and talking all at once, in seemingly a dozen different dialects. Water fights and splash dancing and beer froth doused everyone. The children were already soaked, but the girls now looked like contestants in a wet lingerie contest. The fiesta gained momentum with each passing beer.

"It's impossible to wreck the joint," the steward laughed to Ricky, surveying the scene of stacked furniture and pillows and crucial equipment. "It's already wrecked."

It turned out that the owner of *Paraiso* was off high and dry in his villa, leaving only his teenage nephew to bartend, and the six young lovelies to keep house after the typhoon. Presumably nobody expected company. The opportunity presented itself for a grand release of tension after the storm, since the lifestyle of these maidens of pleasure certainly did not lend itself to partying on their own time. The girls instantly sensed they could really let their hair down, without having to act in a way to impress their usual clientele of boorish businessmen, patricians and politicians. They quickly unfurled colors of liberation, their youthful spirits bursting forth after nights of repression, dumping all inhibitions in an unexpected holiday of joy and frolic.

Through the afternoon the partying went on. Both Ricky and the steward had danced with all girls present, including a wide-eyed 5-year old sister of the *almirante*. "See, Cowboy," yelled Ricky. "I told you we'd find the hidden virgins of Elysio!"

Finally, as Ricky had struggled up on a table island to rest, one of the girls whispered something to the bartender, who in turn leaned over to get the ear of the underage admiral. The ten year old smiled his toothiest grin of the day, and then gathered his eager crew up on the log again, announcing, "It is time to go. We have to go home."

The bartender waded over and climbed on to the log. "Take me with you, Juanito. I've got to take this to my uncle." He had a tin cashbox under his arm. "I'll be back about 7, I hope," he called over to one of the older girls. "Take good care of our treasured guests." The log shifted away from its berth.

The steward reached down into his shirt pocket and pulled out a soaked five dollar bill. He sloshed his way over to the admiral and his crew. "Here ye are, Lilliputs..." he addressed each one of the wet bumps on the log as he gave their leader the bill. "Take her home, *Almirante*. Thanks for the use of your fine ship."

The children's eyes popped at the sight of so much money, gained in the company of this funny stranger with the blue-eyes, and they almost tipped over the log as they all reached in a futile grab for their share.

Then, amidst a blast of language better befitting the captain of the motor launch he had used earlier in the day, the merry crew and their new passenger paddled the craft back out the door in a flurry of splashes and laughing and cheering and waving. The steward stood on the bar and mocked the shrill sound of a bosun's pipe.

"Srrreeeeeerrrrrp! H.M.S. Victoria, departing." He followed with a formal salute, then fell forward like a timbered giant, face down into the water, still saluting.

Ricardito lay on a stack of pillows, exhausted from dancing and laughing. One of the girls, a pretty, tall thing about 18, shimmering in a shiny wet silk lounging robe and little else, crawled out of the stew on to the island and, like some sleek amphibian, slinked her way up on top of him. Ricardito made not a move, but uttered a helpless sigh as she opened her robe and smothered his face with her bosom. As if on cue, *Long Tall Sally* revved up in the Wurlitzer:

"Oh baby, yeah baby! Wooo Ooo Ooo!...

> *We gonna have some fun tonight Ooooo!"*

Suddenly the room went from a palace of rocking laughter to one of sensual stares. Someone turned down the volume, and jumping thumping sank to a subtle throbbing easier on the ears. Then two other girls climbed up on the island and with quiet giggling, struggled to remove Little Richard from his wet pants.

"We're under attack by the sacred virgins of Elysio, Cowboy! It's every man for himself!" Ricky cried out heroically as the two girls stripped down to the buff, then merged into a squirming foursome down under a pile of the large multi-colored pillows.

The steward himself was now surrounded, but underwater. He had been watching Ricky's downfall while leaning waist deep against the bar. Suddenly, one, then another, then the third girl silently bobbed up out of the water in front of him, naked to the waist. Attack of the teenage mermaids. Their fresh, wet young bodies glistened as they approached, mischievous smiles on their faces. The first girl, a sleek nymphet of about 19, the one who had first started the water play at their arrival, slowly unbuttoned his shirt and took it off his arms. Next, the three floated him across the room in their arms, to another table island far across from Ricky, and deposited him ceremoniously on a pile of large dry soft pillows.

A chilled bottle of champagne with a dark yellow label, and flute glasses, had appeared out of nowhere. Giggles accompanied bubbles as a flute was tipped to his lips.

At once completely sober and wide-eyed, the steward lay there spellbound as each girl rose from the inland sea on a hidden stairway of chairs to reveal her lithe young body in all dripping splendor, delicate and graceful and nipples hard. Finally the three stood there over him for a moment, with knowing smiles on their faces. He fleetingly wondered if sacred virgins were still duty bound to perform acts of human sacrifice.

The room spun in a maelstrom of sensation. The last thing he recalled before drifting off into everyman's exotic dream fantasy was the light struggle and accompanying giggles getting his pants off, followed by a soft smothering under the sweetest smells and the smoothest skins he had ever known. The faithful troubadour Wurlitzer shifted background on cue to the jumping pleas of Jerry Lee Lewis...

> *"Shake it baby, Shake...*
> *Ah say Shake, baby, Shake...*
> *Ooooo Shake, baby, Shake...*
> *We ain't fakin'... Oh yeah!...*
> *There's a whole lotta lovin' goin' on!"*

Oh yes. This must be *Paraiso*.

"Dark!"

The steward popped his head up from a pile of pillows and buttocks and breasts, spent of body and struggling to clear his mind. "Oh, Jees!" he thought. "I'm due back to the ship."

He felt a light stirring among his deliciously padded surroundings, and muffled cooing noises from beneath the pillows. Naiads of the highest order were his bunkmates. All happy to be alive. All happy to have the day off. All very experienced in service to mankind, even at their relatively tender ages.

Cinnamon, a sylphid creature with delicate features, possessed a dusty tan to match her name, accented by long flowing black hair, and the longest of fingernails. Cinnamon was the oldest by one year, at 20. She had reluctantly answered his questions during the dancing and drinking, about her and the other girls' presence here. Classic story with a no-surprise ending... Misguided trust in a man twice her age, who shows up in her village in a shiny new convertible, spies her beautiful face in the marketplace, and convinces her parents that she has a future in Manila as a young movie star. Off she goes, to be... A Star in Paradise.

Or Dhania, age 19. With her soft milky tan, large doe-like eyes and the world's smallest waist, setting out even more remarkably the full favors of her other anatomy. Faithfully followed her boyfriend to Manila when he joined the army. He got in trouble and was sent to hard time in the stockade. So she is left in the big city with no place to stay, no funds, no work. An angel lost in Paradise.

Last but not least on this afternoon's sensuous spice rack was Jeera, with the open, hopeful face, age 17. Also deep country, and sold to a family at 8 to be a house servant. Turned out she was made to serve the master in special ways until his wife found out, so she is out in the street at 15 and well on her way to starvation before falling from grace... Paradise Found.

"They all have the same story..." he thought. "Just a different cast of characters and a new slant on bad timing." It was some kind of compulsion in the steward to probe about into the lives of persons he met, particularly with those he liked or had things in common. These young ladies of the night were no exception. Here they were in *Paraiso*... at the top, a very classy, exclusive establishment. Somehow they all started the same way. Somehow they all stayed, and endured. Somehow they all had hopes and dreams beyond their sordid circumstances. Somehow they all knew they would be expelled from Paradise after a certain age, to be misused again in worse ways, beat up, murdered, or left to fall deeper into sticky-sheeted purgatory.

Yet for a few hours, they chose to be seriously warm and wonderful, somehow with him. The key, he had empirically concluded, was in first treating each one gently, as a human being, needing appreciation and understanding and tenderness, and not like a mountable machine.

But these young women were still young girls deep down. Simple in their ways, wide-eyed in their dreams, still trusting a stranger in spite of a world of broken trusts. As he was being pulled down for what seemed to be another of never ending encores, he protested softly that he didn't have any money left.

But Cinnamon shushed his lips, "You don't understand. This afternoon is for you. And for us. It is for your being here. You appeared out of that terrible storm, to us. Call it thanks for giving us a day of joy. We saw. You were generous to the children. You asked nothing of us. You made us feel happy and young again. So this is beyond *Paraiso*. This is for all of us." The rising hot ache in his loins carried him inexorably away from reality, away from his thoughts, and far beyond into unexplored sensations, leaving rhythmic wavelets lapping softly at the base of his island Paradise.

"Don't be cruel... To a heart that's true..." throbbed the juke, into the whirling darkness.

Suddenly Dhania sat upright, and looked at the water ripples around the darkened room. *"Luz!"* she said sharply, watching something different shine on the black sea around them.

There it was again. A beam of light that bounced off the water and exploded near the ceiling on the far wall, and then it was gone.

Cinnamon raised her head, and looked toward the door. She jerked her head to the side, cocking her ears like a cat, and then she whispered intensely into the darkness, "He's coming." Then to the others, to her compatriots wallowing on the other side of the room with Ricky, she hissed out a command, "Get dressed! Lapu Lapu!"

The steward heard Ricky moan into a pile of pillows, "Oh, shit!" which was followed by a scramble of grunts and squeals and thumps and rustles. *"Vaquero!* We must get out of here. Now!" hailed Riccardito across their inland sea in a hushed voice.

The steward somehow fought his way up through a flurry of arms and legs and butts and, stark naked, stood straight up on the tables. He scanned the room, and saw the dancing lights on the water about him, spotting the walls like a spinning ballroom globe. A rush of adrenalin coursed into his body, reviving him instantly. "It must be flashlights..." he thought. "Someone is paddling up the street." He listened a cut above the rustle of his scurrying partners and heard distant cursing and shouting, blended in with a periodic thump of oar against metal boat.

"Who is it?" he asked anyone in the dark around him. "Who is this guy Lapu?"

"Lapu Lapu, the *padrone* of *Paraiso!*" barked Jeera. "He will kill us all! You must get out of here!"

Dhania pushed his shirt toward him. "Quickly! Get dressed and get out of here. Lapu Lapu hates Westerners. They are *tabu* in here! He will kill you!" wailed Jeera.

Ricky sloshed his way over to the table on which the steward stood. "Oh, shit. Oh, shit. I should have known not to bring you here, Cowboy. We've got big trouble now! This place is owned by Charlie Lapu Lapu. Big smuggler. You know, hasheesh, opium, cars, gold. Supplier to the politicians and big families. Anything they want. Oh, shit. This is his place. Oh, god. Oh, *mierda*! He's a crazy! He carries a machete wherever he goes. He'll have our *huevos* scrambled for breakfast."

The steward got the message. "Where are my damn pants?!" he groped frantically about in the now wet pillows. He found nothing but a soggy sarong that he wrapped hurriedly around himself. His shoes were gone for good in the deep.

The noises and flashes got stronger. The boat was banging and bashing about in the darkness, hitting stumps and posts on its way to the casa. With each thump, a bull voice let loose a rash of swearing, inflected every other word with a *puta* or *coño*. Then the voice hailed the casa, now fully highlighted against its surrounding mini-sea, "Dhania! Cinnamon! *Hola*! Where the fuck are you!"

"Quick!" the steward whispered to Ricky. "Get over by the door!" With that he grabbed the three girls who were quivering in unison on top of the pillowed pedestal, gave them a collective hug, and kissed them one by one. "You are each very beautiful," he quickly whispered to their upturned faces. "You live with joy and hope and dignity."

Then he singled out Cinnamon and said clearly, "Courage now. Stay calm. When Lapu comes in, we go out." He squeezed her hand, then half swam half waded his way over to the side of the front door, opposite Ricky.

Cinnamon had taken a stance on top of the table facing the doorway, with Jeera and Dhania huddled at her feet. The flashlight beam bounced around her, spotting her in a key light that accented the plight and drama of her pose. "Is that you, Lapu? Oh, we were so afraid. It is so dark now, and the water so cold."

"Cinnamon!" the voice bellowed. "Are you alright? Where are the others. Ginger! Dhania! Jeera! Haldi and Masala! You are not hurt?" It almost seemed Lapu had real concern for the welfare of his girls, when he added, "*Putas!* The generator's running... Why isn't the fucking roof sign lit? *Paraiso* never closes! Where is my fucking nephew? He's not here and I lose two days business." He banged loudly on the side of the boat with his machete. "*Coño!* I can't even trust my own fucking family."

The steward and Ricky were right inside the door now, with their backs to the wall and squatting up to their necks in the water. The boatmen were banging their way through the outer pillars of *Paraiso*. Flashlight beams filled the hall, picking targets at random.

As the bow of the rowboat veered at last in through the doorway, Cinnamon grabbed the shoulders of the other two girls at her feet and implored, "Oh Lapu! We thought you'd never..."

Her last words were lost as the steward and Ricky, filled with possibly their last breath, ducked silently under the water, hesitated as the massive foreboding shadow passed over paradise's gates, and then both turned and clawed and swam their way outward through the murky darkness and into the space beyond.

After seemingly an eternity under blackness, the steward surfaced like a crock on his back, eyes and nose first cautiously breaking the surface. He was about twenty yards from the gateway, and he felt he was pretty well camouflaged in the mottled light of night. Ricky was about ten yards in back of him, thrashing in some jerky breaststroke, gasping in attempts to regain his breath. The steward waited for him to gain ground, and motioned with his hand for Ricky to stay down and be quiet. Inside the *casa* he could hear Lapu swearing and banging and bellowing, and all six girls sobbing and pleading. He listened for a few moments, then concluded to himself, "Good actresses. They'll survive." Then he motioned to Ricky, and they both softly paddled and waded their way back down the flooded streets toward the distant shore and safety of their trusty Jeep. The steward looked back for a moment. Large dark letters of *CLUB PARAISO*, silhouetted against a half-lit sky, stood menacingly above its shimmering sea realm, as tentacles of light lashed out after them through doors and windows.

"See, Milt? Good guys won. Paradise Lost..." he muttered, and then resumed his progress down the murky sea in quiet mode.

Getting back to the wharf and the ship was even more difficult than the trip up to Elysio. Darkness hampered their reckoning. No utility power was yet in the hills, and only a few lights dotted the city anywhere, probably from lanterns, flashlights or an occasional generator. Car lights, however, flickered here and there, as some other hearties made their way through the maze of now mud and murk. The water levels were lower by about a foot, as thirsty ground and drainage ditches took their toll. Sewer systems seemed only to be in the downtown sections, leaving the hills to run off by themselves. Pockets of water still blocked most roads, but somehow, after two hours of trying, Ricky bounced the Jeepney up to the gate at the pier.

Ricky turned off the engine and leaned on the steering wheel. "*Vaquero,* you dragged me into the wildest day of my life. I get drunk. I get mauled by the hidden daughters of Elysio. I almost get deballed by the biggest smuggler in Manilla. Then I almost drown. Worse yet, I loose all my money. It fell out of my pants in the struggle to get out of there." He sighed and smiled, and stretched his arms out to the side, breathing in the flower scented air about him. "Know what? It's been the best day of my life. Paradise."

The steward reached over and gave him a hug, then shook his hand. "You'll need a week's rest after a day in Paradise."

The little Jeepney driver looked longingly out to the ships moored at anchor throughout the harbour. The bay was peaceful, the morning air quiet and clear. "You're off, then?"

The steward had relayed his schedule to Ricky earlier, knowing he would probably be kept on board the next day during the offloading of cargo, and sailing with the tide the following.

"Yes... I must go now, Riccardito." The steward slowly climbed out of the Jeepney and stretched as the light of dawn escaped the horizon. His shirt was dirty and torn. His feet were bare. His red silk sarong clung gracelessly to his knees.

"You look like Dorothy LaMour in *Typhoon*..." Ricky snickered.

And you look like the world's greatest Jeepney guide..." the steward gibed back at the skinny little man with shorts and no shirt or shoes. "Work on your breast stroke. Maybe you can handle eight next time."

"Go in the hands of the gods, Dorothy..." Ricky called as the steward started down the long pier in hopes of hailing a launch with the dawn.

"Which ones?" the steward hailed back.

The air seemed to freshen, awakening with the growing light. Sounds took on a mystic quality, coming from different directions all at once. The wind laughed softly.

"You must choose."

"Rat guards."

The steward watched in disbelief, as the surly little Philippino in shoes with no laces and a scruffy officer's shirt with some kind of badge on the pocket rocked back and forth like a brooding cobra, head down looking at the deck and avoiding the captain's eyes.

"We have rat guards on our lines..." Eiriksson responded with a curious smile while looming over the petty official like a giant. "It is to keep your rats off our ship!" he added in a ribbing tone.

The little Philippino, no more than 5 feet tall, babbled something in some local Tagalog dialect, intermixed with English, and waved a crumpled piece of paper around. "You ship need rat guards," he then mumbled to the captain's chest, face still down at the deck. "Our rat guards. It is law. Philippinos no want your rats."

"But our rat guards are bigger than your rat guards," the captain poked back. "And Manilla has more rats than anywhere."

"Rats in officials' clothing..." mulled the steward, enjoying this exchange from about 10 feet away on the rail. The Talabot had finally come in to the long pier, starboard side to, at about 0600. Miraculously the first mate had parked the old single screw ship deftly along side without a scratch, even without the help of a tug, all of which were doing triple duty around the harbour, clearing up after the typhoon. The captain, as far as the steward knew, had slept through the raising of anchor, getting underway and entering the pier area, even though the harbour was crammed with assorted flotsam, jetsam, and junk from the storm. Herjolfsson, with the steward as lookout, somehow had zigged a course from the mooring to the pier at position 6, and managed to miss all of Mother Nature's mines and torpedoes that still plagued the harbour. "Not a bad bit of driving in the dark..." the steward had remarked to Herjolfsson after the lines were thrown over to the longshoremen on the pier and secured. Herjolfsson nodded numbly as usual to it all, but he had done his job well.

"Our Norwegian rats wouldn't be caught dead going ashore in Manila," Eiriksson continued to the port lackey. "They put up the rat guards themselves, to protect their daughters from the likes of you."

"No rat guards. No unloading..." the little man hissed back, sheepishly. "I am here to see you use Philippino rat guards."

"No, you're not," smiled Eiriksson with a more serious look down on the little man. "You're here for cigarettes."

The Philippino shifted about again and said something under his breath that the steward could not hear.

"Ok," the captain nodded with a shrug. "Come with me to my cabin." The little harbour official followed Eiriksson up the ladder to his stateroom, like Mutt trying to catch up with Jeff.

The steward shook his head in wonder and disgust. That was the tenth official so far this morning, and not a crate or container or pallet had yet been offloaded. As soon as the Talabot had gently bumped the pier, the captain had appeared, mouth full of raw herring tidbits and a mug in his hand, probably not coffee, on the wing of the bridge. He had leaned over to rest his chest and elbows on the steel railing, head hanging over the side, for about five minutes. He did not move, except for an occasional heaving of his massive chest. The steward and Herjolfsson had watched quietly, waiting for the captain to call the harbour gods by chumming the water beneath him. But once again the metabolic crisis passed, and the Viking of Vikings had risen slowly from his near funeral pyre to stand tall among the living. "O.K..." he had spoken firmly to Herjolfsson. "Prepare to offload."

There had been a steady entourage of uniformed official types arriving that morning, for more than two hours now. Some slick in stripes and braid. One even with jacket and epaulets. Most with weather-worn American officer hats with big centered emblems and scrambled eggs. All, however, had open-collar white or tan shirts with some type of badge hanging on the pocket. Rag tag navy at best," the steward had observed. "I guess they don't like ties in the Philippines."

The stevedores, on the other hand, looked like stevedores throughout the world. Emaciated. Tired. Permanently bent from back loads, bundles, and bales. Torn T-shirts, ragged sandals or sneakers, and shorts the fashion of the day. They all reminded the steward of slaves he had seen in etchings and sketches in a British museum, eulogized in a romantic portrayal of ports and empires throughout history. "Poor bastards..." he thought as one scrawny man struggled to put a monster bundle on his shoulders. "Some things never change. The littlest guys get to carry all the heaviest bags. Big guys direct traffic."

But his sympathy for the stevedores had been interrupted by each official that had climbed the ladder that morning. Each had had words with Eiriksson. Each was then taken to the captain's cabin for a few minutes. Each emerged with a couple of large cases of American cigarettes, some also with a case of Chivas or Black Label scotch. Each then struggled down the gangway and off into their dark lairs of corruption and graft.

"Manila is the worst I've seen," the steward said to Eiriksson in an idle moment between officials. "What's that? Nine? Ten?"

"I don't keep count" replied Eiriksson without emotion. "It is the cost of doing business."

"But don't you get pissed at these little bag men?" the steward asked. "They are really corrupt here. You can't offload without bribing the dock master, the pier boss, the chief stevedore, the medical officer, the local cop, the harbour commandant, and the minister of commerce. Who did I leave out?"

"The keeper of the rat guards..." Eiriksson responded flatly.

"But isn't there some scrap of socially redeeming morality left in the Orient?" asked the steward. "Is everyone a corruptible rat?"

"It is the same throughout the world. Even to some degree in my country," thought Eiriksson. "We represent an opportunity to steal. In the confusion and haste of loading and shipping goods around the world, much is possible. Cultures are different. Customs papers look different. Language is different. Letters of credit are different. Laws and duties are different. Manifests and bills of lading are different. The one common denominator, the one common currency, the one common language, is the bribe. It is all over. It is how things get done in shipping. You Americans have your Longshoreman's Union. Manila has these dock rats. They are all the same. It is a cost of doing business."

"Some cost. Seems you've sent..." the steward mulled and calculated the cost of cases of scotch and cigarettes in estimated prices..."over $1,000 into the sewers today so far. That's heavy bribing in today's values."

The captain looked over at the steward. "It is peanuts. I see you are still young, Steward. It costs up to $5,000 for every day extra we are in port, any port, and not at sea. Dock fees, fuel, taxes, shore power, salaries, food, spoilage, pilferage, damage to cargo... At sea, the shipping business is profitable. In port, we hemorrhage money for each hour extra we must stay to load or offload. If it takes $1,000 to grease the wheels so we can get back on schedule at sea, that is the least cost of doing business. So the key to shipping is to keep moving. Ports are for garbage scows and rats. Ships should be always at sea. It is a cleaner way of life."

"What about the slaves down there?" the steward asked, motioning with a nod to the stevedores busting their humps to drag the bags and boxes over to be snared up by loading booms and cargo nets. "Do they get a pack of Camels out of all this?"

"They get to eat and stay alive," Eiriksson responded. "The fat rats up in Elysio get most of the booty. They have expensive tastes in scotch and champagne and cigars. This is just for the little rats, here, the petty officials, that you see all this little shit being carried off. The big stuff, the heavy smuggling, it is in there." He pointed to a large crate marked 'Machinery'.

"It is all for the honor of doing business in the Philippines. Some countries have a duty, a tax, on imports. Countries like this prefer to take their cut privately, and distribute it to the power players, and not to the slaves. Anyway, champagne tastes better if it is smuggled in, rather than imported."

"You're not kidding..." the steward nodded, looking at the crate now being hoisted up in a cargo net and swung over the side. Down below on the pier, he spied a shiny new turquoise and cream Mercury convertible, pod lights and gaudy chrome across the back, parked on the pier next to a van. Connections rocketed through his brain. "Uh Oh..." he said softly at the pier.

The steward was in his old Navy officer shirt, without shoulder boards, and a pair of khaki shorts. He wore sandals, having lost his brown suede casual shoes on his night in Paradise. Through his sunglasses, he watched as a short husky Philippino climbed out of the Mercury, puffing on a cigar, and started barking commands to the dock masters and stevedores engaged swinging the crate over the side. He was accompanied by two huge goons, twice his size, who had baseball jackets on, probably the Orioles and the Dodgers, judging by the colors at a distance. The short Philippino wore a white pleated *barong* shirt and slacks, sunglasses, and carried a machete, which he wildly brandished about with every bark. The dockworkers gave him space and kept their eyes on the ground, as he strode up the pier to the spot where the crate would come down.

"There's one of them. A more successful variant of Philippino rat," stated the captain coolly as he too noticed the Mercury. "That car here would cost over $30,000 if all the real import duties were

41

paid. A good example of survival of the fittest. You will know a fat rat when you see one."

"I know one..." said the steward, quietly, as the bottom dropped out of his stomach and he had to swallow hard to get his balls back down out of his throat.

The steward's thoughts flashed back a few hours. He had noticed the same new Mercury, grill shining like sharks' teeth, parked near the Jeepney on his quick exit the night before. Questions raced about inside his head... "Could he have been spotted? Were the girls all right? Could they have talked? Was Ricky still in possession of his *huevos*? Did he leave anything behind? Oh, god. His shoes. His pants. Any identification? No. His wallet and passport were in his bunk drawer. Anything from the Talabot? Just his pants and shoes. But in the aftermath of a typhoon, shoes and pants shouldn't be out of place. Or were they left on top of the pillows? Stop. Stop. Cool it. He's down there and you're up here. Safe at home. Home on His Majesty's Steamship. He has no rights here."

"He will come aboard, too." Eiriksson said flatly. "Not only do they bring in all sorts of illegal goods, but the big rats all want the same shit as the little rats. Why miss a good thing? Every case of champagne helps."

The steward felt weak in the knees. "Oh, shit..."

"Stay with me. Learn the ways of the world..." Eiriksson said, as he watched Philippino Johnny Caesar and his goons start up the gangway. The machete glistened in the sunlight.

"But I've got to start lunch..." the steward protested, even though the very thought of food now was tainted with peptic acid.

Eiriksson grabbed him by the elbow with his huge meat hook of a hand, and walked him over to the top of the gangway to greet the arriving guests. The steward looked frantically about for an escape route, but was pulled onward like an old skegg in the wake of the mighty Viking.

The steward mustered his senses and stood at attention next to the captain. He looked straight ahead as the little head in sun glasses appeared above the gunwale.

"Welcome aboard, Charlie," Eiriksson said to the cigar in the mouth. "How long has it been? Two years?" He gave the little Philippino a quick, almost comic salute, towering over him like a giant. Then turning to his brawny bodyguards, "Hello, Gentlemen. Still keeping the flies away?"

"Good God. He knows him." The steward went pale.

The captain ignored the steward, and continued chatting about the weather, the previous typhoon, the damage in the port, etc., as he walked Charlie Lapu and his minions to his cabin. Then he turned and shouted to the blond totem pole with sunglasses still standing at the gangway, "Pilot. Come with me, to my cabin."

The steward weakly staggered up the ladder and into the captain's stateroom, and stood by the door. It was the largest cabin, rather sumptuously decorated, with ornate brass hanging lamps and a fat leather couch, around which were arranged a large rosewood table, brass cornered captain's desk and chairs and bureaus. The bunk, along one bulkhead, was oversized, probably custom made for the Viking, and at least three feet off the deck with drawers underneath. On all bulkheads were assorted maps and pictures of sailing vessels, beautifully framed in gold and rosewood. On the desk was a photograph in an intricate brass frame, of a woman and two small girls.

Eiriksson, without turning from opening a large built-in armoire that resembled a safe, spoke over his shoulder. "Charlie, this is my pilot. He keeps the Talabot out of harm's way."

Charlie Lapu had his head down reading a manifest, and grunted without looking up. The steward nodded mechanically. "Spared!" sighed the steward, hiding behind his sunglasses. The two goons stood like pillars in some temple of greed, aside of their boss, with arms folded.

The captain managed to unlock the armoire/safe and removed a lacquered wooden chest about the size of a breadbox. "Here it is, kept in my personal larder just for you, Charlie. Going to tell me what is in it this time?" the captain asked lightly as he handed the chest carefully over to Lapu.

Charlie placed the chest on the desk, reached in his pocket and produced a small key, and unlocked the top. He opened the top away from all view, glanced down inside, and forced a slight smile. The captain had his back to him, relocking the armoire.

Charlie grunted again, and passed the box to one of his minions. Then he folded his arms with the machete over the top, while the captain went to a large closet and brought out four cases of Chesterfield Kings and two cases of Chivas. The goons picked them up and stood as before, silent and knowing from nothing.

Then Charlie took a legal size envelope from his side shirt pocket and placed it on the desk. It was fat, but neat.

"Two thousand?" asked the captain.

"Two..." grunted Lapu. "Business is done." Then he cracked open into a forced smile, and rocked his shoulders a bit in relaxation.

"Champagne?" asked the captain, as he reached under the desk and lifted out a silver bucket in which a bottle had been chilling, and plucked out a dripping yellow label Veuve Clicquot-Ponsardin.

"Always," smiled Lapu. "It is the one good thing to come out of your part of the world. It opens any door. It seals any bargain. It closes any chapter."

"Good god..." thought the steward. "The sage of the Philippi."

The captain removed the cork with his massive fist, like twisting the head off a fly. He poured two crystal flutes, and ignoring the two pillars of silence, put one into Lapu's hand.

The steward started to feel a bit relieved, as he watched Lapu glug down a goblet of bubbly. Then he noticed it. Hanging over the back of the fat leather couch. The sarong. "Oh shit again," he remembered. "THE SARONG! It was Cinnamon's. Oh ye gods almighty..."

He had returned aboard the Talabot early in the previous morning, only to find Eiriksson standing on the deck alone, watching his approach. It surprised him that the only person on deck at 0530, at dawn in fact, was the Viking. From paradise... back to sobering reality. There he was, old Einar himself, leaning on the rail at dawn! Waiting. The captain did not move, nor hail him as he jumped from the taxi launch to the side ladder. He just watched silently as the steward struggled up the ladder steps in that red silk sarong. LaMour indeed, it was impossible to get up that fucking ladder. Just as he reached the top and entered the gangway, the sarong fell off, leaving him stark naked from the waist down. The steward, however, not missing a beat, turned instead to salute the flag, and then marched barefoot and bare ass double-time off to his bunk area. The captain, who was leaning on his elbows without moving, taking all this in, didn't say a word or crack a smile. He just shook his head slowly, not side to side, but up and down. When the steward was gone, Eiriksson slowly strolled over to the gangway, stopped, reached down, and picked up the sarong. He held it in his mighty hands for a moment, sensing its silken beauty. Then he turned his head back to the sea, and the horizon, and the glow of the new dawn.

The steward snapped back to the present. Cold sweat ran down his face. Lapu was again waving his machete around at his goons, directing them out the door. Then, with his champagne glass high in the air to drain the last drop, Lapu seemed to freeze for a moment, looking over at the couch. Lapu shook his head, almost like a brief shiver, and finished off his glass, and put it firmly on the desk. Eiriksson by this time had put his glass down and was grabbing Charlie by the shoulders in a gesture of obviously false brotherhood.

"Back to business, Charlie. I have a line at my door today." Eiriksson burped unceremoniously. Lapu struggled to avoid the captain's fiery breath, and again glanced by him and over at the red silk, squinting at it and lifting his sunglasses.

Eiriksson noticed his stare. "You like it? A gift for a goddess. One of my beautiful daughters. It is perfection, isn't it? Look at that design. It makes me think of a sun god rising out of the sea. I've never found one quite like it. Smooth as this fine champagne. As someone once remarked, fine silk may be the only thing good to come out of your part of the world."

Lapu looked at Eiriksson and back at the sarong. He shook his head again, shifting his Havana into the corner of his mouth.

"Some things are ours... belong here... should stay here..." he muttered through a tangle of thoughts, passions and loose ends. "Some things... not for sale..."

"I fully agree. It's good that your country has someone as trustworthy as you to look after its best interests, Charlie..." And Eiriksson walked him out of the cabin with his arm around his shoulder, firmly. The two pillars of silence gave a slight reaction to their boss being delicately manhandled by a Viking, but with their arms full of goodies, had no choice but to follow passively along after him, struggling their way down the deck ladder and off down the gangway.

The steward, still at attention and motionless, fell like a timbered fir back to rest against the bulkhead.

"Escorts."

The steward looked over to the horizon in the East, darkening in the twilight sky. He stood on the bow rail, fresh sea wind in his face, watching two dolphins play tag right under the port bow near the anchor, as the Talabot plugged along out into the China Sea. One dolphin would break forth above the waves and back under again, then the other, in a fanciful race with the ship. He tried to keep score, as each playful partner surged ahead a few yards, only to fall from view as the other moved into the lead. The Talabot steadily churned along at 12 knots, with its newfound playmates just slightly ahead, escorting its way.

"Good old international waters..." he mused as he thought about the last few days in this island paradise. Hurried escapes seemed the norm, first from Elysio, then from Lapu Lapu's machete chopping up the pier in a rage. The Talabot had finished offloading earlier than expected, about 1700, and had completed preparations to get underway. The ship had dropped all lines and was slowly moving astern from alongside the wharf, drawing attention in a series of three deep-throated blasts just as the big Mercury roared up the pier and skidded to a stop.

Lapu Lapu's screaming had been drowned out by the horn. As he stood there in the open convertible, shaking his machete violently in the air, the captain had leaned over the railing from the wing of the bridge and hailed, "What's that you say, Charlie?" Then as Lapu started screaming again, the Talabot would drown him out with another series of three ear-splitters.

"So long, Charlie," Eiriksson had hailed down to this Philippine link to a Tasmanian Devil. "See you next trip." Then, after a crisp, friendly salute, he had turned back to the rear, to open waters. The steward had watched this exchange from the hatchway of the charthouse, as the Talabot maneuvered back and out into the harbour, to turn and set a course to the Southwest for the mouth of greater Manila Bay.

The last thing the steward had seen as they picked up way was Charlie chopping up the pier, splintering crates and pilings at random, in a fit of spleen. Even Tweedle Dum and Tweedle Dee had given him ample room, and stood at a befuddled parade rest by the big Merc, as was their habit. "Real nice meeting you, Lapu Lapu..." the steward had mused, leaning on the sprayshield by the bow. "You and your *Islas de Ladrones*." And the Talabot moved purposefully out into the widening bay, aiming straight into a spectacular setting sun off to the West.

"Safe on board..." he thought to himself as he watched the dolphins vying for position below. Eiriksson had unknowingly exposed his butt to jeopardy by keeping that darn sarong. But he had also saved it, maybe not so unknowingly, by ushering Lapu Lapu off the ship. "Back to sea..."

Almost as a self-administered anesthetic to escape from his nerve-racking departure from Manila, the steward's thoughts reflected back through a kaleidoscope of time... to earlier days and events in the log of the Talabot... A montage of images flashed through his mind as he watched yet another city pull back into the distance... "They seem all mixed together..." he mulled as he tried to focus on the last distinguishing characteristics of the retreating cityscape. "So many ports... They look all different on entering. They look all the same on leaving..."

He shrugged, and looked out to sea. Scatterings of Whitman flashed through his view.

> *"Sail forth - steer for deep waters only...*
>
> *Reckless O soul, exploring, I with thee, and thou with me,*
>
> *For we are bound where mariner has not yet dared to go,*
>
> *And we will risk the ship, ourselves and all...*
>
> *O farther, farther, farther sail!*
>
> *Are they not all the seas of God?"*

The two dolphins squealed in agreement, then with a final flick of their tails, plunged back down into the deepening blueblack seas and were gone.

Against the mysterious sheen of the waters racing beneath him, his mind played with time, blurring into vivid surrealism a myriad of images... images of swells and glares and shimmering seas, of shadows and fogs and sunsets and storms, whitecaps and wavelets, sweeping coastlines and beckoning lights, quivering stars in milky darkness, brooding moons over sparkling harbours, luxury hotels along waterfront promenades, water skiing bikinis and dancing crowds, rugged dhows and polished motor launches, menacing Mercedes and fanciful Jeepneys, clashing cultures and diverse ideologies, mosques set against monasteries, opulent palaces surrounded by crumbling hovels, dromedaries and donkeys vying with Daimlers, tall cedar stands contrasting desert barrens, glistening platters laden with steaming feasts, silken sheets and wispy netting billowing in soft night breezes...

On and on the images came, up from a deep ocean of memories streaming along below him... images of a thousand places and faces and senses and scenes... images...

Until, after probing the depths, his thoughts narrowed in, and surfaced once again... to a recent time... to days just gone by... to two large dark eyes, sparkling with merriment... to the cool creamy taste of fine champagne... to the sweet fragrance of Cinnamon... A smile crossed his face, and he involuntarily smacked his lips.

Finally, staring down into his own reflection in the vast dark blueblack mirror racing by below him, his mind settled on one........

The butterfly......

—AT SEA—

"Improvise."

"Improvise?"

"I'll keep 'em liquored up and laughing..." Eiriksson yelled out the doorway as he pulled up his pants. "You keep 'em well fed and in the right bunks, between clean sheets..."

The steward stood outside the head in the captain's stateroom, venturing on in this slightly distant conversation. "But they have had some rather odd requests so far... like for Mr. Landgrave, can I hammer a nail in the steel bulkhead to mount his toupee right over his noggin at night so he won't have to look around for it in emergencies..."

A head briefly appeared around the doorframe, making an expressionless nod.

"Or Mr. Boost wanting to open the water lines in his stateroom head to check the pump output pressure..."

FAALLLOOOOOSSSHHHH. The head again appeared. Another nod.

"Or Mrs. Lovelake wanting just a little neck massage every morning but her kinks that seem to be spreading lower and lower as the days pass..."

Again. Nod, with a half grin.

"Or Mr. Brububber wanting his shoes shined every night... "

"What's wrong with Brububber's request?"

"After his booze bouts with you in the lounge, he's usually sleeping in them..."

"So?"

"With his nose in them?..."

Again. Nod. "Improvise. Nobody said being Ship's Steward was a cakewalk."

"Or Mrs. O'Rouark? Sleeps in her husband's pajamas."

Eiriksson sauntered into the stateroom, adjusting his belt buckle. "So?"

"He sleeps in her nightgown..."

"Hmmmm..." Eiriksson nodded in serious confirmation. "Must find it comfortable...."

"Really, Captain, I signed aboard to be Ship's Steward, not Ship's Shrink. I think some Sterno got mixed into the vodka stock... They're loosing their grip on reality after cocktail hour."

"Maybe just the opposite, Steward."

The steward stood as Eiriksson sat down behind his desk, and took out a fat, messy folder of bills of lading.

"These are nice, respectable people. Mostly retired and happily set in their ways. What are we trying to do to them? Float them around the world in their own drinks?..."

Eiriksson pushed the folder away from the center, and leaned back in his chair. "Well, that's exactly what this steamer cruise is all about, Steward. The passengers aren't looking for reality. They want to escape their old world, their old ways of doing things... They were bored stiff with their old ways. Just for a few months, they have committed themselves to sail around the world! Ah, the adventure of it all! They tell themselves they want to see new things, to have new experiences, to revive sleepy passions, to live again a little before they dry up completely and fade away... and to brag about it to their friends when they return... But first and foremost, they also want their cocktails."

"So, improvise?"

"Give 'em anything they want. They're paying for it. If you can find it, give it to them. If you can't find it, conger it up as best you can. Just keep them out of trouble, give 'em food and drink, and get them home safe in the right bunks."

"Well, I hope they won't be disappointed with this trip."

"Know your *Tempest*, Steward?"

"Tempest?"

> *"'Nothing of him that doth fade*
> *But hath suffered a sea-change*
> *Into something rich and strange...'*

I assure you, Steward. They won't be disappointed."

The steward's midday duties consisted of attending to the needs and requests of the passengers, who in typical good weather conditions sat like a row of chickens nesting on their old cane deck chairs, reading or chatting. Some clustered together a bit; others stayed within earshot but tried to remain independent for a quarter of an hour or so, or usually until the conversations took a turn from mere idle chatter into irresistible backstabbing personaliticide. But for the most part, heads bobbed sleepily over dog-eared pages of hardbound history, esoterica or fantasy.

"Steward?"

"Yes, Mrs. O'Rouark?"

"Come over here, will you please?"

"Yes, Ma'am. What can I do for you?"

"I seem to have something in my eye, Steward. Can you see it? Here, come down closer. Here... What do you see here?"

"Your eye, Mrs. O."

"In my eye, Steward. What do you see?"

"Your eyelash, Ma'am."

"Come closer. Right up here beside me. Now what..."

"Now what what?..."

"What do you see now..."

"An eyelash."

"An eyelash? It feels much bigger."

"It's the whole eyelash, Ma'am. The complete strip. It slipped down off your lid."

"Thank you, Steward. I believe I can remedy things after all."

"Steward?"

"Mr. B.?"

"Ever play football?"

"A little bit. In high school."

"What do you think these Norskies played?"

"Don't know, Sir. Soccer, maybe."

"Don't have any flat land in Norway, Steward. They can't play soccer."

"They could try to kick it over a fjord."

"Goalie's dead if he misses. Keep your head up, Olaf. Don't look dooooooooooowwwwwwwwwwwwnnnn."

"So what sport did the Norwegians play in school, Sir?"

"Fishball. They played fishball, Steward."

"Fishball?"

"Great sport. I can just see them now. Third and six on the foredeck. The Oslo Seals against the Bergen Killer Whales. Seals go for a forward pass. QB fires a herring to his flanker, right over the nose of the Whales. Swooooshhh. SPLAT. Good for five yards, but he steps out of bounds and falls over the side. But, playing heads-up fishball, he laterals the herring back up to another Seal before going under the screws. The Seal crosses back over the hatch covers, around the mast, squirts through the teeth of two Killer Whales waiting to eat him alive, and falls into the cargo hold."

"The Vikings play this game for keeps."

"Fourth down. Hand-off to the fullback, who blasts up the middle, hits the tackle in the face with a codfish, then head down slams into a wall of blubber. Sqwhoosh. The herring squirts out of his hands, and everyone goes for it. I can just see it. Chum all over the deck... Fishheads... Guts... Real Viking fishball..."

"Would you like another martini, Mr. B?"

"I thought you'd never ask."

"Steward?"

"Yes, Mrs. Lovelake?"

"Any bahdy evah tell yoo y'all got a cute butt?"

"Yes, Ma'am."

"Who?"

"My mother."

"Steward?"

"Yes, Mr. Boost."

"You all have one smart Chief Engineer back there. That old Johannes Gynt feller knows his pumps like the back of his hand."

"Good to know that, Mr. B."

"Yeah, he hooked on a centrifugal booster without even looking. Just reached up and hit the switch, and WHOOOOOOOOM! it started spraying shit all over the engine room."

"Ruptured oil line?"

"No. I mean shit. Seems he was working on the drain from the crew's head, plugged up. Somehow he got it crossconnected with the fresh water feed line, trying to blow it out. Hit that clog with 60 psi and WHAM! Shit all over the place. Bulkheads, overhead, even saturated the evaporators."

"Drink bottled water for a few days, Sir."

"You say drink? Don't mind if I do. Usual, please."

"Oh, Steward?"

"Yes, Mrs. Potter-Smythe? What can I do for you?"

"Have you seen my husband?

"A few minutes ago he was filling his pipe on the bridge."

"Good. Then we can talk."

"Ma'am?"

"About his drink today. Before lunch. The Pinkie."

"Was it satisfactory?"

"Alas, not, Steward. I must convey his displeasure to you."

"Can't he do that himself? I wasn't trying to poison him."

"My husband doesn't enjoy confrontation, Steward. So I am bringing it to your very personal attention."

"Ma'am?"

"The drink, Steward. Tony thought it ghastly."

"Too much bitters? Too much water?"

"You used a substitute gin, Steward. Tony can tell. Seems his pipe smoking has sensitized his taste buds. In the future, Steward, use only Beefeaters. Tony only drinks his Pinkie made with Beefeaters."

"Yes, Ma'am. It won't happen again."

"Thank you, Steward. See to it that it doesn't."

"Steward?"

"Yes, Mrs. Lovelake?"

"Your mommie sure knows butts..."

"Steward?"

"Mr. O'Rouark?"

"What's a smart young guy like you doin' aboard a rust bucket like this?"

"Sailing around the world, Sir. Just like you and your Mrs."

"Ever go around the world before, Steward?"

"No, Sir. My first time. You?"

"I mean, really around the world, kid. You know... In and out of different ports... ."

"What?"

"I saw you with that little blackbird back in the last port. The one with the long legs... You know.... Nice and dark... with the full buns... Tryin' to change your luck?..."

"You mean my sister?..."

"Yeah, kid. You and the Pharaohs... "

"Well, she was actually just a friend. We found we shared something in common."

"I'll bet you shared something in common."

"What we shared, Sir, is that we both found human nature to be very odd at times, and usually very predictable."

"Right, kid. You know what I've found on my trips round the world?"

"What, Sir?"

"It may come in different packaging... But human nature's all pink on the inside."

"I would guess that all depends on which end you open, Mr. O. How about another Bloody Mary before teatime?"

"Steward?"

"Mrs. Landgrave?"

"Can you find me another book like this one?" She passed it up to him.

"Let's see what you have..."

"It was delightful. Are there any others by him on board?"

"I don't know, Mrs. S., but I'll take a look in the lounge..."

"That would be kind. I've browsed but can't find things easily."

"I know, Ma'am. The shelves tend to get sort of mixed up."

"One finds Homer in the popular novel section, Steward. Jammed in next to *Gone with the Wind*..."

"And Truman Capote in bed with Epictetus, no doubt. Time to clear things up."

"By the way... What time is it, Steward?"

"I'm not sure, Ma'am. Nearing teatime, though."

As he walked off to the lounge, to try and straighten up the shelves of collective shipboard thought, he opened the sticky pages before him.

> *"And an astronomer said, 'Master, what of Time?' And he answered:*
>
> *'You would measure time in the measureless and the immeasurable. You would adjust your conduct and even direct the course of your spirit according to hours and seasons...*
>
> *Yet the timeless in you is aware of life's timelessness.*
>
> *And knows that yesterday is but today's memory and tomorrow is today's dream...*

And that that which sings and contemplates in you is still dwelling within the bounds of that first moment which scattered the stars into space.'"

"Steward?"

"Mr. Potter-Smythe?"

"I feel I must talk to you about my wife's Pinkie..."

"Steward?"

"Yes, Mrs. Lovelake?"

"Ya think y'all could give me a little ol' massage on this darn ol' kink in mah back a bit?"

"You probably need some exercise, Ma'am. Sitting in that lounge chair all day..."

"Please, Steward... It's drivin' me crazy. Just a little bit... Right down here..."

"O.K. Right about here, Ma'am?"

"Ummmmmmmmm...deeelicious. But much lower, Steward. Much much lower."

"Steward?"

"Mrs. Brububber?"

"Have you seen my naughty husband recently?"

"No, Ma'am. But I saw him back by the crew's galley tossing a herring around. Seems he's trying to get one to spiral..."

"Bilgewater."

The steward finally found the first mate. He was fast asleep. But not in his bunk. Not in anyone's bunk. Bjarni Herjolfsson had created a special lair for himself, up and out of the typical traffic patterns onboard, one in which he could secret himself away from the passengers and the captain and any unnecessary duties at sea. Down deep... In the bilge.

The steward stumbled upon Bjarni's crash pad by accident. He had been exploring the lower spaces, mostly out of curiosity just to see how the old bucket was welded together. But he had also been crawling about out of some practical calling in the back of his mind, to see what emergency equipment the ship had, if any, such as a stand-by diesel generator, an auxiliary fuel oil pump, an extra fresh water pump, and the type of salt water booster pump connected to the fire hose system. His navy days had taught him that it was always good to know where these items were located, and where the power switch was to turn them on, or where a master control valve was to turn them off. Also of strange interest were the two antique bilge pumps that slurped and gurgled at the ever-present slimy black mess that shifted back and forth between the steel hull braces along the keel, in the bilge.

The steward had stepped in through a small hatchway from the forward cargo hold, now half filled with assorted crates and boxes and bags bound from Europe to ports in the Orient, and into an isolated equipment compartment deep under the passenger staterooms. Groping along the bulkhead, he found a switch and clicked it on. One light bulb, barely giving presence to the dark dungeon space, cast a somber glow over a lumpy pile of life jackets in one corner behind the emergency generator. Suddenly the pile moved.

"Yipes!" the steward jumped. "Is that a rat or an alligator over there?" He quickly retreated to the hatchway, trying to make out the shape of the dark mass in the corner.

"*Fi Faen!*" a sleepy voice grunted out. "Can't a man get a little sleep? *Faen ta deg!*"

"Who's there?" the steward asked, sheepishly.

"Poseidon, you asshole. Poseidon always takes an afternoon nap in the gear room," a voice growled from the darkness.

The steward looked around. "Gear room? Looks more to me like the bar room..." he commented as he counted the numerous empty bottles lying about.

"Now that you mention it, now that I'm awake, that's not a bad idea," the voice grumbled. PSSHHHT! The telltale sound of a bottle cap split through the soft hummmm of the pumps and motors nearby.

The steward cautiously ventured further into the gloomy space, trying to see what lay within. There, on the pile of life jackets, lay Bjarni, one hand under his head, pulling on a Tuborg. Near him was a small open cooler, stocked with beer and ice. He reached overhead, and pulled a chain. A reading light snapped on, illuminating the area even more. Upon brightened inspection, the steward was amazed to see the makings of a stateroom within the gear room. Small table, books, blankets, cooler, boxes of crackers, reading light, pillows, cigarettes, ashtrays, all the comforts of passenger class, here, in the bilge.

"So what are you looking at?" Bjarni groused.

"This place is a palace, Bjarni," he remarked. "This can't be your quarters, can it?"

"My quarters on 'B' Deck are about one fifth this size," Bjarni stated flatly. And hot! Too damn hot. So I appropriated this as my own quarters. Got its own air vent. Stays nice and cool down here regardless of latitude. It's become my private home away from home, so to speak."

"At least I know where to find you now," the steward grinned.

"Ahah! I want you to swear you'll never reveal my secret hiding place to anyone. That's why I have it! To get away from all the bullshit problems that keep coming up."

"So you're hiding out?"

"Being first mate on this tub is no picnic. Anything that goes wrong, somebody calls me. The after cargo hold smells bad, call the first mate. Mrs. Landgrave's toilet is broken, call the first mate. Mr. Brububber needs some shells for target practice, call the first mate. The anchor is stuck in the chocks, call the first mate. A seagull shit in the pool, call the first mate. The ship is entering port, call the first mate. The ship is leaving port, call the first mate. The fucking ship is lost at sea, call the first mate. The captain got drunk and thrown in jail, call the first mate.

"So you hide?"

"So I hide. Nice and dark down here. Can't tell if it's day or night. That way I get some sleep and not worry about the time. You're the first person that ever cared to crawl down here."

"I thought as steward I had it tough, with everyone calling me day and night."

"When they can't find you, they call me. *Helvete*! Don't tell me you're hiding out too?"

"I guess so. I bag out on top of the charthouse. That way I can still hear and see what's going on, but stay out of the way."

"I'll keep your secret if you keep mine."

"You have a deal."

"Life at sea is a bitch. Here, have a beer."

"Thanks. Don't mind if I do."

"NOW THE STEWARD WILL REPORT TO CABIN 2, A DECK, ON THE DOUBLE."

"Hear that, Steward? You can run but you can't hide."

"Damn. I forgot. Time for Mrs. Lovelake's massage again. She's up to two a day now. And getting lower every time."

"Why not just push your steak up her crotch and be done with it?"

"I believe in foreplay."

"Three weeks of it?"

"It's the Babylonian method. Learned it from a Eunuch. Keeps one alive. Billy Bob keeps a pearly 45 in his bureau."

"Running."

"Running?"

"It's a running sea," the captain said, looking out at the waves crossing in from the East. "Just like us..."

The steward leaned with his chin on the spray shield, letting the wind run up his face and hair. "I'm not running...I don't think..."

"We're all running," Eiriksson laughed. "From something. From our wives, our families, our debts, our fears, ourselves. That is why men go to sea."

"Not for the glory of Norway and King Olav? Not for adventure? Not for filthy lucre and spoil? Maybe a little pillaging in Sicily?"

"*Faen i vold*!" Eiriksson roared. "Where have you been, reading comic books again? We are at sea because we choose to leave land behind. It's a harsh life back there, *mon nautonnier*! Not easy to keep your self-respect, wallowing around in all the bullshit on land. So we go to sea. Here, at least, we control our own destiny a bit."

"I thought the owners did," the steward smiled.

"Ha! Fat lawyers in striped suits?" Eiriksson bellowed. "They know nothing of the sea. They only care about profits. They can carp all they want to about maintaining schedules and costs in port and cargo rot, but they aren't here, and they can't easily reach us. We have the con over our own lives, here, at sea."

The steward took out a Players Navy Cut and offered one to the captain. He lit both up, then let the aromatic smoke drift slowly from the sides of his mouth.

"Is it freedom out here... or solitary confinement?"

"Freedom!" Eiriksson roared with the cigarette clamped between his teeth. "We have only the sky and the horizon and the sea and the wind and the sun and the stars to contend with."

"And twelve passengers."

"Oh, they are no problem," Eiriksson said, blowing a long string of smoke into the air like a chimney. "They are the solution! Know why they are aboard a tiny freighter like this? They are the means to break the monotony. They are the foil. Without them, we would have a fucking mutiny onboard every ship of this size in the fleet."

"Mutiny?" the steward chuckled.

"It's humanity!" Eiriksson spat out a small piece of tobacco. "Too much of too few people spells disaster. You need just the right amount of human intercourse, my boy. Locked in a small room with only one person and you'd kill him, or her, in a week. Stuck in the middle of a mass of humanity, like in China, and you'd join the military and kill a few million of them, also in a week. But have just the right amount of human kind around, like twelve passengers and ten crewmembers, on a ship of this size, and it is near the perfect voyage through life. I once calculated it exactly. The perfect world has no more and no less than one person every six hundred and fifty-seven square feet. But that is only on board ship. If you take into account the sea, then happiness at sea is one person every three hundred and sixteen square miles."

"What about on land?"

The captain held up his hands in somewhat mock displeasure. "*Faen i helvete!* Humanity fouled its chances there centuries ago. The land is already all fucked up. Many, many too many people. They're crawling all over each other, fucking up the earth and the streams and the air. Killing each other by the millions. And it is getting worse every year. That is precisely why we go to sea!"

"The great escape?"

"*Fi faen i vold!* It's the path to enlightenment, you fool!"

"What about the Norse Norse, on land? Way up there, above the Arctic Circle. There's not many of them per square foot up there. Can a Norseman find real happiness in the snowy wilderness? Or are they screwed up too?"

"Ha!" Eiriksson laughed. "You want a crazy group, that's where to find it. First of all there's not much of anything up there. So everyone goes out of their fucking mind with boredom and booze. Up around Narvik and Tysfjord, they teach the little girls a song up there, before they're seven or eight. Goes like this:

63

>*'Ikka spur, Pul meg.*
>
>*Paa tjukka, Og ta meg med soerpaa.'*

At the age of twelve, they start singing it to every and any man that has the misfortune to venture above the Arctic Circle."

"Cute. What's it mean?"

"Don't talk. Just fuck. Make me pregnant. And take me South."

"So much for population control."

Eiriksson stood looking out to the horizon, hands on the spray shield railing, wind in his face. "So now you see, we Vikings have to get away from all that shit."

"Traded in easy sex and *akvavit* for herring and *akvavit*, right?"

"Yes. We go to sea. It is our Viking heritage. Norway is a great country. Clean. Spacious. But it only gives the appearance of having lots of open land. That's because with just over three million people, two million of them are at sea."

"Anything to escape the midnight sun?"

"Anything to escape nagging wives and girlfriends."

"They can't catch you at sea..."

"Let them sit in the snow and wait."

"What about Erda? Not a threat any more?"

The captain flipped his cigarette over the side, watching the sparks sputter in the air, then snuff out in the sea.

"Somebody has to cook."

—BEIRUT—

"*Coño.*"

The steward smiled at Bjarni's international choice of expletive, supplanting his usual Norse reference to the devil, as he squinted through the compass sight in disgruntled attempts to get a bearing. The ship barely had way on now, as it coasted into position.

"Mark. *Coño,* 078 degrees." the steward called back, smiling.

Bjarni rose from his sighting, frowned, then hailed forward in a loud voice to two crewmembers on the bow, "Drop anchor!" One of them swung a sledgehammer at a toggle holding the anchor chain, letting it race out in a noisy clanking clatter. Everyone watched as the hook unceremoniously fell with a wet KERPLOOSHH into a murky six fathoms.

Bjarni called into the pilothouse to the steward. "Back one third." The steward clanged the engine telegraph back into the correct position. As the headway ceased, then reversed, Bjarni called in again. "Engine stop. Mark the time and wrap it up."

The Talabot had entered Beirut harbour about 1700, with orders to drop anchor for the night, then at first daylight to proceed to a pier for transfer loading. The steward noted the time in the ship's log, 1738 hours, then spoke across the outer bridge to Herjolfsson, who was still trying to confirm their position by sighting on a hotel cupola in the distance. "Know Beirut?"

Bjarni spoke back, still squinting through the bearing finder, "London is the brains of Western Civilization. Paris is the tongue. Rome is the bosom. Beirut is the crotch."

The steward laughed. "What do you mean?"

"Beirut attracts all kinds of women. It's the playground of three continents. Big vacation spot. Women come from everywhere, looking for a little exotic night action. French, German, Swiss, American, British, Spanish, Italian, Turkish, Greek, Syrian, Jordanian, Egyptian... Secretaries, stewardesses, actresses, models, college students, teachers, divorcees, spinsters... From every culture and creed... agnostics, atheists, Moslems, Catholics, Protestants, Druses, even a few Jewesses keeping a low profile."

"So? Sounds like pussy heaven..."

"Nah. Just the opposite. They're all trying to improve their place at the hotel pool."

"Women in Beirut only want to be kept, you're saying?" the steward asked.

"No, fool! They want to keep us!" Bjarni roared back. "Keep us broke, keep us tamed, keep us exhausted. That's how they insure their little place by the pool, simply by toasting their loaves around those skimpy little bikinis. They let us look but not touch. They're not after anything meaningful. Women in Beirut just want *La Dolce Vita*... not to be bothered in the morning or afternoon, but be well fed and entertained in the evening. For a glamorous life, it's a simple formula. Tease with a little skin, and the bloke goes broke."

Bjarni punctuated his aphorism with a snort, then entered the charthouse. The steward stood for a few more moments gazing at the cityscape, with visions of sugarplums by the pool, wrapped in grape leaves...

Beirut, often called the Paris of the Earstern Med, had a sensuous aura about it. The buildings were predominantly European, as one would find on the coasts of France and Italy and Spain, but interspersed among them were the distinctive flourishes of Islam

- here an azure dome, there an intricate tile, and across a narrow street a columned archway. For centuries, sunset in Beirut had been hauntingly beautiful. Progressively a rose colored scrim would slide over the drama of the day, portending of still richer nocturnal things to follow. Shadows cast by tiers of terraces and hotels and domes and spires arose in an animated mosaic. An unsettling vitality overtook the old as both character and costume changed to greet the darkening, blending hues of the night. And like ghostly sentinels of countless cultures that have mauled Beirut throughout ages past, chorus after chorus of hastily built high rises marched their way up into the highlands above the harbourline, inexorably flaring in hues and prominence under the cast of the ruby gelled fireball quenching itself the West.

"There's a mystery to this city that I haven't experienced before..." the steward spoke quietly to his companion sitting in a rocking chair on the fantail of the Talabot, watching the shifting shadows. "You can almost smell it..."

The woman glanced out from her lap upon which she was peeling boiled shrimp in a bowl, looked up to the hills of Beirut, and sniffed the air. "It is history you smell," she said quietly back. "It is also the smell of the future."

"Or maybe the shrimp..." he added. The steward had found a very likable companion in this unique woman. She was the only female crewmember on the Talabot, and she was the ship's cook. It was not uncommon for Nordic vessels to have women onboard, unlike the British and Americans and most other nations. Possibly because their populations were small compared with nautical aspirations, both Swedes and Norwegians had accepted able-bodied females to 'man' the ships. Or possibly for other reasons.

Erda was a motherly little woman, a rather plump five foot three, not visibly old, but probably pushing 55, who had been cook on the Talabot for over 15 years. She had a broad, warm face with an encouraging smile most of the time, and calm, sky blue eyes. She was hard working and steady, never seeming to be overtaxed or frantic. The daily procession of smorgasbords and surprise main dishes just kept coming, breakfast, lunch and dinner, 7 days a week, even if, like this evening, all the passengers were ashore having dinner. She never revealed the depths of her emotions, but the steward thought he could somehow sense what she was feeling. She was never threatening in her manner, always very comforting to be with. The steward had felt very much at home in Erda's galley, from the first day aboard. He had never asked her last name, and assumed she was Norwegian. But Erda surprised him by being fluent in numerous other tongues as well, including fortunately for the less worldly steward, English.

"You are the new steward," she had said. "You do what I ask. You do what I show you, and you will do well in your job." The easy way she had given him his initial brief had set him comfortably on the right course, even though he had just come from giving the orders to scores of men, in a previously more commanding role in the U.S. Navy.

The steward and the cook sat there together on the fantail of the ship, contrasts in just about every visible way, peeling and cleaning a bottomless bowl of shrimp. The steward kept glancing up at the hills of Lebanon surrounding the long sweeping harbour around them. "It looks confused up there..." he said, surveying the involved tapestry of new highrises, hotels, and houses of worship that were interwoven among stone arches and mudded walls and brick dwellings as old as history.

Erda looked up for a moment, then back at her fingerwork. "It is Beirut. It has the misfortune of standing right at the oldest crossroads of the world, its right buttock in the Occident, its left in the Orient." The steward smiled at her choice of image. Erda was not without her own form of humor. "Beirut struggles to survive by balancing the historical interests of all its varied peoples and cultures. Unfortunately, all it achieves is that it continues to bury itself deeper in all their unwanted *baggage du merde*."

The steward chuckled at such a profound observation from the little lady in the apron. "Bjarni says Beirut is a sin hole."

The old woman smiled. "Bjarni knows nothing about sin holes." She shifted about in her chair, replacing some shrimp in her bowl.

"Herjolfsson never goes ashore. How can he ever understand what's actually out there?..."

After a pause for consideration, Erda continued, "Beirut is a city in the path of Pilgrims... For centuries, it has been left the residue of a steady procession of people possessed. Crusaders and armies and nations and religious zealots of all types have trampled through Beirut, banners flying and passions aflame... each never staying for long, but each raising all kinds of havoc, expunging the old ideas and exalting the new... A garbage dump of ideals and a series of never ending holy wars are the result... Even today, Pilgrims come from all over to ravage Beirut, each craving, seeking something. Some come to spread their way, their belief, to impose it throughout the Middle East at any cost. Some come seeking spiritual salvation and forgiveness. Some lust for more sensuous pleasures. Some lust for gold. But in the end, they are all the same. They all fall victim to Beirut's sirens. Bjarni is correct... The seven deadly sins, they surely must have been born in Beirut... Today, these sins are its biggest tourist attraction, and major export."

"Rather heavy condemnation, Erda..." the steward added. "All people can't be that bad."

"Not bad, Steward. Weak." The old woman turned and spoke to the hills. "That is why I am at sea. To escape weakness of all the demanding masses for a little while."

"All except 12 passengers, the crew, and Eiriksson," he laughed.

"Oh Einar?" she smiled. "He is my toy." With that, Erda got up and entered the galley.

The sun had set and the evening cityscape was atwinkle with all the competitive beacons of Sodom and Gomorrah. The steward stood on the bow, actually a small deck area just ahead of the forward cargo well, which housed the anchor chain, its winch, and two capstans for the loading boom. He had finished his duties and was relaxing a bit, leaning casually on the bow gunwale, looking up the wharf and into the city. The Talabot had finished off-loading cases of whisky and champagne, and on-loading palettes of cedar lumber and boxes of dried figs, and was ready to sail at dawn. The captain and the passengers had gone ashore for dinner and dancing at the Hotel Mediterranean, an old, luxuriously appointed grand dame of a building, now crowded in by the bay in the more elegant section of the city, on a slight bluff.

The steward had been ashore earlier in the day, to see some of the city sights and to shop for fresh vegetables and fruit and yogurt for Erda. However, his primary purpose, as it was whenever in a port, was to feast on the local specialties for lunch, today's savory surprise consisting of a whole eggplant stuffed with spicy ground lamb, raisins, and pine nuts, countered by hot peppered cucumbers in yogurt, and all washed down by a bottle of aniseed-flavored *arack*. He had returned, well sated, to help fix dinner for the crew, but with no passengers aboard and light duties now complete, he was debating whether or not to go ashore again for the evening. He looked up to the stepped hillside rising before him, above the lights of the city, up to the crest of a solitary mount, and spied the first bright planet of the evening, Venus, right on schedule, off to the darkening East. He smelled the pungent flower-scented air, and felt the murmuring heart beat of this city of so many seasonings, spread before him. Mysterious, seductive Beirut certainly was calling to him, with each brush of breeze that rustled his hair.

A sudden glare in his eyes drew them to something new. Out of the distance approached a set of headlights, cruising rather quickly down the wharf. As they grew closer, a distinctive mass filled within a cloud of dust.

The open-topped Land Rover popped to a stop right at the forward hawser securing the ship alongside the wharf. A blond headed driver rose up from the seat to sit on the top of the backrest, and looked up at the ship's name on the bow, painted on the side just under the steward.

"Talabot?" a woman's voice called up.

"t o b a l a T..." the steward called back, reading upside down.

"Prick," the voice snapped back, and with a slam of her bottom back down into the seat, the Land Rover peeled rubber up to the gangway, there to skid again to an abrupt stop.

As was usual on the Talabot, nobody was carefully watching the store. Most of the crew had the evening off. The duty officer was nowhere in sight, and the gangway was unattended. Up the ramp strode a young woman in khaki shorts and a white, short sleeve, four-pocketed shirt with open collar. She held her chin high, accenting straight shoulders and an extended neck with long blond hair streaming off behind in two loosely tied pigtales.

The woman looked about at the head of the gangway, and finding nary a soul, strode forward to the bow. She approached the steward. "Is this how you Vikings won the war? Everybody on the beach getting themselves ploughed?"

The steward just smiled. That seemed like a pretty good idea right now, as he sized up the trim, attractive, miffed young woman confronting him. "I'll plough. You reap..." he thought to himself.

"I'm looking for my aunt and uncle who are supposed to be passengers on this tub," the girl said shortly. "Mr. and Mrs. Herman Landgrave. They aboard?"

"Sorry, Miss. All the passengers are ashore for an evening of spoil and debauchery. Can I take a message for the Landgraves?" He remembered the American couple from the Midwest quite well, unique in their futile attempts to inject their Calvinist attitudes into all conversations of the day.

"Damn." She stomped her foot, a dusty desert boot capped by khaki ankle socks. "I drive all the way here from Baalbek just to see them, and they go off drinking. "Please tell them that Liza was here to meet them." She shrugged her straight shoulders, then cocked her head and smiled obliquely up at the city. "I guess they didn't get my letter in time. Damnation."

"I think I know where they are, Miss," the steward said softly. The first evening star flared softly over her head above the crest of the hillside. "I can guide you there, in your Rover, if you wish."

71

The girl finally noticed that the man facing her, in white shirt and shorts with white knee socks, was a person, not a toy sailor to do Shirley Temple's bidding. A rather tall and handsome person at that. She quickly sized him up, extrapolating from her archeological experience at about six two, one eighty-five, mid-twenties. "Could you?" She was all sugar now, realizing his offer of help could just save a lost day.

"But first I am about to have my dinner," said the steward. "Would you join me? It is a light smorgasbord, the choicest morsels selected and prepared by our vigilant steward, just for me. Please join me." She hesitated, surprised by the offer.

"We will eat right here, on the bow. It is a nice view, and peaceful. You look like you could stand a little sustenance after your long drive." She tilted her head, trying to grasp some other meaning... "Please. Join me..." he continued genuinely without inflection. "I have the champagne chilling right here."

The steward reached down under a small table that he had set out earlier on the small bow deck, from experience, in anticipation of any of the passengers who might prefer a touch of solitude for cocktails or dining that evening. He lifted up a frosting silver bucket with a bottle of Dom Perignon probing forth like a golden mushroom through a field of sleet ice. As professionalism would have it, he had also set out two flutes on the pressed linen tablecloth.

The girl looked at him in disbelief. "Who is this creep?" she thought to herself. "Watch out, now... But wait. He couldn't have known I was coming... And I haven't eaten for hours... Sooo..." The steward deftly twisted out the cork at a 45-degree angle as he had been taught, spilling not a drop as frothy mist seeped forth from the bottleneck.

"Oh, what the hell. I'd be delighted," Liza cooed as demurely as she could through a throat parched with road dust. "I can find them later tonight." The thought of fresh seafood and champagne brought a rush of saliva to her lips, after a month's steady diet of lamb and *arack* out in the hills of Lebanon.

He poured two classes carefully, and handed one to the girl. "*Skaal*. As they say in Norway," he toasted her glass. "To your health... and eternal beauty."

"*Boden See*. As they say in Germany. Into the gut." Liza toasted back. As she wolfed down the whole glass in one long draught, she thought, "This Norski is cute. He has a way of making bullshit sound kind of nice."

"Here we go..." mused the steward as he watched a $10 swallow of the Dom slide down her throat. It was fortunate that the deal he had cut with Eiriksson, for his passage to the Orient, was working as steward for no pay but for all he could eat or drink. And the Talabot only carried the best bar stock, tax free at sea.

"If you'd like to freshen up, please use your uncle's cabin, over there. Cabin 6..." the steward said, pointing to a passenger cabin still lit and accessible nearby on the A Deck. Use this master key. Please. The steward and others go in there frequently. I'm sure your aunt and uncle won't mind. And in the meantime, I will have our dinner served."

He watched as first the young woman nodded with a slight smile, then walked carefully off to Cabin 6, climbing the ladder to A Deck quite certain in the knowledge that two eyeballs were sending X-ray beams through the back of her shorts. She added an extra wiggle just for good measure.

The steward broke his transfixation and got to work. First he went to Eiriksson's stateroom and turned on his new RCA record player. Onto it he popped a nearby stack of Deutsche Grammophon LP's, specifics on the labels unseen. After adjusting the volume to medium high, enough to pump sufficient sound forward through the open portholes, he raced off to the galley at the stern of the ship. There he threw two silver platters on to the worktable, slapped on some fresh lettuce leaves, added some endive spears and radishes, then dumped container after container of Beluga caviar, succulent shrimp, pickled herring, six varieties of smoked fish, exotic fruit bits, rich and pungent cheeses, and other Scandinavian delicacies on to the remaining spaces. Along the sides he dolloped gobs of mustards and sauces and herb flavored mayonnaises, flourished by sprigs of dill and wedges of lemon alternating with lime. To this he added rye crisp and pumpernickel squares. The whole display resembled a cross, merged within a circle. Finally with a well-positioned plop of a pink rosebud on each platter, he lifted one in each hand and hastened back to the bow. "Not bad," he thought. "Under two minutes. I'm getting better."

He stood casually by the rail sipping his champagne, watching the rising evening planet off to the East as he heard her footsteps. The table was set, complete with hurricane candle and linen. He turned and bowed slightly to the proud, fresh young face with the slim neck and straight shoulders and golden pigtails and green eyes, looking up to his in the candlelight. Dusted off, she was refined and beautiful. "Your table for two on the bow, *Mademoiselle*."

As if on cue, an accompaniment of deep, rich strumming of double bass and violoncello wafted slowly from the captain's stateroom, urged on by a growing complement of strings, hinting of more rapturous things to come.

"Now here is a guy who has learned how to treat a lady..." Liza thought to herself. The steward helped her into her chair. She noticed that she sat on a slight tilt of the deck, but that the table itself had been leveled. "Keeping me off-balance?" she looked up and asked, noting the difference in the two.

"Being at sea, one learns to keep things in proper perspective," he replied as he served her plate from over her right shoulder. "I hope you will enjoy what the steward has prepared for you this evening." The heroic mid-range of Wolfgang Windgassen could be heard adding tremulent confirmation in the distance.

They ate and talked and looked at the stars and at the cityscape, quite content and alone in their own little world on the bow deck, for about two hours. The champagne helped mold the mood of the evening, as did the music welling and surging from the stateroom... alternatingly soft, then passionate, then increasingly building and more assertive, only to flow onward incessantly, again into another key, another motif, another world.

They talked, and drank, and talked. Or rather she talked, and he listened, with fascination. Liza Landgrave had been on a dig at some tell in the hills for over 6 months now, working as an assistant to one Herr Doctor Professor Wolfram von Eschenbach from the University of Bayreuth. She was here in Lebanon on a field project for her doctorate in anthropology from Champagne Urbana. Her dissertation, soon to be completed, was to be a rather broad comparison study of old cultures and new. She had written of her ideas to this renowned archeologist from the Thuringian Valley, near Eisenach, and was asked by him to join his continuing dig at Baalbek. So far she had found life in Lebanon to be dusty, hot, sleazy, replete with scarab and asp, but just packed with historic and archeological goodies that had made her stay rich in academic adventure beyond her dreams.

But, encamped in the outback, her social life left much to be desired. One big problem turned out to be Wolfie, as she called her boss. She had first thought that this middle-aged pillar of academe was only interested in the quest for truth and beauty, to be found digging into days of antiquity. But she was surprised out of her sleep one night in her tent, by an academic asp slinking in between her sheets, more interested in having a good dig in her behind. She had thrown him out with a well-placed bonk of her dissertation draft, but forever after she had had to keep her rear sensors on alert as she bent over the days' dusty finds. Wolfie, it seemed, now was content to lust after her heinie only from afar, hesitant to incur again the foul-mouthed wrath and impact of weighty research of an American doctoral student, so fair and so faithful to her work.

They talked and talked, and drank. He watched her eyes, distant and aglow, as she spoke of the magical names of history, of Tiberius and Tyre, of Sidon and Baalbek, of Tarsus and Tripoli, of Nazareth and Jerusalem and Byzantium and Alexandria. She spoke of Seleucids and Ottomans, of Phoenicians and Romans, of Arabs and Druses and Egyptians, cultures evoking all the passions and pulls and struggles of the human kind. Her extensive knowledge of the region was fascinating. He listened as a steady procession of deities and semi-deities and kings and mortals fought it out, only to be cast down off their mountain of power by some new upstart, holier or tougher than any of the thou's before. He sat spellbound as she wove overwhelming surges of Islam and Judaism and Christianity into a rich historical tapestry before his eyes. She obviously loved her work.

"So what do you see in all this history, in all this struggle?" he asked softly, at last. "Are we now any different? Have we learned anything?"

Liza stopped short, now diverted from her doctoral diatribe, and shrugged her shoulders. A wry smile came over her lips, as she focused in on his question. "Wolfie found this tomb of an early Assyrian king. Bellabod. Died in 3200 B.C. Wolfie was able to decipher a cuneiform inscription on his sarcophagus. 'Here lies Bellabod, God of Gods, King of Kings, Mightiest of the Mighty, who crushed the Shaldoreans, Great King to all people, King of Tribeab and Murt, of Ald and Cresis, and of all lands and peoples even unto the Jeffer, joined here and hereafter with his beloved consort.'"

"And...?" the steward asked.

"These two bodies, one of them about 45 judging by his teeth, the other about 20... these bones and dust, one on top of the other in an eternal hug, smothered with gems and jewels and surrounded with gold and urns and the most opulent finery.... were both men. The king was a queen," she said flatly. "No... I must conclude... we haven't changed much in 5,000 years."

Liza popped a Greek olive into her mouth, cleared the meat with her teeth, then blew the pit over the side of the bow in a point of punctuation. Then she turned back and smiled, looking up at the steward's eyes. The steward leaned back in his chair, folded his arms, and smiled at this woman of mischievous wit and marvelous dimension, seated before him. They sat quietly for a few moments, searching in each other's eyes for the stars above them. Birgit Nilsson softly began to call to them from the captain's stateroom.

"Here and all around in Palestine and Lebanon there are temples to the sun, to the moon, to stars, to fire, to animals, to mountains, to male and female gods and demi-gods..." Liza continued. "The region could have been an eternal Eden, if all its impassioned supplicants had each let others pursue their beliefs and illusions without criticism. But each wave of these lunies grew so egocentric in their views and self-aggrandizing in their ways, each feeling that their path to paradise was the only true or possible way... that death, swiftly dealt out to any and all who didn't agree, became the obvious means to eliminate any competition. Inevitably, fevered acceptance by the closest of sycophants apotheosized the loudest megalomaniacs into divine rank... The illusion is god... usually revealed in dramatic moments of smoke and fire and zaps of light, confirming that there is only one true path to enlightenment and eternal life."

"There have been so many gods. You say it is all illusion... Not reality?" he asked quietly.

She put her chin on top of her hands, looked off into the deepest night, and sighed.

"Reality? It frankly all had more to do with power and territory and jewels than with any spiritual quests or ideas. It seems that the longer the robes, the grander the trappings, the bigger was the sham. When one deciphers some of the outlandish crap each self-promoting king or priest or prophet set forth in stone, propounding his theories, it is beyond belief. That seems to be what sold in the old days... Things so beyond belief that everyone wanted some, a la mode. The changing fashions of god... this year gilded wings, next a bulls head, someday in a *dirndl*."

"But I see a constancy there, not just frivolous quest for next season's divine fashion," the steward injected. "I see centuries of craving by all cultures, certainly for food and leadership and protection, but more for some form of spiritual assurance, some kind of parental pat on the head, some sage rationale that things were as they were... and are as they were meant to be... for some good reason... and that an explanation of this grander picture, someday, if they were good children, they too would be allowed to see and understand."

Liza looked deeply into the eyes of this stranger, who seemed calm and non-threatening in his argument. His manner was open and inviting, not opinionated.

"If you mean that faith and hope and wonder have always beat in the heart of everyman, no matter how gullible, I agree. That is the one beautiful thread that seems to surface every now and then. But I tend to get a little disappointed at times in what I uncover... a little frustrated. It seems that faith and truth are for the most part mutually exclusive."

"Don't be discouraged. You'll find what you're really searching for..." the steward said, looking into her deep green eyes, sparkling in the glow of the hurricane candlelight.

"I guess life is just one big dig," she added, "with the dusty layer of each generation pretty much just the same as all the ones before, but dressed out in different colors for that year. Unfortunately, the majority of history I've dug out of the ground around here indicates that all those impassioned souls were usually suckered by power-mad charlatans in priests' clothing."

The rich harmonies of brass and bass began to fill the night air.

A slowly moving trail of golden lights snaked its way up the hillside beyond the wharf, voices softly chanting in the fragrant evening air. "Look... up on the hill. Isn't it beautiful?" he asked.

"Pilgrims..." she responded. "Maybe Rosicrucians..."

The light snake worked its way up through the maze of the city, upward into one area of the piedmont beyond, where at the top one clear bright rose light stood calling out across the sea. Nearby to the left, just under the apse of the brightest planet in the Eastern sky, was another hill, its crest aglow with a meld of rose-colored lights, shimmering and moving within a strange amorphous circle.

"Up there... whatever's on top... Very appealing, isn't it?"

"Yes, they both are..." she answered, as a chorus of passionate voices swelled from the stateroom beyond.

"I have an idea," the steward said, taking her hand. Come with me. You need a new perspective on life..." In his other hand, he picked up a fresh bottle of Dom, chilling in wait under the table, and somehow clutched it and their two flutes in all his fingers. Liza offered no resistance to his suggestion. Rather, she seemed to find the idea alluring. Then he led her, slowly, down the short ladder to the cargo deck, across to the base of the mainmast supporting the forward loading boom.

"Up there..." he pointed. "Climb up there."

"You're kidding," she said, looking up a seemingly endless rung ladder, leading to the crowsnest high up on the mast.

"Come on. Afraid of passionate highs?" he urged gently.

"I'm already high, you louse," Liza responded, still looking up. "Oh, what the hell. You only live once." With that, she started up the ladder.

The steward watched her climb, slim long legs in khaki shorts and rugged desert boots alternating carefully up the mast. Then he started up after her, with bottle and glasses in one hand, alternately grasping the next rung with his hand or his free thumb for support. "Whew! Try this one-handed someday," he called up to her.

She paused in her ascent and answered back. "At least I know you're preoccupied and not looking up my shorts right now."

"I'd say you're on top of things. Just don't step on my thumb," he groused back, hanging precariously on to the bottle and mast.

Finally she reached the small barrel-shaped platform that served once as the lookout's crows nest, last used in WWII and now replaced by a small, revolving radar on top of the bridge. "It's beautiful up here," she said breathlessly. "What a view."

"I thought you'd like it here," he grunted as he struggled into the waist-high steel bucket with the bottle and glasses.

"It's spectacular! I am lofted out of my dirty digs, at last." They stood for a few moments, quietly toasting their ascent with fresh champagne, savoring the fresh night air and looking out over the city and the hills. "I wonder what they seek up there?" she asked, nodding up at the hill with a bright light. The snake of lights was half way there by now, slowly throbbing and weaving and winding up its dark path.

"Ask *Rosenkreutz*," he replied. "The meaning of life, maybe..."

"And over there," she said, nodding to the adjoining crest with the rosy glow at the top.

"Also the meaning of life, but looks more like it's *la vie en rose*..." he surmised, judging from its aura.

The sky above was aglow with broad swaths and swirls and crescendos of heavenly light capping the hillside in an unending halo... The air was warm and fresh and and sensuously alive with floral aromas.

The music swirled in the air beneath them, rich deep bass violins slowly setting the theme, first teasing one's passions in a lesser crescendo, then urged on by a full range of strings and woodwinds only to be carried even further aloft by triumphal brass in an ever-building, ever-pounding re-crescendo, finally carrying with it all the impassioned dreams of the chorus... reaching out... longing for the inevitable...

"BUM BUMMMM BUM BUMMMM... BUM BUM BUM BUMMM BUMMM BUMMM BUMMMM BUMMMM..."

He took her face to his, and gently kissed her fully on the mouth. She seemed to stiffen, then shudder, then fall fully into his chest with hers, arms hanging limply down at her sides. She had no difficulty returning his kiss, opening her mouth to his.

"BUM BUMMMM BUM BUMMMM.... BUM BUM BUM BUMMM BUMMM BUMMM BUBUMMM BUMMMM..."

She shuddered again as he slowly reached down to unbutton her blouse, down to the bottom, and then spread it to her shoulders to reveal glorious contrasts in golden tan and creamy white and delicate rose, firm and full and perfection in shape, pointing at the stars. She arched her head back to the sky as he bent to touch his mouth to her. The urgent, incessant music surged about them, filling the night, enveloping their isolated nest with the exultations of a chorus of pilgrims, lifting, swelling, building, impelling their passionate pleas ever upward, lofting all sensations to heights heretofore unknown.

"BUM BUBUMMM BUM BUMMM BUMMM...."

"I love this damn music..." she groaned in ecstasy.

"Ummhhh..." he replied enthusiastically.

"Damn Wagner...It drives me crazy..." she moaned through her teeth.

"Ummmhummmmhhh..." he responded.

"BUM BUBUMMM BUM BUMMM BUMMM..."

"Aaaahhhh, damn music... I'm can't take it any more..."

"Ummmm... Unnnhhhmmmm know what...mmmmhh mean...."

"Oooooohhh....One instrument missing in this orchestration..." she moaned through thrills of unbearable sensitivity.

"BUM BUMM...."

"What's that?" he mumbled.

She fell to her knees, and urgently opened the fly of his shorts.

"BUM BUM BUM BUMMMM BUMMMM BUMMMM BUMMMM BUMMMM BUMMMM BUMMMMMM..."

"The saxophone..." she groaned as she grabbed hold of him with both hands.

"Hermannn!"

A plaintive scream pierced the air, shattering all rapture. The steward looked over and down into the brightness below, on to the wharf, where next to an old Mercedes taxi the driver was helping a frantic, trembling woman to the foot of the gangway. "Help!" she cried up to the ship. "Someone please come and help. We must find Herman!"

"Herman?" A somewhat mussed blond head popped up over the edge of the metal bucket and peered below. "Oh my god..." said Liza. "It's my Aunt Fiona!"

A trio buffo of pleas and calls and recognitions and acknowledgments and curses accompanied Liza's and the steward's stumbling descent down from the outer reaches of heaven. The middle-aged woman, all decked out in high heels and cocktail dress and sparkling necklace and bracelets and rose-flowered scarf, staggered up the gangway and fell dramatically into the arms of her long lost niece.

"Liza!" she pleaded. "Liza! Thank god you're here. You must help me save Herman before he is lost. He has his mind set on going straight to Hell!"

After an episode of arm waving and pointing and breast-beating, the woman sat down in a plop on the deck. It followed in panting narrative that she and her husband had gone with the others and the captain for dinner at the Hotel Med. As usual, some of the passengers got smashed on Beefeater martinis. Herman was one of them. And as the evening's festivities disintegrated with each passing olive, the party started to tear itself apart. Auntie and Uncle had had a public shouting match, she threatening to come home alone, and he saying fine, he was going off with the captain for some real fun.

"And off he went!" she cried. "Without me! To get into all kinds of trouble! There are infidels out there, you know!"

"That's not the kind of trouble I'd worry about with Uncle Hermie, Auntie. Where were they going?" Liza asked.

"I don't know... Something about taking the party to new heights, to some place called... Cytherea! Or something like that..." she moaned.

The taxi driver, who had been standing in silent awe, watching these arm flapping dramatics, flashed a telling smile to the steward, and nodded his head.

"Um hum. One of those. Where do we find Cytherea's?" he asked the driver.

The driver smiled and pointed to the top of the crest above them, to the rosy glow of lights set against the heavens. "Up there."

"I've got to go get him," Liza said firmly to the steward.

"You can't handle this alone. You're a woman in a wild man's world out there. I'll go with you," the steward replied.

She looked into his eyes, somehow already knowing she could count on him. "I'll take all the help I can get, protecting my backside," said Liza, remembering her months with the rear view mirror spent with the boys on the dig. "Let's take my Rover." She started to the gangway, unwittingly buttoning up the final closures on her white blouse.

A small figure stepped forth from the shadows into the lighted deck. It was Erda.

"Wait. You'll need this," she said softly but directly as she handed the steward a black doctor's bag. "All sorts of things in here. Good for all kinds of emergencies." Then she placed a white bundle into Liza's hands. "Here, take this kitchen coat. You should cover up a bit. Some in this city will take a strange view of women in shorts after dark."

The steward and Liza hurried down the gangway to the Land Rover parked on the wharf, followed by night-piercing wails of Birgit and her aunt. "Bring Herman home safely! Please!"

"Don't worry, Auntie," Liza called back as she stuffed her arms into the long white coat, flowing behind her like a train. "We'll keep Hermie out of purgatory." Liza then jumped into the driver's seat, with the steward only half in on his side, slapped the Rover into successive gears down the wharf, courageously roaring toward the increasingly menacing rhythms out in the darkness of the city.

The steward started to rummage about in the black bag. It contained the usual variety of medicines and bandages, a couple of syringes, some strange tools and pliers, a stethoscope and blood pressure band, and rolls of tape. It also revealed an envelope that, upon inspection, yielded ten crisp new $100 bills. "Emergencies indeed..." the steward thought as he realized the captain had obviously had addressed the need for disaster training for nights on the beach before.

Also in the black bag were a few more surprises. A ten inch square sky blue United Nations flag, the kind a tourist buys at the U.N. in New York City. And two arm bands with a red cross on a white field. And a spare pair of the captain's shoulder boards, four gold stripes across black, with a star at the apex.

"Here, put this on." he said to his intent blond chauffer. "We may need some muscle tonight." He then helped her push her arm through the armband and up the bulky long coat sleeve into position near her shoulder. Next he put the captain's boards through the shoulder loops on his shirt. Liza glanced at him oddly, then turned back to her driving, as he too put a red cross armband on his arm. He looked at the coat that hung like a huge baggy robe on the trim, five foot six driver. "Extra large," he chuckled. "Atta girl, Erda."

They raced their way up into the city, zigzagging back and forth, weaving through the terraced streets into the foothills. Suddenly they rounded a corner to come only to a screeeeching halt. In front of them stretched an endless line of people, two and three abreast, mumbling in unison, trudging along dressed in a variety of clothes, and each one carefully carrying a lighted candle. Their faces took on a drunken, transcendental look in the flickering light and shadows. "Aaaaarrrr gooodddaaaiiiss waaaannnnaaafooooooo..."

"Oh, god!" she gasped. "Pilgrims!" She started beeping the horn, but to no avail, as the chanting chain of humanity seemed oblivious to the agitation at the side, or felt that they had the right of way.

"Wait!" he said. The steward jumped out of the Rover and taped the United Nations flag on to the heavy metal grillwork that shielded the headlight on his side. "Now let's try it." He led the way on foot, like walking a camel to water. Slowly the Land Rover moved into the crowd and across. He jumped in as she gunned it, spraying the moaning, suffering masses with gravel and dust.

"Who are they?" he asked in half interest.

"Who cares," she replied. "Maybe some Masonic convention. We have our own journey to worry about."

They roared by street after street, climbing through and out of the city, roaring past surprised civilians walking and driving through, past the local gendarmes standing perpetually angry and vigilant with bushy black moustaches and paramilitary uniforms and Sten guns slung over their shoulders. Each *flic* stared with wonder and probably with some envy, as the blond dish in the Land Rover, flag flying and horn beeping, sped with abandon through their respective intersections of confusion.

Finally they were reaching the outer limits of the city. Liza pulled up to a "Y" at a high point on the road and asked, "Which way now?"

The steward pointed starward and to the left, to the top of the hill, where the rose lights were gaining in intensity. "God only knows. Go that way. Head for those lights, up on top." Off they roared again. "Nice view for a cat house," he mused to himself as he looked back over the sea behind them.

The Land Rover slowed as it approached glow. Cytherea's was a large low building capping the crest of the hill, surrounded by an eight-foot high circular wall and high front gate, all floodlit in red. The whole compound seemed to be swaying and rolling with a strange rhythm, with eerie moaning sounds exuding out of the doors and windows. "Wow! I've never seen something like this before. This place is really hopping..." Liza said with a touch of hesitation in her voice.

They entered through the large steel gateway, elaborately decorated with Islamic heavenly motifs, yet covered here and there with climbing roses. The parking area inside the compound was chocked full... Mercedes and Citroens were everywhere, limos, sedans, sports cars, inter-parked with the occasional pompous Bentley, stylishly plump Jag, or sleek Ferrari. "Not a club for the working stiff," she said objectively.

Liza and the steward cruised right up to the front door under an elaborately pillared portico of Moorish arches. Inside the arched doorway, rose-colored light filtered out from the pink plastered interior. After peering at first into this slowly bubbling cauldron through a layer of sweet, sickening smoke, they strode courageously through the front door, only to be greeted by the roaring scream of a titan at bay. "*Fi Faen*! Devil in Hell! Back! All you fucking worms, BACK! Or I'll bash your heads in!"

Swooshhh! It was Eiriksson. Who else? Eiriksson was standing astride a great round table, naked except for his scant white jockey underwear squeezed down to bikini size by a huge lilywhite belly and barrel chest expanded to their limits, violently swinging a massive smoldering incense brazier on a great chain around his head, like a glowing planet around the sun.

Swooosshhh!! Smoke trailed the perfect arc of the heavy ornate bronze, as it swung past the heads of an assortment of well-muscled gorillas in turbans and pantaloons and curly-toed slippers, trying to get their hands on this raving maniac above them.

SWOOOOOOSSSSHHHHH! "Ah, HA! Almost got you, you teat of your mother's goat! *Fi Faen! Faen i vold!*"

Behind Eiriksson was a pillared platform, enveloped in dense incense smoke through which shafts of light escaped. Opulent velvets and sleek silks in reds and purples and pinks covered the platform. Across a carefully arranged litter of plush pillows and scatterings of rose petals, under a flowing, billowing canopy of sheerest pink voile, lay a voluptuous woman. She was dressed only in see-through pantaloons and necklaces and bracelets and wispy scarves, with long silky black hair cascading down to casually cover her more than ample breasts. Her fingernails, each at least 4 inches long, were lacquered cherry red, matching her wet lips. She was elaborately made up to look somewhere between Liz Taylor and the Bride of Dracula. The woman just lay there, observing, calm and smiling through the tumult around her, as if she had seen it all a million times before.

"Back, you turds of Neptune! I'll smite you right in the fucking face!" Eiriksson bellowed above the din. SWOOOOSSSHHH! Yet again a wave of humanity shrinked from the power of a swinging brazier.

Around the room, spread and sprawled about platforms and flowing pools and pillows and smoking urns and water pipes, other bodies lay focused on their own activities, engaged in an eye-opening variety of intricate intimacies in groups of twos and threes. "Christ..." observed Liza. "I think I've found the conclusion to my dissertation."

The steward stood wide-eyed at the edge of a sunken floor holding an oily pool sprinkled with rose petals, amazed at the commanding power being unleashed by the Viking. "What do I do now?" he asked himself. SWOOOOOOOOSSHHH! A big one! Turbans and fezzes ducked in all directions.

"Here's one for you, you son of a pig's prick!" growled the captain as he took aim with a mighty SWOOOOOOSSSHHHH! The brazier swung again its sweeping arc, just missing the moustache of the target Neanderthal, but in returning from its apogee it found its chain inappropriately jerked, causing it to slam smack into the forehead of Wotan personified, CRACKKKK!, knocking him back off the table in a staggering crash, and into the waiting arms and sumptuous bosoms of Our Lady of the Night. A stunned silence fell upon the room, rhythmic grunts and gyrations and moans not withstanding as here and there eyes looked up briefly from more sensual duties.

"He's down!" gasped one of the moustaches. "Let's get him!"

"Down, gentlemen. *Langsam... Langsam...*" spoke the couchant queen. "Slowly. It is over... He is senseless."

Eiriksson lay there in her lap, out cold, but still breathing heavily. He looked like some fallen wrestler, all blood and sweat and skin.

"*Liebschen... Liebschen...* You are such a foolish man..." this fleshy madonna whispered to him softly while she stroked his hair and forehead, sadly mirroring the passion of the *Pieta*.

Two deep black pools looked up to meet the stare of the steward, as he approached cautiously through the glistening bodies and incense pots and pillows, black bag in hand, Liza trailing closely at his rear. "And who may you be?" she eyed him with a hint of a smile, while licking her red lips to make them shine.

The steward gulped at her calm and measured directness. "I am his shipmate. I will take him home." He added, fascinated by this large, voluptuous woman unruffled by a sleeping titan in her arms, "And you are... Cytherea?"

She nodded slowly, keeping his stare. Then she looked down at Eiriksson, now snoring softly, and said, "He will be alright. I know him for many years. He has the skull of a bull."

The steward leaned up to the platform and looked at Eiriksson. Aside from a reddening horn now growing in the center of his forehead, he looked like he was sleeping like a baby, safe and secure in the bosom of one who loved him.

Liza had stepped up, also to look at Eiriksson. She reached out to take his pulse. "And who are you, my lovely one? Looking for a job?" asked Cytherea, seductively eyeing her blond hair and pretty face. "You look experienced in the pleasures of history."

Liza jumped back. "I'm looking for my uncle."

"Aren't we all..." Cytherea replied idly.

"Really," Liza spat back. "Did someone come here with this ape? A middle aged American man, tall, with gray hair."

"No, Einar came alone... But look about you, pretty one..." Cytherea said as she gracefully waved her hand towards the rose scented, smoky room. "There are many middle-aged men in here for you to choose from. They are the ones on the bottom of their respective piles."

"Einar?" the steward asked. "You know him?"

"Einar and I go way back, to younger days in Bremen. He was a sailor. I was a student of life. We became close friends..." Cytherea reminisced. "Little Einar always comes to visit his old friend Holda when he is in port. I offer him what he doesn't find at sea. The comforting bosom of a woman."

"Holda?" the steward asked. "I thought you were..."

"Holda Gotlieb, *liebschen*. Cytherea is my, ahhh... professional name..." she replied, smiling into his eyes.

"Is this how you treat your friends?" Liza asked probingly, surveying the involved heaps of flesh about her.

"Oh, lovely one... Einar and I are only friends. He comes here to pour out his heart to me... to talk. He drinks so much he can't even get it up any more. He takes off his clothes so he won't seem out of place. Besides, he has always been faithful to his wife and family."

"Talk. Un Huh. So then what was all that ruckus about?" Liza probed.

"Oh, that..." she shook her head casually. "Einar strangled Leda's pet swan after it attacked him. Then he threw the limp carcass back across the room and Leda simply went crazy, so my bouncers took him on too." Holda replied.

"Why did a swan attack him?" the steward asked, afraid to ask.

"Because of that *scheistkopf* who had chosen to party with Leda and her beloved swan," Holda replied blasély. "Seems he lost interest in Leda and tried to bugger the swan. Swans don't like that, I guess... Stupid swan..."

The steward couldn't believe all this. All of a sudden there was a piercing wail, cutting substantially above the din of sinning noises in the pit, coming from a cage lofted by a chain near the ceiling in one corner. "Elizaaabeeeeaaaath! Heaaalllllpp meee!"

Liza staggered back in shock, looking up at the cage, and grasped the steward's hand. She stood there in a spotlight, mouth agape, hands outward and downward in dismay, long blond pigtails trailing down her oversized butcher's coat with blood stains on the side pockets. "Oh god!" she gasped. "It's Wolfie!"

There he was, the good Herr Doctor Professor, naked as a jaybird in a gilded cage about the size of a large steamer trunk. "*Oh, mein Gott. Lass mir auuss! Aaaauuusss!*" he wailed, shaking the cage like a stir-crazy primate.

"Wolfie, you son of a bitch, what the hell are you doing up there!" Liza yelled up at the shaking cage.

"Let me out, Liza. Please! Please don't tell anyone. My reputation will be ruined!" Wolfie pleaded. "I will never work again at Bayreuth!"

"Neither will the swan," Liza snapped back.

"Holda, let us get these two out of here. Please..." the steward asked the blasé madam. "We have a Rover outside."

Holda looked at the steward, sizing him up and down. "They are yours... But someday you must come here alone... Or possibly with your pretty friend here..." She smiled without inflection, "I may be able to teach you both more of life..."

The steward shuddered, somewhere between being nauseated and intrigued. "Deal. Someday. But now... What do we owe you for the mess?..." he asked as he surveyed the destruction, bodies, blood and feathers about him, something out of a Hieronymus Bosch.

"Einar owes me nothing. I owe him. But Herr Professor *Scheistkopf* up there... He owes Leda for that stupid swan. Gimme two hundred bucks," Holda stated flatly, all business.

The steward groped into the little black bag and pulled out two crisp $100 bills. "He put them into her hand, pressed it briefly, and said, "Thanks." She looked back, and nodded her head to the side with a slight shrug.

Then he grabbed Liza, still standing in the limelight, glaring dramatically up at Wolfie, and pulled her over to where the cage's chain was secured to a large iron cleat on the wall. "Let's get out of here," he whispered as he unhitched the crucial link. "While we still can."

WHAM! Wolfie dropped to the floor like a golden bomb. "Come on, Wolfie!" Liza shouted to the dazed aviaphile. "*Aus!* Get out of there." She unlatched the door hooks. Wolfie fell out in a naked heap, on top of three groaning, sweaty bodies, one fat and white, one slim and black, one a curvy yellow. He sat there stunned for a minute, debating whether to slide in between them.

"Come on, you jerk! Out the door!" Liza pulled him up from the *melange* of flesh and swung one of her desert clodhoppers into his bare white backside.

"Wait! My clothes! Where are my clothes?" Wolfie pleaded.

"Here. Put this in front of you." the steward said while bending over to somehow grab hold of the captain. He threw Herr Doctor Wolfie a large golden fringed pillow, stuffed with down. "Liza!" he called. "Help me with the Viking."

Together they succeeded in raising Eiriksson to a seated position, and then pulled him over the steward's shoulder, fireman style. The steward staggered under the massive body. "Out the door! Before you have to carry both of us," he groaned at Liza.

Somehow the foursome, Liza in bloody butcher coat, Wolfie with pillowed fig leaf, and the steward shouldering a fallen Viking in bikini, staggered out the door of Cytherea's pleasure palace, exulting in their escape to the parking portico and fresh air and freedom, only to be greeted by the flashing red lights of local *gendarmerie* jeeps and six large, bushy-moustached policemen, with Sten guns at the ready.

The steward attempted to straighten up and spoke bravely. "We're glad you're here. You can help us, Officer."

A brutish man with a nine-inch jet-black handlebar stepped forward, menacingly. "We hear... report. You have here... go mad... wild bird." he spoke in a gruff, deep broken English, laced with accent and garlic.

"Yes." The steward replied calmly. "Inside. You will find its dead body. A berserk swan. You go see."

The chief looked past him and through the doorway into the red, throbbing smoky den. He licked his moustache but made no move to enter. "Shit..." the steward muttered to himself. Holda obviously had the cops on her payroll.

The lead moustache leveled his Sten gun at the steward and Eiriksson. "You all... come with. Under arrest," the brute growled.

"What?" asked Liza. "Why?"

"Break god's law. Sin. No clothes." he grumbled, and started to pull handcuffs from his belt to put on Wolfie and Eiriksson.

"Stop!" the steward yelled. "Get back! Don't touch him!" He struggled to turn his Red Cross armband into view. They hesitated.

"These two. Sick." Liza took his lead and piped in, stepping in front of the three men, and showing her Red Cross badge and even redder bloody pockets. "Do not touch. Rabid swan. Rabid swan bit them. Rabies, you big knuckleheads."

The lead cop stepped back. The other five, probably not fully understanding, followed his move. "Rabbi bite who?"

"Rabies!" Liza continued, "Rabies!" hissing right into number one moustache. "No touch or dead! You see. Rabies!" she pointed at Wolfie who was frothing at the mouth a bit in shivering panic.

The moustaches stepped another step back, and leveled their Sten guns at Wolfie.

"We take these two to hospital," the steward chimed in, as he staggered over to the Rover and dumped Eiriksson unceremoniously in the rear seat with a thump. "Sick. Do not touch."

He returned to Liza, took the black bag from her hand and opened it, and revealed a 10-inch syringe to the cops. Eyes widened as he spoke softly while holding the needle straight up and flicking the canister as if adjusting a quantity level. "You have all come too close. You will all need to be inoculated."

The moustaches suddenly withdrew into the darkness. "You go. Take to hospital. We guard Rabbi's swan. Go!" number one moustache called back.

"That's our cue, Wolfie!" Liza whispered severely. "Get in the goddamn Rover. Now!"

Wolfie climbed into the back seat with Eiriksson, awkwardly crawling over his slumbering body, slimy nude to grimy nude. He kept his pillow covering his privates.

Liza jumped into the driver's seat, started up and gunned the engine. The steward swung aboard, making sure the syringe was in full view. The Rover roared off through the collusion of luxury cars, out the gate and into the fresh night air. Only after five minutes of fast curves and faster straightaways did Liza, with her experienced glances in the rear view mirror, turn to the steward. Then both broke out into a paralyzing fit of laughter.

Wolfie was hanging on for dear life, sliding back and forth atop of the well-oiled Eiriksson. He yelled forward to Liza. "Oh god! I think he's waking up."

"Good sign, I hope," said the steward.

Suddenly, another screeeeecchhhh of locked brakes and the Rover skidded to a halt, once again blocked by the long light snake. "Damn. Not again!" said the steward.

He had just started climbing out when he heard a colossal blast over his head. "Devil in Hell! Out of the fucking way, you idiots!

Get out! Move!" It was Eiriksson, suddenly awake and roaring, a ghostly white giant standing on the rear seat, one foot on top of the cowering Wolfie, blood streaked hands held out wide, resplendent in shiny *deshabille* and bikini loin cloth, bellowing out into the crowd. "*Jevla in percula*! Zealous fools! The Devil take you all!"

One hundred pilgrims dropped their candles and fell awestruck to their knees, eyes wide, hands clasped, mouths agape.

The Rover accelerated in a roar of dust and gravel through a small parting in the line, off into a wedge of darkness beyond. Eiriksson toppled back and bounced his head off the roll bar, rendering him insentient once again, only to amass himself on top of Wolfie in an even more bewildering replication of the Pieta.

"Oh, god... not again. Just get back to the ship... Just keep going. Fast!" the steward yelled over at Liza. "While he's still out!"

Through the maze of the city roared the Rover, horn blasting and lights flicking bright and dim for attention. Zoooomm past the local moustaches at the intersections, Zooooommm past bewildered passers-by, Zooooommmm down the pier and... Talabot at last!.. Screeeeeech up to the gangway.

"We made it," Liza grinned over at the steward.

The steward looked into the rear of the Rover, at the heap of flesh. A voice hailed down to him from the ship, "Found him, eh?" Bjarni was leaning on the railing frowning, next to him stood Erda, smiling. "Who's the other lost soul?"

"His name is Herr Doctor Professor Wolfie. Do me a favor and don't ask more. Now about Eiriksson... How do I get him aboard?" the steward asked. "He weighs a ton."

"*Helvete*. The way we always do." And with that, Bjarni strolled over to the cargo boom, fired up the capstan, and swung a large mesh loading net slowly over the side and down to the wharf near the Rover.

Liza climbed out of the Rover, white robe and all, and called up to Erda, "Have you seen my uncle? Herman Landgrave? Did he get back to the ship tonight?"

"He's here. But full of martinis, it appears," Erda replied. "Came home in a taxi soon after you left. He and your aunt are both sound asleep."

"Thank all the gods. And thank you. For helping," Liza added. "Your survival kit was just the thing." Erda smiled once in reply.

"Climb out of there, Wolfie, and give us a hand," the steward said to the man huddled in the rear. Liza walked back and took off her coat and gave it to H. D. P. Wolfie, which gave him courage to get up and out to the wharf.

"On three, we lift him out and on to that cargo net," the steward ordered. "One...two...three... Unngghhh!" and out came their dormant load, horizontally with an arm or leg falling freely downward, until he was plopped over the waiting net.

Eiriksson lay there on his back, spread-eagled in the bright wharf lights, breathing slowly and seemingly at rest with the world. "Think he's alright?" the steward asked.

"I'm certain of it..." Liza replied, transfixed. "Look. Apophasis of a Viking."

There it was. A point of interest, protruding upward, pushing the scant limits of the cotton briefs. "My god, he's got an erection!" added the steward. "Quick, smuggle it on board."

Bjarni called down, "Ready?"

"Hoist away!" the steward called back. "Take him to his bunk."

As the captain was swung over the side, snooded securely in the cargo net, Bjarni faked a short ssrrrreeepp of a bosun's pipe and sang out flatly, "Captain, arriving." Then kerplop. The steward and Liza winced, even down on the wharf, at the unkind thud.

The steward turned to Liza and took her hands in his. "Show you the view from my crows nest?"

"Aarruummmmhh..." she groaned wistfully. "But I can't. Only one trip that high a day. Remember Wolfie? I've got to get him home," she said sadly but responsibly. "Come see me in Baalbek sometime. We can explore my... dig."

"Dig we must..." sighed the steward, squeezing, then letting go of her hands. "*Ciao*. We'll meet again."

"In this world, or some other," replied Liza.

"I got him down," Erda called down to the wharf. "He's sleeping comfortably."

"Completely down?" asked the steward.

"I iced him in the champagne bucket," smiled Erda, objectively.

—AT SEA—

"Change..."

"Change?"

Byron Boost lifted his head up and looked out over his double chin and rather full belly at a flat, waxy sea. "Shelley and I came here looking for something different.... So we took this crazy travel agent's advice and signed on to this world cruise thing."

His wife Shelley, clone in size and shape, picked up on his sentiment without skipping a breath, obviously a skill perfected by many years of marriage to the same partner. "Not your typical first class cruise, mind you, with all the luxuries, you know, steamer trunks, dress every night for dinner..."

Back to Bryon, "Oh no!... Shelley wanted the romance of a tramp steamer, trekking about the Orient... It all sounded so great."

Now Shelley again, "And we were so bored sitting about at home after Byron's early retirement. It all seemed so perfect.

Your court, Byron. "We wanted a change. All we asked for was a little change..."

Shelley volleys in, "Something new and different from the local country club..."

Don't bobble it, Byron. "So what do we get? We sit looking at the goddamn sea, day after day, in this goddamn deckchair that has a goddamn hole in the seat, reading the same goddamn books we could have read at home. What change? I ask you, what change?" Byron vented a little steam out of an otherwise bored expression, with an inaudible burp.

The steward listened dutifully to Byron and Shelley Boost, as they volunteered about what was lacking in their current state of being. The middle-aged couple from Montana were occupying Cabin 3, one of the better of the lot reserved for the Talabot's 12 first class passengers.

Byron had sold pumps until his retirement last year. Sold more pumps than anyone in the country, Byron says he did. All kinds of pumps, to hear him tell it. A job of infinite variety, selling pumps everyday for 42 years. Byron sold big ones and small ones and light ones and heavy ones and steam ones and electrical ones and centrifugal ones, all doing the same job of moving some hapless substance from here to there. Byron loved his job. He just pumped along, says Byron, hitting the same customers over and over, selling his pumps whether one needed a good pump or not. Byron loved pumps more than just about anything, including Shelley. The company gave him a gold watch at 62 and said thanks but we're going to replace you with someone half your age and salary. Byron told the Sales VP to stick his pumps up his ass and get pumped. Cataclysmic change. Way to go Byron.

Now the Talabot was doing the same... just pumping along... moving twelve hapless souls from somewhere to somewhere else, all the way around the world.

"Everybody gets pumped sometime," Byron used to say, frequently.

Yet unfortunately, as is the way of being at sea 95% of the time, the old Talabot just kept pumping slowly along... at 14 knots, steadily pumping... day after day... pump after pump... week after week... on a slow cruise from tedium to apathy. The only thing to do on board the Talabot that truly interested Byron was to go down into the engine room and talk pumps with the Chief Engineer. It didn't matter to Byron that old Johannes Gynt spoke only Norwegian.

The steward spoke courteously, "Many a sailor wouldn't have it any differently. A calm sea is a safe sea. Boring, maybe, but seldom life threatening. A stormy sea, or a rolling sea, can put a whole different complexion on things, so to speak. I'll take a calm sea today. Better to let sleeping monsters lie and count our blessings."

The sea was calm... and hot... and flat... and full of sheets of glare... and certainly boring today. There was no wind... not even a puff... offering any subtle surprise, even in spite of the 14-knot headway the Talabot was making, to the hot 102 degrees of the mid-afternoon sun. The steward was making his continuous round of the passenger deck, as he did every afternoon, taking drink orders and chatting with the passengers. He had found that after a few days of posturing in the beginning, most of them were pretty good sorts, who just happened to be trapped at sea, having paid big bucks for their world cruise tickets... on board a tramp steamer.

After eating one's self into oblivion at each meal, reading was the only other routine pleasure of the day for most passengers, both morning and afternoon and evening... that is, if one was not captive, going drink for drink with the captain. Any books that had been brought along had been quickly read and passed on to others. Now, some half way around the globe, the passengers were reduced to attacking the ship's assemblage of a library of salty, dog-eared classics that had been accumulated from over 15 years of world passenger travel. Each passenger had come aboard looking for something special, anticipating a tour of the exciting, expecting to land in exotic ports of call to experience the local sights and savories. In fact, the Talabot frequently spent only one day in each port, usually a dilapidated, rat-infested corner of port at that, as most cargo shipping ports are, and passengers were seldom provided facility or convenience in getting safely ashore for the day to see these exotic cultures first hand. Alas, these intrepid passengers learned more about each country and culture by reading about it, while at sea, than they ever did ashore when in port.

First class? Or worst class? The debate raged daily, in spite of the heroic efforts the steward and crew made to treat the passengers as lavishly as possible on a rusty old freighter. But time and many a full belly finally wore everyone down to acceptance of fate as it was. Swayed by appropriate personal handling and pampering, each passenger finally settled into the monotony, possibly disappointed in the reality of their present lot, but determined to make the best of their days and months ahead, on the jolly Norwegian steamer, the S.S. Talabot.

"Change is all I asked for," Byron went on. "And all I get is the same thing, day after day, smorgasbord after smorgasbord. I'm so bored I could spit." And he leaned forward and tried to project a small bit of spittle over the rail. It blew back unfortunately into the lap of a British woman, Mrs. Anthony Potter-Smythe, dozing on her deck chair, and landed kersplat on an open collection of lesser-known English poets, a tome certainly not sought after as cerebral stimulant in most circles. The steward quietly picked up the volume and wiped off the pages, glancing briefly at the words so ungraciously anointed.

> *"We are as clouds that veil the midnight moon;*
> *How restlessly they speed, and gleam and quiver,*
> *Streaking the darkness radiantly! – yet soon*
> *Night closes round, and they are lost forever...*
> *Man's yesterday may ne'er be like his morrow;*
> *Naught may endure but mutability.'*

"There's change all around, if you only can notice it," the steward offered pleasantly, trying to cheer him up with a daily ration of mental stroking. "Really. The crew of the Talabot does a pretty wonderful job trying to make your stay enjoyable. The cook makes every effort to vary the meals with specialties of the day. We shop in each port for the local delicacies and fresh fruits and vegetables. We have more caviar than the Shah of Iran. There are eight barrels of iced shrimp in the cold locker. The wine list is endless, containing only the best of vintages. I'd say we offer a lot of possibilities for change in your usual bill of fare."

Byron injected, "If I eat another shrimp I think I'll barf."

The steward kept up the subtle pressure, "And just think about it... the sea is always in a state of change. Just look out there. One minute ago it was amber and waxy. Now it has a greenish hue from the shadows of that one cloud there, and a moving shimmer from a patch of wind there off to the South."

"One cloud. You call that change?" Byron grunted.

"I kind of like that little cloud up there," Shelley commented. "It's kind of refreshing. See?.. It has a life all its own. See it changing its shape?"

The steward looked up at the blue glare above, which surrounded the small cloud in every direction. The words of the *New Testament*, probably James, seeped up from the steward's memory bank,

> *"What is your life? For you are but a mist that appears*
> *for a little time and then vanishes..."*

"Looks like a flying fish now. Maybe an angel," Shelley continued.

"It looks like a rotary pump," Byron stated without emotion.

"One learns to read the sky and the sea out here, after a while. Here in the western Indian Ocean, this time of year, with so little weather influences coming off the land, no clouds are the norm," the steward added. "One cloud is a nice change. Two is happiness."

"Other people see meaning in a cloud, Byron" Shelley commented. "Open your eyes."

"Two is happiness... Is three a cloud?" Byron smiled.

"I could stand a drink after that one, Byron," Shelley noted.

"How about a different drink this afternoon, just for a change?" the steward asked. "To celebrate seeing the true depth of that cloud. How about I make you a Koenig's cocktail?"

"What's that? Lowenbrau in a jeweled chalice? Martini with a *knoedl?* Rhine wine in a spiked helmet?" Byron asked, showing a bit of interest at last, smacking his parched lips.

"Champagne and brandy, a dash of bitters and a cherry," the steward replied. "Try one. Put you right on cloud nine, sound asleep on the deckchair this afternoon."

"Better he has an ipecac and soda," Shelley added.

"What time is it, near four o'clock? Naw, just bring us our usuals, my friend," Byron said after trying to taste the new combo in his mind.

"Two Wild Turkeys in deep water, coming up." The steward replied.

"Rocket fuel."

"Rocket fuel?"

"That's what it is. 120 proof alcohol."

The steward cautiously eyed the crystal clear yet oily-looking liquid chilling at near freezing in a glass pitcher. He took a whiff at the top. No reaction other than disappointment crossed his face. Then he poured himself a thimbleful in a small glass, looked once up to heaven, and tossed it down his gullet. A muffled internal explosion caused his eyes to bulge and his ears to vent mist. The captain slapped him on the back.

"Welcome to the religion of the true believers. You are now baptized in the water of life..." Eiriksson said, as he sipped from a coffee mug full of the cherished elixir.

"Whew!" the steward gasped frantically. "Powerful stuff."

"Guaranteed to lift one's spirits in the most adverse of climates and situations."

"Probably has a dampening effect on a few other things, Sir."

"Norway's secret weapon. Sent thousands of Vikings into battle, singing and swinging. Horns held high."

"I thought they were just happy to get ashore again..."

"Pillaged and spoiled like madmen."

"Could have been the fusel oils, Sir..."

"Kept them warm, too. Permanent antifreeze."

"Never found a frozen Viking..."

"From the lowly potato, the beverage of liberation..."

"It certainly opens one's eyes a bit."

"It's our most beloved heritage, our deepest tradition."

"What, Sir? To stay, ah... spirited?"

"To stay happy and warm, Steward. Vikings fed it to their dogs, too. The fucking Russians stole our secret weapon. They fed our Norwegian *akvavit* to that little Laika. Kept her happy as a bitch in heat tripping around the cold heavens up there."

"*Akvavit*. Much better than Doggie Dinner..."

"Russian vodka is bear piss next to our Norwegian *Akvavit*. Russians knew that. Dogs lap it up."

"Couldn't let poor little Laika freeze up there. Krushchev's orders. Bad PR."

"I heard even Von Braun uses it to power the Jupiter-C..."

"*Akvavit*? Come on..."

"Not in the rocket, fool. To power himself!"

"Where'd it come from? You Norsemen never even saw a potato until after Columbus. What did you do before that?"

"The early Vikings? A great tradition. Lost art, though... Fermented ox horns..."

"Wow! Musky stuff I bet."

"Terrible after taste..."

"But better than sitting around freezing and bored all winter?"

"Made the old shepherds up North go blind..."

"Not the glaring snow all year round?"

"So all those young bucks who could still see, went to sea. The first Vikings..."

"That's what sent them searching for the new world? A quest for the potato?"

"It was fate. Potatoes didn't grow in Greenland and Vineland."

"Took the Spaniards to find 'em, Captain."

"Spaniards? Bunch of pussies. Warm weather sailors. They learned pillaging from us!"

"Dumb luck they found the potato first and not the Vikings."

"Took Vikings to figure out how best to use it, though."

"Drink a potato, not eat it?"

"Exactly. It was a critical time for Vikings at sea. Emergency actions were required."

"What did they do? Run out of ox horns?"

Eiriksson raised his mug, and looked at it dreamily. "They had even stripped their helmets by then. All their ox booze was gone. Blown off course. Surrounded by salt water and ice. Near freezing. All hope vanishing..."

"The Saga of Eirik the Red is being born, I trust."

Eiriksson gazed into the mysterious swirls of clear, icy liquid in the pitcher, and held it aloft as if it were some holy grail.

"Like all their other food at sea, it either froze or rotted. This one longboat, it had a load of potatoes. Potatoes rotted, then fermented. Adrift for days, the Vikings were so thirsty they boiled the rotten potato juice to get the maggots out of it. Stirred it with their last ox horn, just for tradition's sake. Tasted terrible, but they drank some anyway and passed out, warm and happy. But... unlike everything else onboard, it didn't freeze overnight. A morning pick-me-up tasted even better. *Voila!* Ox horn flavored potato moonshine. Modern-day chilled *akvavit*..." He took a taste from his mug. "The water of life."

"And the Vikings lived to spoil another day..."

"No, they gave up their old ways of traveling. They stayed home. Became real pirates and went into the commodities business. Cornered the potatoes futures market. Let the Spaniards do all the work, lugging them home. Then robbed them near the coast."

"And invented Norwegian rocket fuel. A major industry."

"Made heavy water in the big stills during the war, too."

"Saved the musk ox population from extinction, though."

"Ah... the water of life..."

"Colder than mothers' milk. Tastier after you're three..."

"Have another teatful?"

"I'll pass," the steward said. "Time to set up for lunch."

"It's good for you. Make you a man before your time..."

"Puts hair on your chest?"

"Never. On your tongue."

"Lots of ways to do that."

"And on the soles of your feet?"

"You got me there, Sir. The deck plates are too hot for bare feet." The steward poured himself another icy thimbleful from the pitcher, and shuddered in anticipation. "To Vikings..."

"And their sacred ox horn elixir."

"To *akvavit. Skall.*"

"Steward, come here please."

It was Mrs. Lovelake, languishing behind large rose sunglasses.

"Afternoon, Mrs. L. Can I get you anything?" the steward said, then gulped as he realized he was reopening the door to trouble.

"Sit down here, beside me," the attractive brunette said, motioning for him to settle on the deckchair near her thighs. "Please. Ah have something Ah want to say to you. Privately."

The steward looked at the leggy, late-forties wife of a Mr. Billy Bob Lovelake, a retired car dealer from Texas, in a turquoise one piece bathing suit with the straps hanging down, by now very well tanned from the hot tropical sun since Suez. Billy was in his cabin this afternoon, resting, the steward was sure. The lovely Mrs. L was sunning in the afternoon, as was her habit, before primping up for dinner. That was when she inevitably called the steward to her cabin - for some kind of help, lifting up a trunk, searching for her earring behind the bunk, buttoning up her gown, always something like that. By then, Billy was usually in the lounge, splashing bourbon about with the captain and others on political or racial or religious matters of major consequence to a big silver belt buckle Texan like Bill Bob. That left his younger wife, Pammy Sue by name, to matters of major consequence to her, namely, getting laid by anyone interested. The steward, every late afternoon, was a prime candidate in her date book. The other male passengers were out of bounds, having their nosey wives aboard, and most were Billy Bob's age, happy to be retired in more ways than one, and content with joining the other old boys in the lounge for cocktails and bragging contests. Yes, given the limitations of her sea-bound ranch, the steward was U.S. Prime beef on the hoof, and in demand.

"Mrs. L, I've got to fill these drink orders," the steward replied. "Can I get you anything to drink?" he added purposefully.

"Please sit down here, honey. Just for a sec," Pammy Sue leaned forward with a whisper. "Really. Ah want to tell you something."

The steward reluctantly sat down on the side of the deckchair, casting about for *voyeurs* and gossips.

"Boy, Ah...." she hesitated.

"Oh, god. Here she comes again..." the steward thought, awaiting the pass of the day.

"Ah..."

Pammy Sue looked out at sea, for a change, and not at the steward's crotch. She didn't smile at him with her typical pursed lips heavy with Chinese red war paint, usually smeared at the corners. In fact, something glistened in the afternoon glare, something wet on her cheek, just under her sunglasses.

"What can I do for you, Mrs. L?" the steward asked, courageously. "What do you need?"

"Ah..." She swallowed and continued in a low voice, "Ah need mah Billy Bob. Ah learned that the other evening when you and the captain..." She kept staring out at the horizon. "Ah want to thank you... properly... You helped save his stupid life..."

"Mrs. L..." the steward started.

"No, honey," she cut him off. "You and the captain gave us both something. You gave Billy Bob his life... and you gave me back his pecker." She turned slightly and smiled at him. "Ah didn't know how important Billy Bob was to me until Ah almost lost him in the charthouse there. Ah'm afraid Ah lost my head, with all the screamin' and everything. Ah thought the wrath of god was comin' down on Billy and me... Ah really lost it. But you kept yours... You and the captain were wonderful... Ah just want to... thank you... properly."

The steward didn't move when she softly put her hand over his thigh, and let it rest there, in public view.

He reflected back to the Red Sea about a week ago, steaming about 30 hours South from the Suez. It was hot. About two in the morning. He had come up to the bridge to get some air and to sleep on top of the charthouse in the breeze. The night was crystal clear and hot, hot, hot. 105 degrees, at night, no less. Cooler than daytime when it was closer to 125 degrees. But still hot. Unbearably hot. And no air conditioning other than a few window fans. And 14 knots headway. Uniform of the Day for the crew was shorts only. Passengers spent most of the day in the Talaboat's round canvas pool, hiding as best they could from the hot rays of the Arabian sun. Shoulder tans and bosom burns blossomed. Bald heads blistered. The lovely Mrs. L, by contrast, took the weather by the horns, adding to her already mellow tan by lying near nude on the top of the charthouse, defying all the gasps and criticisms of the other wives, to toast her white buttocks a bit. That act unfortunately popped a painful kink into the neck of Byron Boost who possibly dreamed, while straining for a better view from the now hot tub, of giving pretty Pammy Sue a little pump or two.

The steward had just found a not so comfortable slab of steel, somehow cooled down by the headway breezes, on the front edge of the charthouse roof, and spread his blanket, then on top, his sheet and pillow. He lay there looking forward into the breeze and the clear night air, seeing only a few flickering lights off to the South, dancing just below the horizon.

"Nothing in the vicinity. I can get a bit of shut eye..." the steward thought to himself, noting that Ole the helmsman seemed quite content on his compass course of a steady 170 degrees, with the wheel tied off to midships, leaning back in a chair and with his feet up on the capstan, snoring sonorously. So much for vigilance in tanker alley...

He watched the lights over the horizon, some forty miles away, dancing... vanishing... dancing... dim... then brighter...

"Interesting," he thought, remembering his Navy training on the bridge, "that one can see better into the distance looking a little to the side of the object being sighted. Just a degree or so to the right or left, brings it more clearly into view... Must be something about the receivers on the back of the eyeball... specialization and all that... or maybe the ones dead center in back of the lens, at the focal point, are worn out and can't handle the minute sharpness or contrasts of distant objects any more..."

The fresh night air tickled by his face and shoulders. His thoughts drifted with the breeze and the engine hum...

"Just specks of light... white, mostly... some faintly amber... bobbing and hiding...way out there... on the horizon... Just like the stars... on a slice of the sky above...little stars bobbing on a long curved line... each a ship... each with a personality of its own... each going its own different way... Just maybe we'll cross paths... maybe not... Somewhere way out there... in a special place... and a special moment... in a tiny slice of eternity..."

The hum of the Talabot underway was like a subtle massage transmitted through the steel decks on his body. The breeze felt good flowing past his sun-baked skin.

"It is easier to see things at sea... few diversions out there... simplified... barely defined... just lights on the horizon... and maybe beyond... across an infinite sea..."

"Ship me somewhere East of Suez, Rudyard..." he hummed. "Where there are no ten commandments..."

He felt a hand on the back of his thigh, and he jumped with a start. "Who in hell?..."

"Shhhh... It's me... Pammy."

A woman's hushed voice greeted him in the dark. "Pammy Sue Lovelake."

The way Pammy Sue said her last name was pure deep Texas sugar, cut short at the end, sounding like Luuuvv-lik. For Pammy Sue, it seemed fitting. But the steward, after first speaking their name the way Pammy Sue and Billy Bob pronounced it, guarded himself against embarrassment by avoiding Luv-lik altogether, choosing to call them Mr. or Mrs. L.

There was Pammy Sue, all five foot eight of her, all Texas long legs, standing tall in the moonlight. She was in a flowing white sheer nylon negligee, trailing in the breeze like a bridal train, now standing there above him, with the moonlight set behind her... Stunning... A beautiful apparition... long firm curves silhouetted in the moonlight... She slowly let the negligee drift down off her shoulders and trail even further back into the moon glow, a lithe sensuous body with facial highlights in the shadow, standing there, breasts head into the cooling night wind, standing proud and confident, like Winged Victory.

If ever they start putting maidenheads... ahh, matronheads, back on vessels, I know the perfect model..." the steward thought in awe.

"Ah knew Ah'd find y'all up here..."

"I... We... Your husband..." the steward stuttered.

"Billy Bob's asleep. Or trahin' to sleep..." she said softly down to him. "He's had too much champagne to drink agin. Says he really aches in his groin tonight... It's no fun with Billy Bob anymore... So Ah came up here for some air."

"Whew..." thought the steward. "She doesn't give up." He just sat there looking up at her attractive body, now stretching slowly in the wind for his benefit, all aglow in the moonlight.

"Ah kind of hoped Ah'd find you up... so to speak..." Pammy Sue said ever so softly down at the steward.

"Ah, Mrs. L..."

"Ah thought we could...ahh...get to know each other..."

"Really, Mrs. L..."

"Call me Pammy Sue..." she said as she dropped slowly to her knees, still upright with the white train in the breeze.

"Ah...Mrs. L..., the helmsman is right below..."

"Ah said, call me Pammy Sue..." She dropped down to all fours next to his white shorts. "Luuuvvv-lick..." and she bent forward to touch her tongue ever so softly on his salty navel.

"Uunnnghhh...., Mrs. L..."

"Luuuvv-lick..." she said as she slowly trailed her wet tongue upward across his chest, slowly across his neck, and more slowly up to his ear, and in...

"Oh, god... here we go again..." the steward groaned. "Wait, Mrs. L. We can't do this..."

"Billy Bob can't, or won't do this..." she whispered, "and Ah can. Ah'm as horny as a three year old filly tonight, honey, and there's only one way to fix that."

"Humh?.."

She slid her body fully on top of his. "The thighs of Texas are upon you, honey..."

"What?..." he asked feebly.

"We're goin' to make luuvv...Texas style..." she murmured as she slid her silky tongue over his eyes and down his nose.

"What's that?" he gasped, weekly.

"It's simple, honey..." Pammy Sue had somehow worked his pants open during her slithering snake dance on his chest. "Just sink yo'self deep into the saddle, grab yo'self a hank of hair, and r.ah.d.e."

"Mrssss... Llllphh..." His protest was quickly muffled by her tongue probing the depths of his epiglottis.

"Paaammmmmmyyyy Sooooooo!"

The cry pierced the night air like a squealing pig.

"What was that?" Pammy Sue bolted upright, strattling the steward on all fours like a bobcat ready to spring.

"It sounded like..." the steward tried to say.

"Paaammmmmyyyy Soooooooooo!!" There was serious pain in the voice.

"It's Bill Bob!" she shot up, drawing her negligee up and over her shoulders. "Something's wrong!"

She hurried to the ladder and started climbing down to the bridge deck. "Ah'm comin', Billy. Ah'm comin'!"

The steward started pulling on his shorts after the third trumpeting cry "Pammmmyyyy Soooooooooooo!" and followed her down the ladder and down to the passenger cabin deck.

"Here Ah am, Billy. Here Ah am. What's wrong, honey. What's happened?" Pammy Sue rushed into the cabin. The steward hesitated at the doorway.

"Oooohhhh. Pammy Sue. Oooohhh my gaaahhhddd. Ah'm in pain. Ah cain't piss. Gaaahhhddd dowg, it hurts!"

"You cain't piss? What do you mean, Billy honey? You can always piss. Like a horse."

"Ah cain't PISS, damn it. Do Ah have to spell it all out for you? Ah ain't pissed at all since last night!"

"Last night?" the steward added in, coming in from his position in the doorway. "That's only eight hours ago..."

"Not this last night, damn it. Last last night." Billy Bob moaned. "Ah ain't pissed for over 30 hours now!..."

"Oh god, Billy. Come on, now, come ON! Let's see you piss."

"Honey, Ah cain't piss. Gawd, Ah wish Ah could. But Ah CAIN'T! Gawd dawg, it hurts! It's my fuckin' prostate again. Ooooooh. Sheee-it. Ah think Ah'm goin' to daaahh." Billy's frantic face looked both green and red together, his pleading eyes bloodshot with strain.

"Oh, Billy. Here, let me hold it, honey. Ah'll make it piss." Pammy Sue offered her nursing training gained during her earlier years as a camp follower in the rodeo circuit.

"Git AWAY, damn it! If Ah'm goin' to daahh, Ah'm goin' to do it mah way. Where's my gawd damn gun. Go git me mah gawd damn gun!"

The steward jumped into the fray. Now he could understand why the reluctant Mr. L kept his pecker out of Pammy Sue's hungry hands lately. "Mr. L, take it easy. Here, sit down, or lay down, or find a position that's comfortable. I'll get the captain up and we'll see what medicine we have for this problem. You're going to be O.K. Just relax. Take it easy for a couple of minutes. I'll be right back."

The steward shot up the interior ladder to the captain's stateroom, knocked once, shook his head, and burst in. Eiriksson was flat on his back in his bunk, still dressed, snoring loudly, arms straight down at his sides. "Captain. CAPTAIN!" he shook him by the shoulders. "Wake up! Emergency!"

Lazarus's eyes popped wide open. He did not stir from his coffin position, but asked, "What's happening?"

The steward quickly explained as he poured a glass of soda water and offered it to the couchant Viking.

"Tappawalla. Over."

"Who?" Squaaakk. Squeeeelll. "Over."

"Tappawalla. My name is Tappawalla." Screech. "Sidhartha Tappawalla. Over."

Eiriksson shook his head. The radiotelephone was doing its typical trick of shorting out and squealing and squawking. At best, it made an impressive wall hanging. At worst it acted like this.

Squeeeeeeeechhh. Crackle. "This is Captain Eiriksson of the Norwegian freighter Talabot. We are somewhere near Djabouti in the Red Sea." Squeeeelll. "Can you hear me, Dr. Tatawala? Over."

Sgreeek. "Oh, yes. I can hear you. Can you hear..." Spleeebbb. "Over."

"I have a medical problem on board, Dr. Tatawala." Scrackle. Screep. "One of my passengers. Over."

Screeppp. "Tappawalla. My name is Mr. Tappawalla." Grabble.

"Aaarrrrrggghh. Ask the fuckin' waog what we should do, damn it!" Billy Bob yelled. "Ah'm fuckin' dahin'!"

The steward had helped Eiriksson carry Billy Bob up to the chart house on the bridge, to be near the radiotelephone. They had plopped him on top of the chart table, a large flat surface in the corner surrounded by an array of calipers and triangles and straight edges used to plot courses. Then he had run to the galley to bring back the black doctor's bag that had been stowed there. The steward arrived back, breathless, to the glow of the nightlights in the darkened charthouse, which made it look like some shadowy red grotto of hell.

Billy Bob Lovelake was a disheveled mess in terrible agony. He looked like a water-filled balloon ready to burst. He sat there, in an open green terrycloth bathrobe, a strained shining belly protruding over his shorts, striped boxer style, and he still wore his traditional silver-toed cowboy boots on his feet which presumably he couldn't bend over to get off. His eyes were wild and bugged out, his face bright red. He sat there on the chart table like some piss-filled Humpty Dumpty, spread-eagled on top of the Red Sea, with Pammy Sue supporting his head and shoulders from behind.

Squaaaakkk. Spuuttteerr. "*Faen i helvete!*" Eiriksson cursed at the phone. "We are better off with flags than this piece of shit." Squeeeelll.

"Talk to the fuckin' waog, damn it. Find out what to do!" Billy groaned.

"Oh, Billy. Oh, Billy. Oh, Ah'm so afraid, Billy. If anything happens to you, I'll just dah!" Pammy Sue wailed in his ear.

"Shut the fuck up, Pammy Sue. Ah'm the one dahin', not y'all!" Billy replied loudly.

"Dr. Tappawalla?" Screech. Squaalllk. "Can you hear me?"

"Yes. I can hear you. It is nice to meet you, Captain Ergson." Squeeekk.

Crackkkle. "Eiriksson. My name is Eiriksson... of the freighter Talabot...in the Red Sea." Squeeeeeeeeelll. "Dr. Tappawalla, I have a passenger with severe pain in his groin, and who hasn't relieved himself...hasn't urinated in 30 hours. Can you give me advice on what to do for him? Over." Squeeeelll.

"He He He. Keel him. Over." Crackle. Poppp.

"What??? Aaahhh Gaaahhhdddd! Ah must be in hell!!! The fuckin' waog is crazy!" Billy cried.

"I didn't hear you well, Dr. Tappawalla. Say again, over." Eiriksson said, puzzled.

Squaaakkkkk. "He He He. I said to keeeel him, captain. By the way, my name is Mr. Tappawalla, not doctor. I am not a doctor. I am a pharmacist."

"Aaaaaaahhhh!" Billy went berserk.

Squeeeell. "A pharmacist? I thought they were going to find me a doctor!" Eiriksson bellowed into the radiophone. "Where are you. What city? Over."

"He He He. I am in Jiddah. I run an all night pharmacy in Jiddah. He He He. I am also a ham radio operator. It helps to keep me awake. Over." Crackle. Sputter.

Squeeeekkk. "Can you find me a doctor? I need to act fast. Over..." Eiriksson asked.

Squaakkk. "He He. There are none up at this hour in Jiddah. It is left to foreigners like me to work all night." Squaaakkk. "Anyway, the doctors here would give the same advice. Keel him. Throw him over the side. It is the kindest way. They would say it is the will of Allah. Over." Sputter. Craaaaak.

"The fuckin' waog is craaazzzzyy!" Billy Bob screamed. Pammy Sue had lost all her tan on that last exchange. "Do somethin', pleeeeze!"

"We can not kill him, Mr. Tappawalla." Eiriksson responded firmly and calmly. "We have some medicines, and a few tools. I need first to relieve his bladder. Any ideas, Mr. Tappawalla?" Squueeek.

"He He. Oh, yes. You will need a catheter. It is a long, curved silver tube, like a sipping straw. If there is none, you will need a large syringe. If there is none, you will need a long narrow knife. He He He."

"That fuckin waog is laughin' while ah'm dahin'! Ah'll kill the bastard. Oooohh, gawd!" Billy roared. Pammy Sue was quivering behind him, causing him to vibrate.

Squeeeekk. "I think I have a catheter here. Do you know how to use it?" Squeeeellll.

Crackle. Creeeeeechh. "Oh, yes. You will need some peetroleeum jeelee. If you have none, use some spit. Lubricate the catheter about ten inches up from the sharp tip. He He."

Billy Bob's eyes were wide as dinner plates.

Squuueeeech. "O.K. Mr. Tappawalla. The catheter is greased. Now what? Over..." Eiriksson asked as the steward prepared the silver tube with Vaseline.

Squeek. Crackle. "Now? He He He. Now you do what you must do. He He."

"Aaahhhhggg...." Billy Bob fainted as the captain took the catheter in one hand like a long shiny saber, and started over to the chart table, a look of serious concentration on his face.

The steward grabbed Billy by the shoulders as he fell over limp. "I'll hold him upright, Captain, so you can get a better angle."

Then, with a wry smile on his face, the captain added, "Mrs. L. You know your job. Hold his penis in both hands. Hold it out steady, like a hose. Don't let go. I will do the rest."

Pammy Sue looked like a ghost. She took a deep breath, grabbed Billy's pecker, and closed her eyes.

"Stop shaking, damn it. We must do this!" Eiriksson barked. The steward put his hand over hers, to steady her.

Squeeekkk. "How is it going? He He He. Is he dead yet? Over."

The captain deftly slid the catheter up and up and up past the obstruction until KERBLAAM! A explosion of liquid blasted forth from the end of the silver straw, spraying a nozzled stream across the chart table, flooding the Red Sea, and covering most of the Middle East with piss.

The flow lasted what seemed like a full three minutes. A sense of relief grew with each passing cupfull. Eiriksson's eyes met the stewards, and smiles crossed their faces. The captain returned to the radiotelephone.

Squeeekk. Squaaalllkk. "We are rich, Mr. Tappawalla. We brought in a gusher. Over."

Squeeeell. "Oh that is very nice indeed, Captain. Now if we could only sell it to the Ethiopians. He He He."

Squaakk. "What next, Mr. Tappawalla? Leave it in? Over." Eiriksson asked.

Squeeeel. "I think so, Captain. For at least until he gets sufficient medication to reduce the swelling and blockage. Have you any antibiotics on board? Over."

Crackle. "Yes. Penicillin. Tablets. Over."

"Give him two 100 milligram tablets every four hours until he gets to a doctor in port. That should help reduce the infection around his prostate. Also give him two aspirins every four hours. He will be in pain. The key is to keep his bladder from blocking again, until he is not inflamed. Keep the catheter in for at least a day. Then try it out. If he can urinate, keep it out. Otherwise... repeat the procedure. Over."

Squeeeelll. "You should have been a doctor. Thank you, Mr. Tappawalla. You are a good man. You helped save a stranger's life. Over."

Wheeeezzz. Crackle. "A doctor...yes. But alas, I am but a pharmacist. It must be the will of Allah himself. Or Vishnu. Or Buddha. Or somebody. Thank you, Captain Eiriksson. Go with god. Your god. He is probably kinder than the one here. Jiddah, out." Squueeeeekkk.

The captain and the steward as carefully as possible carried the deflated and inert Billy Bob back to his stateroom and bunk, and lay him there like a fallen warrior, in silver-toed cowboy boots, and with a silver flagpole sticking up out of his pecker, which Pammy Sue still held in both hands for support. Ah, a kingdom for a lone star flag.

—BOMBAY—

"India..."

Even the air was laden with timeless mystery... A soft breeze lifted gauzy dawn mist above the slowly approaching shoreline... carrying with them hints of sensuous delights... part floral, part feral, part female... all folded into a pungent, intoxicating perfume. There was indeed an air about India.

"In...d...ia." The steward sounded out the syllables. There was music in the very pronunciation of five simple letters. And magic. And adventure. The very name sent a thrill of anticipation throughout his body.

"Indjiah..." he tried again in best clipped British. "It's only a word..." He watched the thinnest sliver of coastline roll slowly left, then right, then left again, stretched across the horizon, as the Talabot churned its way forward into the brightening east. "But quite a word."

History paged through his thoughts. India... A word that enfolds the deepest secrets of the Orient... A word that fuels man's obsession with the mystic unknown... A word synonymous with the highest raptures of spirituality... A word that has driven men mad for centuries... calling, singing, luring the adventurous and the avaricious and the zealous and the ravenous to a self-indulgent feast upon its shores. A young Alexander, emboldened by gods high on Olympus,

117

had trekked well past its borders, bent on civilizing all cultures less perfect than his, while quietly open to a little plundering of vast riches. Columbus, spirited by a Catholic omnipotence that had just pummeled the Moors, had sailed off in quest of it, charged with cornering lucrative sea routes to its foodstuffs and fabrics, and just maybe a few slaves. Even the Disciple Thomas, after the death of his master, had reached its shores, inspired with converting the aberrant souls of this cultural catch basin, only to be tested most personally on his theories of everlasting life. Aryans, early claimants to being the master race, had elbowed past its frontiers intent on conquering the factious clans of a subcontinent, and left it amalgamated with a universal language in payment for their spoils. Moslems too, with scimitars slashing in a craze of religious persuasion, had thundered in to conquer the minds of any wise enough to retain them intact. And most recently, the British, all pomp and polish, sabers in salute, had confirmed that only they deserved to reap the abundance of its labor and resources, realizing full well they had been divinely bred to impose Victoria's rule and protestant order on this lush, lesser-civilized world.

What is India? On the surface, India is the compost heap of time and exploitation. Yet... somehow... its spirit remains pure and unravaged... and is hiding, deep, mysterious, in the earth...

He felt a presence join him at the rail.

"India is a forever ripened fruit, waiting to be plucked and eaten." It was Eiriksson. His hair was protruding oddly, crushed to the left probably from sleeping face down with a pillow over his head. He washed over his teeth with his tongue, and grimaced. It was indeed a surprise for Eiriksson to be up so early, and seemingly sane and sober.

"What kind of fruit?" the steward asked, without looking away from the horizon, as he leaned on the bridge railing.

"Pick any. Plum. Pomegranate. Passion fruit." Eiriksson scoffed as he watched the shoreline emerge from the misty veils that slowly danced in the early morning light. "It does not matter. There's something savory in India for everyone."

"Then why are the Indians so skinny?" Don't they like fruit?"

"Aaah!" Eiriksson mockingly banged his forehead on the railing. "You touch on the age-old mystery of the subcontinent. Monks and hermits have for centuries have pondered this question, and you, a simple American, now stumble on the ultimate truth. They don't eat enough fruit!"

The steward smiled at the idea. India. It was out there, a massive succulent fruit about 25 miles to the East, ripening in the morning breeze, just waiting to be plucked. "I appreciate that the Hindu people had a profound respect for all living things... Animals, bugs, snakes... But fruit?..."

"For time in memoriam, Steward," the captain murmured on, "India has been the ripest, juiciest fruit of the Orient, mustering no tactical defenses such as thorns or brambles or bitter skins, just lying there lushly, waiting to be gorged upon up by whomever could make it through the crazies in the mountains."

"Did you just have a bad dream about fruit? Can I bring you some breakfast?" the steward jousted.

"Really. Out there lies a subcontinent of immense natural wealth and inexhaustible labor. Hundreds of millions of people. Oh, a few tribes in the mountains put up resistance to intrusion, but mostly India just lies there, passive, docile, allowing herself to be conquered and used, over and over again. Even the elephants don't fight back."

"I thought in '47 India achieved independence from Britain in a rather unique way. Just persistent, non-violent persuasion," the steward observed. "Not a massive civil war."

"Non-violent? Hundreds of thousands killed each other in Punjab." Eiriksson added. "In an immigration traffic jam!"

"It could have been much worse..." the steward pondered, remembering the bloody confrontation of Hindus and Moslems as they were forced to repatriate into separate new nations. "Any other country being split into pieces on religious or moral grounds would have butchered itself even more. Look at Ireland. Look at Palestine. Look at the American Civil War."

"Still, it amazes me that 400 million people can over and over again put up so little resistance." Eiriksson went on. "It is more than their religious beliefs. It must be a diet lacking in vitamin B or something. Maybe fruit. Over the centuries, Persians, Greeks, Aryans, Moslems, British, they just walk in, vastly outnumbered by indigenous masses, but are virtually unopposed. They eat up whatever fruit they want, the supply is endless, and when their empires become exhausted by overextension and overeating, they vanish. Poof! And India just lies there, waiting, until the next empire puffs up its chest feathers and thinks itself master of the world."

"So you don't think this new independence will last?" the steward asked.

"It will last as long as it is destined to last," Eiriksson replied. "If history is a reliable factor, their fate will be tested from outside again. The pressure right now is not from the last set of masters - Great Britain is still actually India's friend and benefactor. The immediate pressure is from Mama Rooski up North, who wants warm water ports so badly she is pissing in her babushka. And from China, who wants to keep Mama Rooski pissing."

"Not a more lofty goal, maybe like swaying poor Hindu souls to Lenin's ways?"

"No. Warm water ports. The Red navy is freezing its balls off in Murmansk and Vladivostok. Nature blockades them by ice and sleet and high winds much of the year. You Yanks can take a holiday during that time, if the Reds don't get out to sea before weather sets in."

"But the U.S. has effectively stayed out of India's waters since '48. One would think they would welcome any Western presence, just to temper any ideas of the Reds expanding their empire into India's sphere in any way," the steward pondered.

"The Indians want investment and development expertise. The U.S. is one primary source. Russia is another. So they give the impression of being neutral, bowing and smiling and picking their fingernails at the conference table. They are so neutral they appear to have no personality or position on anything."

"They sent medical and military personnel to Korea..." the steward defended.

Eiriksson was undeterred. "Realistically India has to give the impression of being neutral. They have enough problems at home. They want help, not war. On paper, they may have a military. Unfortunately, it had been beautifully trained by the British for parades and cavalry charges, and it is no match for Russian tanks and cruisers." Eiriksson confirmed his feelings with a pointed burp.

"India doesn't view the Russians as much of a threat?"

"Everyone's a threat. Particularly the Chinese. And the Pakistanis. And the Americans. And the last thing they ever want to do is to invite the British back in to help, in peaceful development or in defense. But remember, these people are pretty experienced at being conquered. They must understand the timing fairly well by now."

"I don't know. I was indoctrinated to think the Rooskies were bent on expansion of their empire," the steward countered. "India would be a jewel in their crown as well."

"Ah, *Faen*." Eiriksson laughed. "India would be a jewel in their asshole, and quite problematic. First, the Western nations would never stand for any overt Russian expansion into the area, such as India giving Russia a naval facility on its shores. Even more a factor, both the Indians and the Russians know that there are vast differences in their cultures and ideologies. India is not ready for Communism. It has just chosen nationalism based on its deepest traditions of theism, not atheism. It has just reborn itself as almost purely Hindu. It has just said good riddance to its Moslems, like a welcome crap after a bad meal. It cherishes opulence and regality, supported by more feudalistic castes than you can count. To have an internal revolution along the paths of communist ideology, it takes masses of people ready and willing to fight. India's masses have never been motivated to fight. They just go along with whatever the Raja's or the governors say, and move out of the way of the fancy-outfitted soldiers on horseback, just like the cattle. The people just endure. Even flies don't bother them."

The steward stretched his arms wide, then took a deep breath of the moist sea air. Then something started to stir a bit under

121

the soft, billowy coverlet of morning mist. A gray-green landmass began to define itself slowly in the East, under a brightening sky of scattered cirrus clouds, now increasingly splayed with shades of pink and saffron.

The steward spoke up again. "I think India has achieved only a facade of diplomatic relations with many of the Western powers. Why are things strained?" he asked, perplexed. "The U.S. didn't particularly back the British or hinder India's independence movement. They went along with the U.N. position. I thought the U.S. tried very hard to stay out of this... this amputation of a major rump of the British Empire."

Eiriksson nodded. "Maybe that's just why. India may have expected more support. Democracy and independence and all that. But the U.S. couldn't actively help in a situation that could hurt Britain, its closest ally. Anyway, India kept the Western nations at a good distance while they got their bare feet under them."

"It's ironic. America has been their friend. It has given India plenty in foreign aid in the past few years."

Eiriksson scoffed. "They will never see it repaid, so they might as well just write it off and forget it. It bought the Americans nothing. It taught the Americans nothing. It's the game of foreign aid. That's why India seems so friendly to Russia now. Looking for another sucker."

After a few moments of silence, Eiriksson stood up, lifting his elbows from the rail. "Our 0800 E.T.A. in Bombay still on track?" Eiriksson asked, looking at his watch and then back at the shore expanding on the horizon.

"Yes," the steward answered. "We're on track." Once again, he had awakened and come to the bridge to see landfall. It was his habit. It had always quietly thrilled him to see a coast appear out of the sea, or out of the fog or misty sky. Particularly a new coast, where he had not been before. One could sense land. One knew something was out there, past the horizon, but it was still an unknown, without shape or color or impact. Its existence was unverifiable, but its presence was very real to some mysterious combination of the senses. Even without the long ranging eyes of radar, one knew when land was near. One could sense a powerful energy, a feeling of impending conflict in the air. A certainty that a new dynamic would arise from the interaction of the sea with the land, of the mariner with the culture. While at sea, the importance of whatever it was out there, just out of sight or reach, was conceptual, not physical. Things at the horizon were defined by impression, or by imagination, not by detail. Only by approaching a new land by sea did the steward feel this way. Never by air. Air travel was too abrupt, to dramatic, to noisy, leaving one culture and entering another almost instantly. But by sea, there was time to adjust again with the world's great common denominator, the sea itself, to purge one's thoughts and feelings about the place just left, and to heighten one's anticipation about a new one, soon to be found, somewhere out there just beyond the horizon.

"Can you smell it?" Eiriksson asked as he stared at the coastline. "It is out there."

"India? Yes, I can..." the steward responded.

"Not India, Steward," Eiriksson said sarcastically. "Life."

With that, he farted, and left the bridge.

The steward had stayed on the bridge all the while the Talabot was entering the port of Bombay. It was a busy port, with commercial ships from all nations tugging on their moorings scattered around four well-anchored WWII vintage cruisers. Around and through them all scurried scores of dhows and sails and patrol launches and island freighters and fishing craft.

The steward still leaned on the railing of the bridge, watching the harbour scene before him, and reflecting on his conversation with Eiriksson earlier.

The killing had been over now for a decade. India and Pakistan had been granted separate dominion, and each a place if desired at the British Commonwealth table. Painfully and finally, more than ten years after Gandhi's assassination, India had evolved into an independent, relatively stabilized nation, riding on an infrastructure built so soundly by the British. As apparent to the eye from the unchanged skyline of the city, India had actually not progressed a long way in that time, from a crown jewel struggling uncomfortably in the war-worn framework of the British Empire, to the evolving independent state of 400 million people, bickering over self rule. The rich and powerful were still so, even more so. The poorest masses were poorer yet. Crop failure and famine were the norm. Unbridled population growth was a specter of threatening proportions. Girls were married by 13, or spinsters by 16. Daughters were sold to potential husbands at 10. The caste system, while politically vilified, still remained virulent. Yet another empire had departed, but daily realities had not changed. Even with all its soul searching and struggle, India still had not found its true self, as various political and religious factions continued to vie for power and influence, all the while espousing India's traditional philosophy of tolerance and benevolence to all living things. Except, possibly, to one's fellow man.

Now in port, the air of India had taken on a different quality. Stink. It was the stink of garbage, of human excrement, of industrial sewage, of oil slicks, and as Eiriksson had proposed, of life. Even the sky itself had a humid, sweaty look to it, as if too many persons were locked up in one small room. The air of India... Reality is often quite different from the illusion, indeed.

The steward watched as a classic split-cabin mahogany motor launch targeted its way out to the Talabot through the harbour traffic. He wondered if there was to be any change in the amount of time scheduled in Bombay. The Talabot had major portions of its cargo to unload here, and more to pick up, so it had booked two full days at pier side, plus one on their mooring.

The launch grew closer. The steward squinted to see the details of a man in maritime whites, standing in the mid-split of the cabin. The face slowly came into focus. He had expected some British type of harbour clerk. He never had expected to see Bone.

As the motor launch pulled up along side the Talabot, a lanky young man in his early thirties, dressed in white shorts and shirt, jumped off and on to the base of the gangway that hung angled down the side of the Talabot's hull. He carried his hat in his hand,

and was bedecked with a colorful splay of campaign ribbons above his pocket and a set of two golden strings around one arm pit, topped off by two and one half stripes of gold on black shoulder boards. As he climbed up the gangway, he popped a white, stretched U.S. Navy officer's hat on to his head, then saluted the stern flag along with the deckhand in a greasy T-shirt that happened to be at the head of the gangway having a smoke.

To give his entrance some substance, the steward whistled from his perch on the bridge wing "Ssrrrrreeeeeuuppp!" followed by "Three Bone, arriving."

The officer looked up to the sound, and smiled.

The steward called down from the bridge wing. "What the devil are you doing here?"

Trowbridge Pierson Bone, the Third no less, looked up and broke into a huge grin. "Looking for you, jerk. "It seems you still owe the PX in Naples 25 cents for a role of bum wad, and the Navy has sent me to collect."

After hearty handshakes, the steward led his old Navy acquaintance to the foredeck for a touch of privacy from the invasion of stevedores now swarming in the cargo area.

"It's a small world," the steward chuckled. "Meeting the Bone in Bombay, amidst three million bones." He added incredulously, "Are you really looking for me? What's going on? My family all right? How'd you find me? Here?"

Bone quickly assured his friend that things were fine, and that he had known of his path and a progress through his exit papers in Genoa and passport checks in Suez and Massaua. The steward's passport listing of occupation, "Lieutenant, U.S. Navy", for someone now serving as a steward on a Norwegian freighter, did raise some notice with passport officials in various ports.

Bone put his hand on the steward's shoulder. "In fact, things couldn't be better. That's why I'm here."

"Oh, no, Bone. I left the Navy. I'm out," the steward started. "I don't care if they want to give me Cat Brown's job in the Sixth Fleet. I served my time. I survived. I'm out."

Three Bone in contrast, had elected to ship over after his first tour. He was now out of line duty and assigned to Naval Intelligence, and had been recently stationed as a junior attaché with the Consulate in Bombay. He was far from any super spy, and intelligence in any form was certainly not his forte, but he happened to have been selected for his impressive credentials - prep school and ivy pedigree, Washington contacts, overbearing height, and big family bucks - as a good person to have shaking hands in diplomatic circles. India seemed a suitable duty station, non-threatening and docile, for one to the manor born.

"We need every able bodied man," Three Bone started saying, urgently and quietly. "Something big is happening, and we need help here. You are to be given an emergency temporary duty assignment, right here in Bombay."

"Big? What's afoot? I thought India was neutral. Nobody's declaring war, are they?" A shiver passed over the steward.

"Not shooting war, dummy. A war of the minds. India is a hotbed of opposing ideologies right now. We want to win their minds," Bone affirmed strongly.

"Good. So you come all the way out here for me, to enlist my mind in a war of minds?" the steward asked. "Bullshit, Bone. It doesn't wash. I'm a civilian, not military. I've got a job, right here, cleaning up enough messes. I don't need yours or India's."

"No. Wait. You miss the point," Bone interrupted. "We aren't in any shooting war. It's a social war. A society war! We need you to go to parties, dozens of them. Diplomatic parties! We need every able body we can get into a uniform. You're one. We don't have many military personnel out here, remember? The Indian government, until yesterday, was at odds with the West. Today, things are dramatically changed. Now they need us."

"Parties!?" the steward asked in disbelief.

"Yeah, parties. There's been a complete policy shift. Instant, overnight. The Indians are rolling out the red carpet for the West. It's already started. We've got flights of military guys scheduled in from Naples and Saudi Arabia and Turkey, but they won't get here for 24 to 36 hours. Remember, we don't have much of a naval presence out here. The only goddamn ship we have nearby is the Edward Moale, a cruddy tin can now in the Persian gulf, and it's steaming here right now, ETA in 20 hours. A couple of new frigates are coming out of Subic but they're two days off. We need bodies, now, today! We can't let the Limeys and the Frogs and the Commies steal our thunder at these government soirees. We have to show American bodies. We'll give you a uniform. We'll give you temporary orders. We'll fucking even pay you! It's just for three days! It's a command fucking performance! The future of fucking India rests in our fucking hands!" Bone was flapping his arms in a crescendo of emotion.

The steward thought of Eiriksson's usual comment. "This is all fishshit." Then he laughed out loud at the absurdity of it all. "O.K. When you use the 'f' word, I understand. My country needs my body. I'm yours for the duration."

After waking Eiriksson from a deep stupor with this outlandish proposition, and watching quietly while he shook his head in incredulity, and gaining a grunt of approval in the presence of Three Bone, the steward packed his toothbrush and shaving gear in a small ditty bag and saluted himself over the side with the Bone, into the waiting motor launch. It was ten in the morning, and the harbour activity was at full tilt. Eiriksson, however, had elected to remain at supine tilt.

"Here's the deal," Bone yelled over the roar of the motor. "Each of the branches of the government and the military are having their own parties. Lots of big wigs, politicians, generals and all their suck-ups. There've been eight parties so far since noon yesterday, and ten more scheduled from noon on today."

Why?" the steward asked.

"You can fit in my old set of whites. They shrunk. I'll even throw in my two and a half stripes. At this point the Navy doesn't care about official rank. The bigger the better. The WOGs won't know or care anyway. But you need ribbons. You have to find your own ribbons." Bone was thrilled with the detailed plotting of it all, like preparing for an imminent great battle.

"Why?"

"Because I only have one set, asshole, that's why. Scrounge your own fucking campaign ribbons. Make yourself out a hero. They like that shit out here."

"No, why? Why is the Indian government going into all this atypical display of diplomatic intercourse."

"How the fuck do I know. I'm in intelligence!" Bone added with a touch of frustration.

"I don't believe that, Bone" the steward looked him straight in the eyes.

Bone looked out at the horizon for a few seconds. "Someone's coming for dinner. That's all I can tell you. We were told to make ourselves conspicuous at every possible diplomatic function. Show the flag. Stand tall. Shake hands in friendship. All that shit."

"Quite a change of policy, considering that yesterday you couldn't even get near Nehru's kitchen to pick up his garbage."

"They got untouchables for that duty. The U.S. Navy is not untouchable. Only undesirable. In most circumstances. In every port."

"Never let your daughter go out with a navy man, right?" the steward laughed, remembering the welcome signs on the lawns in Norfolk, like 'Dogs and sailors keep off the grass.' "We should expect here things are to be different?"

"So now they are pushing every available lovely into our arms. I mean it. Every debutant in the fucking country is coming out this week, at these parties."

"War is hell at times," the steward chuckled and looked out to the approaching shoreline and wharf area, sniffing the pungent, fruity air.

Sycophant.

The word took on a whole new perspective.

As far as the steward could see, there was a bobbing field of black-haired heads and golden epaulets and shiny sashes and plumed hats. All bobbing up and down to other heads and military medallions and diplomatic feathers and finery, some bobbing lower than others, some bobbing only slightly, some bobbed from view completely. Only the steward's head, unaccustomed as it was to such regal and diplomatic courtesies, remained steadily aloof. Actually not knowing when or how or even how low to bow was a blessing in disguise. Anyone who came before him immediately assumed he was a heavy hitter and smiled from their toady perspectives to catch even a whiff of his attention.

Most guests were middle-aged political hacks and their wives, bowing and scraping to their superiors in common agreement with whatever was being said. They were the beautiful people of India, competitively dressed for this brunch occasion, fresh from their pampered palaces and luxurious homes, to see and be seen at this most important event. Striking black eyes darted across the room like inverse fireflies in a mating dance, captured in the soft white glare of midday that filtered through gauzy silks enhancing the tall windows.

Power and prestige stood out in this bobbing sea of flattery. A few grandees, a bit plumper than the rest and usually older, wore loose, casual clothing, a sharp contrast the crisp uniforms and stiff-collared suits and vivid *saris*. They gently nodded their heads in the affirmative at any and all surrounding them. The differing strata of sycophants could be recognized quite easily by their hand motions. Lesser sycophants nervously worked their hands and fingers vigorously in a prayer-like position under their chin. Those more dominant held their hands in the same position, but their fingers were still, and their hands only leaned forward when greeting or saying *adieu* to those beneath them. The lesser sycophants were in a fawning frenzy, feasting on so many important personages all at once, all the while trying to stay lower than each other's chins. Even their sounds seemed in concert. "Yes, yes, yes, yes. Yes, yes. Yes, yes. Oh, yes. Yessss, yesss, yes. No? Oh yes, yes. Yesss, yesss. Certainly yes." In Western terms, both the greater and lesser sycophants had captured the requisite limp handshake quite well, never taking hold of all five fingers. Some of the greater had mastered a two-handed variant of the soft backhand wave of the Queen, and would obviously feel completely at home in the back seat of a carriage or Rolls. Overall, there seemed to be a commonly recognized paradigm in place, as each, in the presence of others, would toad right in with the crowd to predetermined depths, in appropriate respect of superior power and privilege.

The steward watched in disbelief. "It's all a game. They can't be serious about all this," he thought to himself. "It's more of a fashion show than a party. Even Busby Berkeley couldn't dream up something like this. It's *The Mating Dance of the Sycophants.*"

He was standing near the marbled wall of a great hall in some antique palace on the outskirts of Bombay. Somebody lived there, quite well. To get there he had been chauffeured by a marine sergeant named Ski in a navy blue Chevy, through the slums of Bombay, from the U.S. Consulate. Contrast is too weak a term.

The past two hours had been beyond comprehension. He recalled his arrival ashore with Bone, onto the massive stone steps at the foot of a magnificently statued arch known appropriately as "The Gateway to India." Here thousands of British had landed to take up their rightful roles as masters of the Sub-Asian world. Officers and wives and governors and petty officials and anyone stiff collared had come in through "The Gateway to India." However, the footsoldiers and mechanics and engineers and railroad workers who actually made the empire function had probably used some back door, somewhere in the elsewhere of the harbour.

He shivered at the thought of the Gateway. He had just stepped out of a beautiful relic of a power launch, dressed in white shorts and high socks and white shoes, with an open white shirt, looking like any of many mariners or tourists to grace India's shores, nothing impressive. Then out of a swarm of flies and dogs and scantily clad skeletons, out of a thousand hands beseeching alms, appeared one strange old woman, stringy gray hair down to her waist, only a piece of brown burlap wrapped around her hips, skinny legs and dusty bare feet, a mere scattering of teeth remaining, with two flat sacks hanging down her rib cage that one had to surmise were once breasts. Halloween had never produced such a hag.

The steward stopped in his tracks right under the Gateway, and froze as she hobbled forward to him through the retches nearby. She had only a stump of a left upper arm. One of her eyes was a blind hole. With the other, a dark coal of an eye that glowed with a strange wild ember down deep in it, she stared at him fiercely, locking his gaze to hers, and half-screeched, half-mumbled something like "Aaaeeeaaaa... Rraammmmaaa... Purreeteetaawwaannaaa...Wwrraaammmaayyaannaa... Aaaaiiiii... Rrraaammmmmmmmaaa....Eeebbuuuu mmaaatttteee.... Puurreteebannaa...Rrraammmaaachaaanndraa...Llaammmaaaa...." Then she dropped to his feet, grabbed his legs in a fumbling one-handed caress, and began to kiss his shoes.

The steward almost jumped out of his knee socks and into Bone's arms. "What is she doing!" he screamed. "Get her off me, Bone! She's putting a damn hex on me!"

Bone just smiled and softly pushed at the old woman with his foot. "Naw. She likes you. She just wants some money."

"Here. Here! Take this!" The steward put a five-dollar bill in her hand, oddly noting how soft the skin was.

"All right, little missy. Off we go. Back to your post." Bone finally managed to break the grip she maintained on the steward's leg, and shoved her softly with his foot back on to the dusty ground.

"What did she say!?" the steward asked, still shaken.

"Something about Rama. Or Lama. Maybe Ramachandra. Or something like that," Bone added laughing. "Usually they evoke the name of some god when they beg. Relax. She's only begging."

"Begging? She was kissing my feet!" the steward noted with excitement. "What does she think I am, some kind of hero?"

"No, some kind of sucker." Bone chuckled. "She got you to pay up, didn't she?"

The steward shivered again at the thought of the old woman at the Gateway. She had been the first, and most frightening, of numerous beggars to accost him in the next hours - until he had found the bunker of safety in Ski's navy blue Chevy with diplomatic plates. India most certainly was a land of extremes. From abject poverty, to this, a frivolous display of opulence.

The room filled even more with bobbing heads and plumes and sashes and *saris*. Here and there a starched white military uniform stood out in the crowd, usually standing a foot higher then the surrounding masses, but no others appeared to be American. Everyone seemed to be congratulating each other, shaking hands, and smiling. In ones and twos and threes, people in a variety of uniforms and formal wear stepped up to him, unannounced, to shake his hand vigorously. They all had the most perfect rich brown tans, gleaming white teeth, and huge coal black eyes that darted about excitedly. They would all say their names, in a high-pitched lilting voice of many little syllables, all sounding the same. He would simply smile into their eyes, mumble that he was simply their steward, and that if there was anything he could do to assist them he would most certainly do it. They each beamed and bobbed graciously at this, and then fluttered off into the whirling crowd without asking any particulars.

As a U.S. Navy officer (temporary active reserve at best) at this particular party, the steward was a big hit for some reason. Maybe because he was the only American there.

In a country where consumption of alcohol is not part of the culture, and in most cases quite taboo, the steward seemed to be in a zone of diplomatic exception. Everyone was getting blasted on champagne and scotch and gin. Regardless of one's trappings or station, booze flowed without guilt. In diplomatic circles, he was finding, religious restrictions take a back seat. "Only saving souls requires sobriety..." he mused, remembering one of Eiriksson's platitudes on command. "Kissing ass requires lubrication."

The canapés forced upon him were delicious, even considering his own skills at the Talabot smorgasbord, and he took mental notes on combining a world of new flavors and colors and textures.

A little coriander here, on a curl of shrimp...and there a crush of ginger, set against a sliver of goat cheese, and chive, on what? Fennel?...What's that? Maybe a touch of cayenne, a dash of cumin, ringlets of chili set in a countering of yogurt, on the thinnest slab of cucumber... And this? A sprinkling of minced onion, and just a brief hint of garlic, and a thread of saffron, blushing on some kind of delicate fish... And now? A dollop of lemon yogurt over a curl of peppered shrimp couched in a tear of flat bread... On and on the fiery finger-foods came... On and on, and ever present throughout, however lightly, however vigorously, a varied involvement of curries. The steward was in salivatory bliss. Ah, India. Here indeed was something savory for everyone.

The steward took extreme care not to spill on his freshly pressed whites, his only existing set and borrowed from Bone for the occasion. On his shoulders lay the boards of a full commander, all that was available in the consulate, and rather impressive for one so young as he. "Instant battlefield commissions are the way to go," he thought to himself. Then he noted the sparkling medal hanging from his pocket. A beautiful red and blue ribbon supporting a gold emblem about the size of a quarter. Only that one medal did he wear. It stood out beautifully on the whites. Very impressive, he felt. Seen at appropriate distance, it was an award obviously given by the Pope or someone equally important for valor, possibly in the battle of the bars of Antibes. Only upon close scrutiny could one determine that the emblem was actually the imprint of two crossed bowling pins and a bowling ball, to be given for victory on lanes other than the sea lanes, and obtained by Ski from the consulate commissary that very day. He was indeed dressed for diplomacy, outfitted in everyone's favorite uniform - crisply starched, fitted navy whites. Just don't splash curry on the suit, please.

A delicate fingering at his elbow made him look down and to the left. A small Indian man, in his late forties, stood there subtly bobbing and weaving like a cobra in a morning coat, and smiling broadly. The steward looked for any curry stains, then spoke to the man. "Hello. Lovely party."

The Indian placed his hands together in prayer under his chin, and replied most courteously, "How doo you doo? How doo you doo? My name is Shajishiva Shivartsepoor. I am the Assistant Deputy Minister of Foreign Relations. I am the host here, this morning. Welcome to my humble home."

The steward smiled, and held out his hand in an effort to shake the other man's. He kept them in the prayer grip, and bowed low, possibly not noticing the outstretched hand. "And what may I call you, Sir?"

"Steward. Call me steward. Everyone else does."

"Ah, my deeeer Commander Steward. It is marveelous to meeeet you." The fingers in the prayer grip started to interplay delicately. "We are always veery happy to welcome members of the United States Navy to our home. It is a veery joyous occasion, I assure you. And one so young as you, a full commander! You must be veery impoortant to your country, Sir. Veeery impoortant indeeeed."

"Thank you, Mr. Shi..vast..e.."

"Oh, ho, ho, ha, ha, ha. It can bee a veery difficult name for you, I am certain. Shivartsepoor. Shajishiva Shivartsepoor. But you, my new American friend, can call me Shivartse. Every one else in your wonderful America does. Ha, ha, ha, he, he."

"Shivartse?"

"Oh, yes indeeed. When I was studying poleetical science at your Ceety College of New York, oh years ago, after my Oxford days, one of my veery good friends named me 'Shivartse'. Even some of your fine older ladies and gentlemen sitting on the benches of Broadway knew my name. Some, however, got my surname mixed up, and called me Mr. Poorashivartse. I was veery well known, I can assure you." His fingers were dancing together now, remembering the good old days.

The steward looked about at the opulence of the minipalace. "You have done well with your political science, Sir. This is a beautiful home."

"Oh thank you veery much. But I must admit in all truth, it comes from my wife's family. You must meet my beautiful wife, Lakshmi. She brings with her quite a sizable dowry indeed."

"Then you have learned very well whom to have on your side, so to speak, Sir." They both laughed, Shivartse quite loudly, and looked about the room.

"He, he, he. Oh, yes indeed. Look about you. I have learned quite well. He, he, he." The crowd of bobbing heads in unison bobbed his way in acknowledgement, and then resumed bobbing in their previous orientations.

"What is your commission, Commander Steward?" the small man turned his eyes up to him seriously. "Why are you here. I mean, of course, besides to meet all our wonderful friends and colleagues."

"I am afraid I can not tell you that, Sir," the steward responded carefully, "However much I would like to."

"Ah, yes indeed, Commander. You intrigue me greatly. Our mystery guest from America. Greatly indeed. Later, we might have a talk about politics, and life, yes?" The fingers stopped fidgeting and riveted together. "But first, you must meet some of my colleagues."

The gracious host ushered the steward around the sumptuously appointed room, introducing him to a continuing list of titles and ministries and indeciferable run-on syllables and darting eyes and bobbing heads... Mister Balabalaboolabool, Minister of Cultural Affairs... His "niece" he, he, he... Doctor Walawalawalawog, Assistant Minister of Finance and Commerce... His "niece" he, he, he... Doctor Wangapangawongapoon, Assistant Deputy Minister of Antiquities... His male "friend" he, he, he... and this is Mr. Moomapoomamoomapoom, Associate Minister of Ministries... His office colleagues... Mr. Tapawampawillawa, Minister of Ministerial Records... His "friend"... and so on and on... and this is Mr. Nurapurayurawog, First Subordinate Minister of Industries and Agriculture... his lovely young "friend"... and now Mr. Singh, Third Deputy Minister of Foreign Relations... His "friend" Mr. Singh...and scores of others, presumably wives, other friends and hangers-on. Two names seemed to register with their faces, possibly because they were Occidental. The heavily moustached and bemedaled "Major General Anderson-Brooks, of our own splendid Indian Armed Forces... and the heavily garlic'd "Mr. Valery Biewgoff, Assistant Naval attaché of the Russian Embassy in New Delhi..." The names and faces were unending. One thing they all had in common. They were all having one heck of a good time, drinking there in the midday shade.

The men at the party generally were all over fortyfive. They all smiled merrily, as they danced about. The steward had seen it many times before, at fraternity blasts and club functions, everyone fawning to the reigning Alpha male. They had made the big time. They were part of the "important" crowd. The women at the party, however, were of two ages, over fifty, and under twenty five. The older set was beautifully dressed, almost without exception, in *saris* of explosive colors, lush reds and golds and peacock blues and turquoise, all interwoven with silver and golden threads. They stood very still, quite composed and always near their bobbing spouses, and smiled serenely at everything that was said. *A la mode*, their long black hair was frequently wrapped up to the side of their heads, and held in a swirl by a comb of ebony or gold.

These were the dutiful wives. They had stood this same duty many times before. Today was today, and their duty called once again. From all appearances, they enjoyed their duty, placid as they might be.

The younger set, however, were more mobile and more nervous, moving about in clusters of twos and threes, or fidgeting on the arms of the older men. They also were dressed in *saris*, but with lighter, happier colors of fresh mint and jade and rich pink and yellow, with a tighter wrap at the waist to enhance the soft, delicious flesh of their abdomens that reminded the steward of lightly toasted almonds. "The world's most perfect tan..." thought the steward. "Permanent. Perfectly uniform. No freckles or sunburn." The young women were visibly more on the prowl than their older colleagues. Their eyes flashed about the room, to see and to be seen. They seemed to be relatively new to these functions, and looking for some new or more satisfactory relationships to perpetuate their being invited in the future. Some were obviously the girlfriends of the politicals, possessing that look of temporary fulfillment and acceptance of their current role in life, but some were apparently this season's harvest of younger ladies brought forth only on occasion into this world of excitement, diplomacy, and privilege. They too had one thing in common. To a person, they were outstandingly attractive, like the freshest, most succulent fruit.

"Curried fruit..." mulled the steward, touching his tongue to a delicate canapé. "A most intriguing combination."

The steward stood very tall among the crowd, by at least eight inches on average. Had Bone been there, he would have commanded a more lofty view of yet additional inches. Above the milling masses the steward persisted in there, shaking hands and smiling, and staring into the deep black sparkling holes that fluttered and flickered in waves before him.

The steward was dying for another glass of champagne, his third so far in the day. It was hot, not terribly, but close with all the people so near. He looked about, for that waiter in the fancy turban, somewhere about with a tray. "Let's see...I had better pace myself on this stuff... Maybe about four an hour." Quick calculations brought him to a total of 48 drinks between noon and midnight. "On second thought, I had better pass. It promises to be a long couple of days." Boon had given him a written itinerary of the parties he was expected to attend. There were to be lunches, tea parties, lawn parties, cocktail parties, dinner parties, and to cap off the evening tonight, a ball on the Indian flagship in the harbour. That was just today. Tomorrow, the diplomatic and social whirl would start again at noon, and was projected to go to three a.m. at a villa of the commanding general of the Indian military, complete with magicians and minstrels. "And I was given a Consulate advisory not to drink the local water..." he groaned.

He drifted off, oblivious to the chattering and introductions of his peripatetic host for a few moments, as he surveyed the scene. Out of the blur of bobbing and weaving, there appeared one face in the crowd, across the room. He found himself staring at the large black eyes and straight, silky long black hair hung over one shoulder, contrasting with a light milky tan. Only a face in the crowd. But what a face. And it was looking back at him. The face smiled, and he felt a rush in his cheeks. Without dropping its gaze, the face started to move through the crowd, closer to him, eyes in a constant fix on his. The smile defined itself in two full slightly reddened lips, balanced by a single dot of red on the lower forehead set between dark sculptured eyebrows. "Now I know why they wear that beauty dot," he thought to himself. "Gives one something to focus on. It's truly hypnotic."

The eyes and hair and lips and dot continued on their path to him, looming larger and larger, only to reveal, as a bobbing mass moved out of the way, an exploding red *sari* that wrapped the most perfect piece of curried fruit in the world. "I'll take Pomegranate any day..." the steward mumbled. Suddenly the eyes were before him, and a hand was thrust into his.

Shivartse's voice broke the spell. "And this is my niece, Commander. Truly, she is my niece, yes, this time, my real niece, daughter of my wife's sister. May I present Sita? She is my gem of gems, my joy of joys. Treat her well, Commander, or I might become angry. For a Hindu, that is veery serious indeed. He, he, he."

"Uh..Bunh...Veery...Pleases me...to meet..."

"He, he, he... Commander. You speak our language veery well, indeed. He, he, he..."

"He speaks more with his eyes, Uncle." Her voice was like dark sugar. "We understand each other quite well."

They were a study in contrasts. He with his ruddy tan, wild sun bleached hair, blue eyes, blond full moustache, set against starched whites, she with her milky tea skin, sleek jet black hair and eyes, and full lush lips, set against a wispy Pomegranate *sari*. She was tall for an Indian woman, about five eight, with proud chin and fine features and long graceful moves, like a dancer's. Her lips were positively in bloom, glistening in a dash of moisture as she sipped her champagne. "Something savory for everyone..." Eiriksson had foretold.

After a few moments of idle chatter, and goings and comings of others in the crowd, Sita spoke to the steward softly. "You look like you could use some fresh air, Commander. May I show you the grounds?" He nodded with a relieved smile. "Uncle, I will entertain our guest for a bit. You have many others to greet. Is that agreeable to you?"

Shivartse too looked relieved, and continued to play the perfect host to those bobbing around him. "A wonderful idea, Sita. Give our American guest an education. Let him taste of the true India. We will rejoin later on. You are in good hands, Commander."

A deep breath and a tug at the tall starched collar gave new life to the steward once they exited through the massive gated doors into the courtyard. He looked about in amazement at the size of the home and its gardens. "Your uncle is really a perfect host, Sita. He has made me feel very welcome."

"My uncle wears many clothes, of many depths, Commander."

"And your clothes? Of one depth. Very beautiful," the steward countered.

"Thank you. I regret you are incorrect. This *sari* is wrapped around seven times. But enough of clothes. My uncle said to give you an education about India. Is there anything you care to ask?"

"Well, ah...Yes. Much," he stumbled, taken aback a bit. "For example, who is in that statue over there?" It appeared to be numerous semi-armored monkeylike figures in a very involved relationship.

Sita smiled. "Ah, you have quite a way to get to the heart of matters, Commander. That is a statue of our Hindu gods. They take various forms, or incarnations, sometimes monkeys, sometimes man. They are usually represented in a series of interactions, some violent, some loving, some dispassionate. This statue depicts the Hindu god, in three forms of Brahma, the Creator, Vishnu, the Preserver, and Shiva, the Destroyer. Here, Brahma is making love to Vishnu, while Shiva awaits the fruit of their efforts to kill it."

"Making love with a sword hanging over one's head. It must be difficult duty."

"It all depends on your focus, Commander. Our Hindu god is viewed, after all is said and done, as one supreme being, but as one with different phases or representations. It is one's choice to concentrate on preservation of life, or its creation, or its destruction. The Hindu religion can be very accommodating."

"Seems an intelligent approach. Who came up with that? Who created Hinduism? Somebody like Sidhartha Guatama?"

"No, indeed. Guatama, the creator of Buddhism, came long after Hinduism, and a few hundred years before your Christ. Like the Christians, he and his followers never really caught on in his own land, India, and left to preach their teachings elsewhere. His own Indian people did not respond to his new views. Hinduism is more a cultural and religious evolution than one of any one person's invention. It has developed over four thousand years, in bits and pieces, in stories and poems, in rules and changes of rules, adding flavors from all cultures and peoples, and applying them to fit the basic needs of all people. The Aryans first brought elements here in 1500 B.C. and these became blended with indigenous religious customs. Over the millenniums, the Hindu religion has blended itself into all tribes and castes and peoples. It does not dominate. It does not challenge. It does not demand. It accommodates. There is something in it, some version or god form or answer for everyone who wishes it. It requires only that we seek it. I believe it characterizes our country very well."

"But what about all your great thinkers, the swamis and the gurus and the Gandhis and the mystics. Don't they have impact on the people? Don't they try to change things? Don't they preach and teach?"

"Most certainly. But you must acknowledge two factors. First, in years past, there was no radio, no television, no newspaper, no easy means of mass communication or mass teaching. Deeper thoughts and ideas moved in person, first from swamis and teachers, then by their impassioned following. Not a very efficient way to sway the masses, eh? Only a few at a time. Things evolved slowly from one generation to another. Secondly, there were many, many thinkers and teachers. It is a recognized phase in the life of a Hindu to leave society and seek profound answers through introspection. Many deep thinkers were teaching only subtle variations of the same theme. Still today, the Hindu religion continues to feature a philosophy that truth and wisdom are found only through deep personal introspection. Our doctrine of Brahman reveals in mystical terms the absolute reality that is the self of all things, and its identity with the individual soul, or *atman*."

"You missed me."

"It misses many. It fascinates many. That is why they seek."

They continued their stroll down a flower path, toward an open space in the trees.

"But are there no laws, no books, like the *Bible*?"

"Most certainly. The *Veda*, our sacred text, comprises the liturgy and interpretation of the sacrifice, and culminates in the *Upanishads*, mystical and speculative writings which lay out various practices such as *yoga*, or doctrines such as *karma*, according to which the individual reaps the results of his good and bad actions through a series of lifetimes."

"Reincarnation?"

"If you so wish it."

"If I might ask an honest but awkward question, who are you this year."

"I am Sita. A daughter of a noble family. A simple daughter of India. Nothing more, nothing less."

"But very wise. And very beautiful." He could not take his eyes off hers. They were the deepest tunnels of darkest black, and he strained to see the mysterious light at the far end.

She smiled, still holding his gaze. "I believe you are ready for a bit of our third stage of life... *vanaprastha*. It requires you to undertake a forest hermitage."

"For what purpose?"

"Simply to sit and think. Truly. To do nothing but think. Carried to its ultimate forth stage, we call it *sannyasa*, it is the complete renunciation of all ties with society and pursuit only of spiritual liberation."

"I do that with a quart of Black Label."

"We do it to see things more clearly. That means our yogis and deepest thinkers sat in the wilderness and thought about the meaning of life, while others more practical, increased their wealth and power in the active world. By their very hermitage, their thoughts were kept very low key, and away from the problems and passions of everyday living. Thusly, the people were left to adapt their thinkings as they wished, when they finally did shape them, to the actions of their daily lives."

"The swamis made no efforts to promote their views?"

"Certainly, but passively, if persons wished to learn of them. Unlike Western nations, there were no nuns to spank the children if they strayed from a swami's view of truth. The Raja's went about their business, relatively unimpeded by religious dogma. And the common person continued to focus on food and shelter, resorting only in time of need to a diety's influence over fertility, famine, flood, and death. So it has been a practical solution after all. A thinking yogi in his *sannyasa* didn't eat very much, he may even have forgotten about his hunger pains, and he takes himself out of the way for the most part. But a working father with crying children learns to apply any religious thoughts or concepts to a different phase of life, *grihastha*, or householdership, and has no time for the purely ascetic. As I have said, there is something in Hinduism for everyone, without much violent confrontation of beliefs."

"But I thought you have Brahmans, priests, to preform sacrifices and spread the word."

"Close, but not entirely correct. In the earliest days, Hindu was referred to as Brahmanism. The Brahmans were traditional priests, bedecked in fancy clothes, who performed the *Vedic* sacrifice through the power of which proper relation with the gods and the cosmos is established. Stated in modern terms, they were the privileged, protecting their backsides through the spectacle of mysterious rites and sacrifices."

"I think I am beginning to see things more clearly now."

She fingered some white flowers cascading down from a large bush by the path. "Yes? Possibly a night in the wilderness, your own *sunnyasa*, might help even more."

He felt he read more to her reply than was implied. "I saw no priests or religious heavyweights at the party inside. Were they felt out of place in this situation?"

"On the contrary, Commander. You saw many. Open your eyes and your heart to see truth. These people inside, these are the Brahmans of today. All very accommodating indeed."

Sita and the steward resumed their stroll to the edge of a hill, where benches welcomed one to a wide, breathtaking view of the harbour. They stopped, and took in the distance. Yes, the Talabot could be seen, still at her mooring, far off to the West.

"The view is always clear from this high vantage point," Sita said softly. "It is so peaceful. One sees things from a different perspective, away from the bustling crowds. Illusion and reality are more easily defined, and take on new meanings."

"I feel that way at sea at times. One is distanced from the complexities of everyday living and carried on by some grander scheme of space and time."

"It sounds like you are ready for your hermitage, Commander."

The steward reached out, hesitated, then touched her hand.

The peacefulness of the afternoon was fractured by a loud, raucous call, right behind the steward. "Ssrrreeeeaaaaccckkkk!" Simultaneously, a sharp point stabbed the steward in the butt.

The steward jumped, both in fright and in a move to protect, into the direction of Sita. A massive spread of blue and green and jade and turquoise shivered menacingly in front of him.

"Oh, it is only my darling Rama. Come here, Rama, my hero. You have startled our American friend, you silly thing," Sita laughed.

A giant peacock stiffly strutted to her, shimmering in the sunlight, head turning abruptly from left to right, looking critically at the steward. "Come here. He is our new friend, Rama. Be courteous to the Commander." The great bird nuzzled its head against her hand.

"Whew! I've never seen so grand a bird," the steward marveled. "Nor so loud."

"It is a small price to pay, for such beauty," Sita smiled.

His rush of adrenaline had just started to subside when he heard a voice behind him again. "You must learn always to guard your flank in India, Commander. To do less, can be most poignant." A large, very bemedaled military uniform with a very British accent emerged from the flowering hedges nearby. "May I join you three lovely young creatures, Sita?"

"My favorite general is always welcome at my side, Sir," Sita replied with a mock curtsy as she took the older man by the hand. "May I present Major General Anderson-Brooks, Commandant of the Armed Forces in this region, Commander?"

Oddly, in this less formal sylvan setting and not at the elbow of Shivartse, the steward felt it more proper to snap his heels together in quick attention. "The General and I have met." He smiled at the very senior, bushy moustache in front of him. "I'm afraid I didn't take my Kipling seriously enough, Sir. I was indeed lanced by this beastie in the backside."

"In time, you will learn to appreciate him, Commander. His passions run quite deep. Like those of India. One can become very attached."

Sita had curled herself into the arm of the older man. "If I were only but a few years older, this is a man I could choose, Commander," she said, giving him a playful hug. "This general is possibly more Indian than I. Does that surprise you?"

"Everything so far in India has surprised me."

"You flatter me, my dear, and I love it. Please do not stop," the general chuckled. "What she means, my boy, is that I have lived all my life in India, as have my parents, and grandparents. Even my schooling was here, quite untypical among my peers, I assure you. But my Sita here is more worldly, having spent part of her education in the more enlightened cloisters of Vassar and the Sorbonne. Also, quite atypical among her peers."

The steward nodded at the light now shed on Sita's softened English accent. "I understood that the British were sort of...ah... asked to leave, a few years back, Sir. How, or why, are you so lucky as to remain?"

"Yes, lucky indeed, young man. I had served the Crown's India well in my career, I do believe. I was asked to remain, and to serve the new India as well. I think the Indians and I have an understanding of many things, kindred souls, so to speak. While so many of my English colleagues thought of these people merely as... subjects, I fortunately was somewhat alone in my view of them as the finest and bravest men, and women, with whom I had ever served, Scot, British, Yank, Australian, or whatever."

"The general was loved by his troops, Commander," Sita added. "They asked him to stay. They themselves convinced the politicians he was more than valuable to India's military. They respected him as a brother in arms. It is not his fault that his arms have pink skin and red hair, and he is topped by that silly white moustache."

The general smiled and bowed, "Pink skin in this life. That is my *karma*."

"One might say he is the inverse of your Westernized Oriental Gentleman, Commander. He is our Orientalized English General. His life is India. He is now ours."

"I am surrounded by liberated women, you see, Commander. That too, is my *karma*."

"Is your wife here also, General?" the steward inquired, uncomfortably.

"Alas, Sir, she has passed on. But she never once was jealous of my beautiful mistress, here, in all our years together."

"Liberated, indeed," thought the steward eyeing Sita carefully.

"India, my boy," the general chortled as he saw the look on the steward's face. "With India as my mistress, I remain forever young. Who could ask for more?" And with a bear hug and a hearty laugh, he spun Sita free into the fresh coastal breeze.

"Now, I must go. I'm sure I will see more of you in various future functions, Commander. I would enjoy having a private scotch with you, and hearing of your purpose here. But first, let me invite both of you to my own party tomorrow evening at my home. It will feature many surprises, not the least of which will be magicians and minstrels. Please, Commander, bring this beautiful flower so that my drab diplomatic efforts might be enriched by her delightful fragrance. Sita, will you come?"

Sita looked at the steward, and his eyes confirmed her reply as he secretly sniffed her air. "Gladly, General. We will be there."

The general smiled, and bowed. As he backed away, he spoke again, "Oh, by the way Commander. I don't recall seeing that medal before. Might I ask its origins?"

The steward blushed. "It was given to me... by a Polish colleague... It's for service in a...ah... populist league."

"Underground. Quite. Until we meet again."

As the general stiffly walked back up the path, he called out to the bushes. "Hello, Valery. Nice day for the thicket, what?"

An embarrassed Biewgoff emerged to the path, brushed himself off, bowed abruptly to Sita, and walked quickly off in the direction of the party.

Ski had deftly driven to and deposited the steward at numerous parties and social gatherings throughout the afternoon and early evening. Ski was a relatively silent young man, whose god-given forehead had expanded immensely through his shaved jarhead haircut. Ski knew his way around the suburbs of quite well, navigating the streets both ancient and new in a speeding cloud of diplomatic dust. He was also a frustrated travel guide, pointing out sites of interest or beauty, in his eyes.

Bombay was a fascinating city, rich in Portuguese and British heritage laid carefully over the colorful batik of Indian cultures. Bombay was actually an island, created and reclaimed over the 19th century from a series of islets until today it had become a peninsula of the larger Salsette Island to the north, connected to the mainland by a causeways and railway embankments. The city had over the recent centuries grown in importance, as it embraces the only deepwater harbour in Western India, a fact not overlooked by the British East Indian Company when establishing its headquarters. Truly, Bombay was the Gateway to India, far surpassing other upstart towns like New Delhi in imperial grandeur and strategic importance to the West.

"That's one of those Parsi death towers..." Ski pointed out the window. "Tower of Silence. They lay the corpses up there for the vultures to pick clean." He picked at his nose. "Hindus, on the other hand, burn all their dead bodies and dump the ashes into the drinking water."

"Fortunately you drink beer, right, Ski?"

"Fortunately I do, Sir," Ski sniffed. "Otherwise, I'd go bumwad out here. All these skinny little people with no teeth. Begging. Gets to you after a while. They all want something. Old ladies, kids, it's pathetic. Then you see the fat cats like today, you wonder, right, Sir?"

"Wonder what, Ski?"

"Like what they do all day. Like what do they treat each other so badly for? There's more Rolls Royces here needing a lube job than cattle, and there's lots of them needing a lube job too. They're all skin and bones and flies."

"In the positive, I suppose it is all in their tradition of tolerance, Ski. In the negative, it's the caste system. They accept their lot, rich or poor. It is their *karma*. They don't involve themselves in each other's business, or quality of life, I would guess, except to serve or be served."

"Sure. The rich don't ever want to give any fuckin' thing away, or get their hands dirty. The poor are too fuckin' weak to fight for a piece of the pie," Ski snorted, and gunned the Chevy through some fly-ridden cattle in the road. "Look at all these bags of bones. The cows eat better than the people." He sniffed the manure-scented air with disgust.

Throughout the afternoon the blue Chevy roared regally through the suburbs of Andheri, Santa Cruz, Thana and Ulhasnagar, an hour at this party, a half hour at that function, from palace to patio, from garden to grand hall, from lush splendor through pathetic poverty and back again, always accompanied by a strange omni prescience.

The steward made certain that Ski did not wait empty handed in the Chevy at each function. "Remember, Ski. They also serve, who stand and wait." After hours of waiting, a half case of empty beer bottles rolled in clanking unison on the car floor as Ski roared off once again into the fading light, towards the Gateway to India.

The steward glanced down from his protected view of the milling mass of humanity through which they drove. His starched whites were somehow still white, but now quite limp. As he got out of the car, he stretched himself to his full height, in attempts to pull out the wrinkles. "Such is the heat of battle," he thought to himself. With that, he gave a soft backhand wave to a group of children playing at the roadside.

There under the Gateway once again was Three Bone, in the feeble glare of the occasional outdoor lamps, stretching out his own wrinkles. The steward walked cautiously over, keeping an eye out for old one eye herself. "Ready for duty, Commodore. All I need is a stout ship and a torpedo."

"All I need is an Alka Seltzer," groaned Bone.

At the foot of the old stone steps awaited the classic launch. The Steward and Three Bone sprung aboard, and off it took them, into the darkness of the harbour, off towards four Christmas trees of light that graced the outer reaches of the bay. "Who's going to be at this one? Admiral of the fishing fleet?" the steward asked snidely.

"Wait and see..." Bone intoned while holding his temples. "You'll be surprised."

Something in the night air touched his senses. The first impression was... No... Could it be?... Over the muffled mummmm of the inboard, the steward heard... music. Out here? In the darkness of

Bombay harbour? He turned to the bow and looked at the lights of four Christmas trees growing in size before him. "But this is India. What music is that? Radio?" he thought. Scattered notes associated with memories, memories with words... *"Mister Sandman... Buy me a dream... Make it the sweetest, that I've ever seen..."* He now could hear the music more clearly... Fresh out of his recent past, which seemed like a lifetime ago. A hit song. Hitting India?

The glow of the Christmas tree cast a magical spell over the darkness. As they motored nearer, the steward could make out the large, long lines of a hull of a ship, resting at anchor. A big one. Vintage lines. Painted light gray. Golden lights strung from bow to the top of the signal mast and back to the stern. On its fantail there seemed to be a huge canopy or tent, stretched overhead from the after guns to the flag. It too was outlined in lights. Lanterns. And under it there were blurs of vivid colors and whites and blacks. On closer view, it became apparent. It was a dance. A lavish one. On the stern deck of an old British cruiser.

The launch pulled up to the ladderway along side the hull of the giant ship. Other boats and launches had deposited their lot at the ladder. The steward could see animated young girls in *saris* and young officers in uniform, some still going up the steps, to join the many on the main deck of the ship. "Now this is how to run a Navy..." he said to Bone who was still straightening up his wrinkled white uniform.

"Debutantes..." Bone inferred with a toss of his head toward the deck. "And young society women. Backbone of the Indian Navy."

"Most from what I've seen have nice backbones," the steward quipped. His heart quickened to the chase. He wondered whether Sita might be there.

Bone ushered the steward first up the ladder with a wave of his arm. "Stairway to paradise. Going up."

The music had taken on new bounce as he approached the main deck. The upbeat urgings of Hindudanny and the Juniors put a spring in his step as he climbed the ladder:

"Oh yes indeed, let us go to the hop...

Oh if you please, let us go to the hop!
You can swing it, you can groove it.
You can assuredly start to move it, at the hop!"

At the hop at the top, the steward saluted the stern flag, somewhere beyond the tent, then the officer of the deck, a huge man in whites with ribbons plastered all over his chest. "Welcome aboard, Commander. The Admiral asks that you make yourself at ease, and enjoy this evening aboard our flagship."

The steward stepped out onto the freshly holystoned teak deck and looked about at the dancing lights and colors, swinging slightly in the soft evening breeze. The scene was something out of some Oriental Junior League Ball at the Biltmore, but afloat. A ten-piece orchestra, seated on top of the stern 8-inch gun turret, was playing wildly. An Indian variant of Eddie Duchin in a double-breasted tux fluttered a baton with preppy *panache* while grinning out at society's swells from his lofty bandstand. A foursome of singers, nattily dressed in Nehru coats and baggy britches, shouldered about a triangular mike.

Preppy Eddie had struck up his orchestra once again, and were now rendering a most acceptable version of the Champs, punctuating their music with appropriate sinful advice for the evening ...... *"Tequilla...."* On the massive deck below, the young and privileged of India were dancing up a storm, Western style, some in close contact, some swooshing partners out dramatically. Off to the side, standing on the rail, both young officers and women were energetically drinking champagne or mixed punch, and, laughing, held their glasses on high with every ...*"Tequilla..."*.

Music bounced about from cannon and bulkhead. The tent was a massive spread, covering a teak deck the size of a basketball court. The tent was decorated throughout its extremes with long colored lanterns, lit from within by bulbs. The air smelled like Parisian perfume, and the soft glow of the dance floor sparkled with black eyes and pearly smiles.

Bone took the steward by the arm and introduced him to various officers, and their ladies, who seemed to be important. The steward nodded courteously and shook all the appropriate hands, but the sound was intense making it hard to speak, and his eyes kept straying from any idle conversation to scan the crowded dance floor. The Indian naval officers were all with drink in their hands, liberated by years of finest of British tradition. They were serving their country with dignity, even though from the look of the anchor chains securing the cruiser, it hadn't been out of port in months. "War can be hell sometimes..." he thought.

The steward had drifted off from Bone, who was talking into the ear of some Indian captain near the bar. He strolled over to the railing, through many beautiful young couples, dressed to the nines for the occasion. "Something sweet for everyone," he mused. The music had evolved to batter another instrumental, unfortunately more in march cadence than slow dance step. *"Love me tender... Love me true..."*

The steward looked about, anticipating some presence in the crowd. His heart leapt as he spied her face amidst the blending bodies on the dance floor. "She's here!" His heart fell, as he saw she was dancing, although awkwardly, with Biewgoff. The steward resigned himself to watch in silence, as the large Russian pumped his hand in time with the music. "Oh, Valery... Didn't all those years with Lester Lenin teach you anything?"

He did not know whether she had seen him, standing there. He was about to muster up courage to cut in, but the music stopped, and he watched as Sita took Biewgoff by the arm and marched him in the steward's direction. He was in his Navy whites also, but his were crisply starched and carried an embarrassment of ribbons. About his shoulder board on one side hung a series of colored cords, signifying his rank and attaché status. The steward gnashed his teeth quietly. The steward took note of the specs of gold on the stiff black shoulder boards. "Humph. Commander Biewgoff. We start off equal."

Sita did not look up until she arrived directly in front of him. Then she looked him right in the eyes. "Oh, good evening Commander. I had hoped I would see you again here, this evening. I believe you know Commander Biewgoff?"

He took her outstretched hand and held it briefly. Then he looked at her escort. "We've met once. Good evening, Commander. I was admiring your foxtrot. Right out of the twenties. Nice style."

"*Zdravstvutya*, Commander. I am pleased to see you again. I assume we are both here for the same reasons, tonight, not so?"

The steward looked straight at him for a moment, then said softly, "I seriously doubt it, Commander." Then to brush away any mistaken meaning, he added, "But I see we do have a common interest in Sita."

With a smile and a nod, Sita grabbed both men by the elbows and pulled them to her bare sides. She wore a light lime *sari* of the flimsiest voile, and white short sleeved open silk jacket that just barely covered her shoulders and bosom. Her waist seemed more lithe than ever, set against the lime of the silk. The red spot on her forehead seemed darker than he had remembered, earlier in the day. Her skin at night was the color of pekoe with milk, and glowed softly in the ornamental light.

Sita carried on with some gracious commentary for a few moments, while the three sipped from champagne flutes offered to them by formally dressed messmen. The steward admired her warm smile and ability to put people at ease. The evening took on a non-combatant air to it once again, and the music swirled about them. *"Three coins in the fountain... Each one seeking happiness..."*

The steward took out a box of Players, asked and received Sita's permission with his eyes, and offered one to Biewgoff. "Cigarette?"

"Thank you, I prefer these..." replied Biewgoff, taking out a Camel from his own pack. "You Americans are good for some things, after all."

"Indeed we are. Like dancing. Excuse us, won't you?" And with that, the steward put his Players box back in his pocket and ushered Sita, not protesting, to the dance floor.

He spent the next hour in the fifth level of Nirvana, dancing, dancing, drinking, dancing, and dancing some more through the night. It was a grand ball in the manner of *Fair Lady* and *Gigi*, seasoned with a dash of curry and saffron. The evening was a whirl of youth, oblivious to any pressures or difficulties in the world. Life was sweet indeed, when you are among the beautiful and privileged.

She was the perfect dance partner, all grace and flow and rhythm, following his unpolished but acceptable lead like a beautiful shadow. Sita felt warm and supple against him. His hands new more of her than other women, as a good one fifth of her body was bare to his hold. He only wished that he could reciprocate in kind. Her hair smelled of Lotus. With each dance, he found new levels of fascination, searching the secrets of the universe in her eyes.

The music played on and on... almost purely Western, both European and American. Not the original, of course, but in its own way even better, its flavor enhanced by the spectacle of the shipboard dance. "A perfect use for a heavy cruiser," he mused. "Damn the torpedoes... Let's dance." While the diplomacy of the West had had its problems as of late, its cultural influence seemed more than successful. Yet the India of tonight was neither Occident nor Orient. India was India. And very accommodating indeed. *"I could have danced... all night... I could have danced... all night..."* played the orchestra.

Suddenly, everyone was startled by a brief brass fanfare. Standing atop the gun turret in front of the trombones was the Admiral of the Indian Navy. Hushed silence covered the crowd. "Ladies and gentlemen. Officers of the fleet and armed forces. Distinguished guests. I have the privilege to make an announcement. He is safely across the frontier and in India now. In a few hours he will be in New Delhi. He has asked for political asylum. The Dalai Lama has come to India."

A soft gasp coursed through the crowd. Then applause. The steward felt a strange chill, but this was quickly gone at the squeeze he received from Sita. "So that's who's coming to dinner..." he thought to himself. "Everyone expected him but me. Where have I been, at sea?"

He sensed Biewgoff staring at him from across the dance floor. His eyes smoldered, as if he had just given up one point in gentlemen's singles. The steward sensed that game and match were far from over.

He had known from old newspapers and *Time* magazines that China had stomped on Tibet recently, taking control of just about everything but its religious leader. But he had been out of touch with the daily events of the world. He had been at sea. In a way, being at sea was it's own form of *vanaprastha*, effectively out of touch with the hectic pace of world events and concomitant squabbling and fighting. But it was frustrating, upon returning to shore, to find that "Front Page" events had taken place without one ever knowing. Stranger yet is that it really didn't matter. Significance is all in one's perspective of things. Presence, a nowness, is crucial to a passionate response. But one event or ten, one tragedy or one hundred, one killing or one thousand.... viewed out of real time, became yesterday's news. And as such, it was dead history. It could only be reviewed. Each heart-wrenching, thrilling event of today, from the fresh vantage point of tomorrow, loses its very soul to time, to become merely another single item in the great scrap heap of yesterday, to be considered only to affirm or deny some grander theory of life. Who needs a hermitage... Go to sea.

The dancing took a dampening with the announcement, and couples began leaving. The steward accompanied Sita to shore, fully expecting her to be squirreled home by some dutiful chauffer, standing stiffly by a Rolls. When they got off the launch together, Sita surprised him by taking his hand without a word, and leading him to a parking area. She asked him playfully which car would he choose. He looked around at all the stately chrome and paint and leather, into which young officers and girls were being helped by liveried chauffeurs, and pointed to a silver, 7-liter gull wing Mercedes. "That one."

"O.K." she said simply. With that, she opened the door skyward, and slipped into the drover's seat. "Get in. I'm going to take you for a ride."

As she gunned the powerful engine, he scurried to plop himself into the right seat and pull down the door. "Liberated women..." he shook his head. "Any time. Any place."

They roared off into the night, headlights blinking bright and dim to ward off any bodies straying in the street so late. Most were asleep on the sidewalk, in whatever shelter or on whatever curbstone each could find comfortable and forgiving for the night. She was an excellent driver, downshifting at the curves, accelerating and power-shifting when the revs were prime. "Who do you think you are, the Countess d'Portagio?" yelled the steward, hanging on for dear life. "Where'd you learn to drive like this?"

"We ladies of Vassar are taught many things, but not all within the cloister. I had a boyfriend from New Haven whose father spoiled him badly. He would fly over to see me now and then in his Porsche that he had named *Grane*. We would, ah... experiment with new frontiers of speed on the Taconic Parkway. Alas, he immolated his noble steed near Valhalla, and now runs a new branch of his father's bank in Bahrain."

Over hill and dale, through intersection and alley, she knew the shortcuts well. In no time they were climbing into the forested countryside near her uncle's home. He had no choice. Go along for the ride.

Sita downshifted in a blubber of engine noise, then let the sports car roll along at idle, quietly, in through the towering gates and past the sleepy gatekeepers who snapped to attention, and on to the estate. Next she cut the lights, and drove silently up the long driveway, but taking a left on a side road halfway to the house. After a few hundred yards or so, she stopped. "Here," she said after a moment, collecting her thoughts. "Here is where you will stay tonight."

The steward followed her lead, and climbed out of the gull wing. Sita then took him by the hand again, and led him down a flower-lined path to a small pagoda-like structure, at the edge of a lotus petal shaped swimming pool. "It is our pool house. I thought you might like a swim after all that dancing."

"I'd be delighted," he replied. "But...I..."

"Leave your uniform here, on this gate."

She came over to him, and unbuttoned his white jacket and spread it wide to reveal his tanned chest. Then she started to undress, quietly, slowly, in front of him, first taking off her shoes, scarves, and then jacket, and then coming up to him, bare from the waist up, the lushness of her breasts heaving with each inhalation next to his chest. "You must help me..." she said, and she placed the end of her *sari* in her hands. Then she started to slowly turn, no... dance... to unwind herself from the layers of silk, slowly backing away from him all the while, twirling faster, until she was at the edge of the pool. And with a final twist, she broke herself free of the silk and dove into the night, entering the luminous water like a sleek seal in a perfect dive.

"Oh, you monkey gods..." and the steward was out of his pants and shoes and shorts and into the water in a flash.

The monkey gods Ski had pointed out to him in various temples and statues found about the city all seemed to have one thing in common. They were always copulating. In a myriad of ways, in every position, in truly ingenious leverage, they all had toothy smiles on their faces, and were actively engaged in the act.

The steward lit up his cigarette, and lay back down on the expanse of silk cushions, one hand under his head. He looked up at the moonlight causing the folds and flows and drapes of netting that surrounded them to take on an eerie white glow, like flying in a misty cloud. A gentle breeze mysteriously found its way through and into their private white world. Sita was sleeping softly next to him. He had never thought such activity was possible, let along morally acceptable. She had taught him many, maybe most, but not all of the mysteries of the Orient that evening. Together they had intermittently probed the ultimate reaches of the heavens, found in the stars in each other's eyes.

They had not spoken. They had no need to speak with their mouths. Their eyes had said everything that needed to be said. They were now. They were alive. They were burning inside with feeling. History could speak of others, of events, of yesterdays and todays. But history is dead. Living is a now event. Feeling is a now event. Memories can only capture a minute piece, a mere trace, of the sensations and thoughts and awareness of now. Now... is vivid place and time. Now is everything.

She had taught him well. Of delicate caresses, of fingers tracing and exploring, of brushes of hair and lips. Of the most sincere intimate communication without a word being said. She had taught him of freedom, of liberation, from the rest of the world. His body responded with its total being... free from guilt, free from embarrassment, free from concern, free from dogma and stigma and tradition. She had taught him well.

He crushed out the final ember of the cigarette into an ashtray, and sensed the pale light of dawn, somewhere near. The air was rich and still, smelling of a mixture of roasted Maryland cut and lotus blossoms. Finally, his tired body defying his wandering, questioning mind, he drifted off to sleep, a deliciously soft brown body next to his, and a beautiful face on his shoulder, close to his, and the silkiest streams of long black hair cascading across his chest. He could only dream that there were yet higher levels of something to be attained.

He slowly awoke, aroused by a soft tickle along his rib cage, and wet his lips in an expectation of something sweet and moist and warm about to greet him. He could sense the full sun above him, even with his eyes closed, and groaned luxuriously, as if some beautiful succubus was visiting him in his sleep.

"Ssccrreeeaaacchhhh!" The steward leaped four feet into the air. Rama stood there, sharp beak inches from his face, chiding him for his sloth-like habits, indignant and impatient.

"Rama!" the steward exclaimed. "God! If you do that once more, I'll make a hat out of your tail feathers." His heart was pounding.

He stood there naked for a few moments, getting his bearings, and eyeing the giant bird cautiously. Then he noticed his uniform and shorts hanging, neatly washed and pressed, over the same gate where he had thrown them just hours before. Next to them, were two trays, one with a Gillette and China soap cup and brush, bowl and hot water canister, the other with a small glass of vermilion

Pomegranate juice, sweet rolls, and individual tea service. He looked around, saw he was alone, then shaved, ate and quickly dressed. His watch said 11 o'clock.

He set off down the path to the driveway, in search of Sita, to explain that he had been ordered to be at a diplomatic function at the Armory at noon, only to be surprised to see Ski standing by his blue Chevy. "What are you doing here?"

"Someone called me to pick you up here, at eleven, Commander." Ski looked hung over, but his uniform was fresh.

"A man?" the steward searched for a suitable explanation.

"Nah. Strange accent. Sounded like a little old woman."

Duty.

The Duty Officer. The Duty Party Officer. The Duty Booze Officer. The Duty Handshaker. Somewhere his orders so stated his true function in this charade. Illusion versus Reality. Dalai Lama. God or Man. His duty was to get his deified derrière out of Tibet while he could. Not very saintly, but smart. The world had plenty of dead martyrs. He could operate in the land of tolerance. He could do just as well in India, with a lot less clothing on. The steward tried to see the reality in all that had transpired. Now he could see the importance of putting on a happy face to the West, to the Americans. Now he could see why he was being wined and dined by all these sycophants. China had overnight become a bully of the first degree, and India wanted protection from big brother Yankee. Russia's nose was bent out of shape because India now leaned dramatically to the West. Drat. Another decade of frozen nuts in Murmansk.

Duty had called the steward to more parties and functions that day. Everyone was congratulating each other. Everyone but Biewgoff. But something else called him more. He searched faces in the crowds relentlessly. Where was she? His thoughts were occupied with her, although he shook hands and smiled and chatted about the diplomatic and military implications of this unexpected visit by a small demi-god to India.

He had again sipped and snacked his way through the day, taking care to pace himself. But with each passing hour, he felt increasingly apprehensive that they might not meet up again. By dusk, the time he arrived at the large stately stone mansion that was the home of Major General Anderson-Brooks, he had told himself that if she were not there, as hoped, he would surely throw diplomatic caution to the wind, and get blasted. After the difficult duty he had had, he deserved it.

The first event of the evening, proudly announced by the general with a crystal glass of scotch in his hand, was music. The country's most popular recording star was the main attraction. "Ravi's here! Ravi's here!" the crowd buzzed and flitted about until it settled down on the great lawn in front of a low, pillowed platform, lit with lanterns.

Ravi Shankar was his name. Ravi was the local rock star of India. He was a handsome man, immaculately dressed, and sat crosslegged in the center of the stage, surrounded by a back-up combo of drum, fiddle, cymbal and oboe. Young girls swooned at the sight of him, shivering in delight as he came on stage, squealing their approval. Ravi quietly responded with prayer hands and a big smile, and sat down to work. Ravi played some elaborate stringed instrument that had evolved from a huge gourd. He attacked it ferociously, pounding out ten thousand notes a second from its many strings. The steward stood at the side of the crowd, and watched an outdoor musical event in the happening.

He felt a hand slip into his. Quietly. In the mysterious rhythms and ornamentations of the music surrounding him, he somehow sensed she was near, and had actually expected it. He turned and looked into her dark eyes for seconds. Then she led him to an area in the grass, a clearing in the crowd, over which was spread a wide fabric, and pulled him down to a lounging position out of the way of the crowd behind them. She remained close to him, but not touching.

The steward sat there amazed, looking at a blur of fingers and hands, listening to an eternity of melodies and improvisations and themes, played in strange sounds that seemed roughly a quarter of a whole tone of Western music. The incessant picking and plucking crescendoed to a blur, and the sounds from the deep resonance of the gourd almost trance producing, carrying the thoughts of the steward back to the night before. Tonight he was hearing the voice of India. Last night he had explored her body.

After an hour of other-worldly sound, Ravi's amazing performance was at last finished. The crowd, after rising up in a burst of appreciation, started to drift to other areas, particularly the bar. Most of the guests were in fully starched formal uniform, as befitting a party given by a staff officer. The general himself was in a casual white shirt and British pinks, with sandals on his feet. Rank has its privilege. He was attended by a huge shadow in a khaki headwrap, a Sikh colonel with a twelve-inch handlebar, his ever-faithful aide.

Sita led the steward over to the general, and greeted him. "It was truly wonderful, General. You have only the best taste in music."

"Quite, my dear. And you have only the best taste in friends. Good evening, Commander. Welcome to my humble home."

"Your minstrel was fascinating. General. I was dumbstruck at his abilities," the steward said honestly.

"Ah, yes, my boy. Ravi is the musical soul of India, I am afraid. He has a magical gift like no others."

"I found the music close but not quite the same to our Western scales, General. Is it developed on the octave like ours?"

"You tell him, my dear. It is not the stuff of Generals," he said to Sita.

She smiled. "The sitar has a track of 20 metal frets with 6 or 7 main playing strings above 13 sympathetic resonating strings below. Our basic scale is *sa-grama*, which approximates C-Major. But its "octave" is broken into 22 segments called *srutis*, which are not all equal. Then other scales can be derived by moving the fret, thus sharping or flatting some of the intervals or leaving out some tones altogether. Melody is based on a system of innumerable *ragas*, which are melody types used for improvisation, each with a set of rules for improvising. Then to each is ascribed certain ethical and emotional properties, and some are frequently associated with a certain season and a certain time of day. In its complexity, you see, it is rivaled possibly only by the pipe organ of the West. But in its essence, it is the music of India. Complex. Improvised. Concurrent themes and melodies and rhythms. Much like India itself."

"Exactly what I would have said, my dear," the general coughed.

"Thank you. I think I am beginning to see India more clearly," the steward added, looking into her eyes.

"But now, my dear, I must ask a favor. I wish to talk briefly to our guest here, alone. Might I ask your pardon, while I take him in for a drink in my study? There is Valery over there. I think he needs cheering up, don't you?"

"That is a excellent idea, General. It surely hasn't been his week, has it?"

The general and the steward bowed, and moved off into the mansion. "Commander, have you been smitten yet?"

"Sir?"

"Smitten. Has India taken a bite out of your heart yet? Like it has mine?"

The steward sensed it would be better not to refer explicitly to his recent amours. "Only by the peacock, Sir. He has taken a bite, but not out of my heart."

The general chortled, and poured two stiff scotches in to heavy Waterford classes. "Neat? Or fizzed?" He did not have any ice, in keeping with the most difficult custom the steward had experienced out here.

"Seltzer, please." The steward felt he needed pacing on this one.

As he fixed the drinks, the general asked, not looking at the steward, "I do not know why you are here, young man, in India today. Frankly, I do not care. There are more than enough smaggots to go around."

"Smaggots, Sir?"

"Larval form of spies, my boy. You've encountered many these past days. Mostly harmless and easily squished if found early enough." He took a slow healthy taste of his scotch, and sighed.

Then he walked over to the large windows and looked out at the sky and the moon, shining over the white lotus blossoms in the garden beyond. "I do sense you will be moving on soon. What I do request of you, no... expect of you, is that you will take with you a respect for this magnificent country, and entreat your leaders to view her well as an ally. India is young, but she is over 4,000 years old. Her people have developed a wonderful way of life, albeit not in complete concert with the thinking and ways of the West. These, I assure you, are not merely Westernized Oriental Gentlemen. They know, better than most of us, what they are doing. They have worked at their way of doing and seeing, longer. They just might have uncovered and solved a few more of life's mysteries then we. The West can learn much from them. They are wonderful human beings, equally as sophisticated, or unsophisticated, as those in any of the, shall we say, more cultured cultures of the world."

"I have seen that, Sir. Quite vividly."

"India's chief problem, or threat, is not from abroad, not from China or Russia or Pakistan, not at this time. Her monster is inside her body. It is population growth. It will take its toll, in due time, I fear. In too few years India's 400 million will become 600, and then a billion. I do not think her loins can stand such progeny. She must change in the deepest genes of her cultural past, and it will not be an easy thing to do. She must produce a liberated woman, who will lead others to a reasonable birth rate. It may be Mrs. Gandhi, maybe someone else. Remember that Shiva is viewed as a god of both reproduction and destruction. Someone must cover all the monkey statues with condoms, and soon. Or India will literally die in childbirth."

The steward was speechless at the heartfelt seriousness of the old man before him. His favorite mistress was unduly pregnant. He watched as the general downed his glass and went to pour another. "Refill?"

"Yes, please, Sir." He felt it was best to stay abreast, at least for a while.

The general picked up an old cigar box, carved with an intricate montage of monkeys and elephants inlaid in gold and ivory over mahogany, and showed it to the steward, while offering him a cheroot.

"Look at this complexity. The fiendish workmanship. The childish representations. The mix of colors and textures. There is a mystic to this place, my boy. I am fascinated by it. A richer life I could not wish. I truly love it."

"That is apparent too, Sir."

"Then enjoy India, Commander. Take fond memories with you. She needs a special relationship with the West. And you with her. Don't let her be hurt. Treat her gently and with respect. And I believe she will become one of your most intimate friends."

The general led the steward back out to the other guests, into the pleasant night air, shook hands, and took his leave. The moon was on high, and cast a pale glow over the gardens. The steward scanned the crowd, then started down a path, looking for Sita. After turning a bend in a thickness of flora, he saw their silhouettes against the sky. Biewgoff was waving and flapping. Sita was serene.

The steward approached with his trouble sensors alert. "May I join you?"

"Join? It seems to me that you have taken your pleasure wherever you go, Commander. Why should a mere Russian try to stop you here?"

"Oh, oh..." thought the steward. "Valery's been hitting the vodka tonics."

Sita stood there calmly. "See?" Biewgoff went on. "We Russians are not even allowed to put our hands on her. We may desire her also, do you see? Russia may have its own designs, just like the British did for 300 years. But we would treat her with more dignity. She would not clean house for us, as she did for the British."

"What is he saying, Sita?"

"Commander Biewgoff was explaining that he prefers the warm climate of India to that of Murmansk."

"Watch! I put my hands on her, and the world takes offense. She will turn to the West for protection." Biewgoff grasped Sita by the shoulders, and brought her near to his chest. He tried to focus on the red spot on her forehead. "You wear the red spot. Why not make it a red star," he slobbered, nose to nose.

The steward stepped forward, cautiously, and slowly. "Careful, Valery. Too much tonic talking." He spoke very calmly.

"See! You don't even have the balls to protect your interests. But we Russians do. Our clients all over the world respect us." He pulled Sita to him in a crush.

Something came over the steward. Something unnatural for him. Time slowed down. He could see Valery's lips moving, and hear him speak, but in slow motion. He could see ten thousand miles into the Sita's wide dark eyes. He could see something other than the event unfolding, as if he were levitating ten feet above it. It all became clear. Clear like he had never seen before, into the darkness surrounding him.

"This creep is trying to provoke an international incident. Yes, that's it. Russia got the short end of the stick when Lama baby came over to the West. The Dalai's request for asylum pushed India right into the arms of the U.S.A. Even China finessed her trump by scaring India out of further developing any closer relationship with the Russians, preventing that old warm water port from ever happening. So how could Russia now get any kind of standoff out of this at all? By provoking an incident. A fight with an American. Bad press. World coverage. Valery knows where I spent the night. Ugly American puts make on Indian princess while God cries for help. Russian comes to her aid. Pour a little manure on America's new relationship with India. Particularly if Sita gets hurt. 'Don't let her be hurt', the general said. It is all so clear."

"See!" Valery boasted on. "I will protect you, Sita, from this charlatan. I know his type. He is a fake. I see through him completely."

Sita struggled, or was made to struggle, in the Russian's bear hug. The steward moved forward to intervene, not wishing the mess to follow. "Bug off, Biewgoff. Let her go."

"Come and make me, Steward," Biewgoff sneered.

"He knows. He knows! This is all going to be front page..." the steward thought as he grasped the Russian's hand, lifting it off Sita's torso.

"Ssccrreeeeaaaacchhhhh!" The Russian dropped his grip on Sita and lunged into the air, back arched, as if lanced in the spine. "Yyyeeeeooooooowww!" Biegoff screamed simultaneously as if mortally wounded, and fell backward to the edge of a small cliff garden, where he stumbled and slid down into a thicket of dark red berries. His navy whites took on a whole new character.

"Rama!" Sita exclaimed. "My hero! You are here!"

The steward and Sita looked in fascination at the spread of a magnificent bird, standing in full splendor on the top of the cliff, shimmering and shaking in territorial victory.

"How did he get here?" the steward asked. "It must be over ten miles from Shivartse's."

"Rama is the protector of our nation," Sita answered cryptically. "He appears to many people, at many times, in many places."

She gently stroked the neck of the great bird in admiration. "Besides, this is the son of my uncle's Rama. We gave him to the general."

Biewgoff staggered off on a lower path, back towards the main house. His uniform had an interesting polka dot pattern of red on white. "Better go wash your babushka, Valery. It won't look well in any photographs tonight," the steward called after him.

With that, another figure rustled its way out of the dark bushes nearby, and scurried off into the night.

"How did you know?" Sita asked.

"You taught me. Remember? To differentiate between illusion and reality. To open my eyes." He took her hands in his. "In darkness, one can see even more clearly."

165

She stood close to him, looking into his eyes, probing for even deeper suggestions, for the night to come.

—AT SEA—

"Three hundred."

"Three hundred?!"

"More or less. Probably more."

The steward carefully set his freshly honed carbon steel knife on the small ash cutting board, and pushed aside the onion slices into a bowl with his hand. He looked over at the plump little woman with the trace of a cat's smile on her lips, as she slapped a huge fresh salmon onto the cutting table and deftly detached its head from its body with an angled chop of a gleaming Sabatier cleaver.

"How can anyone know over three hundred ways to prepare salmon?" he asked in amazement. "You really have recipes for them all? Or do you just fake it, and add a few more shakes of the wrist into the pot for variation?"

"Please, young man, don't insult my integrity," Erda cut him off with a faint huffiness. "When I say I have over three hundred recipes for preparing salmon, I mean it."

"Sorry, Erda, I..."

"Norwegians eat salmon like Chinese eat rice," she continued. "Salmon is much more than simple sustenance... It is a religious celebration, a gift from the gods. Yet I will admit a Norwegian chef's most highly prized secret is to disguise it to taste like chicken every so often. After all these years at sea I have had ample opportunity to experiment." To emphasize her point, she inserted a long, angled fish knife right up the salmon's privates and with a dramatic flair filleted it, freeing the meaty body of the four-pound headless monster from its bones in flat, from-the-tail slicing motions. The steward made mental note never to argue with any woman in a kitchen wielding a knife.

"But three hundred recipes for salmon..." the steward muttered.

"I'm far from a world's record, Steward. You should see the Portuguese cook cod. Easily eight or nine hundred recognized recipes...." And WHAM, she lopped off the tail with another blow of her culinary ax.

The steward carefully attacked another large yellow onion, lopping off root and bud ends with significantly humbled strokes. "That's a lot of variations on a fishy theme, Erda. The law of large numbers states that eventually you have to start repeating yourself," he laughed.

"On the contrary, my dear Mr. Einstein," she countered. "The principle of random walks predicts that each new voyage, each new encounter, each new port, will provide an abundance of new ideas that will translate into new recipes. And I've only been at sea going on nineteen years now. Still plenty of room for innovative salmon." She picked up a two-pound fillet and pitched it across the table right at the steward, making him drop knife and onion with a clatter.

"Where'd you learn that one?... Random walks?"

"You forget that we mariners have lots of time to read at sea. After digesting all the classics, after all Shakespeare's poems and plays, after O'Neill and Isben and Goethe and Dostoyevsky and Epictetus and Aristotle, one hungers for new ideas. By chance one day I picked up a book on the life and work of Madame Curie, and that led me to other fascinating things like Erlich's magic bullet and Da Vinci's studies of flight. Trial and error, I would guess, is a trait common to great scientists and great cooks. Before I knew it, I had ventured on through Newton's system of calculus and dear Albert's theories on relativity, eventually progressing to Fraser's insights on random walks."

"You?" The steward was flabbergasted. "Into heavy science?"

"Don't try to read a cook by her cover, young man. You may be quite surprised." She tossed the remaining fillet across to the table where he worked. "Here, college boy. Let's see if you have learned anything useful. Skin these. Like I showed you."

The steward thought back to the ship's remarkable library, a small converted stateroom that was stocked full of books, clearly categorized on homemade shelves covering every wall. This floating library of congress literally overflowed into the lounge and decks, where even more small stacks of books occupied corners and nooks and tabletops as well. Throughout the ship, recent best sellers in hardbound and paperback, often brought aboard by the passengers, intermingled with a vast collection of leather-bound classics and scores of some of the most esoteric and thought-provoking tomes he had ever seen. Even in the boiler room, one might find Marcus Aurelius next to H. L. Menken. And occasionally a well-oiled copy of *Ulysses*.

"Where'd the ship collect all those books?" he asked with honest interest, as he secured the skin of the fillet with his left fingernails and started table level slicing up from the tail.

"I bought most of them," she replied matter-of-factly.

"You?"

"In each port, while you and the captain and the passengers go ashore to eat and drink and make merry, I take, as one might say, random walks. I see the sights, sample the local cooking, buy some local seasonings and fresh produce and meat, chat with chefs and bakers and butchers and fishmongers. And always in my wanderings, I find myself discovering a bookstore or two, where in some dusty corner are to be found some of the deepest insights of humanity. Every trip to town yields two or three volumes of interest at, as you might expect, bargain prices. Over the years, in my own small way, I feel I have contributed to the ship's collective thought, by insuring a balance between the trivial and the profound."

The steward found himself standing with his mouth open. "So that's why you stay at sea, eh, Erda? You like to read! You may represent the last frontier of civilization unblemished by watching too much TV."

She smiled knowingly, then dumped the onions he had been cutting into a simmering kettle. "This ship is my home. At sea or on land, home is what you make of it."

"Seems like the captain and the crew make it a floating pub..."

"Much of the time. But they drink to dampen the powers that rage within them. Only on shore, do they howl and fight and race about like madmen. Not so much at sea..."

"And as ship's housemother, you are forever in quest of the ultimate Viking tranquilizer?" he laughed. "I thought music soothed the savage beast. Now you're telling me it's *akvavit*?"

"Speaking of music, I have seen and heard what you did with Einar's new Hi Fi. What a pleasant change from the static and tribal classics we normally receive by short wave radio."

"Thanks. Nothing like musical interludes. Change your mood along with the watch. Think Ole could stay awake if we piped *Die Zauberflote* onto the bridge?"

"Nothing can keep Ole awake, except maybe the smell of my food," Erda laughed. "But I have a new RCA Victor as well. Could you rig up the turntable back here in my quarters, like you did for Einar? And wire a set of speakers here into the galley? I chose the biggest unit, with 20 amps of power. It should handle four speakers all right."

"Seems you're up on your reading in electronics as well. Must have been pretty expensive, no?"

"Ha!" she laughed, and slammed another salmon over to its other side. "It cost me nothing. I traded the owner of a bazaar stall in Port Suez a side of smoked salmon for it. Seems a Jewish man in this part of the world would commit murder for a week's supply of lox."

The steward shook his head at the amazing ways of the world. "We're becoming rather *avant-garde* for a tramp steamer, Erda. Seven seas, sunsets, salmon, and Sibelius, all at world cruise prices.

The owning company could be flooded with new business. You may have to work harder. Push you to the limit, maybe 450, 500 salmon recipes."

"You hang the turntable. I'll handle the salmon."

"Consider it done, soon as I finish this evening's meal. Please be careful when you play your records, Erda. This jury rig is far from perfect. They could get badly scratched if we're rolling too much. Seems to work pretty well keeping the needle in the grove up to about a three-foot swell. Then everything starts to bounce and shake too much. But so far, the captain's musical pendulum is working just fine. Think Galileo and Foucault would be pleased?"

Erda smiled over to him as she chopped off the head of another salmon. "They are but latecomers to the game. You have more reading to do, my boy. The hanging gardens of Babylon are much closer to the inception of your invention." She nodded over to adjacent the galley outer hatchway, where two lush, ivy-like geranium plants swayed happily in hanging pots from the overhead.

"Hearty little buggers, Erda," he acknowledged. "What do you feed them, at sea?"

"Finest fertilizer known to mankind, my boy. Fish heads."

"Plates."

"Plates?"

"Yes, Ma'am. Crates of plates. Mostly eight-inch dinner plates. The ship loaded them in Salonica, a few months before I came aboard. Looks like we have about twenty crates."

The steward stooped to unload the crates, lying out on the deck near a hatchway. Louise O'Rouark glanced down into one open crate, out of which the steward started to lift stacks of white china plates, maybe two dozen in a stack. She bent over from the waist, leaning over the steward's back as he rummaged about in the excelsior for stragglers. He could feel her breath near his neck as she lifted her dark sunglasses for a better look.

"What on earth will the ship do with all those plates? There must be easily a gross in each crate!"

"Break them, Ma'am. Just like the Greeks would've."

"Why, that's wanton destruction! No wonder our passage is so expensive." She stood abruptly up, stretching her neck and holding out her haltered bosom in mock defiance. A long thin leg brushed against the steward's shoulder.

"Seems they're cheaper than skeet, Mrs. O'Rouark. Greeks have learned to make a pretty cheap plate, over the years. Otherwise the country'd go bankrupt."

"Skeet?"

"Clay discs for target practice, Ma'am. Well, normally we sling them off the fantail with a hand slinger... sort of like a slingshot...

"And David slew Goliath..."

"Almost. But this one is a stick, an extension of your arm, more like a tennis racket." He demonstrated with a slinging backhand. "A pigeon flies off at the moment of greatest velocity."

"Pigeon? You men are shooting pigeons back there?"

"Clay pigeons, Ma'am. Shaped like a saucer."

"Just like men. Gunning down innocent pigeons and flying saucers."

"It's actually fun, Ma'am. The crew calls it China Road, back there. Must be ten million plates by now, lining the ocean floor from here to Shanghai. Most of them intact. Anyway it keeps the passengers happy... Certainly your husband and Mr. Brububber."

"Happy? You think the men are happy, making all that racket on the stern deck, shooting at plates? It certainly doesn't make us women happy."

"It's a man thing, Ma'am. Women like to talk to one another. Men like to shoot things."

"You should become more observant, Steward. Women prefer to use a more primitive weapon. Most of the women I know would rather cut each other up with words. Much better results than from bloody conflict."

"Men prefer their guns."

"That, Steward, is an understatement. You men have been fooling around with your guns since you first found them on the changing table."

"Ma'am?"

"Men and their guns... My gun is bigger than your gun. My gun shoots farther than your gun... Each man obsessed with the size and power of his gun."

"We have only a few vintage shotguns aboard, Mrs. O. And of course, Mr. Lovelake's trusty old forty-five."

"With his gun in his hand, man becomes brute. An ignorant, bastardly brute. Taking whatever he wants, whenever he wants."

"Ma'am?"

"Without his gun in working order, man is nothing. Like my husband, for instance."

"Are we talking about the same thing, Mrs. O'Rouark?"

"Quite possibly we are, Steward."

"Would you like to try it, Mrs. O'Rouark? I'll show you how."

She hesitated, then nodded. "Anything to break this infernal monotony, Steward. Yes, I think I would like to see your gun."

"I'll set you up with the 20 gauge single shot. Meet you in ten minutes on the fantail?"

"I was actually thinking more of your quarters, young man."

———

"Reckoning."

"What?" Bjarni asked with a scowl.

"Dead reckoning. I'm plotting our next position with dead reckoning," the steward answered, while sliding a parallel ruler over the chart.

"I haven't used that since my days as a midshipman," Bjarni scoffed. "Nobody told me the Loran was broken." He looked over on the bulkhead of the charthouse at a mounted metal box about a foot square, with a set of numbers on a simple screen display, and tapped the side a few times to jiggle its operation a bit.

"Loran's O.K., Bjarni," the steward replied, without looking up. "I just do this for the fun of it. Also, it makes for a check of our Loran position."

"Some fun. Drawing lines on a map," Bjarni mumbled. "I'd rather take a nap when I'm off bridge duty."

"Since when were you ever on duty?" the steward said jokingly. "I thought at your rank, it was all nap."

"Can't help it if I know these waters like the back of my hand, Steward," Bjarni replied defensively. "I could plot our course blindfolded from Port Said to San Francisco."

"And hit every rock and shoal along the way, I'll bet," the steward replied. "Here comes the Talabot, they say at the docks. You can hear her scraping bottom from miles away."

"It helps to have a shallow draft," Bjarni commented. "This old tub can run over just about anything, and still keep way up."

"There." The steward put down his calipers and pencil, and looked up. "In case you are wondering, we should be... somewhere between Cape Town and Yokohama."

"Some reckoning," Bjarni laughed. "You're lucky to get a fix to fall on the chart."

"You should see my star sights," the steward replied, referring to the other means of positioning a ship. "I can hardly get a triangle fix inside the charthouse."

The steward looked over his handiwork. The chart displayed a pencil line of the track of the Talabot, with intersecting short lines and dots and times inscribed along the way. These were the Loran fixes, found by receiving directional radio signals from various transmitters which by now had been strategically built along the coastline on almost every continent and corner of the globe, with their locations so marked on the charts. A navigator simply had to tune in on the nearest transmitters, homing in directionally, and then on the chart, plot their bearings across the intended course. Where some of these bearings intersected indicated the position of the ship, as accurately as a Loran fix could determine. It was a simple system for near the coast navigation, not subject to poor weather or cloudy skies or lack of visibility, and had come a long way since being expanded globally shortly after WWII.

The steward had drawn a light blue line alongside the Loran track, also with many crossing lines, actually slight arcs, and a series of time notations. He had been plotting a back-up version of the course of the Talabot, as accurately as possible, using the same skills used by navigators centuries before him.

"You know, Bjarni, it amazes me that the old timers got home alive," the steward said philosophically. "There's a whole lot of ocean out here, and they didn't have much equipment that was accurate."

Bjarni grunted. "They had rum. That's all they needed to survive."

"No, really," the steward responded. "I read that the old astrolabes gave a pretty sloppy angle on the sun and stars. With only half of a degree error you're two hundred miles off from where you think you are. And the old hour glasses? I heard helmsmen used to warm them against their bellies. Made the sand flow faster, or so they thought, so they could get off watch earlier. How did anyone know what time it really was, other than it was day or night or high noon. They had no sunrise tables to speak of, no planet tables."

"*Helvete.* They just set course and sailed into the sunrise, you fool," Bjarni scoffed. "They went before the wind. They did it out of lust for adventure and lust for plunder, not for accuracy. Those first explorers were crazed for gold. Fame came not from discovering a new land, but from bringing home the gold."

"I thought it was spices. The Moluccas. The Spice Islands. The Indies."

"*Faen.* It was gold. Drives men mad, even today."

"They put their lives on the line for it, whatever it was. Heading off over the horizon..."

Bjarni continued, "Most of it was luck, or fate, or Neptune's protection or some shit like that. Most of them just went with the winds. They had no choice. They couldn't tack or head into the wind. Fortunately for them the winds blew from the East and West, North and South. With luck, they made a landfall, but probably not the one they were looking for."

"Anyway, the ones from Europe, they had the secret," the steward said mystically. "The one's since Dom Henrique o Navegador, they had old Henry's secret."

The steward thought back throughout history, about the many courageous, or foolhardy, European and Asian seafarers who set sail into the unknown. Some, like Portuguese and British and Spanish fishermen, simply went too far out for fish, lost sight of any known land reference, and stumbled on some new territory. Some, like Antonio d'Abreu, traveled South and East close to the shore, and ventured along it to unknown lands like Africa and India, and eventually to China and the Spice Islands. And some, like Fernao de Magalhaes, ventured West and South past the islands and continents newly stumbled upon by Columbus and Balboa, and ever onward into the unknowns of the great Mar Pacifico.

Henry the Navigator had been a prince of Portugal in the 1400s, who loved to sail. And he loved astronomy. Somehow he, or others before him, had put together a system of navigating that far surpassed anything the world's seafarers had ever known or imagined possible. Before Henry, sailors either stayed near to their homelands or near to the shore, or simply went with the wind. There are no road signs out at sea. But Henry had found the secret. He had discovered the functional use of one star in the sky, one whose position would always give a navigator a very useful advantage in surmising location. Henry guarded the terrifying power of his secret like a new weapon. The secret was Polaris.

The brightest students were brought to Henry's school, to learn the secret. And a secret it was kept, among a select club of seafaring men. It gave one individual, not always the captain, almost supernatural power at sea. That treasured person was the navigator, or pilot as some were called. With the secret of Polaris, the navigator alone possessed the awesome skills to reliably guide a ship to its intended destination. Those with the secret were invaluable, and treasured by kings and queens. They alone could sail a ship to far off lands and ports where gold and spices lay there, just waiting to be plucked for the coffers and larders of the royal families of Europe.

"It must have worked pretty well, as long as one stayed above the Equator..." the steward mused, looking over his reckoning track. "Not bad... I'm only off about thirty miles since Said."

His thoughts pulled up navigational trivia from his N.R.O.T.C training days. Polaris is the true name for the North Star. One can find it in the Northern hemisphere only, by looking up at the Big Dipper, then by following the two stars that form the end of the dipper cup, out in a line across the heavens to the last star on the end of the handle of the Little Dipper. That star is Polaris. It alone has the amazing characteristic of never moving across the night sky, but always staying fixed in space, as if affixed to the farthest end of an axis that projects out the top of the North Pole and continues out into space, aiming exactly and constantly at Polaris. Prince Henry had been one of the first to accept that the earth spun on an axis, and had discovered that this axis, amazingly, always pointed at Polaris. So wherever one was in the Northern hemisphere, one could look up and find Polaris, and by simply calculating the angle it was above the horizon, determine the precise latitude where one was standing, or sailing, on the earth.

Bjarni looked over his shoulder at the plot, and hrummpfed.

"Latitude is half the battle..." the steward continued. "Polaris gives me that, anytime during the night. The rest is seamanship and experience with the seas and winds."

"And luck. And lots of bullshit and rum to keep the crew from mutiny," Bjarni chuckled, now looking over his shoulder at the chart.

The steward moved the parallel rulers up the track a bit, checking his plotted heading with the compass heading, and drew a light blue line projecting out into the ship's recent past from his last firm position estimate. By dead reckoning, a navigator would plot his known position, such as a port or an island, on a chart, however humble and sketchy. Working from that point, he then would plot the actual course held over the last time period, from compass directions crude at best, interlaced with seasoned estimates on wind direction and wave direction and speed, to determine the adjusted, or more realistic, direction he felt he had gone. Along that line, he would add a best guess of ship's actual speed in the water, and time spent. The result was a line, stemming from where the ship had been, or where it was thought it had been, notated with how fast it was believed the ship was proceeding along this projected direction... Thereby arriving at a pretty good guess of where it actually was. Or should be. Or hoped it was. At least in the Northern Hemisphere with Polaris's help. In the Southern, any similar navigation was all balls. Look for the sun coming up and setting. That was East and West. In between, one was on one's own in a massive open sea. Of course, if an iceberg was spotted, one was venturing a bit too far south.

"So where are we now?" Bjarni asked with more than a hint of sarcasm. "Somewhere in the charthouse?"

"We are right here." The steward pointed to the chart. "I hope. We now have a place and time, so to speak, in this grand voyage to somewhere. And it is up to us to set our direction from here, and our speed."

"Our reality is here, scratching our butts in the charthouse. Our destiny we set for ourselves?" Bjarni asked without emotion, scratching his butt.

"No, just our direction and determination. What is out there, passed the horizon, unknown things, things to screw us all up in getting to our destination, is our destiny."

"That's why they call it 'dead' reckoning," Bjarni said flatly. "Many a mariner, using that process, passed through the asshole of a shark."

"Steward?"

"Yes, Mrs. Landgrave?"

"May I talk to you in private?"

The steward walked over to the solitary deck chair where she sat reading, in the shadow of the superstructure and out of the direct sun. "Certainly, Ma'am. What is it?"

"My husband is still grouching about getting that hook installed over his bunk. Do you think you could rig something up, just to quiet him a bit?"

"Mrs. L, I..."

"I never get any sleep with his mumbling and groping about for his darn hairpiece all night long."

"Well, Mrs. L, he asked me to drill into three-eighths inch steel plate. I don't think I could do that, even if I had a diamond bit, which I don't. But let me think on it. I'm sure we can come up with a solution that is satisfactory."

"Thank you, Steward. You are always so obliging. I can see now what my niece found so appealing in you. You know we received a postcard from her from the dockmaster in the last port, all the way from Baalbek?"

The steward's mind flashed back to weeks and ages ago, to mysterious light snakes and champagne and midnight rides in a Land Rover and long blond pigtails and red crosses and delicate rose promontories on milky white skin. "Elizabeth? She wrote?"

"Yes, mostly gossip about her dig and her Professor Wolfie and how sorry she was to have missed seeing Herman. But she did asked to be remembered to you, and wished to thank you for all you did for us that evening."

"Oh, yes? It was my pleasure, Mrs. L."

"It seems you both share musical interests."

"Ma'am?"

"Liza said something I don't quite understand. She asked that you be reminded to keep your saxophone in good working order."

"Steward?"

"Mr. Brububber? What can I do for you?"

"Sit down, kid. I need some advice from a young horse like you."

"Problems, Sir? Run out of guys wanting to play fishball?"

"Nah... That's not it. The captain and a couple of the crewmen and I toss around a herring just about every afternoon now. Seems I've started a national sport at sea. Nah, it's something else... something personal..."

"What, Sir. How can I help?"

"It's my wife..."

"Sir? Mrs. B? She's O.K., isn't she? Everyone thinks she's terrific. Always pleasant, good listener, the passengers all seem to like her a lot."

"Nah... I know all that. That's Belle's outward personality. You don't know what she's like alone."

"Sir?"

"Listen, kid, it's like this. She reads those stupid sexy novels all day long on the sun deck. Then she comes at me like a teenage sex kitten at night, always wanting to be serviced."

"Well... Could be worse, Sir."

"You don't understand. I've been boozing with the guys all day long. By after dinner, I'm blitzed good."

"Pillow feels better than your spouse then, right, Sir?"

"You know it. The last thing I need at ten at night is a good roll in the sheets. Particularly at my age. My body needs a good night's sleep by then. My pecker is already dead to the world."

"You could try something after breakfast in your stateroom..."

"That's just it! That's when she's the wildest! Like she's been waiting up all night dreaming about it. God, I barely get to brush my teeth!"

"Well, Mr. B... Seems like you've got a pretty good marriage going, after all these years."

"Wrong again, Kid. I can't control myself in the morning. No booze to slow me down. I unload faster than a fourteen year old. My wife never gets satisfied, and I feel like a damn fool."

"Single shot. You're exhausted and she's even more hungry than yesterday, right?"

"You know the problem? You been there too?"

"Not exactly, Sir. I'm still carrying a full magazine. But I've known friends in the navy, a number of them, with the same problem. Marriages go on the rocks pretty quickly, when both sides don't make it most of the time."

"Twenty-three peaceful years of marriage, and now on this goddamn cruise she has to prove she's a punchboard. Hell, where does she think she is, the high school locker room?"

"Don't you worry, Mr. B. I have the magic cure. It single-handedly saved the U.S. Navy from mass divorce."

"What do you mean?"

"Sailors come home to their wives, after weeks, even months at sea, without firing off a salvo. Hair trigger on most of them, particularly the ones who are still sober when they hit the conjugal sack. Without the cure, it's marital hell time."

"So what do they do? Put a cork in it?"

"Relax, Mr. B. I have some in the pharmacy locker. Fix you right up."

"What? What is it? An Ace bandage? Asbestos wrap? A tinfoil tube? A rubber sock?"

"Nothing so exotic, Mr. Brububber. Merely a balm of hurt minds, an elixir of infinite pleasure, the caress of Morpheus."

"Cut the bullshit. What is it? What? I'll try anything!"

"Tetracaine."

"Tetracaine?"

"The Pentagon's secret weapon. Just smear some on, and your best friend's numb for at least twenty minutes. That should do the trick, so to speak."

"Steward?"

"Mrs. Boost?"

"Can you interpret for me?"

"Interpret? What, Ma'am?"

"Byron's been spending an awful lot of time with the Engineering Officer. I'm afraid he's learning Norwegian."

"With Mr. Gynt? Well, that's good. He's a fine gentleman. Pity he doesn't speak any English. But Norwegian can be a fun language to learn. Good for Mr. B."

"It sounds like a rather simple language to me, Steward. They don't have too many adjectives it seems, or nouns, or something."

"That's probably true, Ma'am. English assimilated lots of vocabulary from French, Spanish, Latin and Dutch, besides the indigenous tongues. But Norwegian stayed relatively pure. Not so many conquerors."

"But they repeat themselves so much, it seems."

"Ma'am?"

"A limited vocabulary seems to describe a variety of objects. I don't understand what they mean. But Byron seems to. Byron's picked up the essence of the language, and now communicates quite well with many of the crew."

"Good for him. He must have a facility for languages. Norwegian is kind of difficult."

"But how can they understand each other? The Norwegians seem to use only one word to describe a whole variety of objects. Is it inflection? Is it an adjective or an adverb? And how can it show any difference, for example, between a table or a hatchway or a pump? Now Byron uses the same inflection in every other sentence, and seems quite comfortable when he talks to the crew on any subject. Can you interpret the word for me, Steward?"

"What word do you mean, Ma'am?"

"It's the odd way they say it, Steward. It's all sort of natural, like saying blue or brown..."

"What word, Ma'am?"

"I'm not sure how the Norwegians spell it, Steward, but it sounds like this... '*Foakin*'."

"Steward?"

"Is it you, Bjarni? You up today?"

"*Helvete*! I've been up since dawn. Looking for my damn fid. Somebody swiped my damn third fid, the fat one, at the port bow hoist. My favorite fid..."

"Oops. It was me, Bjarni. Sorry, but I should have told you. I used it to make one of the passengers happy. Didn't think you needed it, with the others near by."

"*Faen i vold. Faen ta teg.* You took it! Here I've been yelling at the fucking deck hands to be more careful. Good fids are hard to find, in this part of the world."

"Sorry. I should have told you. You need it back?"

"No. I was just pissed it wasn't in its place. Which of our guests did you slip the fid to?"

"Nothing like that, Bjarni. I jammed it between the bulkhead and the head of a passenger's bunk."

"What the hell for?"

"Better you ask Mr. Landgrave that, Bjarni."

"Steward?"

"Sorry to bother you, Captain, but I think we have a problem."

"What is it?"

"Stowaways, Sir."

"Stowaways? You're kidding."

"Not the normal stowaways, Sir. The six-legged kind."

"*Fi Faen*! It never fails after Suez. Who this time?"

"Ole. And a couple of deck hands. They're doing a lot of scratching. You know where."

"Damn. *Helvete*. Ole will never learn."

"American Navy has the same problem, Sir. It's a floating zoo half the time."

"O.K. Pass the word, quietly. Send the crew up to my stateroom, one at a time. Couple of days with the flit gun will take care of them." The captain opened a closet and took out a metal spray gun from the top shelf. After a quick inspection, he pulled back the handle and then pushed it home, filling the nearby air with a white dusty cloud.

"Days, Sir?" coughed the steward.

"Incubation. Got to go for the eggs."

"I'll pass the word now, Sir."

"Take a good look at the passengers, Steward. You know the telltale signs. We must try to keep this from them if at all possible. Might spoil their idyllic image of a freighter cruise."

"Of course, Sir. I'll give 'em all a good looking over."

"Who are most likely to have contact with the crew, Steward?"

"Mr. Boost, and Mr. Brububber. Initiate them into the club, too, Sir?"

"Yes. Contain this problem, or it will be shipwide in no time. We'll make Brububber and Boost think they have been elected honorary crewmembers or something. How about the ladies? There's always one or two on board."

"Delicate matter, Sir. I wouldn't know."

"Bullshit, Steward. Who are they?"

The steward squirmed. "Ah... Mrs. Lovelake, and Mrs. O'Rouark... I would guess, Sir."

"You figure out a way to handle them, Steward."

"Me, Sir? Wait a minute... I..."

"You, Steward. You have access to their quarters. You administer to their every wish. You have their confidence. I'm just the captain of this tub."

"Uuummm... What a job... Will that be all, now, Sir?"

"Haven't you forgotten something, Steward? You're first on the flit list. Pull 'em down."

"Steward?"

"Mr. Potter-Smythe?"

"May I speak with you? In private?"

"Certainly, Sir. What is it?"

"Something wrong is going on, Steward. Something terribly wasteful."

"Wasteful, Sir?"

"Damaging ship's property, it is. Damnable act. No wonder why our passage is so expensive. You Norwegians can't take care of your own things."

"I'm not Norwegian, Sir. But I think they run a pretty tight ship, actually."

"Tight ship, is it? I just saw that young helmsman, what's his name, Ole... throwing his mattress overboard."

"Throwing it overboard, Sir? The crew is airing out their bedding on the fantail again today. Are you sure he didn't just drop it accidentally? Maybe it slipped off of the railings."

"It looked like he threw it, to me. The cad."

"Must have been the wind, Sir. Took it out of his grasp."

"A likely story. He threw it overboard."

"Maybe it was old. Maybe it was a spare mattress that got soiled in storage."

"Damnable waste aboard this ship, Steward."

"I'll speak to Ole, Mr. Potter-Smythe. Make sure he's more careful with ship's property."

"Barbarians, these Norwegians."

"Must be an old Viking tradition, Sir."

"We passengers are lucky they don't still wear bear skins and horned helmets."

"I can assure you, Mr. Potter-Smythe. I haven't seen one bearskin on board. But in certain rituals, the younger ones still have horns."

"Steward?"

"Mrs. Potter-Smythe? How can I help you?"

"Strange doings on board, Steward. Quite possibly you could tell me what it means."

"Ma'am?"

"There has been a constant procession of crewmembers into the captain's cabin for three days now. It starts at about one in the afternoon, and continues until three."

"Oh, that. It's training, Mrs. Potter-Smythe. It's a three-day program. The captain is teaching them some lessons in maritime damage control. Seeing how well they can contain the spread of problems aboard ship, in an emergency."

"Damage control? Are my husband and I in danger, Steward."

"Oh, no... Not you, Ma'am. Certainly not you."

"Steward?"

"Mrs. L?"

"Did y'all remove my bath powder? Blue Bells and Daisies? Ah always leave it on top of the cabinet. But Ah cain't find it anywhere."

"Actually, yes, Mrs. L. I put it on your husband's bureau. I'm sorry but I spilled a little while I was cleaning up your shower stall this morning. So I had to wipe off the box. I forgot to put it back in place."

"Well, that solves mah little mystery. Thahnk, y'all, Steward. In this heat, Ah do lahk to stay fresh as a little ol' daisy."

"Good you brought that after bath powder, Ma'am. We're headed into tropical air masses, now. The crew and I use something similar. Keeps one feeling clean. You might suggest the same to your husband."

"Steward?"

"Mr. Boost?"

"Bring me a bourbon in a tall glass, please. I'm going to celebrate."

"Coming right up, Mr. B. What are you celebrating?"

"Seems I've started initiation into the crews' private club."

"Terrific, Sir. What's the name of the club?"

"Sacred Order of the Phthirus Pubis."

"Quite an honor, Sir. That's an ancient order."

"Yeah, we had the ceremony today. Everybody in the engine room had a beer, and then took the ritual."

"Ritual, Sir."

"Strange initiation, son. They get drunk and dust themselves with a white powder."

"Wonderful, Sir. I knew you spent a lot of time with the Chief Engineer and his gang. They must really respect your knowledge of pumps."

"Yep. Old Johannes and I get along famously. He sure knows his pumps. But it's a strange ceremony, Steward. Boozing and dusting. They say it's a sacred ritual, carried down from the old Viking days. Everybody tries to look like a Viking ghost."

"Ghost?"

"All that white powder. They really lay it on. All over... head, hair, arms, back, front, down the pants..."

"Hey, Steward."

"Mr. Brububber? How can I help you."

"Bring me another Tuborg, kid. I'm celebrating."

"Celebrating what, Sir?"

"The playoffs, kid. The First Annual Fishball Tournament."

"Yes, I know. Really caught on, didn't it, your new sport?"

"These Norskis love it. They want me and Billy Bob Lovelake to play in the playoffs, the Deck Hands against the Engine Room Gang. Even asked our wives to officiate."

"Wonderful, Mr. B. I'll break out a fresh keg of herring. Find you a nice three pounder."

"Great, kid. Got to hand it to these Norskis. They do take this sport seriously."

"Fishball?"

"You bet, kid. They plan to play the game the way the old Vikings used to, when they went on a raiding party."

"How's that, Sir?"

"Play for keeps, they did in those days. First they got all liquored up on *akvavit*. Water of life. Then it seems they dusted themselves in this white powder, some kind of ritual, to scare their enemies, look like ghosts. Made them kind of slippery when they sweat, too. Hard to get hold of."

"Sort of body armor?"

"Right. And if and when they died in battle their souls were all painted and ready for herring heaven."

"Sounds like you invented a winner in Fishball, Mr. B."

"Kickoff at 1500 today, kid. See you there?"

"Wouldn't miss it for the world, Mr. B."

"Steward?"

"Mrs. O'Rouark?"

"This is becoming an enjoyable cruise after all."

"Glad to hear it, Mrs. O. We do try."

"It seems my husband and I have been selected by the captain to reign as King and Queen of the Tropics."

"Yes, Ma'am. I know. King and Queen of the Tropics? Terrific. You deserve the honor."

"We are to preside at the ship's First Annual Fishball Tournament, this afternoon."

"I'll be there."

"We both are entitled to wear the sacred wode of the Vikings. Some ancient ritual. Everyone involved in the Tournament gets dusted white, just like the Picts and the Scots."

"They painted themselves with a kind of blue juice, Ma'am. The Viking sacred wode is a nicer feeling."

"The captain himself will administer the sacred wode, in a brief ceremony before the tournament begins."

"He's very experienced, Mrs. O. It's quite an honor that your and Mr. O have received. It isn't everyone who deserves such special treatment."

"Steward?"

"Mrs. Boost?"

"I've been honored along with my husband, Steward."

"I know, Ma'am. I've heard. You and Mr. Boost and Mrs. Brububber'll be officiating at the First Annual Fishball Tournament."

"Yes, isn't it exciting? But I'm afraid I don't know much about Fishball or football or any kind of ball for that matter."

"Not to worry, Mrs. B. I'm going to be the referee. You just have to sit there and keep score. I'll help you."

"Thank you, Steward. That's a relief. I understand that I must undergo a special initiation also. Is it difficult? Is it painful or dangerous?"

"Oh, no, Ma'am. Just a silly dusting with bath powder. Gives the Tournament some fun and color."

———————

"Steward?"

"Mr. Potter-Smythe? May I ask your help on something?"

"Certainly, Steward."

"The captain has asked me to request if you and your wife would participate in today's Fishball Tournament."

"Hrumph. I fail to understand why, at this late date. All the other passengers seem to have become involved, but Ducky and I have been bypassed until now."

"Oh, no, Sir. Not bypassed by any means. This is a shipwide celebration and tournament. Everyone is involved. I'm sorry I didn't get around to you sooner, but I've had a lot to do recently. Getting things organized."

"A likely story. Anyway, I can't for the life of me see any redeeming value in a sport called Fishball. Why ask me? It seems to be an American event, the way it's being handled."

"That's just it, Sir. We <u>need</u> you. Your input is imperative to making this game truly international. It's a little like American football, that's true, but it's also very much like British football, you know, soccer, and even more like rugby. Mr. Brububber knows the rules for American football, but the Norwegians play a British version more like rugby. So we really need you to set the rules for this game. Otherwise it'll be complete chaos. Only you can give it the proper order."

"I'm pleased the management of this cruise has seen fit to ask me to officiate, Steward. I do possess a vast appreciation of the rules of game, fairness and all that. Please tell the captain I would be pleased to make some contribution to today's sporting event."

"Terrific, Sir. Now it covers everyone on board."

"How should Ducky be involved, young man?"

"Oh, Mrs. Potter-Smythe is a perfect choice for time keeper, wouldn't you say?"

"Quite. She will be pleased to officiate as well, my boy."

"One thing more, Mr. Potter-Smythe..."

"Yes?"

"You might want to be careful and not try to light your pipe when they're dusting everyone with the sacred Viking wode. I heard it can be explosive."

"Sir?"

"didaliiii... didadididum duummmmm..."

"SIR?"

"DIDALIIII... DA DUM DUM DUMMMM!"

"Captain!? SIR!?"

The captain's hearty humming joined triumphal vibrations emanating from E. Power Biggs' extremities which boomed out of the RCA speakers, inundating the upper decks with Toccata and Fugue in D minor.

"BIBABIIII! BIBABIBIBUMMM BUUUMMMMMMMMMM!"

"Oh, that you, Steward?"

"It's me, Captain," he shouted over voluminous waves of cascading sixteenth notes. "How's your leg?"

"What?" Eiriksson put down his scotch and reached over to adjust the volume down to mere crystal-shattering proportions.

"I said, 'How's your leg?'"

"It'll heal. Only a flesh wound. That fucking turnbuckle was right in front of the goal line. It was like slamming into a steel goal post."

"Sorry you dropped the herring. Would have won the game for the Deckhands."

"I never should have joined in..." He took another calculated sip of medicinal scotch.

"Boys will be boys, Sir. You couldn't let the Snipes best you. Afterall, you do stand watch on the deck, not below."

"Goddamn Johannes. He has to play the whole game with his boys. So he has to embarrass me away from drinking in the bleachers. Come on down and play, he calls. *Fi faen*! The brickhead. I'm too old for this."

"He's older than you are. Anyway, you couldn't say no, with all the passengers and crew watching. It was like the ultimate challenge. The Captain versus Chief Engineer. His fifedom against yours."

'DIDIDIDIDIDIDIDIDIDIDIDI..DIDIDIDIDIDIDIDIDID IDIDI... Fucking herring..."

"Sir?"

"I said 'fucking herring'! Slipped right out of my hands. I would have scored, damn it. It's a tough sport, Fishball, I can tell you. Those lads from the nether world were out for blood. My blood. How many times in maritime history has the crew been given the opportunity to try to murder their captain, legitimately? This was a first."

"Maybe a last, too, Sir. The whole crew is pretty well bruised up from the sport of Vikings. But you're a natural, Sir. Norway's version of Jimmy Brown. You trampled over the boiler room gang pretty badly. They were flying off right and left when you went through the line on that third and four play at the end. Lucky nobody went over the side..."

"The lads really played their hearts out, didn't they?"

"Like true Vikings. Anything to please the passengers. With the O'Rouarks, up on the A Deck, sitting like lilywhite gods on their thrones, waiting to give thumbs down to the losers.

"That's not why the teams played so hard, Steward. The crew wanted my ass in pieces, that's why. After the privilege of sailing the sea with me! I can still hear them laughing when you and Potter-Smythe carried me off the cargo deck, bleeding like a harpooned walrus. I was getting it from both sides... punched by my own fucking teammates as well. That's why I ran so damn hard."

"They were laughing at Mrs. O'Rouark, Sir, not at you."

"Why? I couldn't see."

"That loose herring hit her in the face and knocked her over."

"Anyway. It's done. Did we stop 'em?"

"Your team lost, don't you remember, Sir? The Snipes took it twenty-four to twelve."

"Not the Snipes, Steward. The crabs. Did we stop the crabs?"

"A complete victory. Haven't seen an itch all day, Sir."

"See, Steward? Isn't it glorious?" Eiriksson grinned as he savored another sip of scotch, then dramatically continued to conduct Bach's grand finale with Waterford crystal. "Everything always gets resolved in the end...

UMMMUMM...UMMM...MMM...MMM...UMMMM... UUMMMMM...MMMMMMMMMMMM!"

—MASSAUA—

"Safari?"

"Safari." Eiriksson affirmed. "Want to play Great White Hunter?"

"Really? Go on safari? I thought we were a merchant ship, at sea," the steward asked incredulously. "We shouldn't be cruising about on land."

"Not a big safari. Just a small one. One day. In the desert." Eiriksson went on. "My friend in Massaua will set it up. You, Bwana, would be in charge of leading the passengers who want to go. You can handle it. Just like serving cocktails."

Images of a spoiled, red headed English woman on the rocks near a waterfall washed upward through the steward's thoughts.

The steward and Eiriksson stood leaning, as often these past few days, on the bow rail of the Talabot, to take advantage of the first blast of air as it rose over the bow. The day was hot, about 110 degrees out at sea, as the sun peaked high in the clear blue sky at local apparent noon. Both the steward and Eiriksson wore only shorts and sandals, letting their bodies soak up some very direct and very hot rays. The wise or experienced among the crew and passengers tried to limit themselves to about a half hour a day, as the sun was harsh, particularly on fair Nordic skin such as Eiriksson's.

Eiriksson had been up for about an hour now, shudders and body noises behind him, and was sipping on a frosty Heineken. Beer seemed to be the preferred drink of the day in such blazing dry heat, as one's body literally flashed off perspiration into the very dry air. Dehydration was a potential problem, unless one drank continuously, of water or something more spirited. Alcohol seemed to flash off even faster and left one even more thirsty, yet surprisingly still sober. The Red Sea was a mean passage for any soul, like a trip through hell. Only the most weathered and leathered of seamen could repeatedly survive such conditions, and they were preferably well oiled, inside and out.

"Where do we get gear, guns, supplies?" the steward asked. "And a vehicle? And permission or licenses?"

"Lars Larsson will provide everything. Remember, he has access to the Ethiopian military. They are paying his way to outfit the boats and crews."

The steward had heard Eiriksson's radiotelephone conversation with a Commander Larsson in Massaua, as the Talabot churned its way closer to the Horn of Africa at the end of the Red Sea. Eiriksson had radioed ahead to make an emergency stop to get Billy Bob Lovelake off the ship and to a doctor. The nearest logical port, in Eiriksson's eyes, was one in which he had friends. That was Massaua.

Larsson was on special assignment from the Norwegian Navy, and was being paid by the Ethiopian government to train new crews of the recently created "Imperial Navy" to operate the two patrol boats that Norway had sold to Haile Selassi. Massaua, in the coastal province of Eritrea, was the only suitable port city. Massaua was actually just a fishing and smuggling port, containing a harbour which could barely fit two patrol boats and a few dhows, let alone a freighter. Massaua was a dull and dirty little coastal town, erected from stone and mud brick out of the sun-baked desert that lined the Red Sea, lying just Northwest from the larger shipping port of Djibouti in French Somaliland. Its main claim to fame was that Mussolini's gang used it in '35 as an invasion port in his *opera buffa* war to conquer Ethiopia.

As they approached the jutting shard of desert that was called the Horn of Africa, the steward shook his head in wonder of it all. Here was a simple freighter, with 12 first class passengers, about to make an emergency stop in a strange, dreary little port in the middle of nowhere to dump a passenger into what was commonly felt to be the unwashed hands of a very backward nation. For his health! It was a gamble at best, that Billy Bob would find appropriate medical treatment. Hopefully someone there was educated and civilized, and had proper medical supplies. Ironically, but accepted as normal practice in the shipping business, if the Talabot had had 13 passengers, maritime law would have required the owners to also have a ship's doctor on board. As it was, such duties and responsibilities fell to the captain. Eiriksson was surgeon, psychiatrist, pharmacist, chiropractor and nurse to any and all on board, including himself, in medical need. Personally, he elected to ward off any bugs and germs with extreme doses of alcohol. To others, he pushed penicillin pills for every ailment, from the clap to gall bladder attacks. Such was the primitive state of medicine, at sea. Maybe the pharmacist in Saudi Arabia was right. Over the side is the kindest treatment for someone sick.

"*Helvete*, it's hot," spat the steward, picking up on a favorite Norse expletive. The sun blazed down, making the metal of the deck and railing almost too hot to endure. The heat was radiant, from below as well as from the sun. It was like standing on a steel frying pan, slowly being sautéed in one's own oily sweat. The steward reached down to a cooler he had by his legs, and pulled out a chilled Heineken for himself. "Another?" he asked Eiriksson.

"And another and another. *Faen i vold*. This stuff goes through and out of me like steam from a kettle," Eiriksson gassed.

"I can't understand how Arabs don't drink any alcohol. How can they exist without it? It sure hits the spot..." the steward smacked after a long pull on his beer.

"Simple. They have no ice. Try one of these at 120 degrees sometime. It looses its zest a bit. Tastes like piss. The Arabs aren't so stupid as to drink piss. Unless they're dying of thirst." Eiriksson downed his present bottle, cast it quietly over the side into the yellowish, sizzling sea, and took a swig of the new one. "Also, the everyday working Sheets have no money. Someday, if the common people ever get a piece of all that oil money, you will see their habits and religious customs put to the test. You should see some of the sheikhs in Europe, partying around. They are the big spenders in the discotheques, I assure you, and strong drink is one of their foremost pleasures, along with blond women."

"I've heard their falcons go with them when they travel. Some kind of status thing, like taking your lap dog along," the steward chuckled, "to impress their European girlfriends. But I'd imagine a falcon must be kind of hard on the furniture in the hotel suites."

"So they buy a whole new room setting," Eiriksson laughed. "A good Arab always wants to have a bird on hand when he's having two in the bush."

"Sounds very civilized..." the steward smiled at the image.

"The Arabs? Civilized?" Eiriksson scoffed. "The five pillars of wisdom established strict codes of behavior - for their women maybe. The men, however, are all zealots with moustaches, who have mastered the art of double standards. Just ask the British."

"What do you mean?"

"Is it civilized to keep your women covered from head to toe, and locked inside the house all day, so you can go get hashed all night on hookahs? Is it civilized to publicly bow to Allah five times a day asking for mercy and sustenance, then cut off the hand of a starving man for swiping a loaf of bread? Is it civilized to behead a woman only because she is accused of being adulterous? Is it civilized to lavishly entertain a enemy in your tent like a brother, yet kill a thirst-driven person if he drinks from your waterhole in the desert without permission?"

"What makes them think and act that way?" the steward asked. "I thought Muhammad was a teacher, a prophet, who tried to lay out a code of conduct that would bring fairness and constancy into a wide variety of tribes and customs?"

"He was more of a political leader than a religious one..." Eiriksson went on. "Seems that church and state were one in many of these lands out here. It all gets back to who has, or wants, the power. Then the one with the biggest ego sets out a plan, or code of conduct, to tell all the little people this is how things are going to be, and that's that. And the hot god of the day said so. If the people don't like it, they loose their heads over principle. Remember, many have called Islam the 'religion of the sword'. Believe, or off with your head. No objections after a while. Islam spread real fast with the sword missionaries. Resistance was quickly silenced. But verbal missionaries take much longer, having to overcome debate or cultural resistance. It's more efficient to slaughter opposition than to convince it by reason. That's how those in power keep the power. It has always been so, throughout history. The Moslems are no different from all the other religious zealots history has given us in the so-called civilized world. They all want the power. Their way. Only the rhetoric and costumes and flags change color.

"So what's the falcon? Their symbol of power?" the steward asked, remembering similarities all over the heraldry of Europe.

"Good question. Superficially, a bird of prey is a symbol of privilege and wealth... it's a leisure sport... falconing and all that. But deeper, I think it symbolized that those in control must exercise their control by showing they have power over life of other living things. Very godlike in their aspirations, if you think about it. A rich sheikh and his falcons are just like the English and French aristocracy with their afternoon hunting soirees. Reminds them that they can kill, just for the sport of it all." Eiriksson took a long pull on his beer. "At least the British drank while they were lording it over everybody. That, my boy, is truly civilized. If one must play god, do it blitzed. More laughs that way."

The heat of the sun was unrelenting, broiling their thoughts into fantasies. "Blam! Splash." The captain felled an imaginary albatross off the port side. Only a pull of the cool beer brought back any sense of reason and wellbeing.

The steward thought on his comment. "I think the real genius of the British is that they always had a way to stay suitably blitzed wherever they were called to duty, you know, in Egypt, in India. A real test, what? Never let the climate slow one down, when bashing the great unwashed. Take time for gin at noon, gin at five, whatever the state of the battle."

Eiriksson smiled and nodded. "The British are masters of alchemy when it comes to spirits. They discovered the key... the secret that had eluded conquerors for centuries - gin and bitters - just to kill the taste of gin with no ice. That's why the British stayed so long and so successfully as imperialists. They didn't have the overwhelming desire to run home for a cold drink like the Greeks or Romans. They even invented pink pants so officers could spill their pink gin without messing up their uniforms."

Eiriksson finished off his beer bottle, pitched it over the side, and pulled another out of the cooler.

"What about the Vikings?" the steward asked. How did they survive without ice?"

"Ha!" laughed Eiriksson. "They didn't! In spite of their bearskins and battleaxes, they were quite civilized, actually, if drinking is the gauge. They would drink anything alcoholic, as long as it was cold enough to muffle the taste. They needed the antifreeze in their systems to survive the Arctic. The Vikings knew the only lands worth conquering were the ones with an oversupply of indigenous alcoholic drink and lots of ice. Oh, maybe the Vikings would make a quick sortie down to the Mediterranean, like a vacation... pillage a little here, rape a little there, but they stayed only so long as their ice supply lasted. And when it melted, they promptly sailed off home again."

"To ice..." the steward proposed. "The magic crystal that built the civilized world." Both men toasted with their bottles, and drank heartily, eyes crossed, watching the perspiration mist off their noses.

Lars Larsson had everything ready. He had met the docking of the Talabot in his dusty but trusty open back lorry, and taken Billy Bob to the local doctor at the town square. He didn't wish to frighten Billy Bob, but had whispered to Eriksson that the local doctor was the only doctor in the town, and did double duty as the local butcher. Signore Doctore Professore Emilio de Bono was an expert of sorts. His claim to fame thereabouts was not so much in curing the sick, but in showing the local populace how to prepare preserved delicacies such as headcheese and pepperoni and garlic sausage from animal scraps, rather than throwing them away thereby benefiting only the jackals. Supposedly he had been born and educated in Switzerland - as a doctor, that is, not as a butcher, but he was probably an ex-Fascisti, keeping a low profile and seeking some form of social redemption by continuing his fascination on the merit of intestines. Billy's ailment was in good hands, so to speak, with the local best on *wurst*.

Billy had recovered reasonably well after his ordeal at sea. His silvered flagstaff had been removed earlier that morning, and he had urinated by himself without too much difficulty. He was unfortunately afraid to drink much liquid, in spite of the scorching heat, and therefore his urine had a consistency and color near that of molten gold, and was probably just as painful to all his other senses. The penicillin had quieted the inflammation, it seemed, and although he had no fever, he still turned quite flushed with each passing pissing. Pammy Sue had been the dutiful spouse throughout, keeping Billy calm and horizontal until Massaua, and aiming the silvered flagstaff when called for. She had accompanied Billy and Larsson in the lorry, bound and determined to see Billy's pecker resurrected.

The steward had taken a count after Eiriksson had announced the possibility of a Safari to the passengers. All the men except Billy Bob had instantly opted to go, exposing some latent Hemingwayesque desire to kill something, or possibly just to get away from their wives for a few hours. No other crewmembers opted to go, even to break the monotony of shipboard life. The women thought the idea was insane, particularly considering it was 120 degrees during the daylight hours, but not a one protested her husband's going. The wives too presumably wished to have a few moments to themselves.

After depositing Billy Bob with the butcher, Larsson returned with the comic old Italian-made lorry, pre-WWII, filled with equipment. It was a rather eclectic array of hunting, or killing, gear. Pith helmets for everyone, water canteens, fly swatters, hunting knives, ammunition bags and clips, and an assortment of surplus M-1's, vintage Mausers, and even a Thompson sub-machine gun. It seemed a rather formidable amount of firepower, particularly considering that the largest animal in the territory was a Grant's gazelle, about the size of a small goat.

The passengers all suited up with manly movements and language, checking out their given weapons with feigned dexterity and understanding, and climbed into the back of the lorry. Presumably some had hunted before, for quail, but the steward resisted asking that specific a question for fear of the answer.

Clothes of the day had been donned in a hurry, without seriously considering the weather and terrain ahead. A variety of wild Harry Truman shirts for camouflage, shorts, sneakers and leather street shoes made up the regimental uniform - quickly termed American mufti by the steward. A finer band of middle-aged volunteer mercenaries would be hard to find anywhere. The local Eritreans who worked the piers stood by silently and scratched their fleas, seemingly in awe of the well-armed merry group, off to save the world from a gazelle attack. They stood on, still scratching, as the lorry spun dust in their faces as it raced off into the heat of the noonday sun, off to the desert, off to adventure. One could read their faces. "Dumb Americans."

Larsson's first stop was the local police station, a mud-walled one-room hovel with a rotted thatched roof. As the lorry pulled up in a cloud of dust, two local policemen were questioning a skinny young woman. She was shouting and obviously cursing, and gesturing wildly at a local Eritrean man, about forty-five.

Larsson and the steward climbed out of the lorry and made their way into the hut through an open doorway. They left the other passenger/hunters in the back of the truck, to watch the soap opera unfolding on the street before them.

Inside, Larsson was greeted by the local chief constable, who had on half of a uniform befitting a field marshal. The other half was a pair of scruffy shorts and bare feet. Flies were everywhere. The chief swatted indiscriminately without passion, seemingly keeping mental count of his kills to help pass the day.

Larsson explained in a variety of languages that they were passengers and crew from the Talabot, docked here on a medical emergency, and that these persons wished to go hunting for gazelle, and that the truckload of hunters and arms were under his control and that it had all been approved by the local military in Asmara and that they would be back by nightfall and that he would make certain the arms did not fall into the hands of the rebels. The chief nodded occasionally, shaking his head from side to side with an obvious negative disposition to this idea. Then, after five minutes of explanation, Larsson pulled out a roll of bills and put a wad in the chief's hand. The chief nodded yes only once, and without looking either the steward or Larsson in the eyes, picked up a three foot billy club that lay across his desk, and left to go outside where the noises and yelling of the woman grew uncomfortably louder.

The steward and Larsson followed the chief outside. The yelling took a different tone at his arrival on the scene, one more plaintive and less argumentative. The two local cops just stood by idly, holding on to the woman's arms and shuffling their bare feet in the dust, as the woman made her case to the chief.

The woman was oddly attractive in her own way, long graceful neck, fine nose and features, but filthy. She wore a flowered, short sleeveless dress that buttoned up the front, under which stretched thin bare legs and dirty feet. Half the buttons were open at the top, revealing small brown breasts that jiggled as she struggled to free herself from the hands of the two cops. She weighed in at about half that of Sophia Loren, but exuded the same lusty nature. This woman's animated eyes were surprisingly hazel and very expressive, not with fear so much but with anger. The chief listened and tried to get the facts surrounding the encounter, but the two cops still held her firmly which indicated they felt her to be the perpetrator of some heinous act.

The motley cadre in the lorry sat and watched the local soap unfold, in disbelief. The other man, the co-perpetrator, nervously paced back and forth, saying only a few things to counter the young woman's screaming. He appeared to be a few classes higher up the ladder, and dressed like a shopkeeper or accountant or clerk of some sort, in an open collar white shirt and slacks, but with sandals on his feet. She, alas, looked like any one of her sisters in arms throughout the world... a hooker.

"Eeiiiii! Saaaalllaaa tuuubaaatttooo eetttallleeee." She was screaming now, the pitch getting higher and higher. Something was building to a head. She wanted to show the cops something, at a distance from the station. The local chief finally got passed the point of containing his irritation, and, with a nod of his head, set the two cops into action. Suddenly, violently, they picked up the woman and threw her bodily into the cargo area of a dirty police lorry. She landed on her head on the metal floor, and screamed even louder. The chief gave her a couple of thumps with the billy club over the head, and she shut up for a second, stunned. The chief and the man got into the front seat with the two cops, and off they drove, woman yelling and shrieking once again.

"What's that all about?" a concerned steward asked Larsson.

"Something about a door. She says the man broke her door off her hut, or something like that. Wants him to pay for it. He says she is a prostitute, and had propositioned him. In the heat of negotiations, there was a lot of pushing and pulling, and the door got knocked off the hinges."

"Where'd you learn to understand Eritrean like that? You've only been here a few months, I hear," the steward asked, impressed.

"I don't speak a word of Ethiopic," Larsson laughed. "But I do speak some Italian."

"Italian? I didn't hear any Italian..." the steward pondered, perplexed.

"It's the legacy left by Mussolini. She talked with her hands."

Lars Larsson was all Norwegian, ruddy blond and medium build, with rugged hands and a thick neck protruding out of his white military shirt. He wore his Navy hat cocked back over one ear, but not while he was driving. The locals looked up at the lorry with a stare that showed they had seldom seen either a lorry or a blond man before. Lars would see them look up, dumbstruck, and then gun the accelerator while he laid on the horn. Bleeeaattt! Bleeeaattt! He showed no fear of hitting any of the many wide-eyed pedestrians, and actually prided himself on near misses like a matador. "It's a boring town. A little thrill in their lives is good for them," he smiled after sending one old man sprawling into a pile of baskets.

The steward hung on for dear life as Lars roared through what seemed to be a village square, crowded with men seated at small tables and stools and water pipes, assembled haphazardly amidst the dusty middle ground that no longer indicated where the street might be.

Horn blasting, Lars split the crowd like a speedboat sending waves of men to each side, falling and spilling and crashing about in the dust. "The secret is not to stop, for anything. If you stop, you might get robbed or stabbed. Half of these sticks are high on hasheesh or *khat*."

The roads and streets in Massaua were paved in part with cobblestones, in part with animal dung, and in most part with dirt. The stench was beyond description. Waste and rubble were everywhere. The buildings ranged from mud huts to animal stalls to Moslem minarets to Coptic domes to Arabian arches to an open air bazaar to a few European two story stone structures with balconies and tile roofs and very tired vines somehow clinging to the walls. It reminded the steward of some historic replay, as if, in a remote corner of some long-forgotten empire, some trading center of lesser importance had been overrun, again and again, by barbarians. Everything was filthy and dusty, bent or broken, and probably unable to be repaired. And throughout it all was the heat of the sun. Baking everything. The heat was unbearable. And flies. A billion flies. People just stood there, oblivious to it all from chewing *khat*. The more fortunate huddled in patches of shade, others just hunkered on the ground, or walked around very slowly, without much purpose or joy in their rounds. Here and there, fresh vegetables added a touch of eccentric color to the otherwise drab, dusty shades of brown of the city and its people. Massaua certainly was not any Garden of Eden. It lay somewhere between Purgatory and Hell.

Earlier, while Larsson had been getting the safari organized, checking out the weapons and gear with the passengers, he filled the steward in on some of the history of the area.

Oddly, as the steward listened and looked around, he could see it. And smell it. Even hear it. Massaua had an Italian air about it. As an aftermath of ill-conceived strategies in the game of international chess, Eritrea had been selected as part of a concept to place Italy in the ranks of Big Imperialists. Indeed, this sun-parched region on occasion had some brief strategic importance, laying at the intersection of trade routes between India, the Arabian Peninsula and its Persian Gulf, and Africa. Eritrea formed the Western side of the neck of the Red Sea, in fact it was named after it - *Mare Erythraeum* - but this bathtub of scalding water was so wide at this point that it never could be credited with the strategic importance of Gibraltar. The King of Italy had proudly declared Eritrea and Ethiopia a colony after Mussolini's pathetic pastakrieg of 1935, which pitted planes and machine guns against spears and donkeys. Even today, there were still traces of colonial Italy around. A balcony here, the smell of garlic there, pasta on the menu of the few restaurants in town, a lighter skinned shopkeeper arguing with darker skinned customers, and a scattering of pre-war Fiat taxis. And if one listened closely, one could hear the scratchy voice of Caruso pleading in the distance on some antiquated wind-up Victrola. Ah... still the passions and dreams of *Gloria* and *Patria* lived on, although stranded in the middle of nowhere...

"*Ma n'atu sole cchiu bello,*
oje, 'o sole mio, sta nfonte a te! O sole, 'o sole mio,
sta nfronte a te, sta nfronte a te!"

Both men had subconsciously listened to the impassioned song, strangely juxtaposed against the flat, scorched, flowerless surroundings. At its end, they both had looked up at the blazing sun in the sky and instinctively shrugged their shoulders and eyebrows in Neapolitan empathy, only to resume loading the lorry with gear.

Larsson had continued with his history lesson as they finalized things. Although the British made quick work of the Italians in

1941, and had watched over both Ethiopia and Eritrea until 1949 when Ethiopia declared its right to independence again, Eritrea had retained no visible British flavor. Ethiopia had become a charter member of the U.N. and had dragged Eritrea along by incorporating it in a federation in 1952, much to the disgruntlement of the Eritreans who tribally were far down the pecking order from Haile Selassie and his privileged relatives.

Throughout history, human existence in the Horn of Africa could be described as tribal, pressured by external forces. Eritreans were a regional tribe of people, more akin to Somali's than to Ethiopians. The Ethiopians believed they were descended from the legendary Queen of Sheba, a Semitic tribe which had migrated down the Arabian peninsula to what is today Yemen, and then crossed over the Red Sea to set up a new kingdom in Ethiopia. Through the centuries, cultural and religious persuasions from many other nations, Arabia, Palestine, Egypt, and even Rome, had been forced upon Eritrea in a variety of confrontations, heaping new and conflicting foreign habits and beliefs on a simple nomadic people who wanted only to survive in a hellish part of the earth. Tribal loyalties and traditions were always being tested, as Coptic Christians, Moslems, Catholics, even a concentration of Ethiopian Jews still struggled for viability in very harsh environs. But like so many other nations of mixed cultures, Eritrea had been dominated throughout by one family or tribe who held the power. And that tribe was Haile Selassie's. He was the Lion of Judah, Emperor, King of Kings, descended from Solomon himself, or so they proclaimed. Haile's tribe lived in the high ground of Ethiopia, where the temperature and rainfall were much more benevolent than in Eritrea. Haile had the bucks and the guns. It was his family who were given the jobs of local cops and administrators throughout the land. Everyone else was less, and treated accordingly. Life in the right tribe was at best barely tolerable, in this hellhole. Life in the wrong tribe was at best insufferable, and quite precarious if one protested.

By the tone of his comments, Larsson had obviously been crossing off the days on his calendar, anticipating the day he could finish his duties and head home, out of this *Helvete*, back to Norway. In the distance, Enrico gave scratchy echo to his thoughts.

"Tiene 'o core 'e nun turna?

Ma nun me lassa, Nun darme stu turmiento!

Torna a Surriento, Famme campa!"

The merry band of men on board in the back cheered and joked as they bounced and careened through the dusty streets and milling humanity of the city. The lorry's tired four cylinders grrrrrrrred along like a coffee grinder with an errant bearing in it, but with a distinctly different aroma. At every jerking shifting of gears, one crossed one's fingers. At each flying bump, eyes would look around to see if parts and persons were still in tact. With each diving pedestrian, one's heart missed a beat. Fate, it seemed, was at the wheel for the day.

As they approached the outskirts of the town, Larsson pointed out one small mud-brick shack with a classic painted sign over the door. The sign proclaimed "The Cup of Heaven" over a picture of a wine chalice and purple grapes artistically scrolled around it. "An Oasis of the Gods in this forsaken wilderness," Larsson yelled over the wind and the motor. "A favorite of mine, owned by a gal I call Little Sheba. Got herself regally shafted years back by some guy up north, comes home in disgrace, and she and her son Menelik come out here to bartend. Smart lady. She runs the only place in town with an electric cooler. Must have cost her a fortune. Gets her beer from smugglers probably, and sells it for a hefty price. But it's worth every *Krona*. The men around here would rather smoke hasheesh than drink beer. That's fine by me. It leaves more for me, and the leftover Italians, and the local cops who sneak out here for a cool one."

It only took a few minutes to drive through and out of Massaua. Small buildings and smaller huts became even smaller and farther between, and then suddenly, there were none. Only desert. Dry, scorched, barren rock and dust. No glamorous golden sands, no sweeping dunes, no magical palmed oases. Just barren rock and dirt, as far as the eye could see, occasionally interrupted by a scrub bush and scraggly twig cropping out of a craggy ravine in a pathetic quest for water.

The road paralleled a tired railroad track for a few miles, before turning South. "That's the cog railway up to Asmara, on the plateau.

Mussolini built it to carry his gear up to the front. He beat the Ethiopians and Eritreans without much difficulty - he had machine guns and planes, they had spears. But in the end, the baboons beat him," Larsson chatted as they rolled along by the tracks. "He couldn't sustain the occupation."

"Baboons? A British regiment?"

"Ha! What a regiment! Baboons! Real baboons! The best night fighters in the world. They used to climb on board the cog train looking for food, and throw all the other crap off into the desert while the Italians were drinking wine and sleeping. His trains arrived in Asmara empty! Ha!" Larsson laughed heartily.

The lorry left a cloud of dust for miles behind it, as it bounced and slammed its way along a ridge where, sometime before, some other vehicle had left its tire marks in the dirt. The passengers hanging on in the rear were enjoying the ride immensely, even though they were eating a lot of dust. The steward squinted in the hot glare of the sun, scanning the far hills and valleys for any sign of life.

"How does anything live out here?" he asked Larsson.

"Amazingly, things do. Some gazelle. Some jackal. And nomads. They all somehow survive the heat and dryness," Larsson replied.

"Probably by coming out only at night," the steward gasped in the dusty air. He squinted up at the glaring sun. "God, it's hot. The humidity must be zero!"

Larsson drove on for about 20 minutes, over rough rocky slopes, through dry *wadis*, riding the crest of any high ground, casting about in the heat for any sign of animal life. Suddenly he stopped abruptly at the top of a rise. "Over there." He pointed toward the hills, seemingly miles in the distance. "Grant's. Maybe Thompson's."

"I see them..." the steward replied, squinting to get a focus through the hot air mirage in front of them.

"What are we stopping for?" the voice of Bull Brububber rang down from the cloud of dust above.

"Over there," the steward called up from the cab. "Gazelle."

"Gazelle!!!!" rang out five voices in loud unison. Then World War III broke out with a roar of small arms fire in every direction.

The steward and Larsson ducked down in the cab, and yelled back over the din, "Stop! Stop shooting! You can't hit anything from here! They're miles away! You have to get closer! STOP SHOOTING!"

After the firing had ceased, Larsson raised up his head and yelled back at the hunters, "You can't get them from this truck! Every time we approach, they run away! It scares them away! You have to go after them on foot!"

Before he had finished his sentence, the lorry was empty. Off into the hot desert dust stumbled and ran the hunters, in fast pursuit. "Wait! Take your canteens! Take hour hats! It's terrible out there!" If they heard, no one returned. They fanned out in the dust, chasing off toward the small herd of gazelle now about a mile distant.

The steward moaned, as he got out of the cab with some of his gear. "Oh, shit. How do I get them to slow down?"

Larsson chuckled. "You don't. The sun will."

Then he tossed the remaining canteens out into the dirt, followed by a shoulder sack of cartridges for the M-1's. "See you later, I hope."

"Wait a minute. Where are you going? Aren't you coming along?" the steward protested.

"I agreed to take you idiots on a safari, not to go on it. Well, here it is. Go on it," Larsson laughed. "I'm not so crazy as to go out in this fucking wasteland in the heat of the day."

"But...! But...!"

"I'm going back to Sheba's and sit in the shade and drink cool beer. You assholes can fry your eggs out here if you wish."

He gunned the lorry into gear, and yelled over the roar, "Try to stay near here. I'll be back at nightfall. You'll see my headlights. Just fire a couple of shots into the air. I'll find you."

"What do I do now?" the steward moaned. Then he picked up all the scattered canteens and shells and his M-1, set his pith helmet resolutely on his head, and started off after the merry band of hunters.

The others had distanced themselves from the steward by about a half a mile by this time, in a scattered trail toward the hills. They seemed to be slowing down measurably. One dragged his rifle butt in the dust behind him. One sat on a rock and smoked a cigarette. To the left, another would fire off a couple of rounds in the direction of the gazelle, still far out of range, and scare them off even farther. There was an occasional audible curse as one would stumble over the hot rocks, but somehow they all kept going, ever onward, ever more slowly, in the direction of big game.

The steward kept up a steady pace, and over about twenty minutes had gained on most of them. But they had spread themselves far afield, and he could call to only a few. "Stay together! Stay together! And slow down! Save your energy!" he called, only to be greeted with a "Fuck you! I'm going to kill me a gazelle!" and a few more rounds would punctuate the hunter's zeal, scaring the ever-staring gazelle farther off. Civilized behavior had evaporated. Reason had been abandoned. Such was the passion of the hunt.

They had been in the sun for over an hour now, following the herd, shooting at foolish distances, and then pursuing it once again. The steward had tried to keep a head count visually, but the hunters had by now spread themselves quite widely, in pursuit of a herd of about twenty which had split into two divergent groups. He began to get quite worried about keeping track of everyone. As he would catch up with a hunter, he would give a canteen to any who had left his behind, only to see his advice on conserving the water be drowned in a guzzle, as sun-maddened civilized men gorged themselves on the delicious liquor, only to put out their hand for another canteen without any concern for their distant compatriots in arms. He did convince a few of those lagging to stop, group together, and wait while he and the others would supposedly drive the herd back their way. And so they sat in the blazing sun, out-of-shape middle aged men in white pith helmets, dreaming of Hemingway, killing urges still vital but held hostage to the heat, slowly dying a thirsty death on the desert.

The steward himself was getting a bit dizzy with the effort, but resolutely kept after those in the lead. He finally had grouped three of the hunters in an exhausted string, staggering slowly behind. Still ahead were Brububber, and half mile to his right, Byron Boost. The steward called with a weak, scratchy voice, "For Christ's sake, stop. Wait up. You keep scaring them away. Wait for me!"

This had little effect. Then he added, "I've got the water." Brububber stopped, turned and staggered back his way.

Amazingly, so did the half herd Brububber was tracking. The lead buck, who had always kept himself in between the hunters and the herd of females and kids, was himself turned and headed this way, followed hesitatingly by the herd.

Brububber staggered up. "Gimme some. Quick." The steward gave him one of two canteens he still carried, the full one. He had been sipping on the other.

"God help Boost," he thought. "We're running low on water."

The steward offered Brububber a sweat-stained Players, which he took and lit up. He sat on a rock. His Harry Truman shirt, previously sweat-soaked but now completely evaporated, was covered with dirty streaks of mud.

"My fucking feet are frying," Brububber gasped. "But I'm not finished. I'm going to get me one of them fucking gazelles if it is the last thing I do."

"Bite your tongue," the steward gasped back. "You stay here. I'll go after Boost and bring him back here. On the way, I'll flank the herd and scare them your way. Maybe you can get a closer shot. Just lay low, and save your strength. It's going to be a long day out here."

The steward set off to the right, after Boost. He could see him in the distance, leaning on a boulder, fanning himself with his helmet. He had no water canteen.

The sun blazed down, forcing his eyes to squint against the glare. He looked up into the heavens, and felt lightheaded. "Hey, Ra! Are you there, Ra? Rah, rah, rah for Ra!" Then he adjusted his pith helmet and took a small sip of water. "Watch out... keep your wits. Ra runs the ranch out here."

After another twenty minutes, the steward had reached hailing distance with Boost. "Come this way. Let's regroup." Nothing. "I've got water." The magic word moved Boost's feet uncontrollably in the steward's direction.

After Boost had guzzled almost all the remaining water in the canteen, the steward motioned back toward Brububber. "Come on, let's go back." Boost looked back longingly at the half herd he had been following, and started to move out in their direction. "They have the other canteens..." the steward added, and Feet again did an about face.

As they staggered back toward Brububber, they had indeed flanked the other herd and were moving it in his direction. "Carefully, now, Brububber..." the steward thought to himself. "They are almost in range for your M-1. Two hundred yards. Set your sights and Wait... Wait..."

The steward and Boost trekked on in the blazing sun. Boost dragged the butt of his vintage Mauser in the dirt behind him. The empty canteen hung by the straps from his other hand. The steward looked ahead at the herd, shifting and milling about in the baked earth, always keeping a respectable distance. Thoughts flashed up from his academic past. American Lit... Who was it? Faulkner... No, some bear on an urn... No, it was Keats on the urn... Something about the beauty of the chase...

"'What mad pursuit? What struggle to escape?

What pipes and timbrels? What wild ecstasy?...'"

He snapped back into broiling reality. "What bullshit! They keep running away. Nothing stupid about these beasts..."

They kept their slow, steady pace. The lead buck seemed confused, now, looking back at them approaching, and ahead to where Brububber was but could not be seen. Suddenly, CRACK! A shot split the desert silence. The steward saw a doe fall in her tracks, followed by Brububber jumping up and screaming "I got one. I got one." With that, the herd sprang in the steward's direction, with the lead buck darting back and forth. CRACK! Another shot rang out this time right behind the steward's ear.

It took a moment for the ringing to stop and his hearing to return, and he watched as in a silent picture show as Boost jumped and hopped and flapped his arms in victory. The rest of the herd had vanished, but one tan and white body lay flopping in the dust. The steward started toward the fallen animal. Then he saw the lead buck, standing awkwardly, on a ridge about 150 yards away. He stood there, defiant, proud, looking at the steward. His eyes were like black diamonds, glaring, unwavering. He made no effort to follow the herd that by now was far up the next rise in the distance. He was gut shot.

The steward stood motionless, in silent communication with the buck. He looked at this noble animal, still proud, who now could no longer lead his herd, or protect his species, but who looked this enemy directly in the eye. "Now you have the power..." he seemed to say. "For the moment. Use it wisely."

The steward walked a few yards closer to the buck, then sat down on a rock, took out a Players and lit up. He inhaled deeply, and tried to relax and slow his pounding heart. The roasted flavor of the tobacco was tainted with sweat and dirt. His arms felt numb. He was shivering from dehydration and exertion. Next, he carefully placed the cigarette on a stone nearby. Then he rammed a cartridge home in his M-1, and in a sitting position, leveled his sights at the chest of the buck. The buck seemed to stand taller, awaiting the inevitable hand of god. The steward exhaled, steadied, and squeezed. CRACK! The echo rang through the desert. The buck dropped in his tracks, and lay quiet.

The steward got up, and walked slowly up to the fallen buck. He looked down at the body of twisted legs and blood and tongue hanging out to the side and wide eyes black with no brilliance at all, and said, "Shit."

Boost came running back from his aborted trek towards Brububber, shouting as he came up, "I got him! I got him! Brububber gets a lousy doe, but look at those horns! What a trophy! I got him!"

"You got him," the steward said flatly. "You got him good." And he sat down again on the ground, to finish his cigarette, while

Boost stood there beaming and babbling the obligatory masculine expletives, chest heaving in a surge of adrenalin, his cartridge bag hung around his neck, rifle casually held in one hand back on his shoulder, living the moment found so eloquently in many a red-blooded American novel.

The sun flared even hotter over the antics below. The steward stared at the carcass. He seemed oblivious to commotion around him. "I have never been in such a place before..." the steward thought. "Never in such a predicament... Never so alone... What does the book say?... Wandering around in the damn wilderness for forty days or something... Until he found god... or himself... or water... or something... Well, I've only been here a few damn hours... I've found one thing... You get to a point... where one thinks only about one's own mortality. The others are on their own. It puts a full new meaning to the word life... Watch out... You're starting to drift... It's so damn hot... How in hell do we get out of here?..."

After flicking away his cigarette butt, the steward looked up at Boost and said, "What do we do now? You up to carrying it back?"

Boost looked dumbfounded. "Me? I...I..." The blood seemed to drop from his face, as he looked far back over the hills to the groups of men huddled in the sun. "But you..."

Brububber came struggling over, with about a 70-pound doe over his shoulders, blood dripping down his shirt. The tongue bounced and jiggled like a rubber tie from the limp head, matching Brububber's own. "I got one..." he stuttered. "It's a damn doe, though. But I got one. How's yours?" He dropped the carcass in a plop and looked at the buck, kicking the horns with his foot. "Shit, I thought they would be bigger."

After discussing the marvels of their respective kills at length, the men got down to practical thinking. They were almost out of water. There was at least four hours of hot sun left. They had come at least three miles from the drop off place, maybe four or five. There was no way they could walk back that far, particularly with the extra load of two gazelle.

Brububber had a hunting knife that had been in the pile of gear Larsson had provided. The steward summarized the situation and received no argument as he suggested, "We cut off the head for your trophy. We cut off all the flanks, which we can carry more easily, for a dinner of leg of gazelle. We leave the rest. We regroup, and head back to the pickup spot for the lorry."

With that, he took the knife from Brububber, and starting at the groin of the buck, closed his eyes and slit it up the middle. Boost turned and puked air as he saw the guts spill out on the dusty rocks, sizzling as they hit the sun-baked surface. The steward continued to hack and saw and tear the two joints from the hips, until the flanks and legs were free. Then he tied them together by the ankles with a piece of lacing from one of the ammo bags. Then he did the same to Brububber's doe. Next he attacked the head of the buck, cutting through the neck and backbone as close to the chest as he could. Grabbing the head by one of the 12 inch spiraled horns, he passed it to Boost and said quietly, "Here's your trophy. You get to carry it."

The other groups had seen or heard the action, and slowly came walking toward Brububber, Boost and the steward. Each party approached the other with joyful anticipation of sharing the other's remaining water. There was none. The realities of the day had started to sink in. Slowly, in a ragged, dusty file, the excited band of hunters of the morning started to drag themselves and their butchered prizes and their killing gear back to some rendezvous point on the ever-distant rise. The sun was with them all the way, an unrelenting Grand Reckoner in the sky, saying "Now you must pay me... Pay me for your adventure."

Finally, the group had somehow reassembled itself and sat there on the boiler-hot ground, red-eyed and exhausted and near faint, nowhere near the rendezvous point. The steward had suggested, ordered, the group to sit and wait. Going on was pointless, and dangerous. Heat prostration had already started to rear its ugly head, in the form of fuzzy vision and numbness in the arms, as the sun shone on without mercy. Here they would wait, and dream of the cool sea and their yakking wives and the open bar on the ship and their lost youth and their ever-increasing thirst for living... only to wait... and hope that Larsson could find them in the middle of Hell's skillet.

One of the weary band, Michael P. call me Paddy O'Rouark, seemed to having the worst of it. He was experiencing dehydration in spades, in payment for the fact that he had been deeply into his cups the night before while sailing toward Massaua. His normally ruddy drinker's face looked ashen, his eyes spacey. He was a bit chubby and obviously out of shape, and up until today he had constantly bragged about his athletic prowess in his high school days in the Bronx. O'Rouark had guzzled his canteen right in the first hour, and had been dry now for at least three in the blazing sun. He mumbled and babbled things about mothers and Marys, and stumbled along with his arms spread out to his sides. Long before he had given his Mauser to a companion to carry. He would occasionally spin around in some wave of confusion and look up at the sun, directly, then hold his eyes in pain.

The steward had led the group over to a nearby high spot, where they all plopped down on the ground near some large outcropping rocks that might in time provide a low band of shade from the sun as it fell into the Western sky. There were no trees in sight for miles around, no places to hide from the sun, only some dry twigs that might possibly turn green in the rainy season if there ever was one.

The steward tried to take stock of what they had, and didn't have. They were out of water. They had only ten cartridges left for the M-1's, and two for the Mausers. The submachine gun they had left with Larsson in the lorry, considering it slightly overbearing, one Thompson to another. They were bone dry, suffering from severe dehydration in the early stages, and not able to move. They had seven cigarettes between them, and two lighters that still seemed to have fluid that had not evaporated. No matches, other than those that had been soaked with sweat and were no longer lightable.

The group sat there and waited. The sun, now about at five o'clock local, blazed on. They did not talk. One or two of them shivered, even though it was still about 115 degrees. They looked stunned, dazed, exhausted. And waited for some form of salvation.

Suddenly Brububber heard a noise. He grabbed his rifle, and aimed it at the source of the sound. "Maybe it's a buck..." he whispered. There it was again... A sound of scratching, or snapping...

Over behind a crest about thirty yards away. "Maybe it's a lion," he whispered. "The lions of Judah, remember? This is lion country." Scratching once again… "What is it, damn it?"

After moments of waiting, Brububber couldn't take it. He leveled his Mauser at the source of the sound, and fired. CRACK! Then again. CRACK! He tried a third shot, but was out of ammo. Just then, a terrified native man in a burlap wrap jumped from behind the ridge with his hands in the air, yelling something like "*Saaaalllaaammm! Aaalllahhhsalllamm! Aaalllaaaahhhhsssaallllaaam mm!*" He held a spear over his head, which shook menacingly as he danced in place, yelling and waving his arms. He was about six feet tall, but skinny as his spear, and had a bushy head of graying hair telling of some age. Brububber groused, "Shit! It's only some fucking Q-tip! I was hoping for a stag, or a lion."

Boost chimed in. "Oh, Jesus! We're surrounded. This guy's one of those rebels, you know, the NOMADS! The fucking NOMADS are surrounding us!"

"Calm down, all of you!" the steward barked. "You almost killed him! Relax. Put your guns down. Don't aim at him. He's yelling peace. Can't you hear it? '*Salam*'. Anyway, he can't hit you with the spear from there."

Boost was spinning around, gun at the ready, looking in all directions at once. "Don't trust him. He's a fucking savage," Boost hissed, rifle still leveled at the man.

"Trust him?" the steward asked. "He's the only living thing for miles around, and you bet I'll trust him. If he can live out here, he can get us out of here."

The steward put down his rifle, and stood up. He held one hand in the air, hoping it to be a universal gesture of peace, and started slowly to walk toward the native. "*Salam. Salam.*"

The man replied with thirty *salams* of his own, and came walking to him, using the spear as a staff. When they got close, both stopped. The steward started using words and hand signs and anything that could win a game of charades, to get his message across to the wide eyed old man of the desert. "Lorry… Waiting… Go Massaua… Need water... WATER!... Guide... Massaua... Help us... Pay you... Money... Lira... Water... Pay for water..."

The old man removed a slimy, dirty skin bladder that hung about his shoulder, tilted it over his head, and took a drink. Then he smiled, and closed up the spout and returned the sack to its original position.

"Yes! WATER!" the steward gestured. "We pay you for water."

The old man seemed to understand, and he surveyed the bedraggled band of hunters and game and equipment. Then he spied the steward's boxpack of Players pressing out of his top shirt pocket. He gestured to his water skin, then to the cigarettes, and put his fingers to his mouth as if to smoke.

The steward replied with gestures and nods. "Yes. Yes. You give us water. We give you our cigarettes."

The old man took the bag off his shoulder and dropped it carefully at the steward's feet, and held out his hand. The steward put the box containing seven Players in the old man's palm, and smiled in friendship. "Thank you. Thank you." He started to get out his lighter.

With that, the man took the cigarettes out of the box and popped them all into his mouth, and ate them. Then with a big smile and a burp, he backed off slowly, staff and all, into the distance, and disappeared behind a rise into the approaching dusk.

The hunters crawled and stumbled over to the sack and grappled over it for a drink. "To die of typhoid or to die of thirst... that is the question..." the steward briefly pondered to himself. Then he elbowed his way into the fray for a drink.

There was only about a quart of water in the sack, and it vanished in seconds. But it was ambrosia, a gift of the gods. The group lay there as the sun fell lower on the horizon, and the searing heat started to subside. Down to a more reasonable 100 degrees. The steward looked to the east, back to Massaua. No lights. Only unsettling darkness settling over a bleak landscape.

By now, most of the group were shivering and suffering the effects of sunburn and dehydration. The steward felt a numb tingling in his limbs. His mouth was cottony, and his mind wandered. His arms were bright red from sunburn, as was his nose and neck. His eyes ached. Sit. Wait. He will come. Have faith. He said he will come again.

The stars were starting to appear now. First a few, then a zillion, covered the eastern sky. "Specks of light... Different from those at sea..." he thought. "Here we are... broiled by the nearest one. At sea, one gets boiled..."

Suddenly, he wiped his eyes, and stared at the horizon. One of the stars was moving. It was moving! It was getting brighter, coming closer. Now two lights. Saved! Larsson?

As the headlights grew nearer, they seemed to be going off on an angle from their location. The steward raised his rifle in the air and shot off one round. CRACK! Boost jumped up and spun in circles. "They're back. See! I told you. Don't trust that Nomad. He's gone and brought back his buddies. Oh, shit! Gimme some ammo!"

"It's Larsson, I hope." The meandering lights veered in their direction again.

After two more shots in the air, the lorry bounced its way up on to the ridge near their location and stopped. "*Fi Faen*! Where the fuck are you?" a drunken voice called. "I've been driving all over this damn desert. How did you get way over here?"

After the exhausted hunters climbed or were dragged into the back of the lorry, the numbed steward and the well-oiled Larsson pitched in the animal legs and head and helmets and guns and gear. They all lay in a great bloody pile on the floor of the truck. The steward lifted himself into the cab along with a stumbling, laughing Larsson, and off they drove in a dusty tornado, little engine grinding and coughing, into the darkness of the eastern sky, somehow in the direction of Massaua. The steward, too tired and parched to talk, prayed for no flat tires.

After bouncing through the desert for what seemed like an hour, the lorry approached a few simple lights in the distance. "Massaua..." Larsson indicated. "Not much after dark. Not much before, either. What do you say we get a couple of beers at Sheba's?"

The steward had never heard so sweet an idea.

By reasonable estimate, six natives shit their pants in unison. Some leapt up from their chairs, eyes wide with fear, and dove behind the bar or out of the windows that were near. Others stood there stunned, cowering or paralyzed with fright. Sheba herself stood behind the bar, grinning at the filthy, blood-soaked band of renegades, rifles in tow, who broke through the door and attacked the cooler *en mass*. Bottle caps popped like firecrackers, and foam spilled everywhere, as the nearly dead hunters drained the frothy liquid straight down, then fought for another. The look in their eyes was wild, and they coughed and gagged on the cold brew as they hurried to get some form of moisture back into the deepest pockets of their cellular decomposition. Beer. Beer. Saved from death on the desert. By beer.

After draining at least three bottles each as fast as it would flow out, the band fell back into chairs, moaning and groaning in pain and ecstasy, and drank more slowly. Huge belches punctuated the night air. Bluuuuppph! One could see color beginning to return to their ashen, sun-baked faces. Their bloodshot eyes ceased to wander aimlessly, and focused on the bottles at their lips. Life was returning. Civilized behavior was returning. Buuuupppphh!

The steward had joined his comrades in arms, and was now on his fourth beer. The wetness of life was again coursing through his body. He sat sprawled in an old wooden chair, opposite Larsson, who was probably on his twentieth for the day. Larsson belched profusely as he continued to drink, and laughed and waved his arms around, at bedraggled hunters surrounding him. "Innkeeper!" he howled. "Mead for my men! Tonight we ride!" Then he leaned over to the steward and asked without interest, "We loose anybody? Are they all here?"

The steward lifted his head from its dangling position over the back of the chair and nodded in the affirmitive.

The locals had peered back up from their hiding places, still hesitant to return to the social interplay of before, as there were guns and blood all around them. They had obviously expected to be summarily shot on the spot by this wild band of rebels. Some still remembered stories of the Italian invasion of '35 wherein hundreds of simple Eritrean farmers and their families were slaughtered as they fell into the purview of maniacal machine gunners. Others knew first hand of the unrest in the province, and the popular displeasure of being forced into union with Haile's Ethiopia. Most of the patrons at Sheba's that evening were presumably members of Haile's clan, in that they had both the privilege and cash to go out drinking, and therefore now felt themselves unappreciated guests. One by one, they started to depart, quietly, so as not to upset the delicate liquid truce of the moment.

Soon it was only Sheba and the merry band remaining. Larsson called her over with two more Carlsberg. "This is Bwana Hemingway, Sheba my sweet. Give him the best in the house."

The frail woman peered out from behind an old silver espresso machine on the bar. She had seen younger days, but still had a sparkle in her eyes that betrayed her experience in dealing with men. She wore a homespun cotton dress with vertical stripes, and no shoes. From her ears dangled large golden earrings. A brilliant gold tooth graced her mouth.

Sheba smiled knowingly at both men, and replied, "It looks to me like he would like to sleep for a week, not drink beer for a week like you." She gave the steward a sympathetic looking over, surely having seen many a man barely survive a day journey in the desert. Then she went behind the bar area, and returned with a combination platter containing dried-out looking sliced salami and oily orange pepperoni and lumpy headcheese and pickled green chili-peppers and flat pita-style bread, and some crusty brown mustard in a jar. Everything was covered what he first thought were a couple hundred capers, until a few of them flew around to a better seat at the greasy feast. The steward shooed himself a path into the platter, grabbed a handful of the food and wolfed it down, and, with his mouth full, gestured with his arm to please make the same available to the others. Sheba next went to an open hearth grill smoldering in the corner, and brought out, held high in the air in a victory tribute, a two foot long metal skewer on which was impaled a broiled, shriveled kielbasi-like *wurst*. The steward thought of the doctor/butcher Billy Bob had been sent to, and quietly pushed the plate away.

It was, he felt, a new world's record. He had downed five beers in a quarter of an hour. Then three more in the next thirty minutes. And then two, to complete the hour. He sat there in the cab of the lorry, bloated and belching, but amazed that he had no desire whatever to piss. His arms and legs no longer tingled, or maybe they did but by now were numbed by the alcohol. The others in the back of the lorry were standing along the railings, hanging on as the truck swerved right and left through the streets of Massaua, singing and swearing and laughing with gusto. They were all drunk, but alive. They had made it.

The lorry pulled up to the police hut in a cloud of dust once again, highlighted by the one light bulb glowing over the door outside. Inside, a single bare light bulb was hanging on a cord from the ceiling, casting a strange glow out the windows and into the dusty air. Other than that, the streets were very dark, with only a few lights dotting the black city here and there. Few if any people were in sight.

The steward accompanied Larsson into the police station, to report their return and that all guns had been accounted for. They carried all the weapons in and spread them out on the table, behind which the chief still sat. He too looked a bit drunk, or high on hasheesh, or something. In the corner of the hut in a crumpled heap lay the young woman of that morning, moaning in a pained chant "Aaaiiiieeeuuhhh... Aaaiiiieeeuuhh... Aaaiiiieeeuuhhh..." Her miserable mantra droned on at about ten moans per minute. She did not look up, but as Larsson began to talk and gesture, her pace picked up to 12 or 14 per minute, and the volume increased in a sightless search for sympathy.

The chief, who had been listening to this constant monotone for hours now, got up, picked up his Billy, and went over and whomped the pile of bones and burlap six times hard on the back. The pace picked up immediately to 20 cries per minute, but at an experienced, much quieter level. The steward wanted to intervene, but felt helpless as the chief slapped the club in his open hand with satisfaction.

"Anybody pay for the door?" the steward asked Larsson. Larsson gestured to the chief in search of an answer, and the chief spat on the dirt floor in the woman's direction.

Larsson summarized the situation, and, in an instant amazingly sober for all his previous swilling, stepped up to the chief and looked him directly in the eyes, face to face. Then he pulled out a wad of local currency and placed it in the chief's hand.

"I did," he stated flatly. Still holding the chief eye to eye, Larsson then reached over and grabbed up the Thompson sub-machine gun from the pile of arms he had laid on the table for inspection, and snapped off the safety. With his eyes never leaving the chief's, he went over and pulled up the limp bag of bones to a standing position, and then hoisted her up over his shoulder. Her dress was torn in two from the waist down, revealing bruises on her thighs and buttocks. Larsson slowly turned and walked out the door, not bothering to look back. The steward grabbed the other rifles into his arms, and followed silently.

A flock of worried wives paced the deck, waiting the return of the hunters. One could see them waving and cheering and applauding as they spied the lorry coming down the dirty pier. They were all smiles, until they could see the dirt and filth and blood that covered their spouses' clothes and bodies. Then the chatter turned to wails of concern mixed with stern reprimand. The men, quite drunk by now, laughed and staggered their way up the gang plank, dragging heads and legs and beer bottles with them, and yelling goodbye and thanks and brotherly insults to Larsson he drove off in the lorry. The young woman shivered in the seat next to him, clinging to his arm as if she had surrendered herself to him forever.

The steward watched as one by one, wives pulled the merry hunters apart, and marched them off and closed their doors to their cabins. The verbal abuse continued, more muffled, for minutes, winding down, only to be overplayed by occasional curses and snores, the precursors to dreams of the chase and the kill. And then there was delicious peace, flavored by the distant pleas of Gigli, drifting out of the captain's stateroom...

"*Mettite a frisco 'o vino,*

tanto ne voglio vevere ca m'aggia 'mbriaca...

Chisto e 'o paese d' 'o sole,   chisto e 'o paese d' 'o mare,

chisto e 'o paese addo tutt' 'e pparole,

so doce o so amare,   so sempre parole d'ammore."

The steward finished a final pull on a stale Gitanes he had bummed from Larsson in the lorry, blew the blue smoke up at the stars, then got up from his seat on a deck equipment box, and started to pick up the animal parts littered around the deck.

"Bring 'em back alive, Mr. Buck?"

It was Eiriksson, leaning on the bridge, with a brandy snifter in his hand, obviously late into a night of solo drinking as his passenger buddies had been elsewhere.

The steward glared up at the captain without comment. He picked up the head of the buck by one horn and held it aloft in the direction of Eiriksson, blood still dripping from the severed neck. Then he turned and hung the head by its horns high on a securing cable that stretched overhead near the top of the gangway, a bloody monument for all to see. Then without looking back, he walked across the deck, took a final pull to empty his beer bottle and threw it over the side as far as he could into the black of the harbour, and headed aft to his bunk.

—AT SEA—

"Confluence."

The steward answered the question simply, yet he himself was unsure of the correctness of the term in this case.

"What do you mean, confluence?" Herman Landgrave groused. "I don't see anything except a damn ocean."

"Herman, dear. Watch your language," Fiona Landgrave stated sweetly. "The young man is just trying to help."

The steward stood there, swaying and leaning to and fro, like a circus acrobat perched on top of a flexible flagpole, feet glued to the tip and riding every sway to the maximum while still keeping in counterbalance. He actually enjoyed the motion, and the challenge of keeping one's balance with a tray full of drinks.

"Maybe you're right, Mr. L..." the steward acknowledged. "Confluence implies that... well, two flows of water merge together and flow off in another mutually determined direction." He looked out over the shifting railing at the horizon, tilting back and forth like a far distant seesaw. The day was crisp and clear. The sky blue. The wind about 10 knots off the port beam. The ocean not particularly rough. No wind-driven white caps or rolling waves. Why then, the pitching and bouncing of the old Talabot today? Confluence. Or something.

The steward picked up a book that lay on an empty lounge chair, and leafed through it. It was a pocket dictionary in Spanish and English, Berlitz style, left by one of the passengers.

"I'm sure there's a word for it..." the steward replied as he skimmed the pages. "How about current assimilation..." He was making up phrases as he scanned. "The process whereby one mass or element, such as a minority group, adopts the characteristics of another."

"Bullshit. The sea is the sea," Herman burped to himself.

"Would you believe dynamic abutment? The coming together at the boundaries of two opposite forces or elements?" the steward smiled, trying to sound like the well-read reference book he had just picked up. "Or how about an obtrusion?... Let's see here... To force one's self or ideas upon others with undue insistence or without invitation." He leafed on, searching for the proper term to describe the wave action below. "Or... then there's an occlusion? To force upward from the earth's surface, as when a cold front overtakes and undercuts a warm front." The steward stood there, reeling in time with the deck of the ship against the sky, fascinated with finding the correct technical term for the sea conditions of the day.

"Occlusion is what my daughter has," Landgrave moaned. "Cost me two thousand bucks to get her damn cuspids to fit together like normal people. Any way, stop standing there swaying, will you? You're the obtrusion. Just gimme my drink and move on."

"Herman, really. The young man is just trying to help." Mrs. Landgrave looked up from her novel at the steward. "Please forgive my husband, Steward. He's feeling the weather, I fear."

"I know, Mrs. Landgrave. We've all been there, one time or another." The steward smiled. "Here's your Bloody Mary, Mr. Landgrave. Should help."

"Ooohhh..." Herman moaned. "Goddamn ocean. Doesn't it ever stop moving?"

The swells were not visible, but the action was very real. The ship was rising and falling in semi-slow motion, like being trapped in a berserk elevator, riding up and down two floors, over and over again without stop. But added to the sensation was the fact that the elevator cab was shifting and weaving right and left with each ascension... and fall... a real free spirit of motion, which did not sit well within the inner ear of many a mariner.

The steward looked down the line of passengers, sitting on the deck chairs for their afternoon read. More than just Landgrave looked a little green around the gills.

The secret, the steward had found, was to look frequently at the horizon, thus maintaining a constant reference point in the distance. One's brain, or inner ear, seemed to understand that. There was normality, constancy, levelness. All about was crazed motion. But the gimbals of the brain wanted to be in concert with the level of the horizon. Keep it in view, and one could endure the incessant discombobulation of such sea swells. But read a book? Focusing at a close subject was a perfect recipe for seasickness.

"It'll settle down, soon, Sir," the steward said, reassuringly. "We're just in a spot where two different flows of ocean meet. Like choppy air when you're flying. Makes everything bounce around for a while. Should pass by dinnertime."

"Bounce around... Dinner... Aarrrgh... Shut up, for Chrissake!" Landgrave growled. The thought of food was not an image he wished to contemplate at this moment.

"What's for dinner, Steward?" Fiona asked brightly. "This brisk air has given me an appetite. I could eat a horse."

"Fiona! Damn it, drop it! I'm about to blow lunch, and you're talking about dinner." Herman looked ashen, no pink in his ears, his eyes rolling about like they were free in their sockets, in contrast to the motion of the ship. He took a large drink of his Bloody Mary, then sat there as if it had stopped half way down his gullet.

The steward whispered to Mrs. Landgrave, just loud enough for her husband to hear. "Heart of palm, and pork chops."

"Oooaarrrrr RRrooouuuaaaarrrkk!"

With one swift motion, the steward had his serving tray close under the nose of Landgrave, and a small towel at the ready in his other hand.

"See, Herman? I told you not to eat so much at lunch," Fiona berated him. "And all those champagnes with the captain. See!"

"Bbbblllllooaaarrrrkkkkk!"

The able steward had the slightly used Bloody Mary almost half back into the glass.

"You must learn not to drink so much, Herman. This is all of your own doing. Look at the other passengers. They're all watching."

"Fuck the otherrrr RRroooaaarrrrkkkkk!"

"Here, Mr. L." the steward said after a lull in the action. "Take this towel. It's damp on one end. Put it on your forehead."

"UUuunnnggghhh...." Landgrave moaned.

"Yes indeed, Herman. You are being punished for your sins. You and that drunken captain. See. God teaches one a lesson, doesn't he? Maybe you'll believe what the good book says, now."

"What's it say? That God was a founding member of AA?" Herman groaned.

"That nothing exceeds like excess," Fiona chided. "I trust you have learned this lesson the hard way, and will apologize to the other passengers. You made yourself quite a spectacle here, Herman."

And with that, the righteous Mrs. Landgrave arose and strode off into the brisk air toward her stateroom.

The middle aged insurance salesman from Wisconsin just sat there, with the towel over his eyes. Without looking up, he asked to the steward, "Now I know why they didn't want women on board the old sailing vessels. Isn't there something in maritime law, where it's legal to throw one's wife to the goddamn sharks?"

The steward smiled, and picked up the reference book again.

"Ablution."

"What?"

"Water..." the steward said as he looked out at the shifting horizon, "washes away all sorts of problems. I'll get you another damp towel.

"Steward?"

"Mr. O?"

"Was someone calling me?"

"Not that I heard, Sir."

"Strange... I've been sitting here alone, reading, and every now and then I hear some voice, it's muffled in the wind, coming from the other side of the ship. Was anyone over there calling me? Looking for me?"

"Oh, that may have been Mr. Landgrave, but he's gone back to his cabin.

"Funny... Wonder what he wanted?"

"I imagine he just wanted to share a drink with you, Mr. O'Rouark."

The steward took a few moments from his duties, as all the passengers seemed topped off and stabilized for the time being. He stood at the bow rail by himself, wind in his face, watching the waters surge and fall underneath him, as the Talabot churned its steady path through the swells.

"Strange how the different waters merge here..." he thought to himself. "Must be the equatorial current that heads up the coast, crossing the counter current that flows across. It sure makes for some healthy swells."

He could actually see a difference in the waters, just a slight tint of color, deeper blue coming from the outer ocean current, and a touch yellowish brown from those heading North just offshore. He could almost sense the depth of the forces powering forth beneath the rather uninspiring surface.

He thought about the places where they had been, and the quality of the sea at each. "Kind of like migrating currents... major flows of waters, forcing themselves on others going in a different direction. And where they meet, lots of turbulence. One can actually see the folding of the currents, not in white caps or crests... but in their distinctive colors... Maybe it's the angle of the sun on the different directions of current... Maybe its what the waters carry... like silt or algae... But there's something essential about the sea... parts of it always being carried forth into new territories... Each trailing banners of individuality, only to get muddied into some new mix... And underneath, hidden, the deep swells are always there, all heaving and groaning and struggling in readjustment. All together, it certainly makes for an uneasy passage."

Every person at sea, Landgrave being today's example, was affected by the heaving quite vividly at one time or another. "It usually happens on a clear day, like today..." he thought on. "Not in a storm. People are too busy, or too scared, to be seasick in a storm. But it happens when the sky is clear and the sea looks relatively tame and peaceful. Some set of powerful conditions that defeat one's sense of stability, one's grasp on an accepted constant... like my trusty old friend over there... Dr. Horizon."

"One thing though... It never stops. Always some interaction of these waters. Big... Small... Nature's primeval forces... Nice to know that there are some things one can count on, with no exceptions."

The swells shuddered under him. A hollowness in the pit of his stomach seemed to be thrown up and down, back and forth.

"Conjugation. That's it," he mused. "The infusion of one mass into another to form a new one..."

"Steward, please report immediately to the passenger deck!" The loud speaker crackled against the wind.

"Oops." He started back to the main deck. "Better get the mop. Sounds like the others are following Landgrave's lead."

As he passed under the bridge, a voice hailed down. "There's a chorus of retching on the lounge deck. Monkey see, monkey do."

"Unfortunately, you see. I do," the steward yelled back to Eiriksson, as he picked up a mop and bucket from a bulkhead locker below the bridge. "It's the privilege of command."

"You could get out a fishing line while you're at it. The passengers are chumming up behind the ship quite nicely. Should hook some beauties."

The steward laughed at the image. "How many are hanging on the rail?"

"Most of them. Others in their cabins. Your call board is lit up like a Christmas tree."

"The delights of a freighter cruise, eh?"

Eiriksson had a devilish smile on his face. His champagne lunch had undoubtedly agreed with him. "Look at it this way. You can go light on tonight's smorgasbord. Probably won't get too many big eaters. Even the hearty Mrs. Landgrave fired a little ambergris over the side."

"The great leveler..." the steward called back as he started climbing the outboard ladder to the passenger deck.

"What is? Herring?"

The steward swung his arm out in an arc across the horizon. "This conjugating sea..."

A chorus of voices greeted him as climbed the last steps of the ladder and poked his head above the level of the deck, testing the air first with a wet finger to insure that he was upwind.

"Ooorrroooaaarrrrkkkk!"

"Book covers."

The steward muttered to himself as he paused his way down the row of hard and paperbacks that shielded the faces beneath them from the late morning sun.

"Somehow there's a connection..." He surveyed the row of book covers being held in parallel, angling off in perspective like a picket fence on a suburban street. The passengers lay like a row of seals, soaking up the sun and feeding imaginations in the process. Certainly one could tell them by their shoes, or by their knees, or by their butts or bellies. But, there must be another way... a unique connection.... some sort of literary ESP... allowing one to tell the reader of a book by its cover.

The steward went down the line, checking for pre-lunch drink orders, focusing only on the paper masks in front of him.

First, there was *Atlas Shrugged*. He guessed correctly. "Good morning, Mrs. O'Rouark. Drink order? Bromide?"

"No drink yet, thank you, Steward," she replied, tracing a dollar sign in the air. "I have more important pursuits."

Next came *Caine Mutiny*. "Usual drink before your lunch, Mr. Boost? Bourbon over ball bearings?"

"Yes... No, wait. I'll take a medicinal Brandy and soda today."

Then *From Here To Eternity*. "Morning, Mr. Landgrave. Maggio out of the stockade yet? Drink this morning?"

"Maggio's out, Prewitt's in, Steward. Scotch on ice, with just a splash please."

Adjacent, *Breakfast at Tiffany's*. "Ah so now... Dlink Gorightry with you before runch, Mrs. Landgrave?"

"Make it a Mimosa today, Steward. This poor dear needs a brightener. Holly's lost her dearest cat."

Next, *Lady Chatterly's Lover.* "Morning, Mrs. Lovelake. Drink? Something horsy or something lacy?" Ooops! Missed one. "Excuse me... Good morning, Mrs. Boost. I didn't recognize you."

"My, my, young man, thank you... With my figure, I need such compliments. Let me try something adventurous... an Irish Whisky and seltzer today, Steward."

Here's an easy one. *Lolita*. "Hello Mr. O. Would you care for a nice little pick-me-up this morning?"

"Hmmm... A Virgin Mary would quite suit my fancy, thank you."

Followed by *Peyton Place*. Process of elimination. "Morning, Mrs. L. Drink? I have the good stuff stashed over the stove..."

"Thank y'all, Steward. Ah would lahk a sherry before Ah eat."

Farther out, *Fahenheit 451*. "Drink, Mr. Brububber?"

"Bring me a vodka and a beer. Make that two beers. It's getting hot out here. I'm feelin' very thirsty this morning."

Next, the thick tome of *Giant*. "Morning, Mrs. Brububber. Are you in horse country or hoss country this morning?"

"An Old Fashion, please, Steward. Only 500 pages to go."

Not to be left out, *Brideshead Revisited*. "Morning, Mr. P.-S. Pre-lunch drink today?"

"Ah, yes indeed. My Pinkie, please, Steward, and bring some matches. Two packs if you can manage."

And *Justine*. "Morning, Mrs. P.-S. Care for a drink? Or is Alexandria celebrating Ramadan this morning?"

"Mind your place, Steward. A Pinkie. You know how I prefer it."

Finally, *Catch-22*. "Morning, Mr. L. How's the flak this morning? Feel like a drink?"

"Wheweee! Almost got his bawls shot off, Youssarian did. Yeah, y'all can brang me a bag ole bourbon."

"Eleven out of twelve..."

"Steward?"

"Yes, Captain?" he panted, having covered the two exterior ladders in triple steps.

"What are you doing up here?" Eiriksson asked from horizontal repose in the captain's seat, his sandaled feet sticking out the open front bridge window, toes cooling in the breeze.

"Didn't you just call me, Sir? On the loudspeaker. 'Steward report to the bridge on the double.' I was on the fantail with Erda, peeling potatoes and listening to Orff on her HiFi."

"Open your ears, Steward. Or turn down the volume. You were not called to the bridge. I said 'Steward report to the bridge game on the double.'"

"Drat. The bridge game. I forgot. And the afternoon poker game. Sorry, Sir, it won't happen again."

"Your passengers await their pleasure, Steward. With parched throats. Like Orff has been known to say, '*Quidam ludunt, quidam bibunt, quidam indiscrete vivunt...*'"

"To add to your Orffism, '*Bibit ista, bibit ille, bibunt centum, bibunt mille.*' You have that new Angel recording too?"

"One develops a tremendous thirst playing bridge and poker."

"Or listening to Orff."

"Orff was right, Steward. Man was not intended to be a monk."

"According to Orff, man is a gambler and a drunkard."

"I'll drink to that," Eiriksson smiled, and took a sip of his vodka and tonic. "And I'll wager, Steward, that the afternoon poker game in the mess hall out-drinks the bridge table in the library, two for one."

"It's more like five to one. It's the physical quality of the game, Sir. Poker players sweat and drink more fluids like beer in keeping with their combative facade. Bridge players quietly exude a nervous perspiration, and rely on more concentrated aromatic stimulants like gin to disguise the fact."

"Who are the big winners so far?"

"I fear we have some real hustlers on board, Sir. Pammy Sue Lovelake wins most of the rubbers at bridge. She stuffs her cards in her bikini top so she can gesticulate with her hands. Drives the opposition mad. Chatters them to death. And Bull Brububber is bluffing his way bigtime into some pretty big pots. He's either very lucky or one hell of a poker player."

"I've never been able to figure it, Steward. Is victory at cards related to skill? Dumb luck? Or appropriate intake of fluids?"

"If it's the latter, some of them better change their drinks, Captain. Might change their scores. Like Mr. Potter-Smythe. He talks a superlative game... real tournament bridge...all the rules and strategies and probabilities and contracts and tacticians and famous rubbers. Then Mrs. Lovelake strolls by from the pool and sits in for twenty minutes with the cards stuffed in her bra and beats his pants off with 11 or 12 trump in every hand. Wham! Bang! Another laydown!"

"Who? Mrs. Lovelake?"

"Her hand, Sir."

"It's nice to know she's also good at cards, isn't it?"

"She shouldn't let all that natural bridge talent go to waste, besides playing Stud poker with Ole."

"Ole can slam with the best of them, Steward. He's had four years experience in some of the best rubbers on board."

"What he lacks in finesse, he makes up in a big trump, right?"

"It isn't the size of your trump, Steward. It's how and when you play it."

"Poor Potter-Smythe. Mrs. L just sits there chatting merrily about any and everything, and spits trump out of her bra. He ends up eating his theories and tactics, along with his pipe stem. I've never seen such lemons for hands. Twos, threes, an occasional five, maybe even a seven... He hasn't had a queen in two weeks."

"I didn't know we had any on board."

"Figure of speech, Sir. Only one I know is Erda, our reigning monarch at sea."

"What am I? Chopped herring?"

"No offense, Sir. You really don't qualify as a queen. However, judging from your usual position here on the bridge, Captain, you might just make it as the ship's couchant lion."

"Then drag me a fresh kill up here, dripping with vodka. I'm thinking to do some heavy roaring tonight."

"Deal."

"It's Brububber's deal."

"Shuffle 'em, damn it, and deal."

"Want to sit in, Steward?"

"Thanks, Mr. Boost, but no. I've got rounds to make."

"Bring me a another brewski, kid. One of those Heinekin."

"Make it two. Nice and frosty."

"Make it three."

"Make it a whole case. It's hot this afternoon."

"Can't wait to get hosed down again, Paddy?"

"I see 'em coming up all red this time, boys. You're all going to loose again today. Stay and watch an expert work the suckers, Steward."

"Shit, Bull, you can't pull that flush crap four days in a row. These cards have lost all their pucker by now."

"Maybe Bull knows the card fairy."

"Bull's just lucky."

"At cards. You've seen his wife."

"Watch your mouth. Don't talk about my cards that way."

"Gahd dawg. Ah jist wish I could see four li'l aces once in a whahl. Ah'm gettin' sick to death of seein' pairs all the tahm."

"Speaking of pairs, how's Pammy Sue doin'? Still slammin' it to Puffer-Smythe?"

"That woman is surely well-endowed with good card sense."

"Sure not horse sense. She married Bill Bob."

"Slammed Tony three times yesterday. Two mini's and a grand."

"Heard he bit his pipe stem off on the grand. He had doubled, she redoubled, and laid down in spades."

"First he's run everybody out of matches, now he's running short on pipe stems."

"I'll open with a dime."

"Whew! Big time bettor. I'll up it a dime."

"And another dime. How about you, Herman?"

"Call. You guys must be holding them this hand."

"Bull? Your bet."

"I'll see your piddly thirty cents and up it fifty."

"Here he goes again."

"Sheeit, Bull. You cain't fool us agin. Me and Byron got all the big fellahs on this one."

"You got them split between you. I got 'em all fat and the same pretty shape, this time."

"Bullshit, Bull. I'll up you another quarter."

"See you."

"Likewise."

"Ah'm certainly along for the rahd mahself, Yankee boys."

"Everybody in? How many, Byron?"

"Gimme two. Nice and slow..."

"Paddy?"

"I'm good with these."

"Good? Not gonna be good enough, Paddy. Herman?"

"Three. Gimme three. Make 'em sisters."

"Sheeit. Y'all don't have piss for hands. Gimme three, damn it."

"Dealer takes two."

"TWO! TWO! How can you bullshit us with that flush talk and take TWO CARDS?"

"Brububber, you're full of Bull-shit."

"Bull, you got some balls."

"It's all in being able to play the odds, fellows. It's simple confidence in one's own abilities, and one's opponents lack thereof. Right, Steward?"

"It's bullshit, Bull. You sure got your share of that!"

"He ain't got but piss in his hand, boys. Ah got all the tickies this tahm."

"Then put your money where your tickies are, Bill Bob."

"Ah bet fifty cents, jist to give you Yankee boys a break to stay in the hand."

"Tough Texas talk, boys. I'll up him twenty-five."

"I'll see it and raise it ten more."

"Now we're gettin a pot we can really piss in, gentlemen."

"Bull? You bettin'? Or bullshittin'?"

"I'm in. I call."

"Call!? Sheeit! Big Bull is Sittin' Bull this hand. I'll up it fifty centavos more."

"I'm out."

"You're full of Pecos River cow shit, Bill Bob. I'll call your crummy bet."

"Herman? You in this fray?"

"Come on, Herman. Make Bill Bob rich. Put somethin' in the dang pot."

"I call."

"Bull? You playin' along with the big boys?"

"I up it fifty."

"Sheeit, Bull. Y'all're a slippery rascal, ain't y'all."

"Just happy to take your money, Billy Bob."

"Sheeit. Texas money's no good up north, Bull. Better y'all gimme yourn. Ah up it fifty more. Y'all ain't got sheeit, a'sneakin' in two little cards lahk thet."

"I'm out. Leaves you, Bull."

"Up a dollar."

"Sheeeeeiiittt! Y'all are tryin' to bullsheeit me agin, Bull?"

"Your bet, Texas. Put up or shut up."

"Gahd damn, Bull. Y'all cain't bluff your way around the world, makin' us pay for your cruise. Ah know you got piss-all this tahm."

"My dollar says my piss is better than your piss. What's your bet?"

"Sheeittt! Don't be a'pressin' me. Ah got to do some calculatin'."

"Maybe you should go play bridge with Puffer-Smythe and the ladies, Billy Bob. Poker don't take calculatin'... Just brass balls."

"Sheeittt! Ah call, dahmmit. Beat these five little indians, all in a row, Bull."

"Nice hand, Bill Bob. I just got a bunch of nothin' this time... but they're all bleeding hearts... Sorry."

"Steward... Better bring a jug of sour mash along with that case of beer. It's going to be a long afternoon."

"Mr. Potter-Smythe?"

"Hrumph."

"Bridge game over?"

"It is for me. Puff, puff."

"What are you doing here all alone on the fantail?"

"Alas. Puff. Contemplating ending it all..."

"Mr. Potter-Smythe, you really don't mean you're thinking of..."

"Do not, puff, puff, concern yourself, Steward. I mean bridge."

"Bad rubber again?"

"Disaster, my boy. Real rout. Worse than Dunkirk..."

"Need a refill on your Pinkie?"

"Thank you, Steward, but I'll pass. Just like I have done all afternoon."

"Mrs. Lovelake again?"

"That woman is a... puff... phenomenon."

"Others might concur with that assessment, Sir."

"Look at me, Steward. I appear a civilized, logical, reasonably well-educated man, do I not? Chelsingham School, D Phil Kings College and all that."

"Immaculate credentials, Mr. P-S. You pass as civilized."

"Then why I ask you am I contemplating heinous murder of a fellow passenger?"

"It defies logic, Sir. Whom are you contemplating murdering?"

"That Pamela Sue Lovelake."

"That's locigal."

"She, Steward, defies logic. In fact, she employs no logic. She knows no logic."

"Women use a different form of logic, Sir. That's why many are bookkeepers and so few are accountants."

"What form is that, Steward?"

"It has something to do with their internal wiring, Sir. Women have some other thinking process... It's all part of some great master plan... Sort of got rewired during Genesis, I suppose, to give Adam a taste of hell on earth... It's all quite illogical to us... But in women, thinking's a complex circuit... Sort of like connecting emotional wires in series with their sensory devices, then shunting across in parallel into their paths of recall, then grounding all these to the pelvic bone. Given slightest stimulus and demand for thinking, this tangled ganglia emits forth a burst of energy to servo motors in the hands and mouth... resulting in conduct and verbosity which counter all the theories proposed by great thinkers of the past, Plato, Kant, Edison, Einstein... even Gauss."

"Puff, puff. Interesting metaphor. You may indeed be on to something, Steward. Puff, puff. Do continue..."

"Men are simple circuited. Simple sequential direct current. One and one makes two. Logic feeds more logic. Right?"

"Indisputably."

"Well, women seem to be able to juggle three or four streams of thought at once. You've seen them in a car, all talking at one time, even the driver, all talking and none of them ever seeming to listen? It's amazing that they don't murder each other for interrupting or not listening, but it seems an egalitarian characteristic - they all just assume it's their talk time. It really even doesn't matter what is being said. Opinions don't hold weight. Just participating in the babble is what counts."

"You're shedding new insight on an age old mystery, my boy."

"Or over cocktails, we see it every evening in the lounge. A group of your wives will handle three or four conversations all at one time, never missing a point of what another woman is saying, but still carrying on putting forth their own ideas? Interrupting and juxtaposing one line of thought with another, over and over?"

"Your point is well taken, my boy. A patchwork of non-sequiturs. Women are indeed complex conversationalists."

"Or the fact that they repeat themselves over and over on the telephone, I guess to get agreement from the woman on the other end, but never seeming to get the message across, or maybe not even themselves believing what they are saying? It takes women ten minutes to say what men can say in ten seconds on the phone."

"Quite. An unexpected boon that's not overlooked by AT&T, I might add."

"It's their complex circuitry, Mr. P-S. An impregnable design. Indecipherable encoding. Patents held only by women, for women."

"Fascinating... The ultimate enigma machine..."

"You British should have used more women as radio operators during the war, Sir, like we used our American Indians. The Krauts wouldn't have made any sense whatsoever out of their chatter."

"But I fear the war would still be going on, my boy. We men would still be waiting for clarification of our orders."

"Point for you, Sir. Anyway, when you consider all that, and apply it to bridge, women can frustrate the best of players, Mr. Potter-Smythe."

"I doubt Charles Goren has ever encountered a Pammy Sue."

"I'm sure he has, Sir. And he just stuck to his theories of probability and rules of percentages and look where it got him."

"Gastritis... Emasculation... Even worse... Cannonization."

"I think he got his revenge in the end, Sir. In his bridge column. I think he wrote out his great theories just for the women readers, but they were all a smoke screen. He kept the best ideas to himself, just to make women try to play their game according to misleading rules."

"Obviously not British, fair play and all that... But our dear Mrs. Lovelake is beyond rules. I am positive she has absolutely no idea of what she is doing, either in bidding or playing her hand."

"None?"

"You've heard her bid, my boy. 'Ah bid four of these pretty li'l red diamonds... No waiht... thet's not enough for gahm, is it? I'll bid six, jest to be on the safe sahd.' It defies any concept of bridge. It defies all manner of logic."

"You really can't take Mrs. Lovelake that seriously, Mr. P-S. She's had a tremendous run of cards, Sir. Unbelievable luck."

"For six weeks now?"

"Her cards will change, Sir. Probability predicts it."

"She does not operate on probability, my dear boy. She just sticks her cards in her bra and babbles throughout the play. On eight separate occasions, Pammy Sue has trumped her own Ace and still managed to win the hand. She is truly a phenomenon."

"You can take her, Sir. Just keep playing. Without you, the afternoon game has no character, no direction."

"I feel my only direction is down, Steward. Down, to the level of, perish the thought... poker. I am but another broken man..."

"Now as I think on it, maybe there's another theory, Mr. Potter-Smythe..."

"Yes?"

"She did spend a few years following the rodeo circuit..."

"So?"

"She knows what a gal has riding in her bra trumps horsesense every time."

"Steward?"

"Mrs. Lovelake?"

"Can y'all find a nice fresh li'l deck of cards for tomorrow?"

"Certainly, Mrs. L. Problem with the one you're using?"

"They're gettin' all sticky powdery n' hard to shuffle."

"Steward?"

"Mr. Brububber?"

"It went just like you said."

"He's back to his old self again?"

"Potter-Smythe is puffing away like a proud chimney."

"Hide your matches, Sir."

"Nah, he's goin' back to bridge tomorrow. Head held high."

"The poker game cure was just what he needed?"

"Yep. He won just about every hand."

"Wow! Probability and logic paid off, in spades."

"Big winner. Tony took home an afternoon pot of $7.30."

"What? You guys were betting that on one card sometimes."

"We're not stupid, kid. The p-p-puffer needed his ego boosted, not his wallet."

"He must have a real knack for poker. How did he get winning hands so much in five card draw?"

"After the five were dealt around, we let him choose..."

"Choose? Choose what?"

"What suit was trump."

"Steward?"

"Yes, Captain?"

"I expect you to do your duty."

"I try, Sir. What do you mean?"

"You're letting the afternoon card games get out of hand."

"I am?"

"The poker game has alienated everyone against Mr. Brububber."

"Sir?"

"Whenever he now opens for a dime, the others fold right away."

"Could be they're just bluffing, Sir. It'll pass."

"And what's all this about a fist fight between Mr. and Mrs. Potter-Smythe?"

"Oh, not a fist fight, Sir. She just smacked him in the nose."

"All in a friendly game of bridge?"

"Well, Mr. Potter-Smythe has been wanting to beat Mrs. Lovelake for weeks now, and he finally did it. A little slam in clubs. He was way overbid, but Mrs. L let him finesse a jack and get it through. He thinks it was his superior play of the hand. Logic. Actually she forgot what suit was trump. She could have set him three tricks."

"So his wife socked him?"

"Only after he celebrated his victory by stuffing a handful of cards down Mrs. Lovelake's bra. The second time."

"Second time? What happened after the first?"

"She said, 'Ah enjoyed thet, Tony honey. How about stuffin' the other side too?'"

"Like Orff says, '*Fortuna Imperitrix Mundi...*'"

—CAPRI—

"Sea mount."

"You've seen one, you've seen them all," Eiriksson mused, as he took a range on the peak.

"Really, it's beautiful," the steward continued. "The way it shoots up 2000 feet right out of a blue sea."

It was a perfect afternoon at sea. The Talabot churned along at 14 knots, in the smoothest blue waters of the Tyrrhenian Sea off the coast of Italy, headed for Naples. Eiriksson had chosen an entry to the sweeping Bay of Napoli coming in more below it, from Southwest than West, just to give the passengers a better view of the majestic rock rising forth out of bluegreen waters like the nose of a great dolphin.

Behind Capri, just a hint of a sun-drenched mainland sketched across the top of the sea, stretching back into the hazy distance from the Sorrento Peninsula eastward in a grand arc, punctuated by the perfect cone of Mount Vesuvio rising into a near cloudless sky, only to reach back again to the sea at Cape Misena on the north. Capri. The Bay of Naples. A picture postcard view.

It had been a peaceful passage down from Genoa. The steward reflected on the past two days in his new job. "A quick passage really... Only enough time to serve a few meals and to connect the passengers by faces and names. All pretty cursory... Nice people...

A few seemed bored, but most seem satisfied with their trip so far. Easy duty... but no let up when at sea..."

Adding spice to this was to watch Einar Eiriksson in action. His daily routine was legend, and for the steward it had been indoctrination by fire, as he hurried to keep the captain supplied with the raw herring and hard drink and champagne and liquors from morning to night. He was already a bit exhausted by his new duties at sea, and he looked forward to a day or two in port when hopefully the passengers would go ashore for sightseeing. Maybe give him a chance to catch up on his sleep.

The steward without being asked took his turn at the bearing finder, aiming first at Monte Solaro on the top of Capri, then on Vesuvio, then on the tip of Misena point to the north. He quickly plotted the three bearings on the chart spread out on the table in the bridge house, and noted the position of the Talabot. Then he started to read the chart. Depth 16 fathoms. On this course soon to be 2 fathoms. Or less. In about two minutes. "Does Eiriksson know what he's doing?" he thought to himself. "He's headed right at an underwater mountain!"

The steward rechecked his findings, then hurried out to the bridge wing where a hung-over Eiriksson, intent on his upcoming liquid lunch, was looking out at the view. "Sir." He tried to get his attention quietly. "Captain."

"What is it, Steward? Can't I enjoy a nice view, like everyone else?" Eiriksson said, a little irritated.

"Ah, Sir..." the steward moved closer. "Captain... I don't know just how to put this, being only a steward, and you the captain..."

"What is it, Steward," the captain snapped. "Tell me, or don't bother me. I don't wish to be bothered right now." Eiriksson looked out ahead over the clear blue waters at the ever increasing, lightening color, from deep cobalt blue to a softer, milkier aquamarine. The ship was still about two miles out to sea from Capri, double that from any surrounding rocks and islands.

"We are about to go aground, Sir," the steward blurted out.

"Go aground, Steward?" the captain chuckled. "I don't see any ground. No rocks. No shoals. Don't you think you should stay in the galley and leave the piloting of the ship to me?"

"Captain, you are about 40 seconds from hitting a seamount. It's marked clearly on the chart. 'Under two fathoms.' We draw way over three when loaded. And we are I would guess about half loaded. If you care to check my bearings..."

"Left standard rudder," the captain said casually to the young seaman leaning lazily on the helm. "*Faen i helvete*, Ole, wake up! Turn the fucking ship."

The young helmsman, shocked out of his sleepy state into action, spun the wheel hard to the right.

The steward leaped into the pilothouse and grabbed the large bronze wheel and spun it full to the left. The Talabot lurched first to the left, then leaned hard to the right, as the shifting rudder took hold. One could hear the crash and tinkle of breaking glass, on the deck below.

"Steady up on 020 degrees," Eiriksson said quietly. "Take aim on the most eastern point of Capri."

The steward joined Eiriksson on the wing, and both men looked over the side as a huge blue/green monster moved down along side the hull. The water was so clear that the steward could see the peaks and valleys in the surface below. The two men said nothing as the seamount slid slowly by at 14 knots, just out of reach.

"Don't they put a marker on this thing?" the steward said in dismay.

"They do. It blows away every six months," Eiriksson replied, as he let loose with a deep burp. "The Romans built roads to last millenniums, but modern Italians can't make one stupid buoy to stay afloat for a year."

"That was a close call."

"Not really. We'd have about maybe two fathoms to spare, over its outer reach. Tricky little devil, though. I even gave it a nickname. I call it Homer's Pedestal.

"You knew?" The steward said, incredulously. "You knew about the seamount? And you let me almost have a heart attack?"

"Just a test..." Eiriksson smiled, looking out to sea.

"Test! Testing what! Me?! Why?" the steward was aghast at the irresponsibility of it all.

"I need a clear head on the bridge on occasion. Remember, Lieutenant, I saw your passport." With that, Eiriksson strode off to the passenger lounge to make himself his first mixed cocktail of the day. After all, it was nearing local apparent noon.

The steward stared after the captain, and then at Capri now less than a mile distant, then at the young Norwegian at the helm.

"Damn." He kicked the bulkhead. "I thought I was done with bridge duty." Quickly he entered the bridge house and went over to the chart area and scanned the figures and lines before him. "Aim at the eastern tip of Capri... Deep water here, and here... but rocks here, and here, and here, and here. Damn. I'm supposed to run an obstacle course. Let's see... We take this track to here... off this small hook. Lots more rocks... Then it opens up a bit. Rocks on the right and left... Shoal off the hook... Here it's deep again... Then turn to due North, then into open waters again, then 355 to Naples..."

He quickly looked out the window at the approaching mountain. Then he spoke to the helmsman directly and clearly. "Ole, I have the con. Steer course 022 to the eastern tip of the island. Keep her about 200 yards off the cliff. Any farther out, we cross over rocks. Keep her close to the tip."

The boyish helmsman hesitated. "But you are the steward... The captain has not..."

"Ole, the captain is not on the bridge. I am taking bridge control of the ship. If you do not do what I tell you, we will hit the rocks about 1000 yards off that island, and we will sink. Before I let that happen, I will throw you overboard and steer this tub myself. Now come right to 022 and hold it there."

248

The befuddled young helmsman now looked very much awake. "Yes, Steward...ah, Sir. Steadying up on 022 degrees."

The mass loomed closer and closer. It was a majestic sight, this mighty fist of stone rising out of the sea. Covered with vegetation. Houses, no...villas, lots of them, dotting the sides of the cliffs. Most white, some pink, some yellow. Flowers everywhere, adding bright yellows and pastel blues and rich reds amidst variegated greens. Winding paths and narrow roads, mostly people walking. Occasionally a small car. Here and there a horse cart. Boats and sails anchored in clusters near the shore.

As the Talabot chugged closer to the tip of the island, the steward noted something odd in the water. "What the devil are those floating things, Ole? There, and there, out past the smallboat moorings."

"They look like rocks, Sir. But they seem to be moving about. Sort of wandering."

The steward looked quickly at the charts, then grabbed a pair of binoculars and ran back outside. "They're floats. Or moorings. There are people on some of them. Sunbathing."

"Women, sir?" Ole's interest perked up.

"Steer through them, now, Ole. Don't hit them. You have the wheel now. Weave through them. Stay near 022."

On the floats sprinkled around the point of land were young women, occasionally with a man, stretched out on the slowly bobbing wooden decks, luxuriating in the warm, delicious noonday sun. One fact was obvious as they came into view. The women were topless. Lighter streaks and white areas adorned certain shapely body parts, contrasting against mellow tanned skin. In fact, as the Talabot drew nearer, a few stood up and waved. They were even bottomless. Then a scattering of them plunged into the clear aquamarine water like sleek sea nymphs at play.

The steward stood fascinated. "Ah, an island paradise..." he mused. "What a place..." Then he turned to the helmsman, who was straining to get a view out of the window, "Keep your eyes on the compass reading and on not hitting any of these floats, Ole. I'll tie you to the wheel if you don't keep your mind on your heading." Then he dreamed away silently as he looked ahead, "Mermaids... We wouldn't want to sink anything so beautiful."

The Talabot wove its way through the floats and small boats at anchor, keeping about one-quarter of a mile off the shore. Lazy bodies would sometimes lift a golden haired head to see what was chugging their way, and occasionally wave an arm. Some would even stand up and strike a calendar pose, directly for the benefit of the full crew on the freighter that somehow had learned quickly of the nude bathers so near and yet so far off the beam, and now lined the railing of the main deck in force. Cheers went up from the men as each new bather would display her toasted and untoasted parts to hungry eyes. It was probably the only time the steward was to see the ship's crew assembled all at once. Even Eiriksson was among them, waving and cheering with each new pose of pulchritude.

The steward found it nearly impossible to keep his mind on steering the ship, with all the visual sightings and gorgeous bodies and cheering going on. But somehow, slapped by a puff of breeze, he remembered the shoal and the outlying rocks and barked to Ole, "Now, bring her left to 355. Let's get past the hook up there. Stay in really close, Ole. Keep it about 200 yards off the cliff."

At that distance from the rocky hillside rising precipitously from the waters edge, the steward could see the inhabitants and homes and gardens dotting the hillside quite clearly. He could even smell its alluring beauty in the air. He stood on the bridge wing, strangely bound by the spell of this enchanted isle, smothered in aromatic flowers and stony textures and pastel walls and verdant vegetation, completely fascinated with the view.

"Funny..." he mused. "I hear music..." Above the hummmmm of the Talabot's engine that filled the still noonday air, he could hear a tantalizing sound and rhythm coming from near the tip of an isolated small cliff, clinging to the island, up ahead. He put the binoculars to his eyes. He could hear it more clearly now... "*Volare.....Oh, no.....*"

Scanning the area, he saw a young girl. No, definitely a woman. In a very skimpy, yellow two-piece bathing suit... Dancing subtly by herself on a flowered terrace... Slow beat... Easy motions. Slight movement of her arms... Happy dancing... Smooth, loose... Now he could see her face. Ouch. A classic. Raven black hair streaming down her back. Oooh. He took a swallow. What a figure... Italian figure... full where a woman is supposed to be full... and a waste like a wasp.

The music was clearer now. She was dancing and singing along with the recording, singing freely, openly, with no inhibitions.

"Cantare..... Oh,oooh,oooooh oooh...."

The steward climbed up on top of the pilothouse to reach a level closer to hers on the cliff. Then he grabbed a taunt cable that stretched up the small mast holding the ship's foghorn, and pulled down hard. "WWWWHHHHOOOO OOOOO OOOOO. WWHHOOO...WWHHOOO...WWHHOOO... WWHHOOO." Then he waved, in big broad strokes, to the girl on the hillside.

The music drifted out to the ship like an audible mist, in delicious beaconing. *"Nel blu, dipinto di blu..."*

She stopped dancing and looked up, startled by the blasts so near. He could see her clearly in his binoculars. She came over to the small, pillared stone railing that enclosed her terrace, to a telescope on a tripod, and aimed it at the ship. The steward was dressed in white long pants, a white short-sleeved shirt, and wore a red kerchief tied jauntily around his neck. He waved broadly, and pulled the cable again. "WWWWHHHHHHOOO OOOO OOOO... WWWWHHHHOOO...WWWWHHHHOOO." Then he started dancing to the music, as she had done, right hand on his waist. She waved in return, and then resumed her dancing for a few seconds.

It was all over in about 30 seconds. The Talabot churned by, and on its way into open seas again, headed toward Naples some twenty miles to the north. The girl stood looking at the ship, without motion, for a minute more. The steward did the same, looking at the island as it passed close by, and wondering what pleasures it held, now being left fast behind. The last thing he saw was a burly older man in a white shirt and sunglasses, and a very large dog that suddenly appeared beside the girl, looking after the ship. The girl gave a slightest shrug of her shoulders and tilt of her head in a little body language, followed by a subtle palm-up wave with her right hand. Then she resumed dancing, as the man looked out at the sea.

The steward glanced down to the deck, to see the crew, and some male passengers, and the captain, drink in hand, looking up at him. Eiriksson, smiling, shook his head slowly from side to side. Then the steward climbed down from the overhead and went back to his charts, trying to think of Naples, ahead.

As the Talabot threw over its last mooring line to the men on the pier, Eiriksson turned to the steward who was standing about five yards away on the main deck.

"Come with me, please, Steward. I have a job for you."

The steward followed the captain to his stateroom, and waited at the doorway as Eiriksson went to his desk and took out a small package wrapped in brown paper. "I'd like you to deliver this for me. It will give you some time ashore. Anyway, the passengers will all be going on a bus tour of Mount Vesuvio this afternoon, and will have dinner ashore. You can have some time to yourself. Be back by dawn. We sail at 0700." He handed the parcel to the steward, and started to leave.

"There's no address, or name on it..." the steward replied.

"Just take it to Don Lucci. Ask someone ashore. They'll tell you where he is," the captain smiled.

"Anyone?"

"They all know who he is. You'll find him. Please give him my respects." And the captain went back to his passengers to toast them off on their trip to Vesuvio.

The steward looked around for answers, and finding none, departed down the gangway and into the port of Naples. As in any commercial shipping port, the area was dirty and smelly, and he hurried to the gate. There he showed the bored guard his new Norwegian seaman's papers. The guard started to read them closely, word for word, struggling with the Norwegian. The steward asked, in mock Italian, "Where... *Dove*..ah, ah... Don Lucci? The guard looked up, gave him back the papers and waved him through with no questions or inspection of his parcel.

Once outside, he looked around for a taxi. Finding none, he asked a man walking down the street. "Don Lucci? Ah...*Dove*... *Signore* Don Lucci?"

The man looked him in the eye, smiled broadly, and pointed up at the top of a rising hillside. "*Palatio del Sol*." Next he put his index finger along side his nose and pushed softly to the side, and grinned. "*Il Luce*." Then he walked off.

The steward wandered down the block, amidst narrow valleys of high rising tenement apartments and yelling children and singing men and cursing women and laughing young girls and running boys and a runaway soccer ball and laundry hanging across the street like a thousand flags in the sunlight. Everything and everyone was upbeat and energetic, happy even if they were fighting or yelling at one other. It was like the first act from an Italian opera, with everybody in the chorus doing their stage bits all at once in the big opening scene. "*Vivacci*," he thought. "*Multissimo*."

At two thirty in the afternoon, Naples was indeed larger than life, even comic. People were just coming back from a long and filling lunch hour. Singing was everywhere, rather decent singing, mostly from men and occasionally from women. Love songs, Neapolitan songs, broken hearts, and lots of high notes held as long as lungs permitted. It was a street scene that would have made Giacamo himself proud.

He walked along turning his neck in all directions, watching a basket of vegetables being hoisted up to a small balcony window by a fat smiling woman, yelling joking obscenities at the vendor below. The air smelled of garlic. *Multissimo* garlic. And human excrement. Depressed drainage ditches lined both sides of the cobblestone streets, and contained raw sewage trickling down to grates at lower levels. "Now I know why armies always want to take the high ground," he thought, gagging at the stench. "It flows down hill. Gas your enemy without firing a shot."

Suddenly a high-pitched BLEEEEEEEEEEETTTT behind him caused him to leap to the side. A Lambretta with a girl on the back, side saddle, blasted by him, swerving in and out of the pedestrian traffic and parked cars. "Thanks for the beep!" he yelled at the young male driver, as he stomped the wet sewage off his shoes. The girl waved happily.

Next he heard a loud PLOPPP to his right, as a bucket of kitchen waste and other unmentionables landed at his feet. He looked up, three stories, only to see another fat smiling woman, still holding the bucket, shrug her shoulders as if to be saying. "Damn. I missed. Didn't allow enough for the wind." And then she ducked in to her apartment. "*Core... Core n'grato....*" wailed a live tenor with great passion into the afternoon air.

The steward felt he was under attack by the natives. Quickly he ducked under a doorway and looked about for more trouble. Finding none, he then asked a middle aged woman all dressed in black and carrying a large shopping net full of food up the street, "*Pardone me... Scussi... Por favore... Dove Signore Don Lucci?*"

The woman stopped in her tracks, looked him up and down, spat at his feet, and then marched resolutely up the street without looking back.

Next the steward picked a man out of the passers-by and asked the same whereabouts. The man also pointed to the top of the hill showing above the houses and apartments, and said, "*Del Sol. Palatio del Sol.*" He smiled, bowed, and continued on.

The steward scratched his head. Then he spied a small car, a pale green Lancia Appia, waiting at a corner. Maybe a taxi? A young man leaned idly against a fender, smoking a cigarette, ogling each passing female, young or old.

The steward walked up on the passenger side and asked the young man, dressed in a wide lapel suitcoat covering only a T shirt, the same question. The young replied in broken but very good English, "The Don? Sure. He'sa upa there, in his restaurante.

Every day about thisa time, hesa eat upa there. Palatio del Sol. Get in. I take you there. Don't worry. Cost you nuttin'."

The steward was flabbergasted. What courtesy. What nice people. He even forgot Mama the Bomber, and looked up at the distant hillside. An offer to drive him to the top of a pretty steep rise overlooking the city. For free. "Thanks. Thanks a lot," he replied as he climbed in along side the driver.

"My name it'sa Vincenzo. Whadda you, American?"

"Yes," the steward nodded to his driver. "Where'd you learn so much English?" the steward asked as they zipped off in a squeal of tires on damp cobblestones.

"Lots of soldiers, when I'ma kid. Lots of cousins from America, come to visit. Lots of Hollywood movies," he laughed.

"Not in school?" the steward asked.

"School? Wha school? Fiftha grade and I'm outta school... Now ova dare... she'sa my school." Vincenzo howled as he pointed at the wiggling walk of a well-endowed young woman carrying a basket on her head. "What I gotta learn but to push him up?" He roared past the girl about two inches from her arm with a loud BEEEEP... BEEEEP, followed by lots of wavings and yellings out the window, back in her direction. "*Ciao*, Scicolini!" She did not even flinch.

They raced through the winding streets of Old Napoli, gears grinding and wheels squealing, ever upward toward the sun-drenched ridge above, through narrow laundry-strewn alleys and crowded open plazas, along flower-strangled roadways hugging the hillside, past crowded colorful slums and on past posh antique villas, to the open ground atop the hill, overlooking the spectacular panoramic grandeur of the turquoise Bay of Napoli, arcing on down the peninsula, with Vesuvio towering majestically in the distance, down to a small dot on the horizon with the sea to the East.

Vincenzo stopped at a suitable vantage point, by a crumbling stone railing along the curve of a switchback. He swung his arm in a grand arc along the horizon. "Nice picture, no? We got an old saying... 'See Naples and Die'. Waddaya tink. You ready?"

The steward looked at the man oddly.

Vincenzo caught the look, and laughed. "I mean. You ready to see the Don?"

As they drove on, the steward reflected back on his earlier moments through the slums, and mused, "Smell Naples and die."

The four-cylinder Lancia skidded up to a stop on the side of a small hill near a large villa with pillars and low stone fences and olive trees and flowers. The little engine had done its work, climbing to that elevation at low gear speeds, and it was hot. Parked on a slight incline sideways, the car felt like it was about to roll over and down the hill again. Suddenly, as the steward was about to disembark, the tired little engine, tilted and hot, got a spill of petrol in the wrong cylinder, and exploded in a loud smoky BLAMM! And another. BLAMMM!

The steward staggered out through the smoke to see three large men rush out of the villa front door with pistols drawn and charge out into the bushes and olive trees, looking and yelling and pointing everywhere. The steward and Vincenzo put their hands high in the air, and froze.

Finally, after much shouting, one gorilla of a man came over and with an upward nod of his head, pistol pointed between the steward's eyes, requested clarification.

"D..Don L..Lucci," stuttered a startled steward. "I've... I'ma here to see Don Lucci."

The large man gave him a quick frisk with his empty hand, noticed the package in his hand, and with a couple of quite eloquent wrist flicks of the largest 9mm the steward had ever seen, motioned for him to follow. Then with a couple of backhand counter flips, he suggested politely that Vincenzo scram back down the hill.

The steward walked up to a vine-wrapped metal gate that must have been hundreds of years old. Through it lazed a shady court yard, with a tiled patio area containing four small tables and assorted chairs, surrounded by flowering bushes and hanging plants and a grape arbor and olive trees. A picturesque setting for lunch, if the steward's stomach could just settle down.

Standing by the doorway to the villa, leaning against the wall, was a very large waiter in a long white apron, nonchalantly picking at his teeth with a toothpick. Somewhere inside, a scratchy radio or Victrola played the same syrupy Neapolitan love song of the streets below... "*Katerine.... Katerine....*"

Under a tree, giving a soft mottled light on the white tablecloth below, sat an older man with white hair, in a crisp gray pin-stripe double-breasted suit. He was reading a newspaper, and sipping a glass of wine. He looked up at his new visitor.

"So?" he asked after a moment.

"I'm here to see a Don Lucci," the steward said hesitatingly. "I have a package for him."

"Give me the package," the man said without interest.

"Are you Don Lucci?" the steward asked.

The old man looked up from his paper. "No. *Sono* Santa Claus." Then he said some words in some Italian dialect, and all the other men roared with laughter.

The steward looked about for assistance.

"Relax, kid. Just a joke. You American?" The man put the paper down and looked up.

The steward accepted this as confirmation of the man's identity, and walked up and put the package on the table.

"Know what you brought me, kid?" the old man said in a hushed voice. "Nitroglycerin. Shake it wrong and... Va Va Voom!"

The steward flushed with anger at Eiriksson, that he had set him up as a messenger boy to bring high explosives in to some two-bit smuggler. He could have been blown to smithereens in that hair-raising ride up here. The other men nearby stiffened a bit.

Then the old man motioned with his head at the burly waiter and the two gorillas remaining in the courtyard. Again, one eloquent nod held a clear message..."Give me a moment with the kid." The men exited quietly.

The old man opened his package carefully, to reveal three small vials. They held pills.

"Nitro," he spoke flatly. "For my fuckin' heart." He took one out, and downed it with a swallow of red wine. "The others aren't to know. Think I'm strong as a horse. Now you and I, we got a secret, don't we."

"Yes, Sir," the steward acknowledged in the head nod language.

The old man looked at the steward, and smiled. "So how's America? What's new? Business is good, I hear."

The steward answered, "I don't know, Sir. It's been over two years since I've been there. I've been...ah...traveling."

"I know what you mean, kid," the old man replied with a silent nod and shoulder shrug.

The steward, trying not to acknowledge the silent pause, sniffed the air. It was a beautiful combination of garlic and flowers.

"You hungry, kid?" The old man clapped his hands once. The burly waiter hurried up. "Have some lunch. I ain't seen anyone from America for long time now. Let's talk. Stay. Eat. Let's talk about the old country." With a backhand wave of one hand, the waiter understood the order... a little *vermicelli* in oil and garlic, a little *antipasto*, maybe a taste of veal *picata*, a side of fresh *fenoccio* and basil salad, definitely a little *brodetto di pesce*, maybe a little *calzone* stuffed with chicory and olives, and of course, a little wine. A little light lunch.

The steward looked on in amazement as the array food came right in, freshly prepared and hot where necessary. The waiter poured him a glass from the slightly chilled bottle before Don Lucci, a Gran Furore Divina Costiera. "*Saluto*," the old man clinked his glass and drank. "So tell me... What's wit that dick Dewey? Still makin' waves?"

"Dick... Dewey? Do you mean Governor Dewey?"

"Certainly. Tom Dewey the dick," the old man snapped. "Tell me he's history."

"I don't know, Sir. I haven't heard much from him since Truman embarrassed him in '48. You know him personally?"

The old man looked out over the sea. "I know the guy."

The steward took more than a few bites of the delicious food in front of him. Any reserve was won over by aroma and flavor, and he attacked voraciously.

The old man then perked up. "What's wit Rocky Marciano these days. Think he'll try a come back? He can take that Swede, right? Bam! in the fazool. No trouble, even at his age."

"I...ump...don't think so...Yes...ummph... I agree he can, Sir," the steward replied with his mouth full. This was the time for body language, and he remembered too late.

"Great fighter," the old man reminisced. "43 KO's in 49 fights. He flattened dat Jersey Joe Walcott in '52. I miss him. Watched him grow up as a kid. He had class. Great fighter."

"You knew him too?" the steward asked, impressed.

"I got around," the old man nodded. "So I retired here."

A sudden slam of a car door caught the attention of the other men, and they went outside the gate. There, through the flowered ironwork the steward could see a large black Mercedes sedan. Walking this way, followed by the men from the patio, was a fattish man in a long black robe and a wide brimmed black hat. A black rope tassel swung around his knees as he waddled in. A priest.

The old man stood up, but stayed at his chair. "I want you to meet a friend, kid." To the priest as he came into the patio, he spoke slowly and softly, "*Monsignore* Pulposo. You do me a great honor, that you could come to my hillside. Here, share food with us. You musta be hungry after you trip here from Roma. And some wine. Have some wine. How are all my friends?"

The priest came over and shook hands heartily with the old man. "*Bene. Bene. Tutti...bene.* Ah, my respects to you, Don Salvatore. It is good to see you again. You are looking well. The *Cardinale*, he sends you his deepest respects. I will tell him you are well. The sun and air here agrees with you."

"The sun, the fresh air, and a little wine. I am comfortable," the old man nodded around, surveying his domain under the trees with his shoulders and chin.

"Still tough as nails, eh Don Salvatore?" the large priest laughed, arms spread wide.

"Believe your eyes, *Monsignore*. I can still make my weight. Here... Meet my young friend, here, from America. Hey, kid. What's your moniker?"

Still swallowing a large piece of *scungilli*, and wiping his mouth, the steward mumbled, "I'm...Umm...steward...Umf...Hello, Padre."

The priest bowed and smiled. "Don Lucci knows how to make a guest feel at home, no? Surely this is only your first course?" he grinned, smacking his lips at the spread of food.

Now, time for a shoulder shrug. The steward shrugged politely.

"Here... some wine. Let's all have a little wine," the old man smiled, and waved a hand in the air. The waiter appeared out of nowhere, with a fresh bottle of Gran Furore, all wine glasses full, as did a place setting for the padre.

The priest and the old man clinked glasses, then were about to drink as the downshifting grind of a sports car was heard outside the gate, and the screeching of brakes.

"Ah..." The old man smiled and sighed contentedly, and put his glass down. "My niece. Perfect timing, as usual."

All eyes looked to the dust settling about a red Ferrari convertible, out of which strode a young woman in a white dress whirling just above her knees, and holding a pink flowered Pucci silk scarf in her left hand, up by her shoulder, trailing in the air behind her like a banner, fighting for attention with her long black hair and the two huge dogs that propelled her forward on their leashes. The steward chocked on a piece of veal. It was the girl from the terrace.

"Ah, Ariadne. Ariadne. *Mia cara*. You make my day *perfecto*." The old man held out his arms to the smiling beauty as she whisked in through the gate. The massive dogs, tongues splashing about, dragged her right to her uncle, then fell couchant at his feet, surveying the feet around them. The girl, blue eyes darting about to take in everything, kissed her uncle on the cheek, and gave him a big hug. With a toss of her hair, her proud nose, nostrils flared, surveyed the air like a filly ready to race, exploring the zesty scents of oregano and wild flowers and garlic. She looked the old man directly in the eyes.

"My handsome uncle. You fill my heart," she cooed.

Music drifted out from the villa... scratchy but haunting... the voice of Maria Callas in her more virginal days, swelling the afternoon air with familiar sympathy,

"O mio babbino, caro... mi piace, e bello bello..."

"Where's Scyllato, Cara?" the old man asked softly.

"I left him at the pier, Uncle." She flipped her head with a secret smile. "I have Primo and Sexto here to keep me company." She ruffled the hair on the back of the necks of the two beasts at her feet. "You protect me, don't you, my darlings?"

"Growl. Slurp. Pant."

The priest was already banging the steward on the back as the old man said graciously, still looking at his niece, "Ariadne. Meet some friends. Join us for some wine. You know my dear friend *Monsignore* Pulposo, from the Vatican?" She curtsied reverently, head down, then rose smiling to take his hand in both of hers.

The steward was now red in the face, matching the color of his neckerchief strangling his throat at the moment. He looked at the girl in disbelief.

"And this, Ariadne. May I present a new friend from America. *Signore...*"

She looked over at the steward, stopped her graceful animation for the briefest second as recognition shifted to the present from a recall of telescopic focus, held out her hand and smiled. "Ah, yes. *Teniente* Horatio Hornblower, I believe. How nice to see you again."

Her sky blue eyes seemed to penetrate right through him. He flapped his arms and jumped up and down and gagged and pleaded and took his hands and pointed to his throat. Melodramatic gestures were the language of the day. Ariadne spun him around and slammed both fists together on his back. A piece of veal plopped out on to the tiled ground. One great dog snapped it up, as the other growled.

"Some table manners your friends have from America, Uncle. But they have other skills, I am sure." She smiled and turned abruptly and whirled about the patio, greeting the other men and the waiter, who stood there silently applauding her dominance of center stage.

"Si, si, ci voglio andare! E se l'amassi indarno..."

The steward, normal color regained, spoke to her as she returned to the table. "You... Ah... Thank you, Miss... Ariadne... I think you just saved my... neck."

"It was your veal, I believe, *Teniente*. The *Monsignore* here, he was ready too, to help, I suppose to save your soul. It appears as if I, however, have more influence on your body." And with a dramatic swallow of the steward's glass of the Gran Furore and a toss of her chin, she spirited off in the direction of the villa, scarf atrailing. The music swelled to its highest...

"Mi struggo e mi tormento,   O Dio! vorrei morir!...."

Diva, exit stage left.

The steward, trying to compose himself, joined the other men in reseating themselves, and, while suffering a large set of drooling fangs resting uncomfortably right next to his shoe, followed the lead the priest already attacking the afternoon *abondanza* before them. The conversation evolved mostly between the priest and the old man, bits and pieces about business, ownership of property, expected revenues, sharing profits, interspersed with touches of sarcastic jest or affection about common friends and associates. The steward continued to eat hungrily in the fresh air, and nodded and shrugged at appropriate moments, feeling quite accepted and in good company. One of the dogs chewed silently on a lush black tassel hanging down from the priest's cassock. Feasting, it seemed, was a common denominator for man or beast.

As the conversation went on, the steward increasingly felt, however, that his host had much more to him than just being gracious. In fact, he looked familiar. A face in the news, perhaps, or an actor lookalike. The steward couldn't exactly place it. As the conversation shifted to non-specific comments on shipping merchandise, and port inspectors, and politicians, and longshoremen, and a man named Hoffa who had no respect, the connection with Dewey registered. The steward sat back, wiped his mouth, and looked intently at the gracious old man. One dog laid his heavy wet muzzle on his foot.

The old man noticed his change of demeanor. He took a sip of wine, and said to the steward, "You got enough to eat? Here... Have some more wine. It makes for good friendship."

"Thank you, Sir... But I've had..."

"Here, kid. Fill your glass. We toast to your boss. To the big Norwegian." He poured, then held his glass up at eye level.

The steward held up his glass for a clink. "To the captain."

"To Einer. My friend." He took a swallow, never leaving eye contact with the steward, who now felt even more uncomfortable.

"You wonder if your captain is involved in smuggling, right, kid?" He said casually.

"Ah... What?...No... No, Sir."

"I tell you a story, kid." The old man stroked the head of one of the dogs. "A few years back, I'm on the piers, looking for someone to take some cargo of mine someplace. My assistants..." he shrugged behind him at the other men, now eating at another table, "they go aboard Eiriksson's ship to... negotiate. They enter his cabin. Then I see them one at a time come flying out the door and over the side into the bay. Va Va Voom! Like a sputnik, up and over they go. I don't get mad. I think to myself... Here is a man I can trust. He has principles. His principles. Not necessarily mine. But he can also be made to see the reasons for doing business with me. So I go aboard myself, alone." He took another sip of wine, as does the priest.

"And here's this giant of a Norwegian, standing there with hands on his hips, waiting for me up at the top of his gangway. He laughs. I laugh. He welcomes me into his stateroom, and we have a Campari. Now I know and he knows that he needs fair treatment on the piers of Italy to do his business. No trouble, you know what I mean? And I know he will only go so far, and I know he is a man of principle, that I can respect. He is boss of his world at sea. I am boss of mine on shore. We can do business. Only thing at stake is the action, and the price."

The steward shifted his foot, uncomfortably, away from a slimy growl from below.

"I figure I can find a hundred ship captains that will take my goods and look the other way. Slip a little green, and it's done. But Eiriksson, I can use a man like him different. He's like the *Monsignore* here. A man of principle. We still got to live together. Right, *Monsignore*?" Shoulder shrug, head nod response. "So we find ways to work together. For Eiriksson, he is an avenue I can trust with some things, like this package you brought. I could buy it here, no problem, but then certain people would know. We help each other. This way, Eiriksson gets peace on the piers. I get a package. Personal delivery. We negotiate. Nobody gets thrown over the side like these *buccalados*." Head nod. "They're good boys, but they don't use their heads. Except to hit things with. But Eiriksson. We do business. We give respect. We get respect. Right, *Monsignore*?" A toast of glasses. A smile. A faintest shrug to the left while nodding.

"I think I understand, Sir. Thank you," the steward replied.

"What you don't understand, kid, is that you have the respect of the captain. He don't let just anybody bring the package."

"I...I barely know... He...We only..."

"He trusts you. So I trust you." The old man took a sip, and looked the steward hard in the eyes. "Anyway, we got a secret. Don't we."

"We have a secret, Sir."

"Now, kid, the *Monsignore* and I have some business to talk about. But I have a favor to ask of you. My niece... Ariadne. She'sa the flower of my life. She is the one in my family with a spark. You know what I mean? Life. She'sa got it. A passion for life. I hurt bad when I don't see her happy. But she'sa my niece. The Queen of

England has more freedom. She don't easily find young friends she can trust. You know? I got one of my men, Scyllato, he watches over her. All the time. She goes stir crazy. 'Cause if she goes out alone, she might get in trouble. She'sa my favorite niece. You understand? Some people might use her against me. So I gotta keep her safe. Only with people I can trust."

The old man looked back at the villa, and sighed. "She'sa in there, putting on a fresh face for you, kid. I can tell. So you do me a favor. Maybe I do you one. You take my niece out on the town tonight. Nice dinner. Little wine. Dance a little. Moonlight. She'sa like a delicate flower. *Fiorella mia.* Needs a little watering, a little sun. Tender like. You handle that for me?"

The steward sat dumbfounded. He would give his eyeteeth for the opportunity to take out this gorgeous creature, and here the old man was offering the Contessa di Napoli to him on a platter. "I would be honored, Don Lucci. My ship leaves at 0700 tomorrow. I should make it back to the pier with plenty of time. Eiriksson gave me the night off."

"One thing, kid..." the old man said softly. "You treat her correct. Whatever that is. You understand? No bullshit. I trust you on this."

Ariadne appeared in the archway of the villa door, flowered scarf around her shoulders, flipping back her hair off her shoulders, proud chin and nose held high, a beautiful young flower in an expectant, vibrant pose that would have the balcony screaming even before she said a word. "Floria!...Floria!...*Brava!*"

The steward looked over. Their eyes touched with a sizzle, then danced apart. "I will treat her with great respect, Don Lucci. You have my word."

———

The late afternoon was a dream. Racing around in a red Ferrari convertible, scarves and drool flying, the foursome toured the hillside in animated conversation, Ariadne pointing out antiquities with a shout and a wave of a hand above the wind. The Kingdom of Naples was colorful, confused, and poverty-racked. A maze of flying laundry and singing voices and wiggling behinds and flashing smiles and shrill whistles and idle young men and hand language and bustling street activity and impassioned arguments contrasted with the imposing dignity of the Royal Palace, or vied for attention with nude stone gods bathing joyfully in ornate fountains, or played in counterpoint against the grandeur of the Teatro San Carlo Opera House, or appeared in textured surprises in the Old Spacca Quarter. Everywhere, the loud street scenes provided an energetic opening for any second act. *"La Donna mobile..."* could be heard in numerous tenor renditions echoing through the narrow, hilly streets. Throughout the city, Verdi, and Puccini, and Donizetti reigned supreme. Life in Napoli? Comedy and melodrama at their best.

Ariadne gave him a running commentary on the history of the city as the two, plus hounds afoot, sat at an umbrella'd table at a cozy seaside restaurante in Santa Lucia for a late afternoon aperitif. Ariadne ordered Mistra Varnelli L'Anice Secco Speciale and water, the steward the same. Soon, as the sun sank lower toward the horizon, at Ariadne's casual nod to the waiter they switched to a chilled white Giuseppi Scala Lachryma Christi del Vesuvio.

Ariadne laughed casually as she recapped the checkered history of the area. "Napoli has always been like a seaside resort, coveted over the centuries by waves of wealthy and royalty from all over up north to get away from the cold. I guess strategically it is a decent port, but in reality, there are much better in Italy. It is best looked upon as a playground, with the Napolitani as the children. Nobody wants to work. Everybody wants to play. They play at work. They play at marriage... at religion. They play at politics, just look at the *Communisti* and the *Fascisti*. They play at industry. Naples cannot be taken seriously. It is all *opera buffa*. They play at life. But they have no work, and have no money. So, they fantasize and enjoy whatever they have, and sing, always sing, day and night, of what might have been."

Her face was bright and happy, animated in the soft shadings and terra cotta glow of near dusk. The steward stared into her eyes, which now matched the deepening azure of the bay in the reddening sunlight. "The important Romans, like Tiberius, and Vergil, used

Naples and Pompei and Capri as a resort area. They enjoyed its baths. Before them, the Greeks controlled it for the same reason, until the 4th century B.C. After the Romans, in the 6th century A.D. came Byzantine rule. Then in the 1100s the Normans conquered the city and it became part of the Duchy of Sicily. Then the came French, under Charles I of Anjou, who took control in 1266. Then came many others, like Alfonso V of Aragon, then Don Carlos of Bourbon in 1738, you know him as Charles III of Spain. And on and on. Joseph Bonaparte was made king in 1806, even Lord Nelson rescued it at one time. Finally, to put a finale to these never-ending acts of political intrigue and territorial barter, Ferdinand I took the crown in 1815, and the Kingdom of Naples effectively became Italian, once again. You can see, probably what each of these peoples and rulers really wanted was to own a villa in this delicious climate with its beautiful vistas.... Have a nice bath... A little wine... A place in the sun. We, here today, are the same. The important things, I feel, they have not changed in 3,000 years."

Ariadne looked back to the cityscape rising behind them. "Today, Naples may look fast and furious, but it is pathetic. It is so poor. So decaying. But out there..." Ariadne pointed out across the bay, past the tip of Sorrento. "Out there is my enchanted isle. That is where I live. Along with the rich and self-indulgent from all over Europe and the U.S.A. Out there... is Capri..." She said it with longing. "Here, one visits the ruins. Out there... On Capri... One lives free of cares. One lives with one's heart."

The steward thought it a strange, open, idealistic view for one, as he had been told, forced to live like a beautiful bird in a golden cage, kept secure from harm and human contact by a well-intentioned uncle. "Don Lucci was right..." the steward thought to himself. "This young woman lives with a freshness, a fire, in spite of either her privileges or her restrictions... Her radiance dominates the world around her... Her passion for life transcends any problems of her reality."

Fanciful music played softly in the background. The theme from *La Strada*.... mysterious, strange...

Ariadne slowly rose from the table with a gleam in her eye and a Felliniesque smile on her face. Then her eyes drifted light years away. Slowly, in movements ever so subtle and fully feminine, Ariadne started to dance... She danced by herself about the floor, dreamily, happily, oblivious to, no... quite aware of those surrounding her. Her smile left a trail of pleasure in its wake. All conversation, all other activity stopped. She danced, an expression of life at its fullest... of youth at its most potent... The steward stared transfixed at this captivating creature... in complete control of center stage.

The music played, and jested, and teased, and ended. The activities of other guests and waiters were still turned to stone. An abrupt silence followed the music. All eyes were on Ariadne, as if some explosion was expected. She just stood there, head high, looking out at the sea. A hush covered the dining patio. Yet, instead of an explosion, Primo came over to her side and hunkered down, tongue flailing in appreciation, followed by Sexto, who gave her a huge shlurp on the wrist. The audience in unison stood and cheered and laughed and applauded. "*Brava! Brava, Signorina!*" She turned, and threw her head back to the side, chin proud, freeing her hair with a swish, a haughty smile on her face, as if to reply, "I do that every day." Her admirers, after waving arms and hands and chins about in eloquent reciprocal communication, gradually resumed their eating and chatting.

"Come." She strolled over and grabbed his hand. "We go now." And off she pulled him in a whirl, scarf flowing, waiters bowing, patrons nodding, glasses being hoisted, dogs following at her heels, off not to the red Ferrari parked outside but down on to an old stone pier extending out into the protected harbour, languishing in the setting sunlight with numerous small sails and motor fishing boats.

Diva. Exit rear stage to sea.

At the end of the pier stood a large, sullen man in sunglasses. He had a head like a wildebeest, thick and brooding. The dogs ran ahead to him and haunched, as he held their necks at his sides. Ariadne swept down the pier, and pulled the steward into a sleek mahogany speedboat about 25 feet long, with three individual, cushioned seating cockpits, surrounding an inboard motor amidships.

"Scyllato, this is my uncle's friend. He will be with me tonight," she said haughtily as she turned the ignition to fire up some deep gutteral gurgles at the stern. The two dogs jumped into the boat without urging, and the large man bent to undue the stern line. The steward untied the bowline and climbed in beside Ariadne in the driver's cockpit. As he turned to receive a possible catch of the stern line from the large man, he fell back in a lurch as Ariadne gunned the engine into full forward, and left Scyllato standing dumbstuck on the pier. "*Asta domani*, Scyllato!" Ariadne called back over the roar. "*Grazie!* Have a night off, my uncle said. Don't worry! The puppies will protect me!" Then she started singing with a full voice... "*Ciao, Ciao, Bambino...*"

And off in the fresh night air roared the shining chrome and mahogany, a wide wake of luminescent sparkles trailing behind with her wispy scarf in the moonlight.

The trip across the large bay took about forty minutes. The stars were bright in the summer sky, the moon a plump new gibbous, silver gold and set low in the sky, silhouetting the mass appearing ever larger on the horizon. Stars seemed to also cover the landmass, but golden stars, and pink, and aquamarine, not silver as in the sky. As they drew closer, the lights of Capri dotted the landscape like a festival scene. Above, a scattering of lights played about a black mass below, at the waterline, concentrations and colors and shimmers danced along with the nightlife at the harbour areas. The tiny clusters of restaurants and discotheques and bars had the glow and blur of youth about them. Young men and women in stylish summerwear, whites, pastels, sailor shirts, flimsy scarves, bare midriffs and legs and thighs, sun glasses even in the evening. Bobbing and weaving slowly to the music of the stars, which drifted out to sea like a hypnotic mist, pulling any and all near into the whirl of its maelstrom. A combination of beats and rhythms played for attention as they drew near...

Chanson d'Amour danced along atop the atypical metre of *Mack the Knife*... The simple purity of *Edelweis* poked up past *Love Letters in the Sand*... Charles Trenet could be heard forsaking *Les Ponts du Paris* for *La Mer*...

"St.Tropez... Juan Les Pins... Cannes... Monaco... And now Capri..." the steward reflected longingly as the speedboat whooshed playfully into and out of the small twinkling harbour. "The Edens of the wee hours. After all, God created woman just for such places, didn't he?"

Ariadne did not stop at the harbours near the small town of Anacapri. She continued down the shore toward the tip of the island. The steward looked up in wonder at the villas dotting the hillside, glowing and happy and content in their luxurious dramatic backdrop.

Finally, Ariadne headed inland, throttled the craft to an abrupt coast, and slid amidst its throaty gurgle to a halt in the V of a private dual pier coming out from the shore. "We are here." She turned and smiled, suddenly relaxed and soft after the happy exhilaration of the past ride.

The steward sat quietly, wondering what to say next. Primo growled in his ear, having crept out of his cockpit and come forward. "I guess he wants me to get out..." he said, carefully and slowly.

The steward made the lines secure, and turned to help Ariadne, now standing on the bow like a white apparition of a figurehead in the moonlight, to jump to the pier. She landed in his arms, chest to chest. He could feel her fullness, taste her hair, inhale her freshness, touch the smallness of her waist. She looked up at him, and held his gaze for a moment. Then she gave him a smiling shoulder shrug that said... "Not here. Follow me."

Dogs in tow, she led him to the side of the cliff, to a personal elevator of sorts, a bucket style lift with a gate, suspended by a thick ropes up to a pulley about fifty feet above. "Now you must work," she laughed coyly. Pushing him into the bucket, along with the two dogs, and squeezing in as well, she handed him the major rope, and with a head nod and a big smile, indicated. "Use your arms, dummy. Pull this bucket up."

The counter balance of cement blocks came down past them at midpoint, but the steward was by then feeling the effort. Hand over hand he pulled down on the rope, slowly hoisting the bucket to its intended perch. At the top, he exhaled with pleasure, and looked at the sky and the view and the height and the dogs and finally at her eyes. "Fifth floor. Heaven on your left."

The gate swung open to spill the foursome onto a tiled patio, covered by a flowerladen trellis. Behind, a white stuccoed villa nestled itself into the hillside. No other homes seemed nearby. Only sheer, vertical rock and occasional scrub pines and flowering bushes. The music drifted up from the harbour, quite clearly now... *'I'm just a stranger in Paradise..."*

They started to dance. First apart, he following her lead. Then closer. Until touching. Slow, mellow dancing. Eyes locked. Then arms and fingers interlocking. Then chest to chest. Soft breath to breath. Then closer. Then closer, almost to a kiss. The steward jumped. The hound licked his hand.

"Ah, yes, my pet. You hunger terribly, I fear," Ariadne backed away, smiling. "You have had no dinner." She whisked off to the villa doorways, and swung a set of double doors open. "Hello, Secundo. Tercio, how are you! And Quinto, you beauty! And Quarto, my sweet. How are you all? Have you been good boys?" She bent to hug each one passionately, as four more monster dogs, some cross probably between Mastiff and Great Dane, crowded like puppies about her, lapping and panting and prancing with joy. Then they spied the steward.

He was backed up against the stone railing that enclosed the terrace, bent backward over the sea fifty feet below, struggling to keep his feet against the weight of 600 pounds of well-muscled dog flesh. Hot breath and growls covered his face. Eight fiery eyes glared into his.

"Heel. *Tutti. Pronto.*" Ariadne spoke softly yet clearly. The dogs immediately backed off and sat down, looking hungrily at their prize cornered on the railing. "He is friend. *Amici.*" The dogs lay down in unison, muzzles to the tile, still eyeing their adrenalin-saturated visitor.

"Let me give my beauties some food. They must be starving. Please relax. They will not harm you now." She laughed gleefully, presumably having enjoyed this experience of creature shock many times before.

"This is your cliff house..." the steward sighed to himself. "You have the con." The dogs eyed his every move vigilantly.

After a moment, he heard a single clap from inside the villa. The six dogs stood and trotted into the lighted room.

When Ariadne returned, she had shed her scarf, and fluffed her raven hair back fully onto her shoulders. She stopped a few yards from the steward, and stood looking across him.

She looked out into the night. Far out, to the opposite shoreline, to the dancing lights so faint in the distance. "My uncle is calling us. Excuse me."

The steward had heard no ring. Ariadne walked over to a ledge near the villa and picked up a telephone. "*Si...* We are here, Uncle. *Si.... Si.... Capito. Si*, I understand. *Si...* Thank you, Uncle. *Bona note.*" She hung up the receiver, and walked slowly over to the railing at the edge of the terrace.

"How did you know he was calling?" the steward asked, amazed at her clairvoyance.

"We have a form of personal communication. You are his friend. You may share our secret," she smiled. "See that shore, see Napoli's lights over there?"

He came over and joined her at the railing, offering an experienced head nod in reply.

"That one brightest light, high, on the left?"

Now a shoulder shrug, gives better inflection than the nod.

"That is his *Palatio del Sol.* That light is kept constant, day and night, overlooking his beloved Napoli. All know of it. All are reminded of my uncle."

A head nod better fit the moment.

"When that one light blinks... My blink. Three times... Each minute. Then he wants me. And I respond."

The steward felt now a Polish version of signing, a flat palm to his forehead, was in order. Ariadne laughed, and held his hands in hers.

She looked him straight in the eyes. Sizzle started its crescendo.

"Do you want me?" she said simply.

The steward was stunned. He had never seen such a voluptuous young woman before, vibrant, beautiful, standing in the moonlight, asking him such a dumb question. His face flushed. His loins ached. His heart thumped.

"I... You know I... Your uncle asked that I... " he stuttered.

Ariadne walked slowly apart from him, farther along down the stone railing, and stood there looking out to sea, hands together in mock prayer. The music below had shifted to opera. The purest virginal pleas of Renata Tebaldi filled a silence in the night air...

> *"Vissi d'arte, vissi d'amore,*
>
> *non feci mai male ad anima viva!..."*

She slowly unbuttoned her white dress and let it fall to the tiles below. Then, her bra. Then panties. Next she climbed up on the railing, and spread her arms wide against the moonlight. Time remembered could never have displayed itself in such an hourglass. Still looking out at the sea, she said softly as she took a step to the edge of the railing, "If you do not want me, I shall throw myself into the sea."

The steward started forward. "Oh, my god..."

Then she looked back over her shoulders, and grinned. "If you do want me... You must catch me first!" With that, she dove out into the blackness, a perfect swan soaring out into the moonlight, down, down into the black below, to vanish into an explosion of aquamarine stars.

"How do I get into these things..." the steward asked himself in wonder. "How do I get out of these things... " he found himself saying as he hurriedly pulled off his trousers and shirt and shoes. "Gerrroooonnniiiimmooooooohhh...." His scream pierced the night like a siren as he leapt out feet first into the blackness. Six hungry mouths yelped high on the hillside, as the music swelled in confirmation...

"*E lucevan le stelle...*"

She was a fantastic swimmer. She stroked the water without a splash, keeping at least thirty yards ahead of him, drawing him away from the landing and down the coastline, into the darkness of the sea that everywhere held a shimmering silver/aquamarine glow in the moonlight. The only sounds he could hear were his own splashing as he struggled breathlessly along after her, eyes set on his target, so near yet so far ahead. He was slowly gaining on her, or she was letting him gain. Wavelets of Keats splashed into his thoughts...

"What mad persuit? What struggle to escape?

What pipes and timbrels? What wild ecstacy?

Bold lover, never, never canst thou kiss,

Though winning near the goal – yet, do not grieve;

She cannot fade, though thou hast not thy bliss...

Forever wilt..."

She faded! Out of sight! "Oh, oh..." he thought to himself, senses awakened again. "Where did she go?" He swam up to where he had last seen her, approaching some rocks near the shore. "Did she get into trouble with the rocks?" he worried.

Looking about while treading water, he started to become concerned. She was nowhere in sight. It was now well over one minute since he had last seen her. She couldn't be under water that long. Air would give out. He looked about anxiously.

"Ariadne?" he called into the night. "Where are you?" he puffed. "Are you all right?"

No answer. He checked his bearings again, reckoning where he had thought she had last been. Then he took a deep breath, and dove down into the sea, out of the black of night and into a strange aura of moonlight mixed with minute marine life, giving off a radiant glow like an underwater milky way.

He broached and breathed deeply. "O.K., mermaid..." he gasped, "Where are you?" Now he was truly worried. "Ariadne!"

He took another deep breath, and dove once again. He headed down until his eyes spied a strange glow coming out of the rocky falls below him. It beamed out into the moonlit waters like a beacon, promising of *lux et veritas*. He swam nearer, lungs paining and ears popping as he pulled himself deeper. At last, he reached an opening in the rocks, through which a strange blue/white light blasted forth into the depths. Involuntarily he followed it back, pulled back by the surging water into a tunnel of brightness, back towards its source, lungs bursting, heart pounding. "This must be it..." his thoughts raced before him. "This is how you go. Into a tunnel of light. Never to find its end... Death... Where do you begin?... Life... Where do you end?..."

Suddenly appearing above him was an overwhelming brightness. He instinctively propelled himself upwards, toward it. "Now I see it... A realm where all is pure... Here I come... Here I come... Now I understand..."

He broke the surface of the water to find himself, gasping for breath, inside a radiant blue space filled with the sweetest air he had ever breathed. He coughed, trying to regain his senses. The moonlight bounced around on and within the jelly-like sea swells that half filled the cave. Flying in a blue cloud... Sunbathing in a blue light... The steward could not make it out...

"What took you so long?" a sensuous voice said softly. "Still hanging on to your old life out there?"

Ariadne sat demurely on the side of the seapool, combing her hair down her right shoulder in front. "You..." the steward tried to chide her, but only gagged on some salt water.

She reached down, and grabbed him by the hair to pull his head clear of the water. "*Vene*, Hornblower. Let's make music."

Amazing. Maybe not all the comforts of home were there in the grotto, but certainly it contained the important ones. Placed strategically about the roomy sea cave lay huge white fluffy towels, soft sun-lounging chair pads, an armful of spicy Moscato d'Asti Spumonti chilling in a net low in the pool, goblets, cigarettes, and a selection of rich cheeses and salamis and crackers, all protected in a large tin. Still another tin held chocolate Torrone Amor Pernicotti, and yet another, delicate Amaretti di Saronno. Ariadne had supplied her subterranean lair by first dropping wrapped parcels, weighted, on a line, then pulling them up in to the grotto. Where was he? In an underground world certainly not on the tourist maps. Her own private paradise. There was even a wind-up record player, playing from a stack of 33's and 45's. "*Come prima... Come prima... Banderlo...*"

Ariadne spoke after a while, as they lay there spent and content and in each other's arms. "You found my secret place..." she said, pensively. "I did not give it to you easily. You found it, deep within. You now share a secret part of me."

The steward exhaled slowly from his Chesterfield King. He looked above him at the smooth milky stones aglow with a surreal blue. She had not led him directly there. She had certainly enticed him to follow. But it had taken some Herculean effort, and in fact courage, on his part, to follow deeper into the unknown. Into another person's world... into a private place... this secret space for Ariadne. She had found it by accident while exploring the reaches of her island kingdom above and below the waterline. Even her uncle did not know of its existence. Certainly not Syllato. Its only entrance was by water. Air entered by cracks and minute tunneling up through the cliffside. Moonlight shimmered in by reflecting off the polished rock bottom beneath the pool, which went straight down into the floor of the sea. It was Ariadne's secret world. One into which few, if any, had ever been permitted before.

They lay together for hours, talking, dozing, sipping wine and food, feeding each other chocolates, laughing, touching... and loving... lost from the outside world in an iridescent sea.

With each swell of the sea about them... Time drifted from time... Thought from thought... Sensation became the only reality... Feeling became life itself.

The color of blue was different. The aura in the grotto no longer had the quality of moonlit aquamarine gemstone, but shifted into a more milky azure tone. The sea, too, shifted more restlessly in the pool, no longer raising and lowering in lazy swells. The steward could feel someone watching him, as he lay just at the surface of slumber, trying to register meaning from the dreamlike world about him.

"Oh, my god..." The steward sat upright. "My ship!"

Ariadne was already awake, sitting wrapped in her lush terry towel, and combing her long black hair. She smiled at him.

"Good morning, Horatio. You slept well, I trust."

"Ah...Ah...Good morning. Ariadne..." He looked at her and fell back into his trance. "Ariadne... Come here... "

She came to him, and they held each other closely, softly.

"I must go."

"I know."

"I... I... You are... the most... wonderful... " he whispered to her ear.

She pulled back and put her finger to his lips to silence him. "And you... will always be a part of me..." Then she got up, and let her towel fall to the floor. She was wearing a silver bathing suit. "It is seven thirty. You must go now."

"Seven thirty! Ahhgghh!" the steward moaned. "The ship sailed at seven! Aaaahhhggghh! I've let them...."

Ariadne again placed her fingers to his lips. "Your ship will pick you up... outside. It has been arranged." She pulled off his towel, letting him stand there naked before her. "Ah, yes. I will always remember you, dancing on top of the pilothouse," she said as she tied his red kerchief around his neck, "And... blowing your horn..." she added dreamingly, eyes affixed appropriately.

"And I... You... Hurling yourself off the terrace because of me..."

"When the stars were shining..." she said wistfully.

They hugged softly, smiling. Then Ariadne spoke sternly. "Now follow me. Closely, this time." And she dove straight down into the shifting pool.

The steward gulped a lungful of air and followed, down, down into the sobering chill of the sea, following the fluttering silver fish ahead of him, into the open waters. They broke the surface about twenty yards from the shore. Ariadne came close, kissed him as they treaded water, then pointed out to sea. "That way.... Swim that way... out to sea... until you can swim no more. Then wait. You will find your ship. The gods will be with you."

He had learned to trust this woman, even though he didn't fully understand why. He knew she would cause him no harm. "What about you?" he asked.

"I will return to my world. Do not be concerned for me. I am happy there. For as long as my uncle lives... a little longer, I pray... I will be there for him, as he is for me. And after?... I will do what I do now..." she laughed. "I will live!" And she paddled off in a powerful backstroke toward her enchanted isle, leaving the steward alone in the sea.

He watched her for as long as he could, then he turned and started swimming out to sea. He swam and swam, for what seemed like miles. He could see Capri in the distance, now far behind him. Around its end there steamed a ship. Coming his way. It was the Talabot.

Suddenly his feet touched something under him. Ground! He struggled against the waves, to gain a footing. He stood up, waist deep in the sea, standing, waiting, looking at the island behind, and the ship approaching.

A loud horn blast split the crisp air of the early morning. "WWWHHHOOOOO OOOOO OOOOOO..... WWWHH-HHOOOOO..... WWWHHHHOOOO....."

The ship slowed to near where he stood, and coasted. He could see Eiriksson on the bridge. They looked at each other, without a

278

wave, the captain hung over, leaning on the railing, and the steward, naked in the water to his waist, red kerchief still around his neck.

"Good morning, Theseus," the captain called down. "Enjoy your morning swim?"

"Refreshing, Sir. But I wouldn't recommend it to everyone," he hailed back.

"Don't expect me to get up this early again," Eiriksson spoke down as the ship slowed nearby. "That's your job."

"Yes, Sir," replied the bleary eyed steward. And he slid off into the sea and swam the twenty yards toward the waiting gangway, angling down the side of the ship.

—AT SEA—

"So?"

The steward and the captain sat on galley chairs, feet up on the stern railing, sheltered from the headway breeze by the after superstructure which housed the crew's quarters and the all important galley.

They sat drinking. An unfathomable collection of beer bottles, kept iced in a large barrel, sat at their side. They sat drinking, looking aft out over the wake fanning lazily out behind them like wispy tail feathers on the flat calm sea, a milky haze amidst the blue/green that splayed from right to left as far as the eye could see. They sat quietly, sharing a moment of peace, watching the early evening pulling down on the huge red ball in the western sky behind them.

"So... What, Sir?" The dusk air was warm and dry.

"How's the job been?" The sky was almost cloudless.

"Job?... You mean the experience." His thoughts fast flipped through the past weeks and days, a blur of images and emotions.

"So what have you learned so far...?" the captain said as he pitched an empty Tuborg over the stern, only to watch it bob around in the wake for a few moments and then fade out of sight, enfolding itself in the distant froth.

"I've learned the difference between flotsam and jetsam," the steward replied, also watching the vanishing brown spot. "But I still haven't figured which a beer bottle is."

Eiriksson struck a pensive look. "Depends on how you look at it... Belch." The steward reached down and handed a fresh Tuborg to Eiriksson without being asked.

"Either on the surface, or from below, in SCUBA gear?... Burp..." the steward pondered, trying to imagine the view from underneath the wake.

"What else have you learned?..." Eiriksson popped the cap and flicked it far out astern.

"How to lay out a mean smorgasbord in pretty quick time... " The evening dinner session had finished, and he was now taking a well-earned break.

"True. You're no match for Erda, though..." Eiriksson pulled out a yellow pack of Gauloises Caporal and lit one up with a well-struck chrome Zippo.

"She taught me everything I know about *gjeit ost*... But not yet everything <u>she</u> knows about it *gjeit*... yet... or whatever... Burp."

"Watch her closely...It will all be revealed, someday...Beeeeelllch." Eiriksson inhaled deeply and let a trail of smoke seep out from his mouth in the vacuum of the ship's way.

"I've learned wine doesn't travel... Some of those Lebanese and Italian wines we picked up... like that Coteaux de Ksara... or the Caruso Bianco... the ones that tasted like liquid gold, remember?.. There... They taste like bilgewater and vinegar out here..." He took a long pull from his Tuborg just to clear recall from his taste buds.

"Scotch travels. That's why the British conquered the globe, not the Druse..." The captain reversed his feet on the railing.

"Booze always tastes best in the homeland, doesn't it? Fresh... Alive... Fits in with everything else..." The steward flipped his feet in response.

"Alcohol becomes life... it adds the zest. " Eiriksson pondered as he looked through the brown glass at the flattening head inside. "How could my ancestors be so right? *Akvavit*, the water of life..."

"So what is sleep? An alcoholic stupor?" the steward sighted at the sunball over his bottle neck.

"Alcohol processing... It's simple body economics... The body needs the night shift to get the throughput to keep up with the input that makes the piss output." Eiriksson pulled hard on the Tuborg, holding it high in the warm air to document his theory.

The steward continued on the earlier question. "I learned other things too... A new port is like a new local wine... Fresh and exciting. Even the hellholes... Something unknown awakens the senses... There's always something new to see, something strange to taste... Food is never the same... Every port is an all new experience... gets all the glands and olfactors jumping... "

"And the gut. Burp."

"The locals are no dummies... They master the cultivation of all sorts of weird tubers and goobers and organ meats... for a simple reason... it's all they have... then they learn how to skin it and beat it and boil it, and how to cover up the bad taste with other masking flavors, and then they make a big fuss about how wonderful it all is to eat it..."

"Like tripe... Burp. Pass me another Tuborg."

"I've learned something else, cooking on this ship... We can only approximate the taste and character of some of these unbelievable local foods I've had over the past few weeks... We never match the freshness of the locals... never get the full bloom out of all the varied flavors... like they get locally... And I have learned why... "

"Why?"

"Because the locals keep the best seasonings for themselves... "

"Which?... Belch."

"The air and the hills and the sunlight and the smells of flowers and the sounds of their culture... These are the spices that make the foods, and the wine, so spectacular, on their indigenous tables... Burp."

"I'll stick to herring... Belch." Eiriksson flicked his cigarette butt far into the following air, watching it glow its way down to the wake and snuff out. "Less risk of the runs..."

The steward pondered the red orb that had begun to quench itself in the sea. "Anyway, that, I conclude, is why the local wines don't travel well with us..." He threw his empty Tuborg over and popped open another. "It's a different sunset here from back there. Changes the color of the wine. Even the beer."

"What else have you learned, Steward?..." Eiriksson said after a while.

"It's fascinating out there... More than I ever imagined."

"Why?... Red sunsets are here or on the other side of this old turnip the same way... "

"Naw... There's always something new... Regardless of traditions and religions and antiquities and all the baggage that's been dragged along and cherished as important possessions all the years... Each land, each city, each family has the wonder of living it all anew... some new set of circumstances... some new technology... new individuals... new pressures... You can live with the past... But you can't live the past, or in the past, only the present. Beelllllch."

"Seems to me your historical scenario of life is confused, was confused, and always will be confused... "

"But that is just gives it its spice! That's what makes it fun! Confusion!... A bit of knowledge, a bit of unknown... If we knew what to expect, all beer would taste rather flat, like this one..."

"Have another... Burp."

"Every time I cook one of these meals, with Erda... The recipe is the same, out of a book, the traditional fare from many ports of call... But it's me, though, that puts the extra twist of the pepper mill in it, the secret herb, the dash of Pernod... I'm today... It becomes my creation... even if just for a second or so..."

"Before it vanishes down Brububber's gut, then tomorrow hits the wake as his personal flotsam... Belch." Eiriksson pitched another empty over the stern, and dipped onward and deeper into the frosty continuum.

"You look at people like bugs, don't you..." the steward probed. "Dancing around, silly little creatures... stomping out their passions and parades..."

"Pretty colorful they are too..."

"But they're on!... They're flitting around in the light... They're having a good time... You... You're just sitting in judgment..."

"No... Now I just observe... Someone else can do the judging... if he's not just sitting around drinking beer like us... Anyway, I've had my day dancing around the light... I'm tired of the music. It's your turn, now. Hand me another beer, bug. Burp."

"So you observe... What have you learned, then, through your beer bottle microscope?..."

"First... There are no bad people... Only good people fucking everything up and setting bad examples... "

"That I understand..."

"Second, life is fun and games only after your belly is full and you smell a little of garlic and wine. Then you have a glow on... then life is rich... something new on the horizon, someone new to screw, something new to experience."

"To fun and games and garlic... Burp."

"Third, life is full of shit the rest of the time. Most bellies aren't full, and every day is the same old difficult routine, same old faces, same old sun and moon on the hill, same old fishshit... Routine and boring...."

"So enjoy it when your belly is full?... Right? Bellllllch."

"Fourth and last, the real shit comes in big waves... and when it comes... the big ones... all you can do its to stand there, and admire the grand power and design of it all, before you get buried in fishshit..."

"Here's to fishshit. Burp."

"To fishshit. May it not land on us for a while... You know, Steward... This old superanimal called man was designed with one serious flaw that has caused all his problems over the millennia. Buurrrrppp!"

"Too much fishshit?..."

"No. It's this constant craving, deep down in his soul... Wherever he goes, whatever he does, it is always with him... gnawing at him... diverting him from finer, grander acts... this godawful craving... for... "

"Enlightenment?... Burp. A shapely buttocks?..."

"For beer, Steward! *Helvete*... We're out of goddamn Tuborg..."

"Mark."

"12:03 and 27 seconds."

The steward looked at the angle reading on the sextant, and wrote down the figure. 78 degrees, 15 minutes, 22 seconds.

"Thanks, Bjarni," the steward spoke as he put down the pencil and resumed shooting the sun. "My last Timex went over the side a couple of years ago in the Atlantic, and I never bought another. Anyway, even the better watches used to rot out with the salt spray. I never had any watch in my three years with the fleet that lasted over 6 months."

Bjarni had quoted the time at the steward's mark from the ship's chronometer, a brass and glass-enclosed monster that hung on the bulkhead of the charthouse. He had checked the ship's time simultaneously with his own Oyster. "There's a 4 second difference. Ship's time is faster than mine. Pick any one you want. It's just another demonstration that your sacred concept of time is all relative. We're just a couple of blokes floating along, someplace."

"I'll stick with ship's time," the steward replied. "It's what I've been using all along."

"So that's why you're always late serving tea. Using ship's time, not the passenger's..." Bjarni gruffed.

"Better than sleep time, which you seem to go by."

"Not so, my meticulous *nautonnier*. I go by drink time. And right now it is nearing the critical pre-lunch drink hour." Bjarni was on the bridge for some odd reason, and not as usual in his bunk.

The steward swung the polarizing glass off the sight, and pointed the sextant again at the mischievous sun, now hiding behind a thick canvas of alto cumulus. "Rats. It's like lights on, lights off today."

"*Helvete*. Who gives a damn, anyway," Bjarni groused as he traced over the charts on the table. "We are here, or there, or somewhere just about here... I think. Your noon sighting won't matter at all."

"I know. But it's kind of fun. I've enjoyed keeping my plot all along so far, and why break the streak. The last sun line I actually got to intersect with our course. That's a major nautical accomplishment."

Bjarni laughed. "Ha! But look where it intersected... two hours behind! Living in the past. Even a Norwegian can do that."

"At least we have an idea where we've been, then," the steward chuckled. "Hell, Bjarni, you don't even know what day it is, let along where we're going!"

"It's a day like any other day at sea. Shit boring," Bjarni replied. "I don't give a *fi faen* where we go, or where we've been. I just look forward to my noon ration. That is what keeps me going. Someplace."

"Yeah. Back to your bunk. You certainly have the fix on it."

The steward actually had gained much respect for Bjarni's nautical skills. As the First Mate, he was second in command. Yet seldom did he ever exercise such command authority, as Eiriksson constantly upstaged everyone on board with his booming personality, drunk or sober. Bjarni was content to plot courses, approximately, to guide the ship into and out of harbours when required, to dock and anchor, and to drink and eat.

Actually, Bjarni's main duties were supervising the deck activities, keeping the ship painted and relatively clean when at sea, and offloading and loading cargo when in port. His motley crew of six able bodied seamen, ages and experience ranging from 18 to 60, handled all the winch and boom loading, and policed the local stevedores when they came on board to assist in assembling cargo into the hoist nets. Bjarni spoke English fluently, even without any perceptible accent, as did most Norwegians since their first grade in school. He had other invaluable linguistic skills as well, such as being able to speak about ten other languages in bits and pieces, which he had picked up through the years in dealing with the local harbour officials and stevedores. He could argue, and barter, and bitch with the best of them.

The steward fiddled with some numbers on paper for a moment, matched up the settings in the calculation book, and finally figured the ship's position from his sightings. "18 degrees, 25 minutes, 34 seconds North latitude. Maybe..." Then he transferred these numbers to the scale on the chart, coming to rest near a pencil line heading west to east across the expanse of ocean. "See? I'm only two hundred miles south this time. Should have used your time, not the ship's."

"I know exactly where we are, according to drink time," Bjarni grunted, and continued to plot his own numbers with the calipers. "But Loran puts us here. In the South China Sea. Take any bets on who is correct?"

"Yep. Neither of us."

Mr. and Mrs. Potter-Smythe, Anthony and Ducky to their friends, stood against the bridge wing railing, taking in some of the headwind as if on some highland heath, breathing vigorously and deeply. They had just completed their daily late morning routine, which was to stride around the deck twenty times in a brisk pace, arms swinging like the Cold Stream Guards on parade, corners sharp, even counting cadence, as they walked off the food and drink of the day before. Tony even carried a small bamboo stick, slapping his thigh on every fourth step, with Ducky in lockstep two paces behind. Every day, rain or shine, in cold or heat, they made their brisk hike, husband leading and faithful wife obediently in his wake, but equally determined. The deck was no more than thirty yards long and ten wide, forcing a rather rapid and annoying repeat on all the other passengers trying to sleep or read in couchant deliria on their deck chairs. As the cruise went on, with each circuit some passengers even took to whistling softly a mock version of the *Colonel Bogey March*.

"Steward?" Anthony Potter-Smythe called over.

The steward put down his books and pencil and came out on the bridge wing. "Yes, Mr. P.S.? What can I do for you?"

The lanky university ex-professor kept breathing deeply, face into the wind, as he spoke. "I say... What were you doing... puff, puff... in there?"

"Shooting a sun sight, Sir."

"Obviously, Steward. But why you? You are only the steward, and a very fine one I might add. But determining our whereabouts certainly is not your job too, I trust."

The steward was somewhat taken aback by the simple question, as if he had been caught doing something wrong by a schoolmaster. He looked at the tall man in khaki shorts and knee socks, suede shoes, sweater over his shoulders even in the heat of the day, with the sleeves tied across his chest. Potter-Smythe was seriously British, very proud of it, mid-sixties, and ruddy-cheeked from his routine of fresh air walks and from his cultivated habit of accurately timed boozing. He presented to his public a fire ax of a nose that sheltered a fine moustache matching reddish gray hair, and huge sails of ears, all the better to overhear one with, my dear.

The steward purged his quickening feelings of retaliation and replied courteously, "Ah, I was in the Navy for three years, Mr. Potter-Smythe. It's been a hobby of mine to continue plotting the Talabot's progress, right from when I joined the ship. It's kind of fun, to see where we've been and where we are going."

Potter-Smythe hrumphed. He turned his fire ax out of the wind and toward the steward, still breathing deeply with nostrils flaring. "My dear boy. We are privileged to have thousands of years of history to tell us where we've been, and we still don't know where we are going. And from your comments to the First Mate in there, it appears you have not learned well your skills in school, if you are still some hundred miles off the intended course."

Potter-Smythe enjoyed having a dig at everyone. His methodology was not new, nor limited to the steward. Actually, it was usually well meant, in hopes of sparking lively conversation, but his demeanor came across more as bating and pedantic, as in anticipation of rigorously debating a point.

"Ah, well, Mr. P.S.," said the steward, drawn in. "At sea, it is not critical exactly where one is, unless, maybe, when one is sending an S.O.S. And even then, the seas can be so capricious that a ship might not be anywhere near that exact point when help finally arrived."

"So you advocate being lost at sea, as are we, even now, Steward? Dear me, we are in good hands, Ducky."

"Oh, not at all, Sir," the steward hiked up his shorts for the next round. "The Talabot is by no means lost. We know pretty closely where we are, and which direction we are going. And when we get closer to the next port, or to a critical passage, there are many more land and radio sightings available than out here in the open sea, things like buoys and beacons, which allow us to pin-point our position and steer our course with much more accuracy."

"I recall what Cheshire Cat said to Alice, my boy. 'If you don't know where you're going, any which way will do nicely.' One trusts you do not espouse this theory onboard Talabot?"

Mrs. Potter-Smythe, "call me Ducky, Love", finally came over from her vigorous breathing on the rail and chipped in, puffing and panting and a bit heady from hyper-oxygenating after her walk around her limited metallic heath. "Don't mind the schoolmaster here, Steward," Ducky gasped. "He just likes to badger his pupils. That's why they retired him last year."

"Thank you, Mrs. P.S.," the steward smiled. "I'm sure he was an excellent taskmaster." Visions of a large ruler held threateningly aloft filled his mind.

Potter-Smythe did not let up for a moment, once he felt he had a student stumbling on facts and fear. "How is it, my boy, that you can shoot Noon, and still be over three minutes late in doing so. Rather untimely, what? No wonder you are not able to plot our course with any modicum of accuracy."

"Oh, that," the steward replied, rummaging for the right science knowledge deep down in his mental storage locker. "That is because we shoot Local Apparent Noon, not Noon as you know it from your watch. The sun reaches it's highest point in the sky at apparent noon, which varies from 12 Noon by a few minutes, depending where we are in the time zone, and which season it is, and the fact that we are spinning on an axis, and that we are moving across the surface of the earth, and things like that. It's all very complicated, but also very simple."

"Simple. Quite. That's why the great navigators of yesterday, such as John Cabot and Drake and St. Brendan the Navigator, found all sorts of new worlds, while the Talabot can't even tell what time it is. I dare say, they knew where they were going, precisely. Like we British today. Not like these Norwegians."

"Sorry, Mr. P.S., but the old navigators had much less accuracy than we have today. The ones that survived to tell about their travels had the most valuable nautical tool of all -- luck. Actually, nature provided them a few positives, though. First, they sailed with the wind, always downwind, and barring natural calamities, it carried them to strange new lands. What is amazing is that nature even carried them back, but by a different route, ahead of winds from the opposite direction. The old world is pretty accommodating, when you stop and think of it. You can always find a big wind to take you someplace."

"Big wind. Ha!" Bjarni's voice could be heard in the charthouse.

"Accommodating? They sank by the scores, those early explorers."

"Well, it was all new water to them, Sir. Hidden rocks, shoals, weather patterns. Today, however, we have pretty good knowledge of what lies ahead, from our charts and radio reports," the steward countered. "But you are right, Sir. One must know where one is, or such knowledge is meaningless."

"Maybe that is their legacy to you, Steward." The Great Fire Ax rose smugly, while he dramatically unfurled and read from a mock scroll. "Here, on the Lord's day of 8 September, 1368, for the glory of God and the King whatshisname, our good shippe hit the bloody rocks and sank, all hands lost. Any future souls foolish enough to be mariners, set sail to go another way."

"Some of the first Norsemen and Portuguese had a mean time of it, obviously. I admire their courage, or foolhardiness, to sail out into the unknown."

"Get your facts correct, lad. It was the British who invented Mean Time," Potter-Smythe interrupted. "Greenwich Mean Time. Without it, all your Vikings and Portuguese and Spaniards would still be sailing about in circles, eating herring and codfish."

"Oh, Tony. Don't be so imperious," Ducky added, patting his arm. "The Portugee did a fine job catching fish without clocks. So did the Norwegians. They just happen to be a little late, much of the time."

Bjarni, hearing the exchange, yelled out from the charthouse. "The British invented Mean time, all right. Meaning it was time for civilized Englishmen to get mean and kick the butts of all your pathetic little WOGS around the globe. That's why you British were so successful as swagger stick imperialists. You invented Mean time." He joined the threesome on the outer bridge.

"I say... Greenwich Mean Time set the civilized standard for a very confused and uncivilized world."

"It certainly did," Bjarni came in with eyes sparkling, looking for a scrap. "Stomp on the little people only when it's their time, not before, not after. 'Oh, dear me, it's time to thrash the Hindi. Ah, four o'clock, now bash the Pakistani. Five, flail the Burmese. Mustn't keep the WOGs waiting, what?' Time for their bashing. They do enjoy it so. Mean time maintains a world order, keeps the masses regulated, in their place, what?"

"At least we were civilized enough to know when to have cocktails and when to have tea. You barbaric Norsemen never got out of the cocktails." Potter-Smythe chuckled in return, chin held high.

"Ah, ha! But then all the little Orientals started making all those cheap watches, and sold them to the colonies, and then your stupid empire exploded. You British think you invented civilized time... Tea time! But you were blinded by it... Tea time became your adversary! All your faithful WOGs knew their bashing was soon due, so they would hide and only come out when it was tea time. God knows, the Brits would never interrupt tea to administer a good bashing to anyone. Ha! Nobody to work your damn slave jobs any more. And now all your WOGs are revolting. Ha! The imperial sun is setting at last. Serves you right!"

"Ah, yes...revolting... just like the Norwegians. All you bloody Vikings. You'd stop drinking only to rape our women!" Mr. P.S. retorted, as he took out a pipe, tamped the cold bowl, and tried to light it with a match in the headwind.

"What do you mean, stop drinking! We wouldn't stop drinking, for anything or anyone! Particularly when we're raping some dumpy Brit!"

"Now, Gentlemen. Behave yourselves," a dumpy Ducky chimed in. "Tony, dearest, the officer is getting somewhat touchy..."

"At least we didn't go pillaging around with a stupid pipe in our mouths, like you idiotic British!" Bjarni was a bulldog in moments like this. "We Vikings'd have a man-size drink in our hand!" With that, he stomped off the bridge wing and clambered down a ladder to the deck below, in search of a drink.

"I dare say, this is becoming more than a friendly joust, Tony dearest," Mrs. Ducky quickly injected.

"I think we all can agree on one interpretation of the present time, don't you, Sir?" the steward asked as he squinted up at the sun, now reappearing from behind a cloud.

Anthony Potter-Smythe struggled in vain to light his pipe. Undaunted, after numerous hrumphs and tamps and sulfurous puffs, he put his matches away, and held the pipe firmly in his teeth, chin up, squinting as well up along the steward's line of vision. "The sun is well past the yardarm, wouldn't you say so, Steward? Or have you still mistaken its position?"

"There's absolutely no mistaking its position. It's past the yardarm." The steward took out a matchbook of his own, cupped it in his hands and struck one match against its cover. It flared forth and held, and he offered the sheltered flame to Potter-Smythe, who leaned over to place his pipe under it, and puffed successfully. "Drinks are the order of the hour, Mr. Potter-Smythe. The usual?"

"Yes, my boy. Pink gin for the Mrs. and me, if you please," he phrumphed through his pipe. "After all, we do have a long way to go yet, don't we? Just to get back on course."

"Oh, Steward..."

"Hi, Mrs. Brububber. How goes everything today?"

"Have you seen my husband recently?"

"No, Ma'am. Not since after breakfast."

"Could he be back with the Chief Engineer again?"

"No, Mrs. B. I just passed the Chief in the galley."

"What about on the bridge?"

"Don't think so, Ma'am."

"Please try to find him for me, Steward. Will you tell him I'm looking for him?"

"Certainly, Ma'am."

"Tell him I'm in our cabin, waiting for him?"

"Yes, Ma'am."

"How long now until lunch, Steward?"

"About an hour, Mrs. B. Can I get you anything?"

"Yes, actually. Will you bring a plate of fresh fruit to my cabin, please? With some pomegranates, if possible. And a split of champagne. And also a set of fresh sheets for our bunks. It's been rather hot in the morning hours, recently."

"Certainly, right away. Celebrating something, Mrs. B?"

"You might say that, yes, Steward. We're celebrating..."

"Oh, Mrs. Brububber... You left your book here, on the deck chair..."

"Oh, thank you, Steward..."

"Strange title... *Kama Sutra*. What's it about?"

"Umm, nothing special. Just a silly little romance..."

"Steward!"

"What? Who's there?"

"It's me. Bull Brububber. Be quiet and come on over here..."

"Mr. B? What are you doing in the lifeboat? Planning to leave the ship?"

"Shhh, kid. Damn it, I'm hiding out, no thanks to you..."

"Me? What did I do?"

"You and your goddamn Tetracaine. It's killing me..."

"Sir? Worked pretty well, didn't it?"

"Cripes. That stuff is lethal! No one should use it the way you said."

"Sir?"

"It numbs your dick! But just enough. Just enough to take the edge off, but keep you interested. It's fantastic."

"Great, Mr. B. So what's the problem? Still no satisfaction?"

"Belle's getting so frigging satisfied she won't leave me alone. I pass out on her at night, but boy she's there in the morning, wide eyed and grinning like a hooker, when I wake up. Geeeesus, she's turned on. After all these years, I find I'm married to a nympho. I didn't know you could do it so many ways..."

"I just left her, Sir. Going back to your cabin... She asked me to find you and..."

"Shit! Don't tell her I'm here!"

"Sir?"

"Damn, kid. I've got to get some rest. She's taking everything out of me. I feel like a goddamn prune."

"Gee, Mr. Brububber. Sorry. I had no idea..."

"Just flip that canvass over the top again, kid, and amscray. I'm hiding out here until lunch when I can get blasted with the number one Viking. Talk about drinking to escape..."

"Right, Mr. B. Anything you need in there?"

"Rest, kid. I need a week's rest..."

"Steward?"

"Mrs. Potter-Smythe?"

"I saw what you did, Steward."

"Did? What did I do, Ma'am?"

"I caught you in the act, Steward. Shame on you."

"Ma'am? What did I do?"

"An irresponsible act. Unacceptable behavior, Steward."

"I'd correct it if I knew what I did, Ma'am."

"I have a good mind to report you to the captain."

"Maybe then I'd know what I did, Ma'am."

"I saw you reach up and drop that beer bottle into the lifeboat, Steward. That's what you did. It's not a waste receptacle, Steward. It's not there to make your job easier. That lifeboat is meant for the passengers and crew. It is not to be misused but is to be kept ready in case of any emergency. You, of all people, should know better, Steward. I'm surprised at you."

"Yes, Mrs. Potter-Smythe. I know that full well. Rest assured I will collect any empty beer bottles from the lifeboat right away."

"Steward!"

"Mrs. O? What's up?"

"Emergency, Steward. You must come with me! Quickly. And quietly..."

"What's happened, Mrs. O'Rouark? What's the trouble?"

"My husband. He's..."

"What? Is he ill? What's happened!"

"He's..."

"What? Tell me so I can help!"

"My husband... Promise you will not tell any of the passengers. Not a word of this to anyone. Not a word! Promise!"

"I promise, Mrs. O. Now what's the matter?"

"My husband is... stuck."

"Stuck? Where?"

"In our cabin..."

"How stuck?"

"He's... stuck in the porthole."

"How? You can barely get your head out the porthole."

"That's what's stuck. His head."

"How?"

"I caught him looking at Pammy Sue Lovelake out the porthole."

"How? Where the devil was she? Hanging over the railing on a rope?"

"She... had just finished a swim. She was standing along the rail on the main deck, right above our cabin... dressed only in her shorty bathrobe. My husband... ah... has this thing for shorty bathrobes."

"Let's go try to pull him out, Mrs. O. If we can't budge him, we'll get some butter from the galley to grease his ears. I'm sure the Chief Engineer can rig up a few psi of vacuum through the ventilation ducts. That'll pop him out for sure."

"Steward?"

"Mrs. Boost?"

"Is the sun so intense in these latitudes? It appears that some of the other passengers getting badly sunburned."

"Possibly so. Sun's pretty direct. Why, Ma'am?"

"Mr. O'Rouark is wearing strange bandages on his ears."

"Steward?"

"Mr. Lovelake?"

"Y'all seen mah wahf's shorty robe?"

"Robe, Sir?"

"Y'all know the one. It's thet little ole silky shorty one she weahs to 'n from the pool all the tahm?"

"Yes, I know the robe, Mr. L. No, I haven't seen it today."

"Ah cain't figger it, son. She had thet robe when she went to the pool raght aftah lunch. Ah seen her go up thayh mahself..."

"Maybe our head wind blew it over the side, Sir, or down on to another deck."

"There she was, stuck in the pool, naked as a jay bird for more'n four hahwrs. Finally, after waitin' and waitin' for someone to come by and bring her another, she got thet kid Ole to hep her out. He gave her his T-shirt to scamper on home in."

"Ole's a very obliging crewmember, Sir."

"Now she looks lahk a boiled lobster, boy. Too much sun."

"I'll take a look for the robe, Sir. I have an idea where it may have landed."

"Got anything for sunburn, boy? She turned a bit crispy today."

"Just the thing, Mr. L. Special Viking cure. I'll bring some right up to your cabin."

"What's thet, boy? *Akvavit?* Herring oil? Caviar eggs?"

"Tetracaine."

"Steward?"

"Mr. Boost?"

"This ship is getting pretty darn fashionable, son."

"Sir?"

"You're gonna be upsetting those trends back on those beaches in Cannes and St. Tropez."

"What do you mean, Sir?"

"The fashion up there is going topless. On board the Talabot, they go bottomless."

"Sir?"

"Didn't you see Pammy Sue runnin' by in that wet T-shirt? Whewwwweeee!"

"How's that kink in your neck doing, Mr. B? Any better?"

"Funny you ask. It shifted to the other side today."

"Mr. O?"

"What?"

"You O.K.?"

"Fine. I'm fine."

"What are you doing... up there?"

"Just sitting, kid. Can't a guy just sit?"

"In the cargo bucket? Sure. But it's dangerous up there."

"Dangerous? Life is dangerous. Women are dangerous. This bucket isn't dangerous. It's dirty and safe."

"Like a tree house?"

"Exactly. My fucking tree house... Like when we were kids. The good old days..."

"Kids didn't drink martinis in the tree house."

"Grown-ups do."

"Why did you climb up there, Sir? Any particular reason?"

"Because it's here, kid. K-2 of the sea..."

"Mind if a younger grown-up joins you up there?"

"Suit yourself. There's room for two. Martinis for only one though..." He poured himself another measure of chilled, clear liquid from a silvered shaker he had hidden inside his shirt, being careful not to splash out the olive resting at the bottom of his stemmed glass.

"Whew. Not easy getting out here..." the steward panted after climbing twenty feet up the cargo mast and swinging hand over hand along the guide wire to the end of the boom, then dropping four feet into the two large, hinged metal jaws that formed a bulk cargo bucket. After gaining a firm seat, he took out a softpack of Players, offered one to his bucket host, and lit up.

"Piece of cake, kid. For an old jock like me."

"You played sports?" the steward asked as he exhaled through his nostrils in an attempt to relax. "What ones?"

"Played them all, kid. Football, basketball, baseball, handball... I was the fuckin' King of Washington High... Busted heads lay in my wake..."

The steward looked at the serious stare on a man pushing past 60, sitting on the edge of the bucket high above the after cargo deck. He never turned but continued to stare out to sea, even while the steward made his careful climb.

"And now they don't, right?"

Michael P. -call me Paddy- O'Rouark finally turned and looked at the steward. A flare of anger slowly subsided to a blush of frustration, and his eyes shifted back to the distant horizon.

"I was the king, kid... All City football and baseball. I had offers from three colleges and from two farm teams. I was on top of the goddamn world..."

"Seems like we are right now, Sir," the steward said, looking over the vast realm below them, with the frothy wake waters rushing by under them on both sides.

"And now I'm nothin'... I'm fucking running away..."

"Not as I see it, Sir. You and me and maybe Ole are the only three on board who could make it way up here. And you showed the way."

"I'm over the fuckin' hill, kid. You know it and I know it. And you know what else?... I <u>hate</u> it... I fucking hate it..."

"You, Mr. O? Come on... You're not over the hill. You just climbed up here, didn't you? That's no way over the hill."

"I go to the snip each year to get the lumps and spots off my damn skin. I got half a head of hair. I'm thirty pounds overweight. I can't see a fucking thing two feet away without my fucking glasses. The veins in my legs look like blue spaghetti. I got a double hernia. And worst of all, I got dimples in my knees! Can you believe it, kid? The king of the ball field has fucking dimples in his knees!"

"Sir..."

"Where did it all go?.. I'm turning into a piece of shit. Eiriksson's right. We're all fishshit in the end..."

"You're no way near the end, Mr. O'Rouark."

"Ahhh... You don't get it, kid. I'm the past generation. I'm no longer wanted. Nobody gives a fuck about me now. I'm a has-been... Out with the trash bucket..."

"At 55? I don't except that, Sir."

"I'm 62, kid. Fucking 62. An old man. An old fuck. Out to pasture... And I don't even deserve that..."

The steward looked hard at the miserable aging jock next to him. "Not so, Mr. O. You're just a guy like lots of guys, who had a great time in one phase in your life... in more than one phase... And now they're over and it's time for another phase now."

"Yeah. The fuckin' coffin..."

"You were a big man in high school. A great time. A real peak. Big accomplishments. All City. That time I understand. Then from what I hear you were also a big man in your business. Made lots of money. Influential in your town, Rotary Club, Knights of Columbus... Respect from your peers..."

"As if they give a fuck about me now..."

"So maybe that phase is done now too. Now it's another phase coming, like leaving one port and heading to another one. The beauty of it is you have lots to look forward to, Sir. New things to do, people to meet, places to see, lots to accomplish. Just different from the last port."

"I don't get it, kid. Maybe... Maybe that's it. But it's something else. Something else's driving me out of my mind..."

"What, Sir?"

"I'm over the hill, kid. I don't have it anymore. I can't perform like I used to. I still dream... but I don't have the balls anymore. I can't make it across the goal line like I used to..."

The steward just watched and let him talk it out.

"And you know what really busts me? What really pisses me off? I see young bucks like you. Full of life. Tons of energy and ready for anything. Fucking your ears off in every port and probably here at sea as well... And all I can do is envy you... Envy you! I used to run right through guys like you. And now? I'm an old fuck, just sitting here drinking martinis and dreaming of my youth, and watching you get all the ass. Every time I see all those young girls on the beach... I can't even think straight! Or even Pammy Sue... Not bad at all for late forties... And you know what? All I can do is fantasize. It's makin' me fucking crazy..."

"I..."

He swilled down the remainder in his glass, and slowly, deliberately, poured another measured quantity into his glass.

"Kid, you can make it with every chick you meet. Me, I've been married to the same old lady for twenty-eight years now. She's not a bad egg... but her damn menopause is driving me lunie. Now she thinks she can make up for all those years she wouldn't let me get anywhere near under the sheets with her. 'I'm too busy. Too tired.' Oh, no!.. Now, she sees her faucet drying up and she's out to prove to somebody she can still do it. A couple a punches for the road... One for the memory..."

"At least you have your memories, Mr. O..."

"I got more than memories, kid. I got nightmares!"

"Sir?"

"It's all I think about, all I dream about. Like the night I was banging Bunny Bunzone under the bridge. Or Mona Creamer in the back seat of my old man's DeSoto. Or Megan Moist in the counselor's tent at camp, or Gina de Turbo in the locker room after the game. I can remember all of them, kid. Easily a hundred. Every one of 'em I can still see, the size of their tits, the moles on their asses, everything, every detail, even their smells. I remember everything. But funny thing... You know who never is in my dreams? My wife! Never! And so what? Sebastian just lies there like a dead fish..."

"Sebastian?"

"My dick, kid. Doesn't every guy have a nickname for his dick? I'm about ready to have him cut off. It's like he's made of wood anymore. He's no longer interested. He's probably dead already, and me soon to follow..."

"I'm no shrink, but it seems you just need to redirect all your passion away from frustrations and fantasies back into action, Mr. O... From what I've read, age certainly doesn't bag a man's pecker at 62..."

"That's wishful bullshit, written by doctors who are only 40, kid. Wait until their wives are over 55. Then see if they can get it up anymore..."

"Mr. O, your wife is still a very attractive woman. She has pride in her looks, and she dresses beautifully..."

"I'll grant you that, kid. She's O.K. compared to most women her age. It's just her goddamn attitude that turns me off..."

"Attitude?"

O'Rouark took a sizable sip of his silver bullet. He made a strained look for an answer to his problems somewhere near the olive lying at the bottom.

"She's been into this damn Ayn Rand mumbo-jumbo for the last few years. Now thinks she's better than everyone else. Even me. Thinks she deserves Rhett Butler or King Kong or Napoleon, someone with brass balls. But not me. I'm a has-been in her eyes. She seems to forget she was working in a fucking diner when I first met her..."

"Mr. O... Speaking of that, it's almost dinner time. And it's getting dark. Climbing down from here is going to be much more difficult. How about it? Ready to wash up for dinner?"

"Leave me alone, kid. This is my fucking treehouse and I'm staying in it. You go back and push booze to those other assholes. I've got mine here..." He poured another level of martini out of the shaker, this time spilling some on his crotch.

"Mr. O... Come on down. It's time to join the others."

"Fuck the others. They'll just laugh at me. Me and my fucking bandaged ears..."

"No they won't. They heard you scraped them trying to retrieve a shorty robe of Mrs. Lovelake that was caught down the boiler room air duct."

"Who told them that?"

"Me."

"I'll just sit here and drink my martinis and howl at the moon. HOOOOOOOOOOOOWWWWWWWWWLLLLLLLLLLL... See the fucking moon, kid? It's laughing at me too... HOOOOOO OWWWWWWWWWWLLLLLLLLLLLL..."

"Mr. O... What's with the nightgowns, Sir?...

"Ha! That? That? That's nothin', kid.... Don't you see? That's my ploy! That's how I make her think I'm transhormonal or something, that I don't have any interest in women anymore. Maybe make her think I've gone over to the other side. That's how I get out of any commitment, kid. All she wants is a goddamn Ayn Rand hero now... A King Kong! Like I was when I was eighteen! She can't accept me as I am... and old fuck with no balls anymore. So I took to the kimono trail, kid. One night I was so crazy I put on her nightgown. And *voila!* No more threats under the sheets. No more having to perform, and then wanting to kill myself when I can't get it up..."

"Mr. O'Rouark, I think there's real hope for you, Sir. Seriously. I think your problem is only temporary. You can solve it. Easily. It's in your hands..."

"Yeah, I know. I'm thinking of diving over the side of this tub and never looking back. I can swim it to that island back there... So long, Louise... You should have married some jerk named John Gault... He's all you ever talk about anymore..."

"Mr. O, I had a friend once with this same kind of problem. He was only about 50 himself, but he couldn't, or didn't want to, perform anymore with his wife. The zip was out of their marriage. She no longer turned him on. His sex life was a disaster. He had wild fantasies about the escapades in his past youth... And he couldn't get it up any more."

"Yeah, so?"

"He found a way out of his problem, Sir. Two weeks after taking the cure, he stood straight and proud as a marine. His life was his own again."

"How, kid. How? A shrink? Herbal salves? Monkey glands? Rhinoceros horn? Weekly visit to a whorehouse? Hiring an *au pair?*"

"Nothing so radical, Sir."

"What, then?"

"He gave up martinis."

Silence.

More silence.

"Mr. O?"

More silence.

"You wait here while I climb down, Mr. O... I'll fire up the winch and lower you down in the bucket..."

—HONG KONG—

"Victoria..."

"How old is she, Captain?" the steward asked.

"Oh, about one hundred and eighteen..."

"What? Your daughter?..."

"Oh, Viki's sixteen... I think. I thought you meant the island."

There were lights now appearing on the horizon. Not lights as one would normally see them, but golden flares and reflections in the afternoon sun, shimmering and dancing like a festival dragon far off to the north, calling forth into the open sea.

The captain had joined the steward on the bridge as the Talabot drew nearer to Hong Kong harbour. He was well into his afternoon cups, and held a Chivas and ice in a large coffee mug. He seemed distant, more melancholy than usual.

"Your daughters miss you, I would guess," the steward said as he tried to read the far off look on Eiriksson's face.

"*Faen*. They are teenagers. Viki and Inge... My beauties."

The steward recalled the picture on the captain's desk, of two teenage girls and a handsome woman.

"They hardly know me any more..." Eiriksson continued. "They are all grown up. They have their own lives now, with school and the skiing and all the hyperhormonal boys. They even drive a car now. Watch out, Norway."

"Victoria is a knock-out. And little Inge... Their picture..."

"Ah, my beauties... Yes. Like their mother..."

The steward let the subject rest for a moment, as he sensed the pain of distance smoldering in the captain.

"About an hour before we reach Big Wave Bay and Cape Collison, Captain. 345 still looks good," the steward finally said, to break the awkward silence and resume conversation.

"Watch out for all the damn junks off Shek O point, Steward. It can be like Piccadilly Circus when the fishing fleet comes home. And they are coming home tonight." Eiriksson spoke slowly as he surveyed the darkening horizon to the east.

The weather had been perfect sailing up from Manila. Soft, rolling seas and clear sky with high cirrus for most of the past two days. But as the afternoon crept on, the sky in the southeast changed hazy, to a flat light gray. Then to dull gray. Then to slate gray. Now, as the sun angled lower in the west, the seas and the sky behind them took on an ominous aura. "Why do you say that, Sir? Radio reports don't indicate any weather systems near by," the steward asked, looking east as well. "We should reach Hong Kong with fairly smooth sailing."

"See the sky, Steward?" The captain spoke calculatingly after taking a sip of his scotch.

"Yes, Sir."

"Learn to read the sky, Steward. It will tell you many things."

"I thought I was getting pretty good at it..."

"Shit. You are merely knowledgeable in obvious facts and stars and calculation books and clouds... " He took another sip. "The Vikings used to say that the sky is the face of God, Steward. Learn to read it closely. Its countenance tells of things to come."

"I think I..."

"See that sky over there?" He pointed to the eastern horizon. "It is dull. No luster. No definition. No cloud formations to be seen. All is flat and gray."

"Mystery weather out there, I suppose."

"No mystery about it. The sky can tell us what is in the depths of that gray. You only have to learn to see past it, and into it."

The steward had seen Eiriksson well blitzed before, but this was not his typical sarcasm. He was slurring his words a bit, but otherwise was quite lucid.

"There could be a pressure drop or a warm front behind that gray haze, Sir, but I don't see any nimbus or thermals or stratifications building anywhere..."

"There's going to be a storm, Steward. In about four hours. A severe storm."

"We'll be on the hook two hours before then, I hope, Sir. Barring no junk traffic jams." The steward looked back at the approaching lights, still shimmering and glaring out to sea from the North. "I hear Hong Kong harbour provides a pretty sheltered anchorage."

"Better in there than out here..." Eiriksson grunted.

"How can you tell... about the storm?"

"Look past the face, Steward. Look into the eyes, into the heart of things..." he said after a pause. "Now the sky is flat. You can see at best fifteen, eighteen miles, into that haze. Even with the setting sunlight on it. But soon that haze will go through a metamorphosis right before your eyes, as the humidity increases to saturation levels. Then you will be able to see right through it, for thirty miles, even forty if you go up in the nest... see into the darkness, with great detail, as if through a huge lens. You can see deep into the great beyond, like never before."

"And?..."

"That means that severe weather is in the happening. And exactly then and there, when you're smugly content with all that new found clarity, unexpected violence erupts, right out of what you felt was a finally a calming change."

"Why, out of clearing?..."

"It is the moisture in the air... Builds until it hits its critical new dew point, and goes wild dumping heat and causing all sorts of updrafts and pressure drops and wind shifts. These are the makings of a big one. We are given a clear sign. Get out of the way, get out of the open sea. Get to safe harbour..."

Eiriksson lit a Player's Maryland, took a long pull on it, savored it, and exhaled slowly. His mind was off in the distance. "The sea out there... It's full of all sorts of forceful upheavals, periodic violence, inexorable mergings, terrible destruction... all necessary to fuel rebirth... Irresistible, inevitable change is the only thing that does not change at sea. It goes on forever. We sail into a constant state of dynamic renewal. It is what our little universe out there is all about... All part of some grand master plan far beyond our comprehension... But it is out there. We have only to look out there, keep looking, into the darkness."

He took a swig from his mug, without taking his eyes off the horizon. "Oddly enough, while we are here, at sea, we are able to see things differently... We have a privileged perspective... There is nothing of real importance between us and the horizon out there... On shore, we can't see them coming... All life's surprises, all its subtle and violent changes, all meant to batter us off balance... keep us on our toes, maybe even improve us... We don't see them coming in all the fucking congestion. But at sea, we have space and time and warning. The Vikings figured it out. Out there, past the horizon, it is all written in the face of God, if we can but learn to read it..."

The air took on a sudden damp chill. The low humidity of the day had changed.

"Captain..."

"Yes."

"Which god?"

"The one out there... in the darkness. Tin Hau. Around here, all the others are bullshit."

It was like an opera about to begin. The air stilled. The sun cast broad crimson and golden beams across the waters, painting the center of an opaque gray curtain stretched across the east with mysterious dancing patterns. Suddenly, as if on cue, light seemed to penetrate the scrimmed fantasy of a huge stage front, revealing dark, brooding layers of towering scenery behind, dominated by massive dark thunderheads and powered by silver veins of lightning. The surface of the sea became radiant white with each flash, revealing a chorus of great ominous clouds, cloaked in blacks and deep grays and maroons and violets. They marched inexorably forward, their ghostly faces partially hidden by long swirling sleeves, advancing from the distance like a terrible army, their ponderous cadence made even more profound by the random tinkling of wind chimes which hung in the pilot house to keep the helmsman awake.

To the north and west, the world looked festive and playful in the warmth of the sun. To the east, the sea started to swell, as if in anticipation of quite different fun and games to come.

Eiriksson spoke evenly. "You must get Bjarni up from his bunk, and have him prepare for some heavy weather."

I'll go do it at once, Sir." The steward went aft to Bjarni's stateroom to awaken him, an act he had accomplished on occasion before, with much difficulty.

Upon returning to the bridge, the steward looked about to find Eiriksson leaning forward, resting his head over his right fist on the steel railing, elbows splayed out on the rail, scotch cup in his left hand. He looked like some great hunchback, exhausted by his climb into the belfry.

"Captain?"

"Yes..." Eiriksson replied without looking up.

"Bjarni's up, and so is his deck party. They will get started on battening things down and making the cargo holds watertight. I gave him an estimate of two hours until it hits."

"Good." Eiriksson stayed in the head down position.

"Captain?"

"What is it, Steward?" Eiriksson was more curt in his tone.

"Are you all right, Sir?"

"*Faen i Helvete!*" Eiriksson roared, and stood up, face into the headwind. "Can't a man even pray in peace?"

Scene change.

The weather continued its metamorphosis, accenting the character development of the protagonists. One, complacent, golden and warm, now raised its head and shuddered as it became aware of the other, dark, brooding, menacing. The Talabot sailed due North on an invisible line seemingly dividing the two, holding them at bay from inevitable conflict.

Ahead, still miles from the first of Hong Kong's southern outer islands of Po Toi and Beaufort, there grew assembling an armada of junks and sails and fishing boats and island freighters, now heading for safe harbour at best speed. All had materialized out of the haze, from points East and West and South, and joined in common purpose of getting the hell out of the way of the approaching storm.

All except one.

A medium sized junk lay dead ahead about two miles, lagging far behind its brothers and sisters. It had visibly no headway on, and wallowed side to side in the building swells, taking on water. Its mast was nearly bare, with the bamboo-ribbed sail only about 20 percent aloft, jury-rigged from the aft part of the main boom. The old junk was in obvious difficulty, as crewmen scurried and pulled and tugged to somehow make sail.

The Talabot sailed straight at her. Eiriksson still leaned on the bridge wing, with chin on his fists, staring ahead. "Steward..." he called over.

"Sir?" The steward leaned out of the pilothouse.

"At this speed, how much longer to Lei Yue Mun narrows?"

The steward quickly calculated the distance and time to reach the northeastern entrance point of Hong Kong harbour. "About forty-five minutes, Sir."

The captain looked back to the Southeast, at the blackness soon to overtake them. "Shit..." he spoke softly.

"We've got a junk dead ahead with no headway, Sir."

"I know it, damn it!" the captain groused back slowly. "I'm running for port and I get some dead-in-the-water yellow ass thrown in my path. *Faen. Faen i Vold!*"

The steward came out on the wing. He did not speak.

"Get Bjarni to splay out and double up our stern hawsers. We are going to pull a drogue bucket for the rest of the trip in."

The Talabot slowed its way as it came alongside the junk. Crewmen were jumping up and down, pointing to the damaged mast and back at the black sky, and waving their arms franticly. No other power ships were near. Only the Talabot.

The steward grabbed a coiled, weighted line that was stowed in a small gear locker on the bridge, and dropped the bitter end down to Bjarni waiting on the main deck. Then, climbing to the top of the pilothouse, he swung the lead weight around vertically in ever faster circles and then let it fly across the sea gap toward the junk. The lead weight struck the mast on his first try and fell unceremoniously on the head of a Chinese crewmember. He crouched down in pain, grasping his head. Others grabbed the line and started to haul it over, followed by the double hawser that Bjarni had joined on to the line, from the stern of the Talabot. Once aboard, the Chinese crew manhandled the heavy hawsers forward, leading them to the prow of the junk, where they fed them through a large ropeway under the nose structure and then made them fast to the base of the mast. The sky darkened by the minute. The whole operation took five, as if it were well rehearsed.

The Talabot started forward again, with the junk falling in behind, about forty yards astern. The hawsers hummed as they took up the strain, and shivered off water. At standard power, the ships' headway was now less than 5 knots. The steward returned to the bridge.

"Steward. Take some bearings and get me time at this speed to Lei Yu Mun," the captain called, as he looked back at the junk from the bridge wing.

Swinging sightings from Victoria Peak to Lamma Island in the west, the steward fixed bearings on the chart as the Talabot inched ahead. After quick calculations, he called back "Two hours and twenty minutes, Sir."

"Go below and tell the passengers what we are doing, and what to expect," Eiriksson called back.

"Expect, Sir?"

"Close their portholes and pass out the Dramamine."

A black mantle was slowly being drawn overhead, its darkening contrast made even more striking by the melodramatic glow cast across the decks from the crimson fireball exiting proudly into the western sea.

The sea bounced and pitched and rose and fell and bounced and pitched again, relentless in its efforts to dislodge any food in a person's stomach. The steward stood on the bridge, full face into increasing winds but not yet any rains, as the weather built from astern of the two vessels. The Talabot kept headway as best as it could, as the following seas kept both the ship and its tow in constant disarray. A wide-eyed Ole, again his fortunate lot to be on the helm, cursed and spun the wheel right and left in vain attempts to keep his intended heading. The captain stood out on the wing as before, rock silent and calm amidst all the rolling and swaying.

"I calculate about twenty-five more minutes until we get into the lea, Captain..." the steward called as he finished plotting bearings on the main island now two miles off to his west.

"Maybe sooner, if the towline snaps, Steward," Eiriksson replied. "How are all our little friends? Green with envy that they are hanging on back there and not onboard here?"

The steward looked back with a pair of binoculars. "White with fear, I fear, Sir." The junk swung and rolled violently, like a newly roped maverick, fighting the line that tugged at his nose, restricting any freedom to roam. "They're getting quite a ride back there."

"Better a ride in this direction than one blown off to the northwest by themselves. It's all rocks over there, and they must know it."

The wind had picked up to gusts of 40 knots, jousting the Talabot on each of its burdened rolls from side to side. The hawsers strummed painfully like a bass section each time the seas made them taut with strain. The junk was not that large a vessel, but it was wide and bulky and fought stubbornly through the swells and troughs with its head down, stern swaying and broaching with every wave that pounded upon it.

"I sure hope these lines will hold. This following sea is making it tough. Like pulling a barge of wet rice," the steward punned. "We could spill Chinese sailors all over the place."

"We'll make it, Steward..." Eiriksson said calmly, looking back at the junk with binoculars. "Tin Hau is smiling."

"Tin Hau? Where in all this mess is Tin Hau?"

The captain handed over the binoculars, and pointed to the junk. The steward focused in to see a stunning young Chinese girl, clad in baggy white sailor's pajamas, standing proudly on the highest sterndeck of the junk, holding on to the teak railing with both hands, riding the pounding waves like a circus performer balancing on a lumbering elephant's hind quarters. She was grinning ecstatically, hair whipping back wildly in strong wind, confident and composed amidst the screaming of the maddening elements surrounding her.

Scene change again. Day to night. The waters inside the harbour past North Point were choppy, but a mere sassy offspring relative to the ragings of the outer seas. As the two ships wove their collective way through a maze of junks and freighters and tankers and sampans and boats of all kinds and shapes, a strange lucidity transformed the dark sky and surrounding landscape about them. Victoria stood out clearly in the moisture-saturated air, a twinkling crystal looking out to its more humble partner across the straight, awaiting a torrential downpour like a new bride awaits airborne hail of rice, proud and shimmering and all aglow. Those busy afloat, however, had little chance to witness such a spectacular cyclorama, rising against a dim rose backlighting from the western sky.

The Talabot theoretically had right of way through the traffic mess in the harbour. Signal lights aloft, specifying a ship in tow, should have made all other vessels keep their distance and give way. However, it made no sense to the blur of sailors and ships trying to get in out of the oncoming storm, so it was every ship, and junk, and able seaman, for himself. One smaller junk actually tried to sail in between, only to have its mast and sails garroted at midpoint by the towropes. Sailors in pajamas scurried every which way, in frantic search of any means to keep up headway, hoisting blankets and cargo covers on the splintered spars remaining upright, just missing a bashing by the weighty teak junk in tow.

Eiriksson finally smacked his hands together in decision, and spoke as he signaled to the crew on the bow. "Stop engine. Drop the hook, here."

It certainly was not a perfect anchoring position, but it was one of the few open areas still remaining, and it was about 600 yards off Victoria City and mercifully in the lea for the moment. The ship swung hard on its anchor as it grabbed the seabed, pulling to one side as the junk pulled to the other, causing the two vessels to slam side to side with a loud teak to metal CLUMP.

Immediately, the Chinese crewmen threw over lines to the Talabot and clamored aboard, tying off the lines to whatever clamps or gunwales or pedestals available. Once secure, they all shivered in a cluster on the main deck, in the lee of the superstructure, and congratulated each other in exhausted but animated glee.

The steward climbed down off the bridge, following in the captain's footsteps. A soaked and sorry lot of sailors, indeed. But thankful, so thankful, to be off their troubled junk. As Eiriksson strode over, they fell on their knees and bowed and waved their hands in thanks and praise. "*Xie xie. Xie xie.*" They all spoke at once, tonal inflections pouring out in all sorts of babblings of gladness.

"Get up, you water rats," Eiriksson boomed, smiling. "Come below and get some booze in your amber guts." And he pulled two of them up by the collar, one in each hand, and held them aloft. "The Vikings will dry you out."

They followed after him, two still dangling like waterlogged puppies from his massive fists. Only one person remained on the deck, kneeling down with head bowed. It was the girl.

She was dressed in water-soaked cotton pajamas like her shipmates, but wore her jet black hair tied back now in a bun with a carved ivory spear holding it. She looked up slowly, to find herself alone with only the steward watching her nearby. She kneeled there, with her legs under her and her hands resting on her thighs, smiling calmly.

"*Xie xie.* Thank you," she said softly, lowering her eyes as she spoke. The steward knew very little Chinese. But he, like most travelers, knew thank you in a number of tongues. This was Mandarin, not the words *m goi* one would expect in Cantonese, in Hong Kong.

"Tonight?"

"Now," Eiriksson stated coolly. "Take the passengers ashore now." The captain was changing his shirt to a dry one, as the steward stood attentively in the hatchway of his stateroom.

"Yes, Sir. But why now?" the steward asked.

"This is only the beginning of our storm, Steward. It will be far kinder to hurry the passengers into some dry hotel with a hot meal, than to have them lashed to their bunks on board the Talabot when the wind works up. Still have about half an hour. You should make it safely. I've called for a motor launch from Causeway Bay. Told 'em we had injured that we needed to get ashore."

"Do we?"

"No, but we will, if we don't."

"How about the crew, Sir."

"Staying aboard, of course. Somebody has to watch this tub. The owners' precious cargo, and all that."

"No, I meant the Chinese crew. Take them along?"

The captain thought for a moment. "Take the men down into our crew's quarters, dry them off, and have them change into any old shirts and pants our lads can spare. Throw away their pajamas."

"We have one woman, Sir."

"Get a dress out of my closet over there, a green one, with a flower pattern. It was to be a gift for Victoria. It should fit her. She will have to fend for herself for shoes."

"That's a nice gesture, Captain."

"Steward, I suppose you have noticed these people speak Mandarin?" Eiriksson spoke slowly, as he poured himself a cup of Stolichnaya hi-test from his private stock.

"Yes."

Eiriksson took a long pull on his vodka, neat, without ice, and shuddered as the warmth blasted through his system. "This could be the break they risked their necks for. In all this confusion, they might make it, Steward."

"Make it, Sir?"

"Into Hong Kong, Steward," the captain said, frustrated at the lack of communication. "They're from up north. They're Red Chinese."

The motor launch theoretically held sixteen persons. All toll, the passengers plus the steward plus Snow White and her seven sailors made twenty-one. The launch crew went crazy as the Chinese flocked aboard after the 12 passengers, trying to prevent them from jumping onto the decks. But the water was so choppy, it was near to impossible to maintain a safe position along side the Talabot's ladder with all the people jumping on board, so the launch bosun, cursing and yelling in Cantonese, just pulled off and headed for the protected jetty at Causeway Bay.

The passengers were green, but hopeful. The Chinese crew was yellow again, having flushed their ashen fears with rum and vodka. The steward looked with amazement and even a touch of humor at the strange amalgam of humanity, squashed and seated and standing and squatting together in the bouncing cabin, each hoping the person adjacent would not vomit in the confined space.

As they left the ship, Eiriksson yelled "Take them to some decent hotel. Try the Harbour Hotel in Wanchai. Stay in the low land. Stay off the hill."

"What about me?" the steward yelled back, smiling.

"Oh, you'll find a cozy bunk, I'm sure," he laughed. "Or try the Seaman's Mission."

"Not the Repulse Bay? How's your credit?"

"Just get back here after the storm. We'll have a little cleaning up party."

The launch burbled its way to the shore, swaying with all the body weight, and barely under control. The passengers looked greener by the minute. The junk crew looked more awestruck with each closer angle of the magnificent city towering before them. The young girl hung on the outer deck with her crewmates, serenely smiling and staring up at the explosion of lights and highrises that dominated the hillsides ahead. Her raven hair again blew wildly in the gusty winds, lashing about her green flowered shoulders.

Suddenly the radio crackled and squealed, cutting through the dull motor roar, "Signal Nine is now in effect. All small craft return to port. Signal Nine is now in effect."

"What's Signal Nine?" the steward leaned in and asked the coxswain, a sturdy Chinese busy wrestling with the wheel in the gusty chop.

He looked back and smiled, wide-eyed. "You lucky. Good *joss*. This last trip tonight."

"Why?"

"Signal Nine. Storm growing. Maybe *tai foos*. More better you hide."

"Where do you suggest?"

The sailor grinned. "Kit Kat Club."

The launch bounced about the small concrete pier next to the nearly deserted cargo-handling basin below tiny Kellett Island, jutting out from Wanchai, and all onboard readied themselves to disembark. The partially protected area was packed full of junks and sampans vying for security from the building winds and waves. The launch had plowed its way into the melee, horn blasting, as if the hapless teak fleet could possible move out of its path, until it snaked its way up to its cramped normal mooring space at the shore. The coxswain yelled in Cantonese to his mates, in frantic intonations that any sailor could decipher. "Don't let the fucking launch hit the fucking pier. Get these fucking people off. Fast! Let's fucking tie this fucking tub up and get the fuck out of here."

In the fast-paced confusion fleeing before the storm, the happy seafarers were landed near a closed down cargo terminal, with no police or immigration or customs offices in sight. The Chinese junk crew, eyes darting about uneasily, quite easily leapt ashore, and turned to help the Americans and British passengers who were, by age as well as by varying levels of seasickness, much less agile. The steward thanked the coxswain and his mates and helped them double up and tie off the lines of the launch that would now have to weather the storm right at the pier, behind a very small breakwall. By the time he had finished, all the passengers had scurried away and were far up the embankment and at the terminal gate, hailing the few taxis that still traveled now nearly deserted streets. The junk crew had vanished into the night.

"Oh, oh..." he muttered, hastening to catch up. "I hope they can find that hotel... The Harbour. It must be near hear, from what I saw on the maps." The last sixsome squeezed somehow into a taxi, and sped off into the night, leaving him alone. "Damn. I was supposed to see them there safely. I better hike on up there fast."

The rain had just started in earnest, and with it the wind. Sheets of sparkling diamonds, refracting a myriad of rainbows from the still brightly lighted city, crashed downward only to shatter worthlessly on deserted pavements.

Whatever pedestrian traffic there was only moments ago, had vanished. Even taxis and cars left the scene, finding parking or just hiding out of sight. "Damn. Now where is the Harbour Hotel from here?" he spoke out loud to himself. The steward was about to trudge out into the lashing downpour when a hand grasped his arm. It was the girl.

"Do not worry about them. The Harbour Hotel is only a few blocks from here. They will make it all right. You come with me, please," she said in surprisingly good English. Rain poured down her face, past large black almond eyes that reflected the sparkle of the city, down past a beautiful, broadly smiling mouth that outlined the most perfect row of teeth imaginable. "Come. We must find shelter. My uncle's establishment. It is quite near."

The steward looked with amazement at the young girl, possibly nineteen or twenty, standing drenched in Eiriksson's daughter's new green flowered dress. "I thought she was from up north..." he pondered. "How does she know her way around here?"

The rain really started to pound and the wind gusted in speeds requiring a 30-degree body lean. The steward grabbed her hand and said with a smile, "Let's go, Miss. Lead us out of the storm. I'm in your hands."

Off they ran into the streets, hand in hand, eyes all but covered from the flailing rains, charging across sidewalks and into the lea of buildings, scurrying past intersections, and dodging the occasional car. The streets were a jumble of large and small buildings, dark inside but still brightly lighted outside, with Chinese signs swinging violently from every wall, some with graphics and illustrations, others with characters in Cantonese, but most of them dominated by large vertical neon signs in English, with the familiar sleazy names found in every port... "Kit Kat. Top Hat. Lotus Flower. Golden Dragon. All Girl Show." It was the strip.

They darted into a doorway that gave partial shelter from the sheeting rain. "Over there," the girl pointed. "My uncle's."

The steward looked up the street to a large building with a few windows lit against the darkness, with a sign across the front that said in bold letters "Luk Kwok." It was a hotel. "O.K., he thought to himself. "Her uncle owns a hotel. Good choice."

They started running toward the large welcome structure and were about to reach the hotel lobby doorway when the steward was jerked past the warm, inviting lights. "Not there," she grinned. "That is a house of regret. The next building is my uncle's."

The steward's heart sank as he saw the intended refuge. A small, darkened structure with metal shielding across the front windows, rattling in the wind and rain, and capped by a swinging vertical sign that said in clear English, "Johnston. Quality Tailors."

They darted into the doorway and the girl started banging on the simple glass door that had been covered by a piece of plywood. Finally a light came on in the shop, and the door was carefully forced open into the wind.

Backlit from the glow inside, an elderly Chinese man peered out into the roaring air. "Lei Ling!" He shouted, and pushed the door fully open. "Thank the gods. You are safe! Come in! Come in! Quickly!"

The girl pulled the steward in with her, and the large door slammed shut behind them. They were surrounded with fabric bolts, hundreds of them, piled in every possible corner and against every wall, leaving narrow paths through the interior. The most warming golden glow imaginable, after the raging weather, emanated from a room in the rear. The old man pulled the girl, and she the steward, through the fabric valley and into the light beyond.

"Lei Ling! Lei Ling is here!" a chorus of voices cheered, followed by a cacophony of tonal jabbering.

Suddenly the girl was surrounded by some forty Chinese - men, women, octogenarians, children of all ages, all chatting and cheering and toning and mumbling with their mouths full of food. They had entered upon a major feast taking place in a large, garishly decorated room that lay behind the storefront. A long table was laden with an abundance of food the likes of which the steward had never seen, even on his grandest smorgasbord days. A glazed goose, probably a Peking duck, a barbequed suckling pig, ribs and wings and thighs and gizzards and a whole grouper with eyes and mouth open and bright orange monster prawns and a hundred squid in a silvery sauce and every meat and foul and fish yet classified, lay spread out in splendor before them. It was a feast fit for a queen. And there she was. A blushing bride in traditional white gown, standing next to a smiling young man in a crisp black tuxedo. Everyone, even some of the young, were toasting and swilling down Remy Martin V.S.O.P. They had entered upon a wedding feast.

Also in the room, jumping about and cheering and hugging Lei Ling were the seven sailors, decked out in a garish, ill-fitting display of western sport shirts and slacks received from the Talabot's generous crew. They had arrived relatively dry, yet hugging the girl they took on some of her soak.

Lei Ling turned and broke away from the crowd, to face the steward still standing in the doorway. "Respected Uncle. This is the man from the freighter who threw us the line. Without him, we all should not be here tonight."

The white haired man came over and grasped the steward's hand. "Thank you. Thank you. You make an old man's heart burst with joy."

He then dragged the steward around the crowd, and each person, young or old, bowed vigorously and grinned and toned a hundred syllables in Mandarin and Cantonese, interrupted with an occasional "Dan Kyoo." All the while, others were pulling off his wet clothing and wrestling him into new slacks and sport shirt that miraculously appeared, in a perfect fit, from the tailor shop.

The girl, in the same timeframe, somehow changed into a lime colored, high collar silk *cheongsam*, perfectly cut to every curve and much more stunning with its ten inch slit up the thigh than the flowered dress. The girl rescued the steward from the adulation, and leading him to the spread, said, "Please. Share our humble table. Share our happiness to be alive." With that, she grabbed a plate and started serving him a portion of everything, not overloading but carefully placing each tidbit in a prearranged position on the plate, as if to aid in an orderly selection of flavors and textures when eating. The steward could barely control his internal growlings as she added choices to her own plate. She then motioned him to follow to small chairs where they sat and began to ravenously devour the most heavenly combinations from Column A and from Column B he had ever known.

Presented to him were the most incredible selection of foods. Lei Ling would urge him to pick up a new morsel in his chop sticks, (amazing how adept one becomes when hungry), and then after he had tasted and swallowed, she would with great solemnity covering secret inner glee, tell him what he had just eaten. He felt lost in a theater of the absurd, all cooked and sauced to perfection. Goose webs, cow's innards, snake soup, cockerel's testicles, minced pigeon and plum sauce wrapped in lettuce, steamed eel with ginger shoots, chicken wrapped in lotus leaves and baked in clay, bamboo fungus, fried shrimp in toasted sesame... his taste buds swooned in a symphony of flavors and textures that was fit, obviously, for a Chinese emperor.

"We have a saying." Lei Ling smiled. "Anything that keeps its back to heaven, is fit for cooking." And she reloaded his plate.

The feasting went on for four hours. The food supply seemed endless. Every time the steward would feel he should rest, his plate was reloaded with yet another series of new delights, snails laced with garlic, octopus cooked in its ink, turnip pancakes, shark fin, soft-shelled crab in a fiery black bean sauce... like their forerunners each just cooked to a delicate doneness and exuding a complexity of the most subtle, sweet, sour or spicy seasonings. Only when the steward took a large black beanlike item in his chopsticks did the girl shake her head sideways and say, "You will regret it." Too late. The steward gasped at the fireball exploding on his tongue, and coughed out the chili, only to wait breathlessly as the girl refilled his glass once again with frothy Mackeson's stout.

"I warned you," she smiled sternly, while wiping his brow and beating him on the back to ease his inhaling.

The steward lay back in his chair, distended and exhausted by his overzealous attack on the light night snack that had awaited them. "Do you people always eat like this?" he gasped.

Lei Ling laughed. "Wait until you see the main course!" to which the steward's eyes rolled back into his head. "No, we don't," she continued. "This is a joyous occasion for our family. We are all together again, to witness the wedding of my cousin. We have much to celebrate, much to be thankful for."

The steward looked at the merry crowd of jabbering, toasting people. "It's good to be alive. And dry. And among such warm happy people," he groaned blissfully.

Lei Ling, who had kept pace with him chop stick to chop stick, looked no worse for her indulgences. Actually she rather improved in her inner glow now as she sat, upright but relaxed, next to him. With no food in their mouths, they now could converse with more than eyes and hand motions. "Who are the couple?" the steward asked, surveying the crowded room and smiling faces and bride and groom.

"It is the marriage of my cousin Vanessa Chih Nu, to her betrothed, Winston Chien Niu," she replied. "But it is much more. It is the beginning of the Festival of the Seven Sisters. A minor holiday but one that is celebrated throughout China. It is for young lovers who are finally able to get together after long periods of separation. As you see, certain couples have already paired off, now that their strength is restored."

The steward looked about the room to find the Chinese sailors, almost comical in their ill-fitting western drag, sitting closely with young women, talking quietly and personally, as he was with Lei Ling. "But... But you were all... at sea... Coming from..."

"Yes," she interrupted demurely. "They are from Red China. All but my brother, Reginald Pak Tai. He and I have lived here, in Hong Kong, since just after the Japanese were defeated. The others, including Vanessa and her sisters, are recently from our ancestral home, up the coast about two hundred miles."

"Just down for the weekend?" the steward asked sarcastically.

Lei Ling laughed, and looked out over the crowd. "No. We went to fetch them, in that old junk, the Magpie. Our relatives are here for good, now, I hope. The young and old are no longer separated."

"Where did you learn to sail?" the steward asked, fascinated at the accomplishment of this young woman.

"Ha!" Lei Ling laughed. "I never did. Maybe that is why we were adrift, with no sail. But my brother Reggie, although he studies to become an engineer, hired out as crew on a fishing junk for a year, and learned enough to get us there, and back. Or rather, almost enough, it seems. Again, thank you for saving us from the sea dragons."

"It was the only thing to do, take a distressed vessel in tow before a storm like this."

"No. Many Chinese would not have come to our aid..." she said pensively. "Many sometimes are too self-centered, and would not wish to risk their own lives. Many are also, in occasions of stress, quite religious, and follow certain Taoist doctrines to a fault."

"I thought Lao Tze was the compassionate one," the steward interjected.

"Compassionate?" Lei Ling went on. "He left the Chinese with something that even today causes us problems. *Wu wei.*"

"Whoo Whee. Yes it is hot in here..." the steward confirmed. "What did he leave?"

"*Wu wei.* His philosophy of doing nothing. He meant well. 'Do nothing, and nothing will not be done'. The idea is to remain humble, passive, non-assertive and non-interventionist. Your western version is 'Live and let live'. Lao Tze taught that one should do nothing to upset the harmony of the universe, and things will work out as planned in a great master scheme. Keep to one's own business. Don't make waves, as you say. One should do nothing to take the lead in planning affairs, or one may be held responsible. This runs directly contrary to your western notion of taking decisive action and getting things done quickly. Had you practiced *wu wei* our junk would now be scattered on the rocks, and we, a festival feast for the squid, not vice versa."

"I thought that Taoism was fading out of prominence. You now have many religions practiced here, don't you? Buddhism, Confucianism, Christianity..."

"True. And Fatalism, and Pragmatism, and Capitalism and Communism. In Hong Kong, we still will practice them all, just not to offend any of the assorted gods and priests and demons. It is not uncommon to see a Hong Kong citizen seek out a fortune teller for advice on love or business, worship his departed ancestors with elaborate offerings of food and incense and burnt paper, ask a Taoist priest to exorcise his home of unhappy ghosts, gamble late into the night with all his savings, pray to Buddha for fertility, and then take Christian communion. We are pragmatic. We may accept our *joss*, our fate. But we hedge our bets, as you say."

"But Hong Kong is more cosmopolitan than mainland in their thinking, are they not? The British influence...?"

"Many of the traditions of older times still are followed, even passionately, by the Chinese, both here and quietly on the mainland, regardless of the new teachings of our self-declared Red Messiah and his wife. People of Hong Kong have by necessity learned to adapt to Western ways. We now have our own version of *Teo Te Ching*, which translated means The Way and Its Power. We call it M.O.N.E.Y"

"What?"

"We have had so little control over our lives for centuries, first with the emperors and then the war lords and now here with the colonialist British, that we have evolved in our thinking to place a fatalistic dependence on *joss*, luck. Luck is what will be, and we cannot change it. So we avoid philosophizing about what should be. We just put our heads down and direct our energies, not on worrying about the unfair government restrictions or lack of democracy or what is the right path to salvation and wrong way of treating our neighbors, but on making money. It is really very simple. We are here today. Life is today. Joy is here today. Money buys happiness, for today, not tomorrow. Tomorrow, there may or may not even be a Hong Kong, particularly if the Communists have their way."

"Then why did you risk your neck to get your whole family out of Red China?" the steward asked softly, looking into her dark almond eyes.

She smiled. "That, too, was my fate. I was born on the birthday of Tin Hau. My family believes that I have a calming influence, so I was elected to go along on the junk for good luck."

The bride and groom had slowly made their way over through the crowd of well-wishers and now appeared smiling before the steward and Lei Ling. "We wish to thank you for helping our cousins to arrive in Hong Kong safely," the groom spoke as he bowed slightly, bride on his arm. The steward struggled to sit up in response. His empty plate rested on his knees.

The smiling bride suddenly went pale, and gasped as if hit by a thunderbolt. Her eyes stared down at his plate.

Lei Ling reached over and moved the steward's chopsticks, which he had placed together pointing vertically up from the bottom of the plate, to a position horizontally across the top. She then rose and hugged her cousin, and started jabbering in Cantonese. The steward rose as well, and placed his plate on a nearby table. Soon the smile returned to the bride's face, and the party went on as before.

After the bride and groom had chatted niceties with the steward and Lei Ling for a few moments, they were spirited away by others for a series of more toasts. The whole group was by now getting quite loud and colorful, as the effects of four hours of brandy took hold.

"What was that all about?" the steward asked. "She looked like she was about to faint. Did I do anything wrong?"

Lei Ling put her hands over his arm. "You had no way of knowing. The way your chopsticks were positioned on your plate, it resembled the Taoist death sign. We Chinese are very superstitious. My cousin is quite sensitive to such signs, and it frightened her. But she will be fine. I have calmed her fears."

The evening went on for a few more hours. Occasionally, a party member would look out the front door, into the blast of rain and wind, and then let it slam back shut. There was no way people were going to be able to leave in a Signal Nine storm. The rain was torrential, the wind hurricane force.

The uncle and a few of the male relatives started carrying first the sleepy children into the front tailor shop, and then progressively some of the more drunken grown-ups. After the crowd had diminished by half, Lei Ling pulled the steward over to the doorway of the darkened room and peered in. There, lying alone or in twos and threes, on the several large cutting tables that occupied the floor space, were sleeping bodies. They snored contentedly in various harmonies, warm and secure under blanketing pulled out from bolts of fresh flannel, pin stripe, serge, twill and broadcloth.

"Come," Lei Ling said softly, holding him by the arm closely against her. We must find our nest as well. It has been a long day, and there is more to do tomorrow."

The steward followed her into the darkened room, stepping quietly and carefully through the litter of bodies, over to a corner table that was still not occupied. There, Lei Ling spread out a bolt of soft English cashmere, perfect for a blazer, in layers of three or four across the hard wooden tabletop. The light was dim and mysterious in the corner, and the noise from the other room seemed a thousand miles away. Next she pulled off her silk dress, carefully laid it on a chair nearby, and her stockings, and clad in her undergarments, climbed onto the newly formed couch. "Come up here," she said sleepily. "We must measure you for a suit."

By the time the steward had removed his shirt and pants, and climbed in along side her, she was fast asleep.

The tonal commotion grew in intensity, and finally woke the steward. Jabbering parents, grandparents, and children were awakening and rising from their welcome piles of fabrics. The steward looked sleepily about, wondering where he was for a moment, covered with a rich caramel cashmere blanket.

There was light coming in through the front windows, and the door opened and slammed closed occasionally as small groups ventured out of their makeshift flophouse and into the morning daylight.

Lei Ling was not there. In her place and hanging on hangers, however, were his clothes, clean and pressed, Victoria's flowered dress, clean and pressed, and her own green silk shift, also clean and pressed, with a note on it. "Good morning. Please deliver this present for the captain's daughter. You will see me later. Lei Ling."

The steward looked about, and attempted conversation with those nearby to no avail. Smiles and jabbering greeted him, but no English. Finally, he put on his own clothes, picked up the other garments, and ventured out into the bright street.

The storm had been a big one. Typhoon or not exactly, it had caused lots of minor damage in the waterfront area where he walked. Signs were down everywhere, electric wires sparked angrily here and there, and large puddles flooded each intersection. There seemed to be a constant muddy runoff flowing down from the hillside that rose directly up from the waterfront flats, replete with wicker baskets, foodstuffs, an occasional chicken, and dozens of flip flop rubber sandals. The steward looked up the hillside, and saw the numerous flashing lights of police and fire and ambulance vehicles engaged in a variety of catastrophe activities - digging out, bailing out, handling electrical hazards, and tending the injured. The streets were now crowded with many persons, scurrying to work or home to relatives, happy that the crisis had passed and anxious to get on with their primary pursuits of M.O.N.E.Y. Vendors appeared from nowhere, hawking their goods and foods. Out of the rubble, it was business as usual, although covered with mud.

The steward made it back to the pier where he had landed ashore, only to find no launch in sight. He stood there, looking out to find the Talabot still swinging on its anchor in the harbour, cheerily highlighted by the late morning sun that beamed through the broken clouds racing by above.

Whistling shrilly, the steward flagged a small sampan waddling across the protected baylet. Ever vigilant for a dollar, its oarsman waved back and altered course to paddle over to the pier. The steward leapt aboard and pointed to the Talabot. "Take me to that ship, please?"

The sampanman grinned and bowed vigorously, and held up two opportunistic fingers. "Two dolla. Two dolla."

The steward looked about the harbour as they waddled out from shore. Ships seemed to have survived the heavy winds and rains. At least most seemed to be riding high in the water, with masts in place. The previously assembled fleet of junks and sampans where he had come ashore were gone, off to their appointed rounds, or a tea break, or something. Harbour business seemed to be almost back to normal.

After paying the sampanman, the steward jumped over to the ship's ladder, garments hanging over his shoulder, and climbed up to the deck. There was Eiriksson, leaning over the railing and looking down at him. "Been shopping? You'll look lovely in Jade."

The steward presented him with the loaner and gift dresses, and briefly recapped the story of the night ashore. "Any word from the passengers? I got separated from them. I stopped by the hotel this morning, but all had already checked out."

"Oh, they're probably alright and off on a shopping spree. Wet bargains. They will show up sooner or later. Time now for us to bale out this tub and get the cargo ready for offloading."

"What can I do to help?" the steward asked.

"Go over the side with your friends, and help get that damn junk out of here. I'm getting a bad reputation as a softy. Not good for Vikings. Pillaging and spoiling fits us better."

"They're here? Already?" the steward expressed surprise.

"They been here since 0700. Even your young friend. What the hell were you doing all morning? Oh, I forgot. Shopping for your silk dress."

"Lei Ling's here?"

Eiriksson sneered and shook his head. "Ensign Romance. Snoring the day away while his pretty pal gets calluses on her delicate hands."

The steward hurried over to the other side of the Talabot and peered down. There was the junk, still lashed to the ship, but now sitting higher in the water by about two feet, with its main decks clear of trash and rubble. The seven sailors were at work feverishly, some pulling and separating its halyards and lines to clear all tangles, others repairing the mainsail that lay drooped over a portion of the deck. And at the bow was Lei Ling, cooking over a makeshift grill. She looked up and waved. "You're just in time for lunch. Come on aboard."

"Captain?" the steward started.

"Get out of our way here, Steward," Eiriksson scoffed with a backhand wave. "Go help your new friends. We have work to do here. Later today, just find our scattered passengers and tell them to get back here by tomorrow at 1100. We sail at 1300."

The steward climbed over the rail and lowered himself hand over hand down one of the tie ropes.

"Good morning." He smiled down at Lei Ling and the others, who returned his greeting with waves and jabbering and smiles.

"Here. Help me cook. These men are hungry. They work, while others I know sleep the day away," Lei Ling joked as she handed him a wok shaped skillet. "Just keep things moving. They're done when they start to get pink."

The steward assumed her stir frying with a small wand of bundled, floppy chopsticks, mixing the red peppers and strips of ginger and chilies and spattering oil about the large succulent prawns that dominated the wok. Lei Ling then fired in a dash of black pepper, followed by a generous glug of soy sauce and a fistful of chunked scallions. "They're done. Quickly. Get them on to this platter." She smiled as he reacted correctly, and turned to the finishing touches to the large whole crabs that crowded the center of a simmering curry bath in another large skillet. The steward had never seen food cooked so quickly and so deftly, arms and hands flying with no superfluous moves. Lined up on the deck were large bowls already filled with glumps of steaming glutinous rice, and large mugs of steaming green tea.

She did not even have to call her crew. They knew instinctively by the sizzle or the smell, and flocked around like vultures, faces buried in rice bowls with chopsticks a blur. Lunch was consumed in a matter of seconds, followed by sighs and burps and laughter and a moment of needed relaxation.

"These men are from up north. They like their food a bit more spicy..." Lei ling said as she again banged the steward on the back and held the tea mug to his gasping lips.

The sail to Joss House Bay was idyllic. The majestic Victoria Peak was clear of clouds and bright in the afternoon sun, standing out like a tribute to the queen with its mantle of sparkling highrise jewels spread about the harbour and up the hillside. The steward stood on the bow of the junk with Lei Ling, looking over the spectacular harbourama, inhaling the freshest autumn air.

Lei Ling looked up at him. "We go now to return this junk to its owner. And to continue our celebration of life, some of which you witnessed yesterday evening."

"Not another wedding feast?" the steward asked in mock fear.

"Actually, yes," Lei Ling laughed. "Yesterday my cousins were married by an Anglican priest. Today they will have a Taoist ceremony."

"Hedging their bets, as you say in China..."

"Possibly. But actually, pleasing all the parents and grandparents," she replied.

The junk slid along in the brisk afternoon breeze, rolling softly in the slack tide and feeling right shipshape after its stormy journey. They entered the harbour in full sail and proceeded straight toward the shoreline above which stood a quaint Taoist temple overlooking the ragtag fleet of junks and sampans, at anchor or berthed side by side below. The steward looked at the families who crowded together in the floating neighborhoods, inhabiting the aging craft as houseboats. Children played on the rigging. Women washed clothes in water bucketed out of the bay. Laundry hung from every boom and railing. Men and women staggered across the assembled gangplanks and decks with bundles of food and supplies and sticks or bags of charcoal for fires. On the fantail of one junk, a toddler was being held out over the stern, hunkered down on the end of a plank, bottom bare, his coach pleading for the child to defecate more deftly.

The steward was shocked at the contrast. On one side of the hill, opulence and grandeur and sophistication; on the other, a floating slum, rivaling the grimmest, grimiest ghettos and *favellas* in the world.

"I am glad that you are able to see all aspects of Hong Kong," Lei Ling said softly. "Even its backside."

"Isn't disease a problem?" he asked, looking at the crowded floating apartment complex stagnating in its own sewage.

"Less than one might expect," she replied. "The tide washes away all sorts of wonders. And an occasional child."

The junk inched up to a group of other junks rafted together, and clumped along side. The crew jumped to and tied her fast to the group. "Please come below. We must change into our Sunday best again."

Lei Ling pulled him across the main deck and down through a hatchway into the sterncastle. "One moment." Then she stepped behind a door in the junk cabin and donned a coral silk *cheongsam* that clung to her like shrink fit plastic wrap on a Coke bottle, with a knife slit just starting up the side.

As he stood mouth agape, staring at her beauty, she then presented him with a newly tailored navy blue cashmere sportcoat, a perfect fit complete with double vents, flap pockets, massive gold navy buttons, and a fiery red satin lining.

"How in the devil did you measure..."

333

"No, we did not make it from your impressions left on the table," she laughed. "Remember, my uncle is an expert tailor. He saw how the other clothes, the dry ones, fit you, and had the sportcoat made this morning and tailored accordingly. It is his small way of thanking you for coming to the aid of our family."

They danced in a Conga line along the narrow planks that connected the bows of about seven rafting junks, each careful not to fall into the bay in their fresh clothes. Families smiled and children hid and old ladies laughed and jabbered happily as Snow White and her now eight henchmen tripped through their living rooms toward shore. Pots were steaming, dogs were barking, toy instruments were banging and tooting as the rafting families huddled in neighborly bliss amidst their tired teak harbourview apartments. So much for privacy. Yet, for most of the boat people, many of them fishermen, it beat any affordable lodgings on land.

Once ashore, Lei Ling led her merry band up the hillside toward the garishly ornamented temple the steward had seen while entering the harbour. Standing outside, waving and waiting, were many other members of her family, some of whom he had met the previous evening in the tailor shop.

The steward and Lei Ling were slightly behind the other seven sailors, walking more slowly up the hill to take in the sights.

Strange sounds could be heard near the temple. Music of some sort, from the distance, grew louder. Or was it music? It sounded much like the banging of cymbals and drums and sticks and gourds, and the squeaking and thweeting of reed instruments, accented by a few horribly sour notes on a trumpet. A procession began exiting the temple and weaving its way down the hill towards the harbour. It grew in size to about 100 persons, slowly walking behind the most comical ragtag band the steward had ever seen. As it approached, he stopped and stared in amazement. Some members were outfitted in dirty white uniforms, the type for selling ice cream, with broken peaked hats to match. Others wore a variety of pants and shirts and pajamas. Some were barefoot, others in sneakers or sandals. Still other marchers carried heavy ornate metal incense burners that gave off billows of thick blue-white smoke, obscuring the remaining part of the procession in a periodic fit of coughing.

The motley train worked its way closer. The procession reminded the steward of a Chinese film version of some New Orleans jazz parade, but with the sound track played backwards. The noise was absolutely without any unifying rhythm or group harmony, let alone any one theme or melody line. Everyone seemed to be playing at once, to whatever instrumental solo came to mind. No doubt about it - it was an Oriental Dixieland Jazz Band at its wildest, playing versions of *Tiger Rag* and *Dippermouth Blues* simultaneously.

Hong Kong's own Louis Arm Fong led the group on a crumpled cornet, backed-up by King Oh Lee and Bix Bei Dee. They were followed by Kid Oh Ree and "Tricky Sam" Nan Ton on battered bones, then James Dor See and Buster Bai Lee on licorice sticks. Right out of step came along Coleman Haw Kin and Donald Red Man on tenor saxes, Charles Dix On on banjobox and Ed Ei Lang on a retread guitar, pah pah pumped along by Cyrus Sai Clair on a very tarnished tuba. A straggling of others stumbled behind with mysterious forms of gong and oboe and fife, followed finally by Gene Kru Pa on a monster wheeled kettledrum that two young lads had to help drag along. The steward covered a low cough with his hand, trying to disguise the uncontrollable twitching in his grin muscles.

"It is a funeral..." Lei Ling stated softly, holding his arm. "Someone who died yesterday in the storm, no doubt. This area is sacred to Tin Hau, the guardian of seafarers and fishermen."

The steward nodded, and they watched quietly as the procession filed past in all its cacaphonous smoky splendor.

"It could have been one of us. Or all of us..." Lei Ling finally said, looking out at the mourning family members who followed along in the rear with a priest in silk ceremonials. A small handwagon with large wheels that was being dragged along with the group. It was filled to overflowing with a huge pile of small brightly colored paper models and other paper objects - cars, a house, numerous junks, even a television, recognizable food like oranges and biscuits and cakes, small bowls of rice, and stacks of fake money. Lei Ling reached into her garment, through an open placket slit near her bosom, and pulled out some Hong Kong dollars. Then she walked down to the procession, bowed, and placed them into the hands of one of the younger members of the family. She bowed low to the elders of the family, and once they were past, returned to join the steward.

She again grabbed his arm, and held it closely to her bosom. "They are a family of fishermen. Three sons were lost at sea yesterday in the storm. All they are able to mourn is their memory, unfortunately not their bodies. Very bad *joss*. The deceased have become 'Hungry Ghosts', condemned to wander homelessly forever."

The two stood and watched for a few more moments, as the clanging, banging, squeaking procession snaked its way down the hillside to the shore. There, it stopped. A still noisier ceremony unfolded in which, amidst fire crackers and assorted bows out to the sea, the paper objects were placed onto some floating platform, set ablaze, and launched from the shore. The smoking raft drifted off the shore and out into the sea beyond. The paper fire burned out in a few moments. Incense continued to smoke for much longer, as the raft moved slowly out into the great beyond, leaving a wisping trail that dissipated quickly in the freshening breeze of today.

"The music alerts the gods that the dead are coming and to be ready for them. The burned paper items are gifts to the dead, to help them on their way in their next life," Lei Ling said, after the procession began to break up. "It is not a frivolous custom. It is meant to transform the dreams of wealth and cars and luxury items that these poor people could never afford in this hard life, and sends them along with the dead. Just possibly, in their next life, they may be allowed to be more comfortable. It is part of our way of saying goodbye."

"And your gift?" he asked, appreciating her gesture. "A Taoist tradition also? Or are you a Christian today?'"

"We Chinese are many things, as best fits the times. The gift was a little something I was going to give to my cousins today, for their marriage. But this family needs it more. My cousins would agree..." she replied, still looking down at the ceremony. The steward squeezed her hand in his. She continued, "But the act could also be viewed as Confucian. Remember, he too, invented the Golden

Rule. Or Buddhist. Giving up worldly goods brings one closer to Nirvana. But it does not really matter, does it? Compassion exists in all cultures. One only has to recognize it, and exercise it, on appropriate occasions."

The steward and Lei Ling silently resumed their climb to the temple, turning their thoughts now on what lay ahead. "This is *Tai Miu*..." she spoke as they neared the entrance. "The great temple where our families have come to give thanks to the Queen of Heaven, Tin Hau, for our safe deliverance from the storm."

With that brief explanation, Lei Ling left the steward and followed the others who had entered the temple. Inside, she joined those who were involved in saying prayers and lighting incense sticks and candles and bowing before the various gaudy icons and banners and brightly painted dragons and ferocious figures that guarded the mysterious temple interior. The steward stood near the door in silence, looking in awe at the intricately carved figures and thrones and panels that adorned the room, as the seafarers and their families performed acts of thanks and worship to their patron goddess. He found himself even giving a few thanks of his own, for his and their good "*joss*", to whatever presence or spirit that truly occupied, along with thick blue smoke, the inner sanctum.

After a few moments, a priest came forward to an alter-table carrying heavily-smoking incense sticks, and placed them around with circumstance. Next, Chien Niu and Chih Nu appeared, dressed in classic silk finery, he in an embroidered jacket and pot hat, and she in a shining gold and white silk gown with precarious headdress that shook and twinkled and shivered as she moved. The priest joined them before an alter area and began chanting and toning and replaying a ritual born thousands of years ago and refined throughout the years. Parents and close family stood transfixed nearby, and received bows from the bride and groom and others as the service went on.

At occasional moments, the smoke was so thick that the steward could barely see the celebrants. Out of the haze, Lei Ling emerged, smiling. "Now they are properly joined. Today's ceremony acknowledges the past. Yesterday's, the present."

The steward watched with Lei Ling, as the couple and their family members filed out of the temple, smiling and jabbering. All expressions of seriousness vanished, and the young couple freshened as if great weights had been removed from their shoulders.

Outside, near the entrance to the temple, a mandarin-suited fortuneteller, possibly the temple keeper, beckoned to the couple. After much giggling and jabbering, the bride shook out one piece of wood from a cylindrical box onto a well-worn cloth spread on a small table. The fortuneteller nodded over and over and, eyes closed, cast a mysterious smile at the happy couple. Then he said something to them that left them perplexed, yet still grinning. Someone else in the crowd made a comment that made everyone laugh heartily, and off they went towards the grounds entrance, family and friends in tow.

"Come." Lei Ling grabbed his hand and followed the throng. "Now we go to the opera."

Outside awaited a dozen rickshaws, manned by human toothpicks in tattered T-shirts and shorts and Ked-style sneakers. The bride and groom were taken up by one elaborately decorated rickshaw filled with flowers, and amidst a loud crackle of fireworks that some of the party had seen fit to light, jogged off into the road. Others then in pairs jumped into rickshaws and followed, urging their skinny drivers into higher gear. The steward and Lei Ling caught one near the end of the line, and climbed aboard.

"Catch up!" Lei Ling cheered the emaciated, leggy driver on.

The happy group rolled and bounced back down and across the hill, through houses and buildings that at first seemed right out of history. Narrow streets, crowded even more with pedestrians and vendors of every object and bauble and bird, hawked their wares relentlessly. Passers-by waved and bowed and called to the wedding party, only to be greeted in return by blasts of firecrackers flung like rose petals from the procession vehicles.

"Do they always drive like this?" the steward laughed as the rickshaw driver rested casually on the pullrails, precariously balanced and coasting along with both feet off the ground, as the rickshaw sped straight ahead with apparently no steering, down the bumpy street. Smiling pedestrians scurried out of the way, as each rickshaw roared past. The steward repressed the desire to snap an imaginary whip alongside the driver's ear, from their lofty double sulky seat.

"Faster!" Lei Ling called, laughing as the vehicle careened down the hill. "We'll pay you double if you pass the others!"

On and on they sped, laughing all the way, knocking over a pile of baskets here, a wagon of paper gifts there, spinning a pair of woven cages containing geese, suspended on a stick and carried on the shoulders of a man struggling uphill with his load. Two, then three other rickshaws were past, as if in a *grand prix* of Hong Kong. At last, as they gained near to the bride and groom, the driver came back down to earth, and screeched rubber soles as his feet took up the speed of the rickshaw in attempts to slow it down. "Not bad!" Lei Ling exclaimed. "We came in fourth!"

They climbed out of the bright red rickshaws amidst the laughing and jabbering of all the others, and one of the middle-aged men paid off the panting drivers, double going to most of them for their racing efforts.

The group then entered a large old structure that looked much like the tailor shop in the front, rather non-descript and with vertical signs hanging above the door. Once inside, however, the space opened on to a very gaudy, brightly lit stage with an ornate multi-colored brocade curtain, embroidered in gold, and heavy with gold tassels.

The steward jumped at the metallic CLASH! of cymbals followed by a huge resonating BWOOOOOONNNGGGG! The opera was well underway, but they had entered during a moment of instrumental and vocal silence. That was shattered in an instant, and followed by a series of other world sounds - squeals, bangs, crashes, bongs, thumps and booms, reedy horns and shrill flutes, a full orchestration of haphazard noises that put the hired funeral band to shame. These accompanied the irritating squeekings of the lead actors as they spoke, sang, shrieked, posed, melodramatized, shuddered and swooshed their ways back and across the stage.

Make-up was applied by the pound, faces painted into grotesque caricatures and expressions. Costumes consumed full bolts of silks elaborately set off with sashes and embroidery. Wings and satin slippers and headdresses and capes and billowing sleeves and feathers adorned every available space. Here was presumably a world of oriental understatement, in classic Cantonese format.

"It is an opera celebrating the Seven Sisters Festival, very fitting on the occasion of the marriage of my cousins," Lei Ling whispered. "I will try to help you understand."

The steward rolled his eyes around in their sockets, then struck a melodramatic facial expression. "Oh, you will do nicely as a leading man. You get the girl, in the end," she laughed.

Throughout the riotous mixture of singing, speaking, mime, banging and bonging, shaking and shimmering, acrobatics and dancing that droned on in front of them, Lei Ling attempted to make sense of the action. "The female lead is Tin Hau, Queen of Heaven. She is the one with the long pheasant tail feather protruding up from her headdress. How she shakes it determines many of her moods and expressions. See? First she was disbelieving. Now she is angry." The feather quivered in rage.

Dancers thrust themselves forward, only to be forced back again by imaginary onslaughts of water. "Those are seafarers. They are being thrown about by a great storm, caused in part by her rage."

"What is she angry about?" the steward asked, by now totally confused by the melee before him.

"There are evil forces attacking the sailors. The villains are the ones in bold gowns, with the big hats and masks. See how they shake their masks, and thrust themselves at the sailors?" The steward nodded. "The one in red, holds a small red book aloft. His threatening gestures make the sailors cower in fear. The next, in black robe, shakes a small tablet. He to, confuses and frightens the sailors. As does the one in saffron, with the scroll. And the one in blue, with the lance, and the one in brown, with the scimitar. The sailors are drowning in the protestations of these evil forces. They struggle to stay on course. Their craft is thrown against the rocks, and they flounder alone in the stormy seas. Their leader, the large man in the white and gold, is Huang Di, a mythical emperor of China. He is not able to aid his fellow sailors. They fear they are lost in a storm of confusion and rage. But then Tin Hau steps out into their violent world. Her rage is supreme, her will invincible. She alone has the power to drive the evil forces off, and calm the raging waters. Finally, as you see, the sailors are saved, regroup around Huang Di, and sail off confidently into the new dawn."

"Incidental Music" punctuated the strident drama with surprising accord, its profound brass BLATS and booming timpani CRASHES and nettlesome reed THWEETS and stringy TWANGS and TWONGS competing with off-key singing reminiscent of simultaneous performances of Strauss's *Elektra* and *The Chipmunk Song*. After what seemed like a lifetime of shakes and shudders and fist bashing and arm posing and eyebrow raisings, Tin Hau finally drove all the intruders off the stage. Her confident strides calmed both the troubled waters and the sailors, and harmony among fellow men became increasingly apparent, although countered by the far less harmonious instrumentalization from offstage. The steward yawned uncontrollably, and leaned back in his seat, confounded by the spectacle of subtle and not-to-subtle symbolisms still quite obscured from all levels of Occidental logic or comprehension.

"Come," Lei Ling laughed softly, as she urged him out of his seat and out the door. "You have had enough for one day. Possibly for a lifetime. And that was only Act I!"

Once outside, the steward looked about at the neighborhood. It contained a maze of stalls and shops and carts and baskets and cooking pots and simmering woks, competing on every inch of available pavement for any and all passers-by. The buildings were only two and three stories, and packed with people hanging out windows and on roofs and in ground floor shops, haggling and hustling and negotiating. The whole world seemed to be doing business. Whatever in one's wildest dreams one wished to buy could be found within fifty yards. In this one aromatic, riotous microcosm existed the world's most dense variety of cameras and fabrics and shoes and sweaters and silks and dried ducks and fresh chickens and chili peppers and *dimsum* fast food and fruit and prawns and paper money and dolls and binoculars and toys and antiques and ceramics and leather and watches and ivory and rugs and furniture and teas and hi-fi's and designer clothes and perfumes and cosmetics and jade. By comparison, the steward noted, India was boring bliss. There may be more people in total in Bombay, but per square inch, Hong Kong broke all records for people and merchandise piled all together.

Lei Ling dragged him slowly through the milling crowds, pointing out objects of interest, like blue exotic birds in cages or mink skins hanging like rodents from a rope, or freshly caught squid laying shimmering on a screen, or giant sienna crabs hanging on hooks in a window. And all about were a confusion of bold signs and streaming banners in reds and golds, hawking the wares and prices, surrounded by an army of ornamental dragons and demons who protected the merchants from harm or theft. It was, in a word, fascinating. It was also, in another word, overwhelming, and the steward urged Lei Ling to escape the selling frenzy and move to more open spaces farther up the hillside.

"Whew!" the steward sighed. "That gives new meaning to the word bazaar!"

"We have such streets all around the island and throughout Victoria City," Lei Ling replied calmly. "It may be that you are not used to such active crowds, coming from your quiet life at sea."

"Is it like this every day?" he asked in disbelief.

"It is Hong Kong. Business as usual."

They walked for a few blocks up the hillside, with no particular destination in mind. The steward noted that higher on the hill, above the markets and shops, rather precariously there stood, or huddled, hundreds of shacks and makeshift dwellings constructed out of old barrels and boulders and sheets of plywood and cardboard and tree branches and corrugated tin and any material that could be found to hold up a roof or serve as a wall against the elements. The sorry structures seemed to be all leaning on one another, as if collectively they could lend support to the spontaneous engineering concepts that produced each domicile. People and children scurried about from doorway to doorway, amidst thick bluish cooking smoke that drifted out from every window or door or crack in the roof.

"They are the more recent immigrants from the north," Lei Ling said, noting his interest and gaze. "They have not yet found adequate work so that they might move their families to better quarters. But they will. And then others will take up their places here. After the Japanese were driven out, Hong Kong had less than 650,000 residents. Now we have well over two million, and receive thousands of refugees each month."

"Doesn't the government want to prevent more from entering?" The steward surveyed the steaming hillside of huts and hovels that stretched for hundreds of yards, limited only by the edges of gullies.

"Yes and no..." she replied. "The government has a policy that tries to stop the refugees from entering, and will turn them back, to keep the population under control. But if a group of refugees makes it into the colony, as my cousins all did yesterday evening, they are allowed to stay. It is like a children's game you play... if you can touch base, you are home free. Besides, our manufacturing businesses are expanding at such a pace that they hire the new residents soon after they arrive. 'Made in Hong Kong' is taking on new significance."

The steward looked at the pathetic poverty and filth in which these new residents lived, and then looked back to the lights now decorating the dynamic highrises and modern office towers and opulent villas that walked up other sections of hillsides quite nearby. "It is a disturbing contrast," he noted softly.

"On the contrary," Lei Ling injected. "You must look at things from the other person's perspective. These new immigrants may have had a terrible life under the Communists. Their living conditions here, for the moment, may not be that different from what they had known. But their lifestyle is vastly improved. Here they have relatives who will help them, who will feed them and find them work. Here there is opportunity, a priceless commodity they did not have in the north. Here is far better food, education, health care. You may see poverty on the surface. But they see that their *joss* has been very good. They are happy to accept their fate. They made it to Hong Kong. Relatively speaking, they are the lucky ones."

The imaginary breath of two fiery red dragons greeted him as he ascended the small ladder up the side behind Lei Ling and peered on board. The sampanman nodded graciously below them, happy with his fee and proud to have ferried such an illustrious couple to such a magnificent junk. The steward pulled himself onto the deck and looked around in awe.

"It looks like a fairyland. It should be in a museum."

Lei Ling laughed. "It belongs to one of my uncles. Run Run Shaw has used it many times as a setting for his 'sword movies'. It really is quite magnificent, isn't it?"

"It certainly isn't your everyday working junk..." he said in disbelief as he surveyed the opulence and zaniness of the junk's topside structures.

The decor was beyond belief. Dragons and warriors adorned every pillar and post and railing. Freshly holystoned teak decks glowed in the evening moonlight. Incense burners were lit and smoldering on each deck, either to keep the bugs away or the evil spirits. The elaborately carved woodwork was a mastery of snakes and dragons and lions and tigers and demons, guarding the hatchways and ladderways adjoining every room and deck level. Lanterns hung from rigging throughout the overhead areas, creating a festival sky that twinkled and swung about in a thousand colors. It was a floating palace, protected by the images of every god and guardian known to ages of emperors.

As he walked about the decks, fascinated by the wildness of ancestral imagination, he backed into a fierce dog head, and jumped as ten inch fangs probed his backside.

"If you're thinking of casting me in one of your 'sword movies', my *kung fu* is a bit lacking, I fear," the steward said, looking for a dozen warriors to leap out from behind the masts.

"Don't worry," Lei Ling laughed. "I have protected you all along."

"What does your uncle do?" he asked, bewildered by it all.

She smiled, and lowered her eyes a bit. "He is in... shipping."

"Shipping? This is his flagship, obviously."

"The *Fung Shui* is purely a pleasure craft. Many of the more wealthy residents now are having them built, for weekend outings and parties primarily. But my uncle has a small fleet of working vessels. The Magpie, which you so courageously took in tow, is one of his."

"Ah. Your brother worked for your uncle then," the steward nodded. "That's where he learned to sail the Magpie so well."

"Something like that. Both my brother Reggie and I on occasion are asked to help my uncle Tai Ping Shan."

"Oh? What do you do?"

She looked back out to the city. "Whatever he requests..."

They stood in silence at the rail, looking back at the splendor of the city rising to the heights a few hundred yards away. The sea was flat and black, and reflected an almost perfect reverse image of the sparkling cityscape, marred only by the waddling trail left in the wake of the sampan that had brought them out to the mooring. It was a beautiful night, calm and balmy and well received after the storm of the previous night, and the setting was spectacular.

"This has to be the most beautiful harbour in the world," the steward said softly. "Thank you for showing it to me this way."

"Most travelers flock only to the peak tram, and see Hong Kong from the top down," Lei Ling said, looking off to the city lights. "Few have an opportunity to see the real city, like this. One's perspective is so different. Illusion transcends the reality. The city reveals so different a character, when one can find a bit of isolation from the crowds."

They had spent the afternoon after the opera trekking about the streets and markets, sampling hundreds of foods and shopping for nothing in particular. She had bought the steward a tiny cast

345

metal vase, carved and painted with flowers and kilned to radiance. "An urn for your tears," she had said, somewhat jokingly, as he had gagged on another hot chili snack. "Put them away on a shelf someplace and enter the future with confidence."

In return, he had bought her the smallest jade tear, a perfect green, that hung on a hair-thin silver chain. Nothing dramatic, and a quality well within his limited budget, nevertheless the bauble had a purity and simplicity that caught his eye and made him think of Lei Ling. She accepted the token with great delight, complimenting him on his miraculous ability to choose such a perfect jade piece, for only two Hong Kong Dolla.

The wedding party had dispersed after the opera, families and relatives returning to their soggy dwellings to prepare for tomorrow's businesses. The bride and groom had retreated to share their humble new home, a collection of three small rooms that leaned precariously out on the hillside, propped up on stilts and stones and roofs of other squatter huts that jammed together below it, atop the wholesale markets and nineteenth century tenements of the Western District.

"My uncle Tai Ping Shan had made this all ready for them," Lei Ling said as she looked up to their general neighborhood on the hillside. "For their wedding night. But because of the storm, they shared their conjugal bed on the cutting tables, as did we. Tonight, they chose to sleep in their new home. They both must go to work early tomorrow."

"It is a shame they can not enjoy it. It is really quite beautiful out here."

"It is a shame..." Lei Ling spoke softly, then took his hand in hers. "But for us it is our good *joss*."

The steward sensed a greater depth to her meaning, and said nothing as they looked at the hillside, and contemplated the unfathomable workings of *joss*. After a moment, she silently led him over to the gaping mouth of a monstrous dragonhead that surrounded the central hatchway. He followed her through, as if in a dream world, down into the belly of some strange nether land, down into the master cabin.

Made in China indeed took on whole new meaning.

"*Fung shui!*"

The steward heard the voices on the main deck above. Something had happened. Lots of jabbering and toning, of the excited, frantic kind, woke him from a deep sleep. Words needn't be clear. Something bad had happened. Lei Ling was not in the opulent bunk, leaving him to awaken in subtle light to the demons and ghosts and dragons of another world, scaring the wits out of him as his eyes began to register.

He groped about for his clothes, and struggled into them, minus one elusive shoe. Then he scrambled up the ladder to the main deck, to see Lei Ling standing among three wildly gesticulating relatives. She stood passively, a sharp contrast to their wild, animated storytelling. The steward joined her silently.

The three men pointed to the hillside and back again, describing with their hands and faces some grotesque event and agonizing end to something. Lei Ling stood without visible emotion or reaction, and listened as they repeated their vivid portrayal. Tears streamed down the cheeks of all three men, so great was their passion in telling the tale.

From the hint of a glow in the east, it was probably about 4 a.m. The steward kept his silence, but was beginning to understand. From where the men were pointing, something tragic had happened to the newly married couple. It became obvious. Mud slide.

Lei Ling walked silently over to the railing and looked up at the rising hillside. She seemed lost in her thoughts, and made no movements or displays of emotion. She stood there for interminable minutes, silent amidst the wailings and tears of her relatives. "Bad *fung shui!* Bad *fung shui!*" they cried over and over.

Finally, she turned and faced them, speaking in Cantonese. They nodded and scurried down into the waiting sampan that had brought them out to the junk. Then she came over to face the steward.

"They are dead. Mud slide. Caused by the rains. It weakened the foundations of a whole section of their neighborhood, and let loose. Many persons were killed in the slide." Her eyes betrayed her hidden emotion, tears now rising to the surface. "Chien Niu and Chih Nu... are dead." She choked on the phrase.

The steward made a slight move toward her, offering physical support. But an opaque curtain quickly lowered over her eyes, masking any show of emotion within. She stood even straighter, and turned again to look at the hillside. "Our good fortune... their bad fortune. It is *fung shui*. Chance. This is how the gods speak to humans."

The steward kept his distance, dumbfounded by the stoic stature of this young woman who calmly accepting the folly of chance as the one and only logical reason for such a pathetic tragedy. The fact that in such poverty, dwellings were built compounding one layer of unsound construction technique upon another, had nothing to do with anything.

"Lei Ling. Let me take you back to your family..."

"No. I will go alone," she replied softly. "Please return to your ship. You will leave in a few hours. We both have duties, now..."

He helped her climb down into the waiting sampan to the outstretched arms of her cousins, and then he followed, one foot bare. No one seemed to feel like laughing.

—-AT SEA—

"Nearwhere."

"Excuse me?"

"Nearwhere. We are not really there, nor here where you think we are, or should be, but we are near. We are still on that chart. That is good enough. We are nearwhere."

"Have you invented a word?"

"Somewhere near where you think you are. It is actually where you are. Not nowhere. Not somewhere. Nearwhere."

"Why not herewhere."

"Now you're getting it."

"Getting what?"

"Getting somewhere."

"Wherever that is."

"Precisely."

The steward scratched his head in awe of this descendent of some great Viking and his aboriginal form of seamanship. Then he returned to his labor over the charts, struggling to plot exactly the position of the Talabot as it chugged through the open seas. Landfalls were still far beyond the horizon. The sun was obscured by a thick, hot haze. The Loran was on the fritz. The last known exact position was Beirut. The course was basic South, with a small correction for compass variation and minor adjustments for current drift. Dead reckoning was his best last resort, for finding where the Talabot actually was, in the heavily traveled eastern Med.

"Don't worry about our position, Steward," Eiriksson mused casually as he sat in his bridge chair, huge bare feet up on the compass pedestal in the hot afternoon air.

"Don't you care where we are, Sir?" the steward asked, not understanding his drift.

"It doesn't matter," Eiriksson went on, taking a swig of a Tuborg out of the bottle. For a captain, he looked particularly relaxed, bare feet on the compass, shorts torn at the fly, white shirt hanging out of his waistband, and a beer dangling in his hand. Maybe even a little bit extra blitzed for the heat of the afternoon.

The steward shook his head in dismay. "So this is what's left... the ultimate heritage of those infamous Viking merchant mariners who explored new corners of the globe, and brought us all those cultural advances, like pillaging and raw herring," he mused to himself. He resumed his diligent search for knowledge on the charts, hoping he would not find any hidden sea mounts for an afternoon surprise.

"Really, Steward. You needn't try so hard. It does not matter exactly where we are. We are somewhere near where you think we are. Thus we are nearwhere, and that is, like beauty, truth, and all you need to know..." Eiriksson enjoyed exploring a good beer philosophy as well as the next barfly.

"But all my training so far..." the steward tried to say.

"Pure fishshit. It means nothing. Three years in your navy and you know little about the sea. Your navy has its head stuck up its own scopes and tubes and radars. It has forgotten the sea, and what it means to be a true mariner. The sea is the Great Mother. She gives birth, she nourishes, she punishes, she guides the way. She makes all things possible, after all. Your navy has forgotten how to appreciate its mother. It might as well be on land, pushing all those buttons and looking at all those little blips of fishshit on the screen.

"Mother of us all?" he smiled.

"Believe it, Steward. And never forget your mother. She deserves your appreciation and respect like no other creature." Eiriksson pulled a long swill on his bottle.

"Without her we wouldn't be Mother's little mariners?" he replied.

"Careful. Mother can hear you." Eiriksson's voice grew more mysterious and distant. "And she can be very touchy, if you don't show her proper respect." The steward tossed down his pencil and backed off from the charts. "I can't get a bearing on anything around here, let alone on your meanings, Captain. Do you love the sea, or down deep do you really hate the sea, Sir?" the steward asked, partially in jest and partially in a serious probing of what really makes a man like Eiriksson.

"Hate it?" Eiriksson asked incredulously. "It is the mother of life in all its magnificence, Steward. It would be a sad commentary on one if one hated it..."

"You really don't care exactly where we are, do you, Sir?" the steward sought to alter the conversation to a more practical course.

"Ahhh, fishshit, boy. Don't you get it?" the captain grew more impatient. "We are in the eastern Med. We are sailing 190 degrees, at fourteen knots. We have direction, and way on. We have purpose, a destination, a goal. We are near here. We are going there. That is all we need to know, at this exact moment."

"What about calculating our arrival at Said?"

"It will come about in ten hours, if the weather holds and the boiler doesn't blow up again. Fate often plays a part in your calculations, too." He finished off his beer and, after a huge fiery belch that rattled the windows, slung the empty over the side, right through the open hatchway as if bearing witness to years of practice, far out into the sea. "We are near where we should be. We will know where we will be, only when we get to that point. And even then we will also be nearwhere. Not somewhere. Not therewhere. Because we still will only be near to where where is supposed to be. Nearwhere tells it all. We are nearwhere most of the time. Only when we encounter other things and other people does it matter a

351

little more precisely where we are as we sail along in life. And even any of those notable encounters - a fresh landfall or a clean bearing on the cupola of the Hotel Intercontinental or a surprise ship on the horizon or the buoys at the entrance to a port of call or a strange woman between the sheets - is an event which happens somewhere where we are. We can try to re-plot it in our memories later on, but that same event that happened, somewhere, once again becomes a nearwhere, and that is close enough for nautical work. Got all that, now? BELLLCHH!"

"Somewhere, I became dead in the water between nowhere and therewhere. I most certainly am not anywhere near where you wish me to be, which is supposed to be nearwhere?"

"He's got it. By George, I think he's got it." Eiriksson rose from his supine position and danced a little jig to stretch out his legs.

"So much for sloppy chart work?"

"No," Eiriksson said, "You keep right on plotting our supposed course to somewhere, from wherever we are supposed to be. May come in handy some day."

"But I haven't any idea where where is, Sir..." he pleaded.

"Why, Steward. I'm surprised at you. We are on the bridge, of course.

"I'm on the bridge..." he replied. "You, Sir, by all my calculations, are somewhere else."

"Not exactly, Steward," the captain said as he looked at his watch. "But I will be shortly."

"Sir?"

"Cocktail hour, Steward..." he laughed as he strode off the bridge toward the lounge. "Passengers are waiting. I'll have my usual, please."

"Nearwhere on the rocks, coming right up, Sir," he replied crisply, as he took one last look at the chart for hidden sea mounts in the area.

"Steward?"

"Mrs. Boost?"

"My husband got grease on his best resort pants. Have you any spot remover?"

"I believe we do, Ma'am. I'll go check."

"If you see Byron, please ask him to come to our stateroom."

"He was back in the rudder compartment with the Chief Engineer, last I knew, Ma'am."

"Heavens, what pump is he inspecting this time?"

"None, Mrs. B. That's where Johannes keeps his private stock."

"Stock of what? Pump manuals? Pump parts?"

"Viscous liquids, Ma'am. Chilled *akvavit*."

KNOCK. KNOCK.

"Whoall is it?"

"The steward, Mrs. L. You rang?"

"One minute, Steward.... Gidddyyrrrdaahmmpahnnssonn... Gid ddiimmmonnfaahhsst.... Ddaahhhmmm... Ssshhheeeiiitt..."

"Pardon, Mrs. Lovelake? I didn't understand."

"I'll be raht theyah, Steward."

She opened the door and peered around from behind it. "Theyah now. What can Ah do for you, Steward?"

"It was you who rang me, Mrs. L. About twenty minutes ago. I was quite busy or I'd have been here sooner."

"Ahhh, yes... Have y'all seen mah Billy Bobby recently?"

"Yes, Ma'am. He's taking a nap on the starboard lounge deck."

"Good. Please bring me a rum and Coke and a beer, Steward."

"Yes, Ma'am."

"That'll be all, Steward."

"Yes, Ma'am. Are you feeling alright, Mrs. Lovelake?"

"Ah'm just fahn, thank y'all. Whah?"

"You didn't ask for a neck rub."

"I've found someone else who has stronger hands, Steward. Don't y'all be hurt or disappointed now."

"Stronger hands?"

"Your young helmsman, Ole. He's bin ashowin' me how he can hold his rudder nice and straight, even in the roughest seas..."

"Steward?"

"Mrs. Brububber?"

"I thought I heard you in the passageway. Have you seen my husband recently?"

"Not since this morning, Ma'am. He was having target practice... Calls it Viking skeet... shooting beer bottles off the fantail with Bill Bob's 45 caliber."

"Empty or full?"

"The bottles're empty. He's full."

"Has he hit anything?"

"Got the smokestack once. Dotted the 'o' in Tryggvasson."

"Oh dear. Did the captain say anything?"

"'Good shot'. He's the one who suggested throwing the beer bottles. Seems they ran out of herring..."

"Steward?"

"Mr. Potter-Smythe?"

"Come in here and close the door, please."

"Sir?"

"We must have a talk.... Man to man..."

"About what, Sir?"

"The ship has failed to keep up to its responsibility, Steward."

"How do you mean, Sir?"

"A tragedy approacheth. The whole ship is about out of matches."

"Matches?"

"I smoke a pipe, Steward. Special blend... Quinlan-Lazenby Tobacconists Number 58. I'm certain you have noticed."

"Yes, Sir. Strange aroma... Smells a bit like old Argyles..."

"Well, there are no more matches aboard. I've searched fore and aft. None to be had. I'm down to my last two here..."

"You've smoked a bunch of matches, Sir. One might suspect you've developed a craving for sulfur fumes..."

"Are there no more matches to be found aboard? Oh, drat. It's the ship's responsibility, Steward. You must do something."

"I will make it a priority item to buy a carton in the next port of call, Sir. And if I might say so, Sir, you've used them all... Trying to keep your pipe lit in the deck winds."

"But you can do it, Steward. I've watched you. One cigarette, only one match. Even in the damnable wind. Lit every time. How on earth do you do it?"

"Will you step outside, Sir?"

The steward and P.-S. climbed out of the hatchway on to the main deck, where the wind was ripping by at about twenty knots.

"Mariner's secret. Hold the match like a pencil stub, but inwards. Strike it and instantly cup it. It helps to be facing directly into the wind. For some reason the air blows by your hands better that way, and the match is fed from the bottom of the cup. Scrraaatch and cup...See? Just like a chimney."

The steward lit up a Players from his box, and pitched the match overboard. "Good in a fifty knot gale. Now you try it..."

P.-S. struck. "Damn. Damn. Damn. How's a body supposed to light his pipe at sea. Damnation."

"That's what they have stewards for, Sir... Allow me..."

"Steward?"

"Mrs. Landgrave?"

"Where's my lemonade? I ordered it hours ago."

"Coming right up, Mrs. L. Erda is making it right now."

"Well make it quick. Seems like everyone is slacking in their duties today."

"Anything else, Ma'am?"

"Yes. Yes. I've been looking all over this stateroom for my reading glasses. Have you seen them topside?"

"Yes, Ma'am."

"Where? Where did I leave them?"

"Top side of your head, Ma'am."

"Don't get cheeky with me, young man."

"Sorry, Ma'am. I'll get that lemonade now, Ma'am."

"Forget the lemonade. Ship's cook makes terrible lemonade. Bring me a Perrier with a twist of lemon instead."

"Yes, Mrs. L."

"And two of your famous APC's."

"Yes, Ma'am."

"And I mean today, Steward. Not next week."

"Hello, Steward."

"Hi, Mr. Landgrave. You wife seems to be under the weather a bit. Just bit my head off."

"Weather hasn't anything to do with it, kid."

"Oh?"

"It's the moon. Perigee. Apogee."

"Moon?"

"You'll learn, kid. Learn to read the phase of the moon."

"What phase are we in now, Sir."

"The I'm a terrible husband phase."

"What's after that? Gibbous?"

"Yeah. The I look fat and don't like myself phase. Followed shortly by the sleep over on the sofa phase."

"Then what? Full?"

"I got a hot flash for you, kid. Once a month they're all full of it. It's a cosmic certainty."

"Another, ahh... Bloody Mary, Sir?"

"Not this afternoon. Gimme a beer. I'm going back with Boost and the Chief."

"Steward?"

"Mrs. O?"

"Have you seen the book I was reading? Did I leave it in the lounge?"

"What title, Ma'am?"

Tropic of Cancer, Steward. You should read it. Opens some interesting portals of imagination..."

"You might try Henry's upside down side... *Capricorn*."

"Ah, yes, interesting... his upside down side..."

"Here, Mrs. O. I did find this other book near your husband's lounge chair. Thought he might still be wanting it..."

"Which?"

"That new one by some guy named Nabakov."

"Steward?"

"Mrs. Potter-Smythe?"

"I must speak with you, Steward. Please come in."

"Yes, Ma'am?"

"I would like you to speak with that Billy Bob Lovelake person. He's corrupting everyone on board with his crude remarks and distasteful actions."

"Ma'am? What's he done?"

"He has secretly been reading the most vile magazine. One newly printed in your country, I believe. And then he hides it around the ship. He even hid it in my husband's research papers. I threw it overboard."

"Which magazine, Ma'am."

"It's called something disgusting and frivolous like *Playyard* or something..."

"Oh, *Playboy*. That was Mrs. Lovelake's magazine, Ma'am. She was answering one of the ads in the back. Something about a vibrator for her lower back..."

"Steward?"

"Yes, Captain?"

"Passengers are all happy?"

"Seem to be, Sir. Everyone's still standing. At least up until cocktail hour..."

"Any requests we can't handle?"

"Only one, Sir. Seems a group of them are tired of smorgasbord every day."

"Tired of the world's finest caviar and lobster and shrimp and cheese? What on earth do they want?"

"White Castles."

"Steward?..."

"Yes, Mr. L. What can I do for you?"

"Y'all got any sivver pahlish?" The pudgy man mumbled as he lay on the deck chair, double chin strangling against his chest as he attempted to see the top of his protruding belly.

"Sivver? You mean silver?" the steward asked, confused.

"Thet's whut Ah saihd. Sivver pahlish."

"We have some back in the galley, Mr. Lovelake. I'll bring it right up. What's the problem? Your silver dollars getting tarnished in the card game?"

"Naw... It's mah damn belt buckle," Bill Bob Lovelake grunted as he forced his head up even closer to the large metal object gleaming so proudly in the late morning sunlight. "Bought it from some damn Jeewboy in Dallas last year."

Bill Bob Lovelake had been laying on the after part of the main deck in a lounge chair, throwing beer bottles out over the fan tail and trying to blast them into smithereens with his trusty pearl-handled Colt 45 pistol. The acrid smell of spent gunpowder hung in the air, in spite of the breeze over the stern. A series of beer bottles bobbed in the wake for miles behind, not in the least humbled by the aspiring shootist.

The steward bent over and inspected the three-inch buckle as Bill Bob thrust it upward to his view. "Impressive piece of metalwork, Mr. L. Must be heavy. Keeps forward lean on, I bet."

"Damn thang is startin' to rust. Here, looky at it..." he said, pointing with the barrel of his piece. "Gettin' all crusty and brown.... Must be the salt air, son. Mean stuff."

"Don't shoot yourself in the gut, Mr. L.," the steward said, partly in jest.

"Sheeit, boy," the reclining marksman replied. "We Texans 'r weaned on these tohys. Ah knows whut Ah'm doin'."

"Silver shouldn't rust, Mr. L. But let me have it. I'll give it a good shining up. Make your belt buckle gleam like the sheriff's in *High Noon*."

Bill Bob lay back, stretching the kinks out of his neck again. He let the 45 drop to rest along his leg, and then squinted up at the steward standing over him. "Sivver's s'posed to stay braiht and purty, ain't it, boy?"

"Just like our tableware, Sir. Everything gets a bit tarnished over a couple of weeks, but never rusts."

"Think thet Jeewboy sold me tin?"

"You Texans are too sharp for that, Sir," the steward smiled. "Must be an exotic alloy. Maybe tantalum or something."

Bill Bob strained again to see his buckle. "This is s'posed to be some rodeo rahder's personal prahze buckle. Pawned it after he broke his ass bone and quit the circuit."

"Nice design. Eagle spread over bucking bronk rider... And you got it in a pawn shop?"

"Dang! He sold me tin, he gets his balls shot off when Ah gits home, boy."

"How long had the pawn broker been in business, Mr. L.?"

"Donno, boy. He jist set up shop downtown. Mebbe a few weeks. 'Wildcat Izzy Geltbenkian - Top Grade Pure Sivver'..."

"Name doesn't sound Jewish, Mr. L. Armenian, maybe."

"Don't git many Armenians in the State of Texas, son. Jist Wetbacks... Naw, he's a Jeewboy, ahwlright."

"How do you know that, Sir?"

"He got a brother in Lubbock, son. Sells diamonds. He's a one who sent me to Wildcat Izzy in the first place. An' his name's nowhere near Geltbenkian. It's Moe Glatt, just like his damn brother Izzy. Isadore Glatt. Them Jeewboys sure got some balls. Changin' names from a Jeew to a Armenian..."

"I'm sure they value their balls too, Sir."

"Seems they do, boy. Izzy's got three of 'em ahangin' outsaihd, up over his door," he replied, sighting down the barrel of his pistol. "An' Ah'm goin' to shoot all fahve of his balls off when Ah gits back home."

"I would think you could trust him, Mr. L. He probably wants to develop a business."

"Business? Izzy Glatt first come to Dallas to trah to git rich on a piece of all the oil raahts action. Had some hairbrained scheme where he'd do some wildcattin' in the desert an' he'd git 5% of evrythang. Somethin' about negotiatin' an' redrawin' property lahns an' raahts, and sellin' them off to Yankees. Some kahnd a tax dodge or somethin'. So he changes his name to Izzy Geltbenkian and says he's got a cousin to some rich Woag in the Middle East. Thought it gave him credentials."

"Did it?"

"He fleeced a few hundred folks, for a couple a years. But then all the fields went drah, an' his company all a sudden was broke. Wildcat Izzy embezzled all the cash n' run off. Three million buckeroos. Good Christian folk don't take lahtly to thet, boy."

"He get caught?"

"Yep. Found him hidin' in the trunk of a '55 Cadillac headed across the border to Mexico. S'prised ever'one, son. Findin' a body in the trunk, headin' South. Border rangers grabbed him real good. Before the week was out, Wildcat Izzy was ihn his own steel cage ihn a West Texas jailhouse, eatin' garbonzo beans n' rahce."

"How'd he end up back in Dallas?"

"Served only six months. Somehow he got off for good behavior. Meanin' he bought off the district judge, prob'ly some other Jeewboy."

"So he set up shop in Dallas, selling silver?"

"Saihd all his belt buckles were 100 percent all pure solid sivver. Hammered out on Indian reservations."

"Big market in Texas for big beltbuckles, Mr. L. Izzy could do all right."

"Saihd he got religion in the can, boy."

"Maybe he did. Now he's helping the reservation."

"Saihd he had the exclusive, and thet's whah he could sell 'em cheaper 'n Neiman's."

"Izzy Glatt comes out clean, after all."

"Yeah. But will his beltbuckles?" Bill Bob strained again for a closer view.

"Well, let me have it, Sir. I'll put a shine on it."

"Here you go, boy," said Bill Bob as he struggled to unclasp, then remove his buckle, leaving his belt in place. He handed the prize up to the steward without ever raising up off of the deck chair. "Ah raight thenk y'all."

The steward took a close up look at the piece of metal. "Hmmm... Whatever it is, is flaking off a bit, Mr. L. I don't think it's solid silver. See here?..."

Bill Bob leaned up on one elbow, interested. "Lemme see. Sheeeit. Did Ah get me screwed by thet Jeewboy Armenian, boy?"

Both men scrutinized the metal object at eyeball distances appropriate to age. "See what I see, Mr. L.? That color there?"

"Where the sivver's come off? By the eagle's ass feathers?"

Bill Bob grabbed the buckle back, for a closer personal inspection. "Sheeeeiiit!"

"Umhum. This was hammered out in the jailhouse, Mr. Lovelake."

"You'all mean this ain't 100 percent all pure sivver, boy?"

"I'm afraid not, Mr. L. More likely pure silver paint over pure license plate."

—SUEZ—

"Guineas."

"That's who dug the canal?"

"Actually, yes. Guineas." Tony Potter-Smythe puffed casually on his pipe, as he leaned back to the railing, looking aft into the distance, back toward the narrowing coasts that necked into the Mediterranean mouth of the Suez Canal. All ears strained his way, as the passengers realized that undoubtedly they were in the presence of a true Egyptophile.

The sides of the canal had quickly merged out of nowhere into tight parallel embankments of sand that ran straight and as far as one could see into the desert before them. Gone was that unique feeling of freedom at sea, the lack of constraints, the options of direction. Now the Talabot was channeled in behind a nautical caravan, number five in a string of twelve assorted tankers and freighters, all churning primly along at seven knots, one after the other like painted steel camels in tow, now truly ships of the desert.

The ambient world had changed, dramatically, right before their eyes. It was almost too severe a change to accept. Five minutes before they were rolling softly on the high seas, awaiting the formation of the caravan by number. Then suddenly, as if passing through a thin screen of date palms that divided one world from another, now they followed a watery gash through the desert, followed faithfully along, without choice, followed blindly along, back deep into the sands of history.

The steward stood with the full contingent of passengers along the rail near the bow. All had grouped there as the Talabot had approached Port Said, a flat, non-descript collection of buildings and cranes and wharves and warehouses at the northern-most mouth of the canal. A small launch had gurgled out to greet the ship, and off-loaded a pilot who, by regulation, would command the Talabot through the canal. Eiriksson and Bjarni, relieved in more ways than officially, had immediately hit their bunks for a nap, both having made this passage many times before. The Egyptian pilot, flouting his authority, dismissed the steward forthwith from the bridge, refusing to believe that he could in fact be the chosen one, one who could be called upon to control the ship in more difficult passages. A common steward? Never.

"Guineas. That's what they were called," Tony P.-S. gnashed gutturally out of one side of his mouth while clamping on his pipe stem with the other. "Italians, mostly... Quite stupid enough to be lured into the adventure of digging in the 125 degree sand, and poor enough to justify it to their wives."

The historically novice crowd nodded in agreement as they looked about at the increasingly hot desert sands and sizzling dry air now surrounding them, inland, yet but a few miles from the Egyptian coast.

"Not Egyptians?" asked Fiona Landgrave. "I thought they were the master earth movers of all time."

"Wrong. They were people movers," spoke up her husband Herman. "The Egyptians developed a lot of experience, from years of flagellating all those slaves. Over the centuries, they had watched millions croak in the heat. They knew better. So they watched the Italians bust their butts this time."

"Bust their butts...this time?" asked Louise O'Rouark, in her soft low voice that always sounded sexy, regardless of time or place.

Potter-Smythe set a half smirk above his pipe in a moment of superiority. "Ah, yes... This is the second Suez Canal. You must realize we are passing through what was a very advanced civilization in ancient history. The Egyptians dominated the region for a thousand miles in every direction. Indeed, recognizing the importance for trade and travel even then, the Egyptians built a canal in the 20th or 19th century B.C., possibly right on this track. It connected the Mediterranean with Lake Timsah, about 30 miles up ahead, which was the northern most point of the Red Sea in those days, before the sea level dropped. Later Xerxes I, I believe, extended it as the waters receded. About the 8th Century A.D., the sands took it over."

Eyes widen with wonder as they looked forward into the flat desert sands, at the shallow saber gash full of salty water that stretched southward without deviation to the horizon. Heads shook slowly at the Herculean effort required in digging even one bucket of sand in such heat. A sprinkle of pedestrians in drab desert mufti strolled the embankment on the eastern side, and occasionally looked up at the passing convoy. No one seemed to be working.

"It's funny... Guineas seem to do their best work standing in a ditch," muttered Michael P. O'Roaurk around a stubby Camel Filter in his teeth, as he tried to envision the enormous enterprise in progress. "Something about fear of heights, I guess."

Self-professed Professor Potter-Smythe droned on, oblivious to the sophomoric chatter about him. "de Lesseps and his team of French engineers imported what they felt were more experienced and reliable European canal diggers, who were periodically paid something like one English Guinea for their heroic efforts. Thus, these labourers became known as Guineas. In point of fact, no self-respecting Egyptian would ever work all day in the sun for so paltry a fee. It was quite insulting."

Byron Boost chimed in, "I thought it was because their algebra skills were lacking. The Egyptians couldn't figure out how one Guinea could actually be worth something like one Pound plus one Shilling, and make it add up in hieroglyphics."

"All part of British strategy to keep the WOGs in confusion, dear sport," Brububber quaffed, in best British mockery. "Wreaks havoc on the decimal system, what?"

"Then how did they build all those pyramids and temples way back then?" Pammy Sue Lovelake asked. "Import the Italians?"

Shelley Boost answered before Tony Potter-Smythe had fully finished his pre-verbal tamp and puff. "I thought Yul Brunner built the pyramids."

"You mean Charlton Heston," Fiona Landgrave corrected her.

"Them Jeeuuws... Ah... 'Scuse me...Hebreeuuws..." added Billy Bob Lovelake, sniffing the sizzling afternoon that was fast taking on the air of body odor and pipe smoke. "They beeilt the pyramids. Eeegyptians ahr teeoo daahmb and scraaawny."

Anthony Potter-Smythe was gracious in bypassing this opportunity for community disdain. "Regrettably, I can see my fellow passengers don't understand the profound significance of the magnificent history of this area," he puffed professorially. All ears leaned again his way.

He waited just the right extra pulse of time, then set his hook gently into gaping mouths. "Obviously, the Egyptians built the pyramids, and the early canals. They did not build them for money. They built everything for the glory of their gods of the moment, who just happened to be embodied in their pharaoh, so they believed, usually a sickly little chap with a sizable army, a very good public relations agency filled with priests and a shrewd accountant known as a scribe."

The others were taking it all in. Completely hooked. Tony was in his element. His meticulously honed Cambridge accent grew dryer and crisper, as he savored each wondrous moment of history, and played his catch.

"Common man would plant and reap during the Inundation, a period of possibly three or four months when the Great Nile flooded everything near its banks. The Nilotic peoples became quite prodigious farmers for their ancient time, and grew nearly everything they needed to make it through to the next year, plus a surplus. Other tribes and nations would actually come begging to purchase grain from the Egyptians during periods of draught and famine, further increasing their wealth and power among the fledgling nations of the area."

Everyone smacked his or her lips, as the dry air and expanse of sand conjured up images of famine without smorgasbord tonight.

"You all of course remember the story of Joseph... Genesis... ahh... XXXVII, I believe? Joseph was the second youngest son of the rather polygamous Jacob, son of Isaac, who was the son of old Abraham himself. Poor Joseph was drummed out of the family by his stepbrothers for being too goodie a lad. Seems he snitched on them when they were bad. One day they decided to kill him. Fratricide was popular then. Threw him in a pit, they did, to die. But in a moment of indecision and greed, they decided instead to sell poor Joseph for twenty pieces of silver to a caravan of Midianite merchants en route to Egypt, where he was then resold to Potiphar, the captain of the Pharaoh's guard, who had a thing for light-skinned Hebrew boys. Somehow in a few years our little bugger dramatically improved his lot from a teenage slave to become the chief minister to the Pharaoh himself. Rather rapid rise for a Jewish lad, what?"

Many nods of agreement. From experience no doubt.

Puff. Puff. Puff puff. "And then in a period of great famine throughout their Palestine homeland, up near Sechem, these same unscrupulous stepbrothers were sent by Papa Jacob to buy grain, which the prosperous Egyptians held in surplus. And from whom did they have to buy it? Ah, yes, good plot writing here... their long sold-off little brother Joseph, now Viceroy of Egypt. One might say Joseph was now in position to command a good price..."

"Stick it too 'em. Jist like a Jeewwboy..." Bill Bob confirmed.

"Well, in fact Joseph did not. His price was actually to trick his bad brothers into pleading for the life of the youngest and still innocent brother Benjamin, whom he had set up falsely as a thief and was about to place into slavery, just as had he been. But Joseph it seems was truly a good lad at heart. Alas, his actions mark a rare point in history when compassion overtakes vengeance."

The desert yawned in the afternoon. Eyes and ears were on the self-esteemed scholar, as, methodically, he tamped his pipe in deep concentration, each precious tamp causing levels of anticipation to rise. Finally he went on.

"Joseph, his victory complete as his brothers fell shamed at his feet, forgave them all. He even brought his father Jacob and all his family to live in Egypt, saving the whole clan from certain death by famine. That, in point of Biblical time, marked the beginning of major Hebrew settlements in these lands between Egypt and Palestine. Not in 1948, as we have all just witnessed in the bloody culmination of today's Zionism, but in some 2000 years B.C.... Right here... a mere few miles from where we are now sailing... In this Hellhole in a sea of sand... This godforsaken plot... This sun-bleached wilderness... This unending desert... This scarab haven... This roasting realm... This... Egypt..."

His words trailed off into the distant mirage of history. A thousand images filled the minds of all the passengers, standing like school children along the bow rail, mouths agape, trying to piece together all the bits of fact and fable that had seasonally inundated them since childhood, and out of it all, infuse some logical meaning into the wondrous words "hope" and "belief" and "faith."

The group stood silent, looking off into the desert. Nothing was in sight, to either side, except sand. Miles and miles of sand, all the way to the horizons in every direction but fore and aft. Time, and sun, and sky, and heat, and sand, and sand, and sand. And through it, straight as an arrow, cut this water-filled ditch, surrealistically out of place with its natural surroundings but reassuringly alive with wavelets washing up the slanted sides, splashing and lapping upon the desert itself, the following wake of yet another waterborne caravan, rippling its way through the barren expanse of sometime in history which was today.

"Drink time, don't you think, Steward?" Potter-Smythe said, finally.

They lined the bow rail, fellow Talaboteers, leaning on forearms in mirror image, feeling the hot breeze rise up from the shallow ditch and into their faces, singeing their nostrils with each new breath. Drinks rested casually over the rail, sparkling in the hot early afternoon sun that blazed overhead. The steward knew each passenger now not so much by name, but by drinking habit. They were all here... in a line... Mr. Bloody Mary extra heavy on the pepper, the Two Wild Turkeys and water, Mr. Pink Gin, Mr. Dewars on rocks, Mrs. Pink Gin heavy on the bitters and water, Mr. Vodka Martini straight up with an onion, Mrs. Rum and Coke, Mrs. Seagrams 7 and ginger ale, Mr. Jack Daniels rocks, Mrs. Dry Rob Roy, Mrs. Beefeaters Tonic big slice of lime. Tray empty, the steward himself joined the line, popped, then pulled on a chilled pilsner, Mr. Heineken, wetting his ever-dryer whistle.

Potter-Smythe savored his Pinkie, and swung his hand out across the sands toward a sudden splash of green that appeared to the west, obviously irrigated fields fed off the nearby Nile delta.

"They were ingenious masters of flood control, those early Egyptians... Building dykes and containment basins... Channeling the flood waters into a vast network of canals and growing fields that literally lined the length of the Nile from Aswan down to the Mediterranean Sea." Better pause for a couple of puffs, Tony. Pipe's faltering. Everyone must wait.

"But then eight months of the year, the Nile would recede and the land would go bone dry, leaving the farmers little much to do. Oh, they could just sit around and gripe at the heat. Maybe go to war again with the Nubians... that was always fun. But they could not farm. It's pretty miserable here in the dry season. Eight months of a hot bed, if you will, for social unrest."

"No 'telly', eh, Tony?" Herman Landgrave piped in between a pause for new matches.

Potter-Smythe did not miss a puff. It was his lecture time, leaning there on the bow railing, fire ax nose cutting proudly into the light wind. "This inevitably gave rise to the Pharaohs, who were no dummies, mind you. They presumably were descended from a rather enterprising family of warrior types, who saw an opportunity to reap a ripe piece of the farm, so to speak, but without doing any of the hot dirty farm work themselves. So they set about to create and implement one of the truly great concepts in the history of mankind..." Tony drew the phrase out so profoundly and so eloquently that he himself enjoyed hearing it, and puffed a triple just to savor the echo.

All ears flapped forward so as not to miss the secret of life...

"They created 'Organized Religion'..." A gasp in unison from the others.

Tony watched his pipe smoke drift skyward for a moment. "Oh, there were numerous *ad hoc* religions in that day. Church and State were for all practical purposes the same thing. But the Egyptians forged one of the best... Possibly long before anyone else in so sweeping a concept, and cloaked it in ' The Great Promise'... a tantalizing concept well used thereafter throughout history... the promise of a better afterlife. But!...herein lies their genius. The great promise could be redeemed only at a certain cost..." Quiet anticipation........ "Taxes!"

Double Gasp!!! Eyes darted about as if someone had farted.

"It took a major selling job. The pharaohs and their advisors the priests and scribes, created a huge public works program for the off seasons, which just so happened to be designed to keep everybody thinking the pharaohs were indeed sons of the gods and could fulfill the great promise. The small people bought into it. Actually they had no choice, for to fight so grand a concept meant slavery or death. Regardless, it beat the boredom of the dry season. For their construction work, the pharaohs in turn would give the little people food and sustenance out of crop taxes they had taken from them in the first place. The Egyptians didn't invent taxes. Every leader since the beginning of time, has extorted taxes from his minions. Even prehistoric great apes charged one banana per family, assuring that the biggest ape stayed stronger than all the other apes. Your modern day Mafia learned its skills from these great apes, I do believe, and even today remain traditionally simian in how they administer it." Everybody chuckles.

"Sadly for us all today, governments have always been involved in the very same process of legalized social exploitation. They too call it 'taxes'. It still amounts to extortion by the strong, made palatable to the weak by some mysterious promotional hocus pocus, unintelligible terms and nebulous accounting practices. But in concept, quite effective. Politicians still follow the concept explicitly. Don't vote for me, and you'll have trouble and even higher taxes. Vote for me and I'll make sure you get back for your family pot one chicken... one of the three which I will first have taken from you in taxes..." More chuckles.

"These pharaoh fellows were smart. They mobilized the peasants during the dry spells. Don't want them sitting around getting soft, what? Or carping about the astrologers or priests. If there were no wars to be fought, then let's get the small people building something. Make it big. Impressive. Ready, people? Dig that ditch. Lift that boulder. Stack them higher and higher. Do it for your god, and I promise you you'll have a better life next time. Don't do it, and your god will have your head."

"Typical terms for a contract..." Landgrave confirmed. "One side always gets screwed."

"Actually, it was a pretty good contract for both sides. The Pharaoh... the word pharaoh actually means 'great house'... took 20 percent of their crops after harvest for his personal warehouse, just enough to make sure the little people and their families would be hungry a few months later, and then would sprinkle back 5 percent to the peasants in a gesture of royal beneficence if they burst their hernias building earthworks and monuments. Amazingly, the concept worked, and it has continued working for the better part of five thousand years."

Boost injected an observation learned from years of on-line experience with his pumps. "Why change it if it works, right?"

"And there you have it... starting 4500 years ago. Continuous stabile government. Homogenous thinking. Everyone working for the benefit of god or king or queen. Just like Great Britain."

Chuckle. Puff, puff.

"Oh, the Egyptians had their fair share of slaves brought from wars here and there, and more than a few dissidents. But here was a homegrown style of government that few others throughout history can rival for its longevity and effectiveness. Officially, here, in Egypt, began the world's first, and most successful, version of..." A motionless hush awaited his words. "Dreaded Socialism." Shudder!

"What happened to the slaves and dissidents?" Pammy Sue chirped in. "Were they sold to the A-rabs?"

Tony Potter-Smythe shook his head in dismay. "Ah woman," he puffed on fatherly, "Have you ever seen Egypt on a map? Its total population lives only within one mile inland from both sides of the Nile. That's it. A country of 25 million living only in an area seven hundred miles long and two miles wide. The rest is desert. Until air travel, there was only one practical way in and out of Egypt. Up or down the Nile. So the Pharaoh's palace guard could always police who went where, when, up or down the Nile. Troublemakers became crocodile bate."

"So that's where we learned it..." Bill Bob inserted. "But them Heebreews got out..."

"Certainly they got out. Moses struck a business deal with the Pharaohs. Actually, Hebrew tribes had lived in Egypt for hundreds of years, most of which were not in bondage. They lived side by side with the Egyptians, and many prospered. Quite conceivably too much. In most ways, the Hebrews became Egyptian. Profligate buggers, the Hebrew contingent grew in numbers until they posed a serious threat to the indigenous Egyptians. Worse, they had continued to espouse their own preferences for civil and religious dogma that did not include Pharaoh in its hierarchy."

"Sounds like Orval Faubus's niggras..." Billy Bob muttered.

"My guess is that the Hebrews were causing many Egyptians to question the current system which provided so much privilege to the pharaohs. Social unrest was on the rise. Famine grasped the land. Blood was starting to flow in a political chess game. If you take my first born, I take yours. So when Yul Brunner thought he saw an opportunity to rid his country of a tribe of troublemakers, he bade them go and good riddance. Alas... poor Egypt has regretted it ever since."

"Why? I thought Egypt and the Jews were like oil and water." asked Byron Boost, true to proper hydraulic metaphor. "At best a messy mixture where one always floats to the top, and the other is kept on the bottom."

"You may have a point in that phrasing. Ironically, the lineage of Hebrews and Egyptians are both from one family. They are truly brothers. Or half brothers. Really. Old Father Abraham, I think it is in Genesis XX or about there, is the Patriarch of both lines."

"I know that story", Brububber broke in, trying to rid center stage of Potter-Smythe and his tampous pipe. "Here's Abe an old man, and he badly wants an heir. He's not getting any younger, at 80 or 90 or something like that. He's concerned about establishing his family line, one that some voice in the wilderness told him would be famous. 'Time to get serious, Abe.' the voice says. Abe has this younger wife, Sarah. A real knockout. His niece actually. Families were extremely close, then, I guess. At one point, Abe even lets the Pharaoh take her into his harem. Says Sarah's his sister. Abe will do anything to stay alive. Eventually, Pharaoh gives her back. Too bitchy maybe, for the harem. Regardless, Abe wants heirs. Maybe his wife Sarah has a headache. So first he knocks up this Sarah's handmaiden, Hagar, who is an Egyptian. History can't fault him for a little fun in the back of the tent, right?"

"Particularly if the stories of Jewish wives are true when it comes to sex," Herman Landgrave interrupted in proper accent. "Abe, the tent pole needs painting..."

"But then Sarah, the first wife, Abe's got a few, she gets pregnant. Now Abe's starting to create real difficulties in the tent. Sarah's handmaiden, Hagar, she gives birth to her son Ishmael first. Then Sarah has her son, Isaac. But in Abe's tribe's traditions, it's the firstborn son who gets the inheritance. Here old Abe makes his first of two fatal mistakes. He acknowledges his second son Isaac, the Hebrew son, as his true son, and throws his Egyptian son Ishmael and his mom out into the desert with nary a shekel. How do you think the Egyptian kid felt. Not too happy, right, when he saw all those goats going to his younger white brother."

"Just like Orval's niggras..." Bill Bob confirmed again.

"O.K., so again we might forgive Abe for this. Maybe he's cruel, or Sarah's got him by the matzos, or he plays favorites like most of us. But oh, no... then Abe has to make the big one. The cosmic error. The mistake that has caused trouble between the Jews and Egyptians since history began..."

"What's that?" voices asked as one.

"He let somebody write it down."

"He what?..."

"Somebody, probably a shyster lawyer from Jerusalem, writes the whole story down, and it gets published in the *Bible*!... For everyone to read and remember for all time. This guy is the original 'Schmuck'! So what if Abe bopped the colored maid. So did Jefferson. So what if he shafts his first born son. Lots of pigheaded kids get cut out of the will. The boys would have fought it out for the inheritance after he was dead, or their families and their lawyers would have settled it somehow, and it would be forgotten in the dust of time. But no... Somebody writes it down. Maybe Abe felt that was the way to insure his second born son could keep all the goats. But all it has served to do is to keep reminding the Egyptians they got screwed, that they were not as good as the Hebrew side of the family. That's like spitting on someone for four thousand years. You don't easily put aside a continuous insult like that. No wonder the Egyptians are still fighting mad at the Jews. They think the word 'anti-Semitic' has been misapplied all these years. The Egyptians are the real victims of discrimination. Bastard sons of Abraham. The world can forgive Abe's amorous impropriety. But it has never been allowed to forget the awesome power of the written word that painted the Egyptians as second class forever. There are too many books in circulation."

The sun beat down on the captive human cargo of the caravan, philosophically sipping their way across the sands of Goshen. On the shore of the canal, standing on top of the sandy embankment, was a small Egyptian boy, about ten, dressed in a long dusty striped *jalaba*. Nearby stood, or slept, a skinny gray donkey. The passengers waved at the boy as the Talabot slid quietly past. The boy raised his third finger high over his head in international salute.

As if cammed in unison, the thirteen took a sip of their drinks, and looked back out ahead, at the dirty stern of a Liberian freighter in the line before them.

Tony Potter-Smythe took over the fable. Puff. Puff. Go Tony.

"Many Arabs believe that Ishmael was the true sire of the chosen race, not Isaac. They believe that he was the one chosen to father a great nation, the Arabs, and that the size of their numbers and success of Islam over the centuries has proven it. After all, the Moslems do control just about everything from Gibraltar to Istanbul. And if our friend Nasser gets his way, he will be the likely heir to it all."

Interrupting their reverie, the rusty remains of a scuttled old freighter, a reminder of events of a few years just past, passed close by them. It was wedged awkwardly against the embankment, leaving barely enough room.

Suddenly the Talabot's horn blasted the tranquility with a deep menacing THHHUUUUUUUUUUUUUUUUUUUUUUUUTTT! The steward turned to look up on the bridge, where the Egyptian pilot was doing a wild Dervish dance, running around in circles, arms flapping and voice screaming in gibberish. Quickly looking forward, the steward saw the distance closing rapidly between the Talabot and the Liberian ahead. Looking astern, he saw the Chief Engineer, old Johannes Gynt, and two of his snipes standing at the side rail, smoking and drinking beer, just as they were, and looking up at the ship's horn in wonder.

"Oh shit, nobody's minding the store!" he thought to himself. He ran back toward the old engineer, waving his arms. The craggy Norwegian, still some fifty feet away near the after superstructure, noticed him with a smile and waved. The steward stopped in his tracks, jumped up on a cargo crate, and did the best Charades interpretation of his life. "Ship ahead. Collision! Engine Telegraph. All back full!"

For never having played the game, the old chief got the message, tossed his bottle of beer into the canal, and vanished down a hatchway into the engine room. Within seconds, the Talabot shuddered and shook as the propeller reversed itself and disgorged a huge wave of brown froth over the embankments and into the desert. Then the desert air was pierced by a monstrous throaty roar, as near as possible imitating the voice of some god or at least one of his messengers, as the safety valve on the boiler blew, venting a towering plume of superheated high-pressure steam into the heavens. It vanished instantly as it struck the bone-dry air, a momentary vision of some holy ghost, just as the gushing wave had vanished into the sands of time.

Now up and down the canal, a chorus of seraphim joined in, horns tooting and screaming their own variety of danger signals and reverse engines and S.O.S.'s and nautical swearwords, as the caravan slammed itself into a massive snarled traffic jam, the bumpings and crashings of bow to stern and side to sand rivaled only by those on a Los Angeles freeway. All hell had befallen the ships of the desert. Bows dug into sandy walls, metal scraped upon metal, water overflowed embankments, and a hundred scruffy local Egyptians appeared from nowhere to gawk and laugh and jump up and down. Arms flapped across every bridge and deck, startled seamen scurried to and fro, horns blasted, sirens wailed, tempers flared, and steam valves blew their tops in frustration. Yet, miraculously, as sounds and signals drifted off into desert nothingness, no major damage occurred and not one person seemed to be injured. Passengers at the bow never moved, watching this majestic display of seamanship in silent amazement.

Just as suddenly, piercing the momentary silence, blasted the powerful, structured sounds of the Triumphal March from the second act of Verdi's *Aida*, booming out of Eiriksson's stateroom at full volume on his Hi-Fi. *TAH TA TA TUMP TUMP TAH TAH....* *TAH TA TA TUMP TAH TATUMM!...* A vision of an Egypt in all its splendor filled the canal, parting the narrow sea of confusion with an air of magnificence and grandeur, calming the trauma of the moment and filling every impassioned pilot and sea captain with awe. Arms stopped flapping. Yelling and screaming ceased. Seamen rose from frantic searching for possible damage over the sides. A host of Egyptians miraculously materialized out of desert mirages. *Gloria! Patria!* The canal had survived intact. And once again, a Guinea appeared, musically instrumental in its rescue.

In mere seconds, all eyes from every ship in the jam turned to the source of the magnificent sound. And there, above it all, there, standing on the bridge wing with a beer in his hand, naked except for a skimpy pair of white briefs barely visible under his huge white chest and belly, stood a red-eyed frowning Eiriksson. His eyes panned the scene of near carnage, glowering fiercely at the other captains and officers and pilots in view. Then he raised his bottle to the sky, as if to toast the blazing sun overhead, and squinting, head back, drained its contents to the vary last.

With a sidearm flip he sent the empty bottle over the side and over the embankment, nearly sculling an Egyptian onlooker in the process. Then he frowned down from his temple of authority, down at the steward still standing on the cargo crate, and shook his head slowly from side to side. The steward looked back at Eiriksson, standing erect, ready for punishment, awaiting noble edict.

"You woke me..." Eiriksson mouthed slowly above the crescendo of brass and strings. Then he turned and re-entered his stateroom, into the deafening cauldron of full orchestration... *TA TAH. TA TA TAH. TA TA TUM TUM TUM TUM TUM TA TA TA TAH TAH TATUMP!*

"Under attack?"

"Bumboats." Bjarni replied. "Here they come. Battle stations everyone! We are now under attack!"

No sooner had the hook splashed into the salty waters of Great Bitter Lake than a cloud of floating locusts began converging on the Talabot. Bumboats. By the score. Coming from every point of the compass. Paddling their way to the sides of the ship, merchant skippers jabbering and yelling and hawking their wares. It was an onslaught from a floating bazaar, come to greet each and every ship that ever dared pass through the canal. The attack of the dreaded Sea Peoples.

Sailors aboard the Talabot scurried to close any hatch and batten down any cargo cover or container. Portholes were slammed and locked. Bjarni grabbed the loud speaker on the bridge and passed the alarm, "Now hear this. All passengers and crew are advised to secure any valuables. Merchants and thieves are descending on the Talabot in numbers, and will steal anything in sight. Protect your valuables, please. This is no drill!"

The steward had experienced these aggressive merchants before, on his previous passages through the canal. But this time, they were landlocked, not out in the relative safety of the harbour, outside Port Said or Port Tawfig at the southern end near Suez. Confusion resulting from the implosion of the caravan in the canal had delayed the procession by some four hours. There now was no way the string of ships could make it through the 100 miles of narrow canal during daylight hours, so an administrative decision was made to anchor the ships in Great Bitter Lake, that large body of water between opposite coasts that once was part of the Red Sea itself. This was not too unusual, as frequently during periods of heavy traffic, caravans were held there while caravans bound in the opposite direction were allowed to pass.

Great Bitter Lake was a wide shallow expanse of very salty water, located in the middle of nowhere. Neither tides nor canal currents had any daily effect on the exchange of its waters, and year after year, century after century, as it's water slowly evaporated, it had become yet another of the supersaturated salt lakes of the region. But there were settlements around it. And where there were Egyptians, there were peddlers... for all Egyptians are born salesmen.

Now the Egyptians attacked in waves, targeting in on each vessel at anchor, paddling, motoring, sailing, converging as fast as each could, aiming for the more affluent of ships, merchandise held aloft like battle banners, jabbering and yelling at the tops of their voices, each bumboat racing to be the first at the feet of the hapless victims on board. Ah! Tourists! It was going to be like shooting fish in a barrel.

The passengers did not heed Bjarni's announcement, but lined the rail in delight and fascination. Oh, goodie! Souvenirs to buy! Something to send back home to Aunt Maud!

To their dismay, the first grinning Egyptian to climb over the gunwale and stand there panting, holding his baubles and beads aloft, was unceremoniously picked up by two crew members and tossed back overboard into the sea. KERPLASH! Collective jabbering from the bumboats rose a half tone higher. Then another grinning face appeared above the rail, only to be met by a fist, and fall back out of sight. KERPLASH! Then another grinning face, and another, only to sail startled off into space, again propelled by the sinewy arms of Viking seamen. KERPLASH. Then KERPLOONNK! One of them must have landed back in a bumboat.

They were undaunted, revealing the stuff of their great warrior ancestors, and kept coming in waves. Determination and optimism are the mark of any great salesman. And they had that aplenty. The passengers stood in amazement, as the melee continued for at least fifteen minutes. Every time an Egyptian would climb on board, he would be launched into the evening air with aplomb. KERPLASH!

Finally, Bjarni and some deck hands hauled out fire hoses fore and aft on both sides, and pumped them up to blast strength. "This'll stop them," he yelled gleefully. "Pour it on, mates!"

The Egyptians finally realized that this tiny nation of Norwegians, like the Israelis, possessed more sophisticated arms, and held a redoubt of formidable resources. So they backed off, yelling insults and shaking fists but still in full grin with all their teeth, to an encircling encampment about twenty yards off the ship, out of range of the fire hoses. Every now and then, one brave soul would venture back along side, only to be bombed with a bucket load of garbage from the crew's mess hall.

Actually, it was a melee of great fun for both sides, a replay of events held a myriad times before. After a while, both sides rested, knowing full well that some negotiated trade agreement could be reached benefiting both, and one which the wetter side would quickly break if wily enough to find a novel way aboard.

One by one, each passenger started talking down over the side to a merchant in a bumboat. "Wait a minute! Wait a minute!" Bjarni called out to the hungry lot. "There's a science to all this. Better learn to do it right or you'll get screwed royally."

With fire hose at the ready, he called over to one particularly grinning Egyptian, holding long cotton *gellabiyyas* high over his head from a small canoe-like craft filled with bundles. He motioned him closer with one hand, brandishing the long brass nozzle with the other. The peddler eased cautiously over along side, and smiled up with great teeth that contrasted against his dusty skin color and surprisingly light hazel eyes.

The trading began slowly, then increased in intensity.

"How much for that cotton *jalaba*? Which cotton *jalaba*? That one in your hand. This *gellabiyya*? This beautiful robe belonged to the great Khedive Said himself. See the fine embroidery. For you $100. WHAT?! O.K. $50. Ridiculous. For you $20, my best price, for you are a gentleman. Get fucked. All right, $5. I can go no lower. I'll give you fifty cents. Three dollars. Naw, I don't need it. Two dollars? Fifty cents. O.K. one dollar. Throw it up here. Throw down the one dollar. Put the *gellabiyya* on this string. The dollar is coming down on this other string. Very good business. My pleasure. Any time. How about this *gellabiyya* too? $20. Ridiculous. It belonged to King Farouk. He weighed 400 pounds, and that looks like a small. Oh, you are right. I meant his son, who went to Harvard. It is his *gellabiyya*. That was the Aga Kahn. Oh, yes, my mistake. Only $5. I don't need it. One dollar and fifty cents? Why? The other was only one dollar. My mother is dying and needs medicine. Let her die. Fifty cents. One dollar? Seventy five cents. Done. Lower the money. Raise the *gellabiyya*."

The passengers watched in total stupefaction. One by one they moved to inspect the soft, long Egyptian dayshirts made of the finest pima cotton they had ever touched. Seventy-five cents? Bjarni turned to the peddlers waiting hushed at bay, and smiled. "O.K., they're all yours."

With that, the bumboats made a rush to the sides of the ship, scarabs and sphinxes and brasswork and *gellabiyyas* and carved wood and stone idols and perfumes and leather sandals waving ahigh, all teeth and jabbers in the soft twilight of the day. It was like a feeding frenzy of locusts, tender green dollars being eaten alive like never before, and passengers loving every exotic bite.

"Moses?"

"That is my name. And you are, I would venture, the steward?"

The small Egyptian stood in a shallow reed craft, something out of Lake Titicaca. He was about fifty, maybe five feet five, and looked very thin in his light blue *gellabiyya*. But he was sprightly, and his eyes sparkled in the glow of the ship's deck lights.

"Why aren't you selling, like the others?" the steward called down to him.

"Why aren't you buying, like the others?" Moses replied with a toothy smile.

The steward laughed. "No money."

Moses hailed up, "No merchandise. I have only my wits to sell."

"What should I buy, from your supply of wits?"

"I would suggest.... a party." Moses stared up to the railing, and looked fore and aft, surveying the quality of the ship.

"A novel idea. We only have three parties a day on the Talabot."

"Then make it a special party. A costume party." Moses geared up his argument. "I will provide an exotic dance band, exotic dancers, and the exotic refreshments. You provide the basic food, the soft and alcoholic drink, and the room or deck space. Your passengers can quite adequately provide their own costumes. There is enough in all their purchases of merchandise to dress an army in mufti."

"A novel idea. A costume party," thought the steward. "How much is your fee."

"Moses pondered some algebra for a moment. "With a straight face, he replied, "$2,000."

"What?"

381

"But for you, because you are such an intelligent gentleman, only \$100."

"For everything?"

"For everything. The band, the dancers, the savories, and my fee. Total. Complete. Everything."

The steward tried to fathom the reasoning of this wisp of a man. "He didn't really haggle. He knows I liked the idea. He set a fair price, if he pays for all the bodies. What am I missing? Is this guy straight, or really pulling a fast one? After all, his name is Moses. That should give him a touch of credibility. Or does it."

"Yes?"

"I'll be right back."

The steward climbed to the captain's stateroom level, and knocked on his door. Surprisingly, Eiriksson was up and dressed in khaki shorts and shirt, and reading. The steward started to relay the proposal, when Eiriksson silently interrupted him. He walked out to the railing and peered down to the reed boat below.

"Hello, Moses. How'd you find us way up here?"

"I have special connections, Captain."

"Yes you do indeed, Moses. Bring them aboard."

And with a wave of his hand, a new fleet of ten small bumboats appeared from out of the darkness to join Moses, white teeth shining in the reflected lights and music blaring from an assortment of exotic instruments. *"Oh when those saints.... Come marching in...."*

The party of the gods had begun.

Transfiguration.

The steward watched in awe, as this new wave of more civilized locusts overwhelmed the ship, hoisting huge bales and bundles and baskets aboard by pure manpower.

It took only fifteen minutes for the enterprising troupe of minstrels, waiters and dancers to erect flowing webs of sheerest cotton voile across the cargo booms and halyards and masts and forward superstructure, transforming the cargo deck and bow into a light floating cloud. Soft evening breezes wafted across the deck, moving the billowy fabrics in graceful dance overhead. Paper lanterns were hung on crude hemp lines from every mast and boom. Flowers appeared in hanging baskets, and an assortment of large satin pillows mushroomed up in corners and on top of cargo boxes and hatch covers. The most exotic scents filled the night air, as if out of a dream, wafting about in soft plumes from smoky incense that smoldered in hammered brass braziers. The whole process seemed to be well choreographed, as if erected and performed by these skillful artisans many times before. Animated jabbering and bowing accompanied every act, from hanging wispy streamers from the guy wires to sprinkling rose petals across the cargo hatch. Grapes and pomegranates and dates appeared in abundance in woven baskets. Throughout it all, Moses himself presided over the production of every aspect, rivaling even C. B. De Mille in his directorial sway.

As if on cue, music transformed all activity into a mood of Oriental grace and splendor. Some ten musicians in Masonic mufti, sitting on the foredeck above the cargo holds, began a sensuous series of heartbeat rhythms and lyric lines that evoked mysterious ancient Scottish rites. Bystanders found themselves lured into subtle, hushed swaying... to and fro, like reeds being teased by a gentle wind.

Two by two came the passengers, two by two, out on to the open deck, themselves bedecked with the most innovative exotic combinations imaginable of recently purchased craft items and ornaments and opulent baubles and blowing scarves and flowing *gellabiyyas*. As each couple ventured timidly out onto the floor, small searchlights mounted on the wings of the bridge would seek them out, highlighting their costumes and in some cases revealing, through the severity of backlighting, their rather strange and intimate underpinnings. At first the passengers were shy and hesitant to display their creations, but as the efficient Egyptian waiters placed large brass cups of very potent fruit punch in their hands, they livened considerably while laughing at each other's costumed finery.

Most of the men wore long cotton *gellabiyyas* accented with some kind of statement made by an unusual hat. Landgrave sported a red fez, purchased at the usurious sum of one dollar, Boost had donned the removable white fabric top of an officer's cap, and Billy Bob Lovelake wore his favorite trucker's cap with the IH logo. Brububber decked himself out in an antique pith helmet along with brandishing an ornate dagger, and O'Rouark had wrapped one of his wife's silk scarves up into a turban, and carried a small water-cooled hookah upon which he puffed vigorously. Almost as expected, Potter-Smythe ceremoniously entered in a long white *gellabiyya*, curly toed slippers, white bed sheet flowing over his shoulders as a cape, and pillowcase draped back and down from his head, secured with a brow cord fashioned from an old school tie. In his hand he carried an ebony fly flail.

The ladies of the night, however, had gone a bit farther in costume invention. Pammy Sue looked quite intriguing in flimsy harem pants over her red bikini panties, with numerous beads and baubles festooning out of the strapless brassiere that struggled to contain her ample bosom. Shelley Boost came in an embroidered open cotton robe that hung loosely about her pink nylon nighty, and had a white rope mop draped over her heavily painted eyes like some sun-bleached Nefertiti. Ducky P.-S. followed in as handmaiden to her husband's lordly ways, dressed in dusky brown *gellabiyya* with a tattered sheet pulled over her head and shoulders, coyly enshrouding her body and her face, and leaving only her eyes to flutter out to the crowd. Fiona Landgrave had aspired to be a priestess, wrapping herself in a long white sheet and sporting a golden tiara and a heavy beaded breastplate necklace. Little Belle Brububber had painted herself head to toe with Max Factor number 6, assuming the part of a plump slave girl in burlap rags torn from potato sacks scrounged in the galley, and had unwrapped strategic locations to reveal just the right amount of brown pork belly. Louise O'Rouark surprised no one by coming dressed in red fez, dark sun glasses, white officer's shirt with captain's boards, long white slacks, and black pumps with high stiletto heals. Her hand held a jeweled handled fly flail, which she snapped against her hip in appropriate gesticulation, all the while strutting about like Bette Davis as she puffed impatiently on a Pall Mall in a ten inch ebony holder.

The crew involved in the party scene also wore cotton dayshirts or whatever items they had scrounged in trade. The steward himself was dressed in white shorts and sandals and brass armlets, and had wrapped a piece of cargo chain about his neck. On his head, he wore a pillowcase, secured by another piece of chain. His duties it appeared would be limited to the preparation and serving of ice and hard liquor and showing Moses's cooking gang to the galley. Moses's troupe of assorted waiters, now actively engaged in plying food and drink to the passengers, were dressed in colored balloon pants and open vest tops, and individualized by a variety of moustaches and hairdo styles topped with beanies or fez. All guests were greeted with a barely decipherable "Good evening. I am your waiter Omar. How may I serve you?"

Moses flitted about the gathering crowd, bowing and jabbering and grinning and hosting the affair with the skill of an impresario. Everyone quickly became intoxicated not only by the punch, but by the exotic airs of sandalwood and frankincense and rose petal that exuded from this miraculous floating oasis. The passengers had finally realized their dream status in life. Oh to be wealthy, in days of yore. Sure beat baking bricks.

The band itself was a marvel. There, somewhere sifted through the sands of time, sat the Orient's answer to Occident Swing... There were the brothers Abdul and Amahl Dorsey on sax and bone, Big Mohammed Herman next to sidekick Rashib ben Goodman on reed sticks, a wild-eyed Fayez iben Krupa on kettle and cymbal, Ishmael Brown on alto sax, Caspar Cugat on gourds, and Haji James on trumpet. All led in the mellowest of big band sound by the quietly animated Abrahim Miller on rather bent trombone. *In the mood?* Let's dance.

The passengers took to the elevated dance floor atop the cargo hatch like true sons and daughters of the depression. Two steps led to fox trots and on to jitterbugging, with occasional stops for yet another chalice of pomegranate punch and a puff on a Camel. A wind chime hung in front of a bridge spotlight tickled light across the crowd like the wandering rays of a ballroom globe. Even the steward was pulled from his personalized drink orders and on to the floor, first by Louise O'Rouark who grabbed him by the neck chains and held him strangely near to her warm, sensuous tobacco breath, and then by an effervescent Pammy Sue, who flapped her way around the floor like a berserk chicken.

Exhausted, the revelers fell to cushions in every corner, and had thrust into their hands chilled refills of punch, which were downed in an instant. The local Egyptian waiters knew exactly when and where to appear, with fresh chalice or grape or fig or even a welcome fanning from palm fronds. The steward marveled at their knack for anticipating the sensuous cravings and primitive urges of their clientele. Quietly, ornate *hookahs* appeared at every cushioned corner, smoking seductively.

"What's that strange smell?" the steward asked into Moses' ear.

"Oh, do not worry. There is only a mild form of hasheesh, blended with a Turkish tobacco. It will not hurt them."

Hurt them indeed. Within minutes after a few experimental puffs of the exotic water pipe, by all passengers, they were feeling nothing at all. They lounged stunned on the pillows, laughing ridiculously at nothing in particular, and munched grapes or dates or guzzled punch. The mood grew more pagan by the puff. Never before had these stiff, conservative, retired Americans and British, been so delightfully stoned.

An Oriental riff cut through the sensuous cacophony, and a hush fell as Moses took center stage, bridge lights upon him, his gilded front teeth sparkling like midnight suns.

"Esteemed Ladies and Gentlemen of the Great Ship Talabot. I have the honor to present to you, in this most beautiful setting of sand and sea, our main attrrrrrraction of this evening.......... The World Famous... The One and Only... The Exotic... Sensational... Reigning Princess of the Nile Delta...

.... Miss... Thais!"

A hush fell over the crowd. Swallows of punch halted half way. Lights simultaneously went out, as if in one breath the gods had extinguished the world's candles. All except one. One solitary taper in an ancient golden holder flickered softly on top of the bow capstan. Mysterious reedy sounds, more tonal than musical, mischievously pierced the silent Egyptian night. Distant at first, then growing nearer, a mystical rhythm... at best the faintest *TUMP* of a drumbeat, began to emanate from the swing band. Then it built and grew and built anew, *TUMP*, quietly at first, *TUMP*, then ever more urgently, *TUMP TUMP* until it broke TUMP TUMP into the pulsing, pounding *TUMP TUMP TUMP TUMP* heartbeat of history itself.

Out of the darkness, a hand mysteriously appeared near the candle, gracefully, slowly waving and stirring, casting ghostly shadows upon the gossamer tenting overhead. Then an arm extended from the darkness, into the candlelight.... Followed by a second hand. Next a scarf, long and whimsical, began drifting to and fro in the flickering candlelight. The scarf strangely increased in size, swelling to create a ghostly flowing scrim, behind which in sensuous silhouette metabolized the recognizable lines of a female body. Hands joined with arms, arms with shoulder, it with flowing hair, it with long neck, neck with back and waist, waist into hip, hip into leg. All the while the music coursed forth in a long, impatient crescendo, ever beating more strongly, more purposefully, more urgently, until, bursting its bounds, it exploded into a passionate, agitated scream which fired darting tones aloft like shooting stars. More, the beat demanded... *TUMP TUMP TUMP TUMP*... More, the notes sang out. More.

The expressions on the faces of the passengers confirmed the cry. Goblets drained into mouths and spilled down chins. Water pipes glowed red with heavier puffing. All eyes fixed on the aerial scarves and body parts flashing before them. More. Don't stop here! More!

As if pulled against her will, Thais slowly, painfully began to increase her gyrations behind the flowing scrim of her many scarves, her silhouette turning and twisting and whirling and teasing the straining eyes trying to grasp a clearer vision of this unreachable loveliness before them. Stronger and stronger her movements became, propelled on by the urgency of the music that surrounded her, that goaded her, that lashed and pulled at her passions. Suddenly, music reaching a vehement release, through the blurring mist of scarves burst a beautiful young body, all glistening with oils and sweat, whirling long legs and belled ankles enfilmed by the flow of airy harem pants, sumptuous sweat-laden breasts exquisitely contained only by the tiniest of stringed bikini top. A flailing of thinly woven pigtails that if stilled would hang below her naked waist down to her ample hips and supple buttocks, spun about her head like a halo. Topping off this exotic sunday were armfuls of golden bracelets and a gleaming ruby gemstone the size of a fig, grasped somehow by a navel of undoubtedly epic proportions, cresting deliciously upon a glistening bare abdomen.

Thais.

"ABOOMDADABOOMDADABOOM!" the music called.

"ABOOBDADABOOMDADABOOOOMMMMM!" the undulating hips responded.

The stoned passengers lay sprawled about each other in this smoky other world, transfixed in some hypnotic spell, eyes locked on to the rapidly gyrating gemstone, totally lost in their exotic pleasure dome. "Gahd Dawg..." breathed Bill Bob heavily. "Will yeou lookie at the duggs on thet Niggergirl." Even Pammy sue gawked with envy.

Thais knew how to play a crowd. She danced and swirled and slinked her way down from the bow deck, scarves wrapping in the air behind her like airy pinwheels, sliding her way down the arm and body of Tony Potter-Smythe on to the cargo deck, drawing her scarf slowly across the neck of Herman Landgrave, trailing long ropes of her hair through Bill Bob's gaping mouth, brushing her breasts ever so lightly over Byron Boost's balding head, shimmying her gemstone madly in front of Brububber's bulging eyes, and finally, gracefully spilling her body up and onto the hatch cover dance floor. There she lay for a brief moment, chest heaving, heart pounding still to the rhythm of the drum, one arm outstretched to the sky as if imploring some greater force to release her from her passion.

"More. More! Do not stop! More!" the music screamed forth the demands of the audience. *ABOOMDADABOOM...* "More!"

As if carried on inexorably by some primitive undertow, first rippling as a wave in the breeze, then wriggling like a snake getting into forward gear, Thais began again, moving, slinking, twisting her way along the hatch cover, her body throbbing to every pulse and plea of the music about her. Finally she rose in a dreamlike trance and began gyrating, her hips beating and grinding in wild circular rhythms, her ruby shimmering, her belly quivering and flipping beads of sweat off into the crowd.

ABOOMDADABOOMDADABOOMMM!...

Faster and faster she drove her hips, pounding and quaking past a threshold of pain, on into deeper passion, into a new demonic pursuit... Spinning... first slowly... then faster and faster and ever faster, hair flailing fully about her head like a whipping halo, spinning and twirling and spinning about, wildly chased onward by the very demons she craves to seize, until her face arched upward to the great sky above.

ABOOMDADABOOMMDADABOOMMMMM!.....

Onward and onward she spun, arms outstretched, beseeching, pleading for deliverance, screaming for release, driving further and further into the outer reaches of corporal sensations, hands grasping out for the stars, reaching out beyond the stars, out beyond the universe itself, reaching out into the very infinities of ecstasy.....

THHHUUUUUUUUUUUUUUUUUUUUUUUUUUTTTT!

The ship's foghorn roared into the night air, its hoarse steam spewing droplets over all the wispy cotton streamers. The startled steward quickly looked up to the bridge.

There was Eiriksson, leaning on the railing, smiling broadly, his mischievous hand still on the horn cable. He was obviously well-oiled himself, both inside and out, and his nearly nude body glistened in the moonlight. A stunned crowd gaped, breathlessly. Thais fell to the deck, a panting, convulsing mass of flesh and hair and sweat.

The band, its rhythmic inertia in disarray, made a feeble attempt to resume playing.

Thais looked up into the sky, her eyes reeling about in a near swoon of exhaustion. "Eiriksson... You....pant, pant.... fucking....

389

pant, pant....bastard....pant, pant...pant, pant..." she gasped upward toward the bridge, her fist raised in its direction in weak defiance.

"*Helvete*, Thais honey... I like to enjoy a good climax too," he called down with a grin. Then out of the darkness, he was joined, one pressing on each arm, by the shining specters of two long, fleshy Nubian girls who were bare-ass naked, except for tons of gold necklaces and beads which cascaded down sweaty black-tipped breasts that pointed up at the stars.

"Come on, my lovelies, let's get on with my massage..." Eiriksson laughed heartily, picking them up in one swooping motion, and carrying them off to his stateroom. "Ha! Ha! Steward! Champagne for everyone!" he called back from the distance in a booming laugh.

The band struck up another haunting theme, led by mysterious harmonies of mandolin and oboe and flute in light fast pursuit of each other's tails. The passengers puffed vigorously, chasing frantically after the remnants of their shattered trance.

Then CLAPPPP! Moses, taking command again, clapped his hands, once, causing dreamy eyes to look up.

Waiters dressed in their open vests and bloomers and embroidered beanie caps came out of every corner of darkness laden with trays overflowing with racks of lamb and plump roasted chickens, surrounded by juicy melon slices and dates and saffron rice and ripe olives. The crowd, its hash high now at a ravenous peak, dove into the hot, steaming flesh and chilled fruit like vultures. In seconds they were covered by the juices and bloods of ceremonial sacrifice, and screaming for more. On and on came the fantastic spread - platters of paprika grilled pigeon stuffed with green hulled wheat, bowls of cayenne powered *hummus* chick pea puree and mashed fava beans and sesame seed *tahini* with slices of red pepper, cucumber and feta cheese, trays of mullet roe spread on freshly baked *'aish* flat bread, trenchers of braised veal shin and lamb kidneys and fenugreek flavored pastrami and spicy meat balls in garlic onion green pepper tomato sauce, and on and on with an assortment of mouth-watering, finger-licking, hand-dipping succulent savories. Following the captain's orders, the steward poured rounds out of a Rehoboam of Heidsieck Diamant Blue, often by request right into the brass punch chalices, to wash down the spicy feast. Like the bacchanal scene from *The Ten Commandments*, Moses stood silently aside, surveying the growling swarm of bodies and flesh and flies.

"Is it always like this?" the steward asked.

"Always," Moses answered. "If we but had a fatted calf, we could continue for days."

"Eiriksson has thrown these parties before, I can see."

"Yes, indeed," Moses smiled knowingly. "He is a loyal client. A true Viking appreciates pagan excess."

Moses stood quietly surveying the progress of the festivities, his hands clasped behind his back, his beaded head cap propped straight and erect on graying, slightly fuzzy hair. "How do you seem to stay calm amidst all the melee?" the steward asked, looking at all the passengers joining so readily into the orgy of the feasting.

"I have seen life at its best, and at its worst. This is somewhere near the middle," the little man replied. "You should see a boatload of Germans."

They moved from their position in the shadows of the superstructure, over to the port railing, out of the way of the frenzied splashing of food. "Where did you get all your friends, on such short notice?"

"Oh, we follow the ships, and greet them usually at Port Tawfig. Your traffic debacle this afternoon forced us to bus up here for the festivities tonight."

"Roving minstrels and entertainers, right?"

"Exactly. A troupe of traveling players are we... and yours for only $100."

"Where did you find the... girl?"

"Ah, Thais. She is from the exotic sands of Brighton Beach. Come, you must meet her."

"Brooklyn?!! Not Cairo, not Alexandria?"

"She is the niece of my cousin Abrahim, who now lives in your country. He had the good fortune upon return here for a vacation,

391

to marry one very comely lass from the Upper Nile. Their rather succulent offspring you see there, now known throughout Egypt as the famous Thais, a belly dancing legend in her own time, is none other than one Rebekah Nahor, no longer willing to perform her art of Exotic Dance in your Port Said restaurant on Manhattan's Eighth Avenue. She has, as you say, aspired to higher profits, more in the traditions of her Hebrew forefathers, and has returned to Egypt."

"She's Jewish? I thought the Egyptians just finished a bloody war with Israel. How is she allowed to remain here, let alone stay alive here?"

"My dear young man. We Egyptians are all a bit Jewish. And vice versa. And we are also a bit Persian. And Assyrian. And Greek. And Roman. As you have just witnessed, there are moments when our women are most difficult to resist, and the various conquering armies over the centuries have happily sewn their seed quite prodigiously in our more fertile valleys."

He looked up to reveal his own light blue eyes that stood out like jewels above his dusky skin tone.

"And you, Moses? This is your living? Producing Bacchanalia?"

"Actually, just the opposite. I keep such revelries in check. They would happen anyway, so I have taken it upon myself to regulate our primitive desires and passions by a few simple rules, and in the process, take a small fee for my services. If I did not produce these festivities, someone less disciplined would, and persons would undoubtedly get hurt. At my functions, everyone gets mellow and well fed, and if one wishes to be amorous, one can be assured of a *kosher* partner."

"They are all Jewish?"

"By all means, no. Most are Egyptian. I meant clean."

"What about morals? Aren't you fostering pagan revelry?"

The small Egyptian placed his hands together in prayer mode, under his chin. "Dear young Steward. People throughout the world still display and even enjoy the most primitive passions, lusting after all sorts of life's splendors that have by some civil or religious law been made taboo. In fact, such laws only inflame our desires.

These activities are pleasurable. They tease the body. They excite the senses. They vent primitive forces corked inside us. So people invariably invent moral or legal ways around such obstacles."

The steward scratched his head in disbelief. "You are saying there is no fundamental law for the conduct of life?"

Moses smiled. "Certainly there is. Live it." He waved his hand across the crowd, now dropping juicy morsels into open mouths of partners. "Laws, we are told, are created for our own benefit, to prevent physical and mental abuse. But such laws are easily circumvented. For example, in Judaic/Christian law, and too in Islamic law, adultery is taboo. Thou shalt not lust and covet.... But Moslems and Jews throughout history have had no problem justifying multiple wives, even harems, and sex slaves, or in marrying sisters. Christians have no problem justifying multiple divorces, or enjoying premarital relations. The fact is, in all cultures, we can always repent at the end, and be forgiven our transgressions. So we enjoy life. One needn't be a Cenobite to be a decent person."

"But there must be some fundamental law. Or we would all murder each other."

"Alas. We continue to murder each other regardless of any law. War is an inevitable part of life. Without question, in retrospect wars are terrible and bad, especially if one loses. But so far, in spite of our veneer of more civilized behavior, we have not been able to prevent or eliminate war. War remains a primeval passion, one that to date cannot be reigned in or channeled to more positive pursuits. So we adapt our professed beliefs and bypass our laws, to justify war. We glorify war in the name of our god, calling it his will, and kill our brothers without mercy, and certainly without guilt... Regardless of our instruction in *schul*, or sermons in church, or the laws of the prophets. At the sound of the battle horn, we passionately follow our leaders into bloody combat, knowing we are in the right. We elevate war to holy status. So, unfortunately, do our enemies. All to some pathetic end, where only a few profit."

"You are a reasoned man, Moses."

"It does not take any special talent, other than opening one's eyes to reality. The one law fundamental to mankind is a desire to maintain power and dominion. Freud calls it one's *Id*. But it is more that mere survival of self. It is the jawbone of an ass that keeps man in power, or the spear, or the sword or the gun, or the control of food, or the secret wisdoms of the priests, or the private knowledge of the lawyers, the private cache of the king, or the intricate theories of the scholars. Each within his own craft will create his own fundamental law, to be forced upon minions less in an attempt to regulate humanity into non-abusive behavior, but more to maintain a position of privilege and power. If one doubted the Pharaoh or envied his privilege, the Pharaoh would declare that the sun is god, and that he was his corporal form, and that the sun god would punish everyone if they didn't adapt to the wishes of the Pharaoh. Civil law and religious law have throughout history been one and the same, even though we make pompous attempts to distinguish between them. The Torah, the Talmud, the Commandments, the Pillars of Wisdom, the Way, the Path, or Leninism or Maoism or constitutional law... all are painted with the same brush."

The feasting and drinking had reached a seriously mellow period, with the band rendering an Oriental version of "*Mamoouuud Indigooo*" in the smoky, still night air. Sweating, bloated bodies lounged all over the pillowed deck, some as if still stunned from their feeding stupor, others slowly gyrating and moving to the music as if in some couchant pagan dance. Most couples were joined in the correct match-ups. Some displayed various levels of romantic pursuits, dreaminess, or delirium. The pungent smells of hasheesh and Turkish tobacco enfolded themselves within the delicately teasing aromas of frankincense and sandalwood. The steward watched as two dark shadows silently withdrew from the deck area and climbed in and under the canvas cover of the whaleboat. One was a slim Egyptian waiter in pantaloons. The other looked like Louise O'Rouark.

"All this doesn't cross over into fostering the concept of sin?" the steward asked as the shadows vanished from view.

Moses smiled and looked out over the flat waters. "I, for one, recognize it more as a concept not of sin, but of foolish indiscretion. And wherever there is a fool, there is opportunity for profit. I provide what the fool desires. I keep the peace. I employ the Egyptians. By orchestrating life's festivities to some degree, I am able to extract a humble fee for my services. It is merely business. Thus, I am able to support a quiet but respectable life style for my wife and twelve children."

The small Egyptian bowed slightly and silently exited off into the shadows.

The steward looked off into the night, off toward the horizon where a canopy of a trillion stars trailed across the sky, trying to find some other meaning in the little Egyptian's logic, trying to find some better, more reasonable master plan to it all, written in the splendor overhead.

The band responded with a Coptic version of "*String of Pearls.*"

His duties now less critical as bodies began sinking back into oblivion, the steward lit up a Chesterfield and blew smoke into the night. But rather than the aroma of tobacco, he sensed a more sensuous air about him. A dusky voice behind whispered, "Got another fag?..."

He held up his Chesterfields without looking over. A slim hand pulled a cigarette from his soft pack. Then two long fingers grabbed his from his own, and transferred the light. Lungs inhaled deeply after a strong pull, and exhaled forcibly. The glow lit up a shining face with sticky, half inch black eyelashes arched below a pound of pasty malachite eye shadow.

She moved along the railing in the shadows, fluffing her pigtails back off her shoulders to give them a splash of fresh air. "This rock is killing me," she groused, as she plucked the fig ruby from its fleshy mount and popped it into his hand.

"You can still mesmerize 'em without the rock, you know."

"I doubt it. They'd focus in on my stretch marks."

There was something charmingly disarming about this young woman. She had on the outside everything one would dream about in one's wildest exotic fantasy. The finely braided hair of a Nubian princess, replete with beads. Shiny light brown skin, smooth as silk and oiled and scented to perfection. Teeth of ivory. The waist of a wasp. The long proud neck of Nefertiti. The thighs of a panther. The just fleshy abdomen of a Nile fertility goddess. The breasts of Anita Ekberg. But when she opened her mouth... the tongue of an asp.

"I assure you, everything is a blur. You really dance up a storm."

"Every time is a challenge... A blend of speed and agility. I like to see how far I can sling sweat from my belly."

"Some of it still hasn't landed out there."

"I sunk six bumboats in the final spin tonight, didn't I?"

"You've come a long way from Brighton Beach."

"Moses give you the word?"

He nodded. "Another act coming up tonight?"

"Nah, I've done my gig. They're all passing out anyway. Now it's up to the waiters to hose 'em down."

Even the band was winding down. "*Sometimes I wonder why I spend the lonely night... dreaming of your...*"

"What's next for you? Put your feet up?"

"My one vice. I'd kill for some champagne."

"I'm keeper of the keys." The steward walked back into the light, to a small bar area he had set up earlier, and lifted a fresh silver bucket from below the tablecloth. After scooping up some fresh ice, he plopped in a Magnum of Roederer Cristal Sec, and grabbed up two crystal flutes.

Upon his return, she reached down into the ice and plucked out a few slivers in her hand, which she then applied to the back of her glistening neck. "What I wouldn't give for a swim right now..." Then she spit over the side. "But Yuckkk! Not in this inland sheep dip."

"Come with me." He took her gently by the hand. "I know just the place."

They left the others sprawled and strewn about the foredeck, groaning and snoring, and drifted aft to the center cargo area. The round canvas pool was as yet undiscovered. In the dark shadows of the superstructure, they both started to disrobe, being particularly careful to remove all the weighty chains and bracelets and amulets. They quietly climbed up to the wooden platform around the edge of the pool. Clear, cool, fresh water glistened in the starlight. Thais wriggled out of her final wet flimsies and stood there, quiet and proud, in the moonlight. The steward, mouth agape, inhaled the tantalizing airs of rose petal and sandalwood that wafted from her gleaming, sweaty milky-brown body.

The steward grasped the Cristal and twisted off the wire safety. KAPOPPP! FLUuuussshhhhh...

"Shhh. Don't blow your wad yet," she whispered. "The evening is just beginning."

"That was just my ruby."

"Hey! You're not in the Exotic Dancers' Union. Is nothing sacred?"

"Harem life is hell. Shut up and get into the pot, slave."

"Watch yo mouth, boy."

"AAAAAAAAAaaaaaaahhhhhhhhhh. Inundation at its best."

"AAAAaaaaaaaahhhhhhh. Liquid paradise..."

"Our own private Egyptian bath..."

"I sprinkled some rose petals to screen us from any *voyeurs*..."

"I saved the cork for your navel, later on..."

"Gimme back my ruby, you brute..."

"Ummm. You're starting to make waves..."

"Um Huuummmm. Don't spill the Cristal."

"Uummmm. Then keep your hands off my flute."

The band drifted into its final set of the evening... *"You made me love you... I didn't wanna do it, I didn't wanna do it...."*

"Want to dance?..."

"Um Huummm..."

"Uuummmmm....You're starting to make bigger waves."

"Wait 'til you see my egg beater act under water."

"Promise me I get to lick the spoon..."

"Pahtooie!"

"Who's Pahtooie, some Pharaoh?"

"Ah was jist gittin' the dust out of mah mouff," Bill Bob spat out miserably. "This gawddamn bus rahd is worse 'n on a pickup in West Texas... Gawd dawg, I'm feeling poorly..."

"The damn WOG's only learned to build canals, not roads..." Brububber noted, sympathetically.

"We need the Guineas back out here. They built the Apian Way..." Byron Boost muttered.

"*Make straight in the desert a highway... Every mountain and hill made low... And the rough places plain...*" Fiona Landgrave hummed as she looked out of the dust-caked window.

"God, its ridiculously hot in here..." two or three tortured souls mumbled together.

The bus careened along through the paths of antiquity, passing sands and scenes that had not changed for thousands of years. For most of the way from Bitter Lake, over through Mahsama and westward ho to Abu Hammad, they traveled primarily along a bumpy, dusty road through desert sands that paralleled the Isma'iliya Canal. They followed this major branch that cut down off the Nile, originating near Cairo, and traversed east to connect with the Suez Canal. Sand was everywhere, on the horizon, in the air, in the bus, down one's garments, in one's nostrils, on one's tongue. Sand. An ocean of never-ending, searing sand.

Yet as they tripped along, the western horizon took on a hazy look. A hint of green first appeared, miles away. Mirage? Or something else? All eyes strained to the West. An oasis? Maybe Cairo? Maybe Giza? Maybe the end of this heat?

Closer and closer came the fuzzy green horizon. Here and there one could make out patches of palm trees and waving reeds and then shifting fields of green and stark poles and huddles of huts and an occasional fence... until at last... a real cow!

As they approached the small settlements near the canal, the nearby land went through a complete metamorphosis. On both sides of the road lay flood field after flood field of cultivated farmland, green and flush with new crops of vegetables and corn and rice and wheat and cotton, all segregated into neat plots and rows by water-filled canals and moist irrigation ditches. Even the air assumed a hint of humidity.

The passengers scanned the countryside from the windows of the dilapidated little bus, as it bumped its way through a section of the increasingly verdant flatlands spilling out from Cairo. Here, at last, appeared the first smatterings of human existence since the bus trip began. Here were farms and villages and donkeys and camels and cattle and goats and sheep. Here were people, dressed as if out of some lithograph in an antique family Bible, working with tools and animals alongside the canals and in the fields just as they did over 4000 years ago. A man swinging bag loads of water from a canal into a field, using a sack-like bucket hanging down from a long, counterweighted boom pole. A smiling boy, riding high on the hips of a scrawny donkey, feet dangling down to the ground. Here was history reliving itself, captured in time by the sand and the heat, yet re-vitalized by the seasonal reliability of the flood plains, just as in generations ages ago. Here was the renewal of life, nourished and sustained by that amazing presence that trickled quietly into the desert once a year, and made it bloom. The Nile.

"Damn it, Moses, you said just a few miles," groused O'Rouark. "We've been in this damn bus for over three hours."

"Just a few more miles..." the little man replied. "Then we will be there."

"A gotta pee..." Brububber mumbled.

"Really, Bullock, you should have taken care of that before we started," Sarah Belle Brububber scolded in a hushed voice.

"I'd kill for water. Who's got the water?" Herman Landgrave gasped, pulling his shirt buttons farther open at the top.

"Steward? Pass up the water," Shelley Boost called back to the rear of the bus. "Before we have a death on the bus up here."

Byron countered her quickly. "Better yet, pass the beer."

The steward opened a large cooler box, filled with sandwiches and Carlsberg and water and soft drinks and ice, now quickly melting. He sent the appropriate offerings forward according to the requests of hands waving in the air.

"I see a mirage out there... That strange brown cloud..." Louise O'Rouark pointed out the dirty window.

"That's no mirage. That's the stench that hovers over Cairo," commented Brububber.

"Who's stupid idea was this, anyway?" inquired an increasingly irritable and uncomfortable Shelley Boost. "Riding in the hot sun all day..."

"Ah gotta pee... bad!" moaned Brububber, finishing off his brew with a wince.

"Stop the damn bus. Moses, stop the damn bus," bitched O'Rouark. "Brububber has to relieve himself. Me too."

The little bus pulled over to the side of the road, next to the levee. Stagnant water filled the ditch below.

"Don't fall in the canal, Bullock."

More than one male passenger followed Brububber's lead, and wrote their names in the sandy roadside.

"That's not a canal... that's a sewer," Bull Brububber chuckled as he climbed back aboard.

"So's this bus, Brububber," retorted O'Rouark. "How much longer till Giza?"

Moses turned around in the driver's seat and spoke back to the group. "About thirty minutes. See... Over there... the peaks of the pyramids? We are getting close."

The bus trip had become a trip into another world. A day trip back into time... From out of their safe, cradle-rocking bunks of the Talabot at anchor, to the torn, unforgiving stiffback seats of the old six wheeler that bounced and banged its way across the desert roads paralleling the irrigation canals. Off to adventure ventured the merry Talaboteers, roaring across the seamless sands of history, dust plume flying.

"That bastard Eiriksson..." Brububber grumbled. "He's probably still getting a massage from them two colored gals in all the right spots. We get one on our butt bones..."

"Great idea he has. We got to suffer," Boost agreed.

"I didn't want to see the damn pyramids. I just wanted a Bloody Mary..." Landgrave moaned, holding his head.

"*For He is like... a refiiiiiiiiner's fire...*" Fiona mummed.

"We all agreed. We go together. We stick together..." the women sang back in chorus.

"But we didn't know we'd be going straight to Hell in a schoolbus..." O'Rouark muttered.

"Pass the beer," more than one male voice commented.

"Pass the fruit," more than one female voice commented.

"Oohhhh...Uurrrp... Sheeeeit..." Bill Bob Lovelake commented.

"Pass a barf bag. Bill Bob's getting sick," Brububber commented.

"Oh, not here. Open the windows," most of the women commented.

"They are open..." the men commented.

"Throw Bill Bob out..." someone commented.

"Make him ride on the roof..." another commented.

"Spread-eagle him in the sun. That will dry him out..." another sadist commented.

"Y'all be nice to mah Billy Bobby..." Pammy Sue spoke up, while cradling her husband's head in her lap as he hung his feet out the window. "He just had too many of those pomey granut punches, that's all. He'll be just fahn."

"Burp."

"Punched out by a pomegranate. How embarrassing."

"Urp."

"Y'all jist hang in thahr, Billy Bob."

"Gahd dawwwggg... sheeeiit... Ah thenk Ah'm goin' t'... Buuuu uuuuuurrrrrrruuuuuuuuurrpppp."

"So that's what magma looks like..."

"Bullock. Let Billy Bob die in peace."

This merry band of peripatetic mummies had somehow arisen from their deepest slumbers with the rising sun, a miraculous act considering the festivities of the evening before. Many, those unable to move, had simply slept on the deck. Some had made it to their bunks, while others had found succor in more secretive surroundings. But hangovers were the name of the game that morning. Coffee and sweet rolls and eggs and orange juice and more coffee, along with a couple of magic APC pills handed out by the steward, had miraculously brought everyone back from the outer reaches of death, to life. Or at least near life.

So it came to pass that this group of exhumed drunks had been impressed into tourist duty by the wicked captain. Eiriksson had arranged with Moses to have them all taken in the old bus to El Giza, from thence to meet the Talabot near Suez later in the day, after the convoy had completed its journey through the remaining 40 miles of the canal. This seemed preferable to staying on board an anchored ship in 120 degree heat, waiting to resume breezy way again. Now, that most logical decision seemed in question, judging from the impending mutiny aboard the hot, dusty bus.

They had crossed the slow, exhausted expanse of muddy waters, surprisingly unbefitting of the name Majestic Nile, at least a couple of times, bouncing over tired Victorian bridges just downstream of the outskirts of Cairo. The major flows were still impressive, but by then quite diminished by the irrigation which had taken place upstream and by a fan of fingers now coursing out into the lower delta. As far as the eye could see were all types of river steamers and *dhows* and *feluccas* sporting high triangled canvas, a design of thousands of years ago found successful in catching the upper breezes that skimmed over the riverbank. The lazy dissipation of the muddy waters belied the massive flow that stretched back for hundreds of miles up into the highlands.

"Not particularly a font of aqueous energy..."

"The Monongahela is bigger than this..."

"Damn Eiriksson's hide..."

"Moses! These pyramids better be good!"

"I assure you you will be impressed."

BUMP.

"They better be really big. Americans like things really big."

"They are big. More massive than your Empire State Building by some good measure. See them in the distance? They dominate the skyline for miles."

BANG. THUMP.

"My, my. All that for some poor little Pharaoh?"

"Some incestuous little queer in lots of jewelry, you mean.

"That boy must have had some ego, didn't he?

"A final home befitting a god, no?"

BLAM, BUMPP! BOUNCE.

"Pass the beer."

Buuuuuuuurrrrrrruuuuuuuuuppppppp!

"Somebody help me hang Bill Bob out the window..."

Potter-Smythe, quiet until now, felt he had found yet another opportunity for mounting bully pulpit. P.-S. stood to face the captive busload excepting Bill Bob who had his head in a tourist acquisition - a leather water bag. Then he sat himself sidesaddle on one of the seat backs, and began tamping his foul-smelling pipe. All eyes looked up at him in dread. Oh, god... another lecture.

"Pyramids like these at El Giza were built some 4500 years ago. The largest one, there, was the tomb of the Pharaoh Khufu, sometimes referred to as Cheops, and was built in approximately 2680 B.C. Its bases stretch some 230 meters, its height over 145 meters. Quite a prodigious effort, in any century, what? The smaller two beheld the

Pharaohs Khaf-Re and Men-kau-Re. These pyramids here at Giza are the only remaining wonder of the original Seven Wonders of the Ancient World. There are some half dozen near and around Giza, large and small, and some 30 in Egypt up and down the Nile. Up river, in the Sudan, there are some 60 more, of varying smaller sizes. One should note that all are built on the western side of the Nile, on the side of the setting sun. The ancient Egyptians believed that the path of the sun represented life itself, man being reborn each day in the East, like the Scarab god Khepri, then ascending to manhood at noon in the godform of Re, then setting in the West as a tottering old man in the godform of Atum."

"That's one big pile of rocks, Moses," someone said. "Big big."

"That took a few Guineas to build..."

Tony caffed onward, well stoked and fuming. "You may note that the pyramids are aligned with their sides pointing truly East and West, North and South. The opening is always on the North Side, on the side of Osiris, god of the dead. Ancient architects were able to achieve this feat quite exactly... simply by drawing a line from the point of sunrise, to the point of sunset. A simple use of high school geometry, that we often overlook. Simple, what?"

"Shit. Any Boy Scout knows that."

"Bill Bob, you hear? We're going to lay you up on the North Side. You just hang on till we get there, then you can die correct like, and not in this crummy bus."

"Hell, he's already dead. Look at his color."

"Come on, Bill Bob. You can make it. Here, have a sip of beer."

"The ancients used a kind of salt called *natron* to extract all the moisture out of the dead body in the process of embalming. They would remove the organs and the brain, and fill the cavities with more *natron* to remove all moisture."

"Just like Bill Bob. Salts pullin' on him good. He beginnin' to look like a white raisin."

"Next the embalmers would coat the body with special oils and preservatives and perfumes, and wrap it in fabrics. The whole process took something like 28 days. But such mummies have lasted over 4500 years. Rather remarkable accomplishment, if I do say."

"Bill Bob became a mummy in only four hours. Lookie, he isn't even sweating like the rest of us."

"Then the heirs would cart the Pharaoh up to his tomb, led by a band of professional mourners, playing lutes and harps and pipes and everyone weeping wildly and casting flowers along the path."

"Nothing like a good parade. Carry Bill Bob out in style."

"Carry him right up the center of Bourbon Street. We'll hire you a good jazz band, Billy Bob. These niggras here haven't changed in 4000 years."

"Inside the pyramid are tunneling pathways leading to various chambers. One is the King's burial chamber, in which his body was laid to rest, but accompanied by an abundance of items to help him enter and then enjoy the afterlife. Favorite foods and drinks and oils and gilded goblets and crowns and weapons and jewelry and model boats and grains and perfumes and spices. All the little necessities of life. Even his favorite sex partner might be placed in the tomb with him, along with a few slaves to clean up after them.

"Alive. In the tomb?"

"Alive. For only a short while, no doubt."

"All those jewels and gold?..."

"You see? You can take it with you..."

"Alas, not so. In spite of the colossal size and complexity of the tomb, and all attempts to design a structure that would seal and secure the king's burial chamber from sacrilege for all time, practically every Pharaoh's or nobleman's tomb was robbed of all these worldly valuables, within a few hundred years."

"Just like the lawyers... Pick you clean when you die..."

The eyes of the passengers grew wider and wider as they approached the monoliths that angled to the sky before them. The great pyramids of Giza... Their massive, graceful, incisive lines contrasted with the random terrain of the barren desert near the outskirts of Cairo. Images of thousands of slaves, prodded on by whip-wielding masters, ponderously hauling and ramping their ways to the summit with enormous blocks in tow, filled their imaginations.

"Wheuuuweee! Look at the size of that pyramid...."

"How the hell did they make these monsters, eons ago?..."

"Very Slowly..."

"Very carefully. They have lasted some 4500 years...."

Awe was the expression of the day. The pyramids of El Giza... filled all on the bus with profound awe.

Even before the bus had completely stopped, the attack commenced. Peddlers and camel drivers and guides and pick-pockets and laughing children and blind beggars and hobbling cripples and somber veterans and soft drink vendors converged on the bus like flies in large numbers. So did flies.

"Shooo! Scat! Get back. Get your hands off my purse. Don't touch my wife, you bag of dirt. Get away. Get away! Moses! Moses! Save us!"

Moses clapped his hands loudly, and the vendors and beggars and peddlers stopped for a second and looked up. "I will make purchases for these tourists," he said to the assemblage of peddlers. "I will resolve a fair price for both sides. Tell me what you desire, and I will make it all possible."

Amazingly, they all nodded and grinned and placed their fervor into neutral. Moses seemed well known, and to hold great sway. The peddlers eased their crush, and backed off. Even the passengers advanced him a few dollars with explicit purchases in mind. Ah, Moses... Herein lies the origin of *viggerish*.

After all the obligatory photos were snapped cheesing proudly on the backs of dromedaries held by surly one-eyed drivers, after all the scarabs and fly swatters were inspected, after all the cotton dayshirts and brass jewelry and carved sphinxes and inlaid boxes and alabaster pyramids were considered, after all the purchases seemed to be negotiated, Moses bade the peddlers stay by the entrance while he guided the thirteen into the mouth of the passageway which led to the interior chambers of the great pyramid. From blazing brightness into instant darkness, the escape from the heat of the desert sun was a great relief. Until one inhaled.

The so-called air inside of the pyramids had to contain molecules from 2500 B.C. Some slave or worker, not allowed a union break, had relieved himself somewhere, possible in the Queen's Chamber, and the stink, with only one small exit passageway far below compounded by no cross ventilation, had hung around for centuries.

"Aaahhhhh!" cried the group. "Aaarrrggghh! Peeeyyooohhh!"

"The stink should have kept the grave robbers out. What did they use, scuba gear?"

"Pheew! If this is a whiff of the life hereafter, I'll try my chances in Hell."

"This is Hell, asshole. Heaven was last night."

"With my wife? Heaven?"

"So this's what the little woman meant when she told you to go to Hell."

"You made it, Buster. Hell. Right in here."

"If this is the way the Pharaoh's were buried, what about the poor slobs?"

"They were tossed in the Nile to feed the gators."

"Why don't they have some more light in here?"

"Cause there's nothing to read but these hieroglyphics, and you don't need light to read them... You can feel them."

"I just felt when the Pharaoh married his sister..."

"I just felt where..."

"God, this air is awful."

"What air. This is pure hydrogen sulfide."

"Don't light a match..."

"Now I know what's meant by being in the bowels of someplace..."

Moses, oblivious to all the catty chatter as the group groped its way up the internal ramp into the depths and core of the pyramid, finally reached a landing that opened into a large room. It was lit by one light bulb, casting grotesque shadows as the tourists moved about, and revealing dank, dingy walls covered with chiseled glyphs. "Here is the Queen's chamber. We are now some 200 feet above ground, and near the center of the pyramid. Above us some 70 feet, lies the King's chamber."

"Were they both buried in here? Together?"

"Sometimes. Each had a chamber, if needed. But usually the surviving widow went on to more amorous, profitable relationships with the priests and generals, and left her dead husband to the ways of Osiris."

"Where did he live?"

"Oh, Osiris, god of the dead, ruled in the afterlife. The ancients believed that life would be better in the next world."

"How could it be better for the Pharaoh? He got all the nookie and beer he could handle, and got to flail the hell out of anybody anytime he wanted."

"Bullock!"

"The common person was less fortunate, and had a hard life. Farming and toiling in the sun. Building these magnificent structures..."

"Anything in life hereafter would be better than in this shithouse..."

"That is precisely what they believed. That was the basis for their faith in an afterlife."

"Not so dumb after all, I guess. Keeps you going..."

"I'd like to get going... back to the ship."

"Seen one pyramid... seen 'em all..."

"Except Jane Russell's. She's got two."

Finally back down the dingy ramp of a tunnel, the group groped its way out into the sunlight like prisoners suddenly released from a dungeon. The great god Re was at his mightiest, blazing down upon them from ahigh. Gasping to inhale the relatively fresh air, this time reeking only of camel pee, the passengers staggered and stumbled their way out into the open and back toward the bus. "Ahhh!... The real world... Air..."

> *"The people that walked in the darkness have seen a great light..."* hummed Fiona. *"...They that dwell in the land of the shadow of death, upon them hath the light shined..."*

Blinded momentarily, they were instantly put upon by the swarm of flies in *gellabiyyas*, jabbering, grinning and pushing and shoving.

"Back! Get off! Get away from my pocket. Get your hands off my purse. Gimmy my camera, you jerk! Help! Moses! Get them away! Steward! Help me!"

This time Moses' sway had been diffused by his absence guiding his peoples through the bowels of the afterlife. The peddlers attacked in ever increasing numbers, swarming over the twelve passengers plus their faithful steward like flies on a cowslip. Struggles led to pushing and shoving, flailing arms became weapons, fists found grinning teeth to manipulate, cameras became cudgels to be swung about the head, and personal items started to grow wings as the pickpockets probed in and out of the melee with remarkable impunity. A staged event?

As they tried to advance to the safety of home base in the bus, the peddler attack grew in intensity. Even camels came into the fray, one of them slobbering on Fiona Landgrave in a fit of spite, or spit of fight, or something. Another, a large old beastie named *Ba'alzevuv* with a tattoo on his lip, took a nip at Belle Brububber's buttocks that strained imaginatively in her sweat-soaked white slacks. The camel driver laughed openly.

"EEEEKKKK!"

Bull rose to the occasion. "No goddamn camel's going to nibble my wife's ass. That's my job!" He took up two large sun-baked bricks that lay in the sand, and, one in each hand, struggled out of the pack and up behind the offending camel. "I'm going to show this stupid WOG how to brick his camel... Hey, Habeeb, you fuzz head! Watch this."

Brububber slammed the two bricks together as hard as he could, right on the camel's testicles which hung down like two grapefruit in a long sack, almost dragging in the sand. The camel did not make a sound. It just looked up to the heavens in pained amazement and inhaled deeeeeeeeeply, then fell to its knees with a wild-eyed stare on its face. However, the cry of the camel driver filled the desert like an aggrieved banshee.

"AAAAHHHHHHHHHHHIIIIIIIIIIIEEEEEEEEEEE!"

From every distant corner of the valley, from every rock, from atop every camel, from under every bundle and bale of touristy junk, a host of Egyptian eyes zeroed in on the bloodcurdling scream.

"*Jahid! Jahid!*" Someone called out. "*Jahid! Jahid!*" others cried back. "*Jahid! Jahid!*"

"Oh, shit, Brububber. You've started World War III!"

The peddlers and drivers began to converge menacingly upon the unfortunate tribe of tourists. Someone threw a rock, just missing the steward. He whirled about, awaiting another. Adrenalin poured into veins. The crush was on. Hands and fists began flailing about in the air above their heads, while a thousand fingers darted secretively into every pocket and purse.

"Quickly! Quickly! Everyone! Into the bus!" Moses shouted.

Suddenly, Moses flung a fistful of money up into the air, high above the heads of the scrimmaging drivers and peddlers. All Egyptian eyes left their human targets and followed paper and silver in an expanding upward arc. As squints into the glaring face of great Ra himself were held in rapt attention for a brief second, Moses and the steward helped the twelve passengers scurry away and onto the bus. Door and windows slammed behind them as they reached sanctuary within the metal walls of their mobile fortress.

"Floor it, Moses!" Brububber yelled. I'll pelt them with ice cubes out the back."

"Let's use our secret weapon! Bomb the bastards with Bill Bob's barf bag."

"Get moving, bus! Don't fail us now!"

"Damn, that was a close one. Let's get the hell out of here!"

"Just don't throw the damn beer at them. We got a long trip back home across the desert."

"Can this old bus outrun those camel drivers?"

"Sure we can. Maybe not the camels, though."

"Pedal to the floor, Moses. No time for sightseeing."

"We going to make it?"

"They're eating dust. We made it."

Back in the distance, the camel drivers were dropping off their pursuit, and regrouping. Strange, but they changed course and headed off in a gallop across the sands at almost a right angle to the road, fists at the high and headdresses flowing.

Moses looked all around and back nervously, out through the rear window, as he gunned the bus along the bumpy road.

"Don't look now, Moses, but I think they are trying to cut us off at the pass. The road takes a turn up here, and puts us right over there by that irrigation canal..." the steward surmised, sizing up the lay of the land.

"Where's John Wayne when we need him?"

"Those guys look serious. What's *Jahid*?"

"Holy War. Death to the infidel. Brick my camel and die."

"Don't worry. We still got the bomb... Bill Bob's barf bag."

"Hell, bomb 'em with Bill Bob. He's dead anyway..."

"Naw. It's our responsibility to carry his bones out of here..."

"Better yet, bomb 'em with Pammy Sue. She used to take on the whole rodeo circuit..."

The steward listened quietly at the frantic clamoring and bazaar behavior of supposedly civilized men and women under stress, alone with their ways in a strange land, stirred with passions and fears that had filled this very same valley before.

Fiona hummed on, more nervously... *"Why do the nations... so furiously rage together?... Why doooooooooooooooo...."*

"Moses... Get us out of here!"

"It will be close. But I think we can make it."

The steward knelt in the isle beside the little Egyptian driver as he yelled over the roar of the little engine that could.

"We must first cross this canal, up there, at the high point in the levee. It is but a narrow passage, yet it should provide us the escape we need. Otherwise, the camels will cut us off before the bridge."

The bus leaned precariously as it edged its way down the soft, sandy embankment and into the nearly dry canal bed below. Then once level again, the bus chugged up the bumpy bed for a few hundred meters, until it neared a low spot in the embankment on the far side. Then, its ancient engine racing, it ground into low gear, and strained and gunned and spun and slipped its way back up the to the top of the levee. I think I can I think I can I think I can...

"We made it!" everyone cheered.

The bus skidded to a halt in a cloud of dust and sand. "Quickly, Steward." Moses and the steward scrambled out of the bus and ran back to the canal and over to large wooden sluice gate that blocked a new, higher level canal's waters from junction with the canal out of which they had just risen. "Pull. On these hand winches. The gate will rise. PULL! PULL!"

As if in nervous encouragement, Fiona sang more vigorously out the bus window, *"Lift up your heads, O ye gates...And be ye lift up, ye everlasting doors..."*

The camel drivers were approaching the dry canal, some two hundred meters below. They were wildly spitting and screaming expletives and waving fists and daggers in the air. The camels were frothing at the mouth after their three-mile run across desert sands. "Abalabalabalababallah! Death to the tourists!"

The camel cavalry kept on plopping forward, padded hooves pounding in the desert sands like impassioned heartbeats. Suddenly, the screaming band turned and slid down the embankment and into the dry canal bed where the bus had entered.

"PULL!"

The waters began to gush forth in great waves, spilling into the dry canal bed as the gate squeaked its way up. Greater and greater in quantity came the entrapped waters, spilling under the gate like a great inland sea, bursting its bonds into freedom. The muddy froth spilled past the gate and over the embankments, and a great wall of water rushed forth toward the camel drivers.

With expressions of fear and disbelief on their faces, the camel drivers and the camels reeled and scrambled to escape. The ardor of their pursuit was quenched by a great wave of water, possibly one meter high, that blasted into the camels at their knees and caused them to buck and stumble and bolt about uncontrollably. Drivers fell from their humps and saddles, and submerged into the muddy froth. Instantly they stood up, water to their waists, fists shaking and curses flowing freely, chasing after their aberrant mounts. It seems that camels are quite heroic in their drinking abilities, but hate to bathe.

Moses and the steward stood on top of the levee, proudly accepting the cheers of the passengers leaning out the bus windows, banging madly and blowing the horn with abandon.

Fiona could be heard singing boldly above the din, *"The trumpet shall sound... and the dead shall be risen, incorruptible..."*

Even Bill Bob raised his head to see out.

"You did it, Moses..." the steward nodded his head knowingly. "Now I see how."

"We are not yet out of here, my young friend," Moses smiled back. "Alas, we are left on the wrong side of this deeper canal."

"Let's swim for it. Lead the way, Moses."

"There is a better way, particularly in that I cannot swim," the little man replied. "Please follow me."

Moses and the steward ran up the new canal some fifty meters, to a lanky T-shaped mast-like contraption that poked skyward at the side of the canal.

"It is a *shaduf.* To bucket water from the canal into the fields. Let us hope it can bucket us to the other side."

The camel drivers were staggering out of the lower canal, pulling their disoriented animals up behind them. "Looks like they are planning another attack, Moses. You first."

No, my friend. You are heaviest. I will hang here, on the counterweight, and you on the bucket. Take a good run, and you will, I pray, deliver yourself across to the other side."

The steward nodded and, as the little Egyptian clung like a kitten on the lower weighted end of the top boom pole, tested the balance. It seemed close to neither teeter nor totter, so he grasped the leather bucket hanging down on its rope, and sped toward the canal as fast as he could. At the top of the levee, he leaped out into space, and glided softly across the top of the waters as the creaking T-arm swung its way over the canal. With a plop, he landed in the muddy field along side the levee. On the far side, Moses too landed with a plop as the short end of the cross pole dropped abruptly after weight aborted from the opposite end.

Then he dipped the bucket down into the waters to fill it, so to balance the stone weight on the other end, *sans* Moses. After dragging it back as far as he could, he ran and hurled and swung the bucket back over the canal. Moses ducked as it swung by, but grabbed the line. Then he dumped the water from the bucket, and hanging on the bucket, tested his small weight against the stone counterweight. Satisfied, but without alternative as the enraged camel drivers were now pounding down upon him, only meters away, Moses lifted his eyes to heaven, shrugged, and as fast as his little legs could carry him, ran to the edge of the canal and launched himself into space, leaving the exasperated camel drivers naught but to spew invective into the canal.

They had made it. Back to the Talabot. And the safety of the Red Sea.

The story of Moses' leadership in successful flight from the Egyptians... soon to be spread throughout the land by postcard and slide show... would become legend.

—AT SEA—

"Livestock."

"Ridiculous!"

"Really..." the captain commented blandly. "They are classified as livestock. On the bill of lading... One hundred twenty-six ethnic Japanese... destination Yokohama."

"But these are people, not cattle..."

"My young *nautonnier*, we have twelve passengers on board the ship. They are people. They have paid a pretty sum to travel with all the comforts of home the ship can muster."

"But..."

"But the sorry beings you see down there in the cargo hold, they are traveling steerage. They are numbered, not named, in the manifest. They are a commodity, like grain or cattle, handled in bulk by an opportunistic shipping agent. They are paying the lowest possible rate for their journey -- steerage class. They are willing, very willing, to suffer both the momentary and physical hardships to fulfill their goal, to reach their ancestral homeland."

"But they are people. Human beings. It's like the dark ages..."

"Dark indeed. But functional. They are the lucky ones. They have the chance to travel from countries not favorably predisposed

416

to them, where they are the minority and the outcasts and the spit-upon, to one of hope, and maybe even equality."

"But this is the twentieth century..."

"You think this is something new? Steerage class brought millions of huddled masses to the shores of your country, even in this century. Zionism ships Europe's unwanted cattle to the Holy Land, even as we speak. Where there is a boat, there will be boat people, traveling in steerage, fleeing adversity through adversity at sea, only to find it again on opposite shores... Our guests below are not being expelled from back there... They follow a dream."

"But look at them, all hunkering down there in the hold... How do we feed them? Keep them dry?"

"We don't. They will feed themselves from the barnyard that accompanies them. They will drink from a line directly from the fresh water tanks, there in the corner, drinking the same water we do. And there is a crew's head just behind that bulkhead, impersonal but functional. They may stink a bit by the time we see old Fuji, but they will make the journey just fine. And after all, it's only five days..."

"But look at them... what a flea-bitten lot... "

The steward stared down from the deck into the after cargo hold. In it were one hundred twenty-six awestruck men, women and children, dressed in a variety of pajamas and quilted jackets and straw sun hats and canvas sneakers, squatting on their haunches near bags and bundles of belongings. About them lay numerous wicker cages crammed with chickens, a few pigs tethered nearby, a few dogs, baskets of vegetables, and one very loud rooster strutting madly about on top of the bundles. They were all smiling and chatting and jabbering amongst themselves, and the children were playing and exploring the walls of great cargo crates the formed the outer limits of their sunken universe.

"Indeed, look at them, Steward. Are they unhappy with their lot?" the captain asked. "After all these years in distant lands, they are going home! Do they look miserable to you?"

The steward surveyed the smiling, wide-eyed bewildered faces, filled with simple confusion and wonder, but also filled with hope and dreams. "Wait until we get on the open seas, Captain..." he answered. "Then I will give you your answer."

"Steward?"

"Mrs. O.?"

"Where have you been?" she asked in her typical hushed, Bacallesque voice. "You've kept me waiting fifteen minutes. Where is my Rob Roy?"

"Sorry, Ma'am. I had some chores to attend to aft."

"Are you back chatting with the... little people again?" she mused impatiently, grinding out a Pall Mall on the steel deck.

"I was just helping them to clean up a bit, Mrs. O."

"Ugh. Why must you do it, Steward. Can they not care for themselves?"

"They are awash in a sea of their own making, Ma'am. I just hooked up a hose for them."

"Steward?"

"Mr. Brububber?"

"Bring me another martini, please, Steward..."

"Another?..."

"I've been watching those Chinese gooks back there..."

"They are ethnic Japanese, Sir..."

"I've been thinking. They need some excitement down there. This is a party ship, isn't it? Seems to me we could hoist a few up on ropes from the cargo boom, and then swing them back and forth at each other. Sort of like a Chinese joust in the pit. Let 'em get a bit of exercise... bonking heads and kicking about."

"I would prefer that we let them up on the after deck for a bit of sunlight and fresh air. It's like a sewer down there."

"Great idea. Maybe we could teach them a Chinese version of fishball. They could use that damn rooster... toss him back and forth a bit. Might shut him up."

"Maybe you should have a Perrier instead, Mr. B. Cleanse your taste buds. Dinner is coming up soon."

"Steward?"

"Mrs. Landgrave?"

"What is that awful smell back there?"

"It's is coming from our friends in... Second Class, Ma'am. They're cooking their meals."

"But they cook all day long."

"So do we, Ma'am. But there are quite a few of them, and only a few hibachi's and WOK's. They really keep the food moving on and off the fires..."

"I heard terrible screams at night, Steward. What is going on back there?"

"Just their ceremonial rights in preparing their food for the next day. They brought along chickens and a few pigs."

"Ugh. How distasteful. It's a pity the poor souls can't enjoy the smorgasbord and delicious entrees you and Erda so beautifully prepare. Like those special dishes last evening. They were marvelous."

"Thank you, Mrs. L. But we didn't cook your meal last night."

"No? Who did?"

"Our friends back aft. They do wonders with a chicken or a pig. We gave them smorgasbord for a change of pace, and they made dinner for us and the crew."

"Mrs. Landgrave?"

"Steward?"

"Mr. Potter-Smythe?"

I do believe it's time you changed to a new bottle of bitters, Steward. This Pinkie indicates frequent use has altered the consistency of the Angostura. See the color? No longer pink but bordering on a deeper rose. The air, my boy. Air is the bane of all good Pinkies."

"New bitters. Consider it done, Mr. P.-S."

"Steward?"

"Mr. Boost?"

"You'll never believe what I saw back there."

"Try me."

"I was down in the engine room, working with the Chief on his starboard feed pump, and I had to take a leak..."

"No leaks in the engine room, I trust."

"Right. So I climbed through the hatchway into that little head up behind the boiler, and what do you think I saw?"

"What, Sir?"

"A bunch of yellow assholes staring at me."

"*Voyeurs?*"

"Oriental grommets, kid. Nipponese assholes."

"Oh, they were using the heads..."

"That's just the point. The crapper is the old trough kind... with the water flowing down the ditch under a row of seat boards. They didn't know how to use them. There they were squatting down on their haunches, up on top of the boards. Their feet were where you're supposed to sit, on the seat boards. There they were, hunkered down on the seat boards like three little Buddhas, assholes in the air, grunting and squinting like no body else was around."

"What did you do, Mr. B."

"I watched in disbelief. When they saw me, a white man, they got all flustered and started jabbering and squirming around, and their feet started slipping off the seat boards and down into the trough. Wow, did they ever yell, struggling to get their sneakers out of the shit trough and back up on to the seat boards. They were falling all over each other, and finally one of them fell completely back into the shit trough and pulled the others in on top of him."

"And you offered a hand to pull them out, I suppose?"

"Are you crazy? I was doubled up in laughter. So bad, I peed my pants."

"When East meets West..."

The evening air was moist and warm. "Change coming," the steward thought to himself. "Something's not the same above." The Talabot churned its way along through the rough expanse of ocean known as the East China Sea, rolling and bobbing about like a small toy boat in the bathtub splashings of some playful god.

Some twelve hours after leaving landfall off the Asian mainland, just as they were crossing out off the continental shelf, the seas took on a dark brooding quality, stirring and shifting from side to side and up and down in slow, rhythms of discomfort that were quickly transferred to all the passengers, fore and aft. The ship's groundspeed had picked up perceptibly as the effects of the Japan Current carried the Talabot onward to the Northeast. The sky was quite clear, and while evenly washed across with the last remnants of the sun fading in the West, it held forth a foreboding aura. Stars, now appearing by the score after their more assertive brothers had popped out, had taken on a strange shimmer that made them look even larger.

"Moisture in the air," Eiriksson muttered. "Weather's coming."

The captain sat in the wheelhouse on his official bridge chair, welded sideways on the forward bulkhead near the bridge windows. He lounged down in the seat, his head resting on the padded back, feet across on the compass pedestal, sipping a Berlinerweise from a heavy goblet.

"Radio reports have indicated a low developing off to the southeast, but no specifics. Also, no mention of anything severe, as yet..." the steward offered, pleased that he had sensed the change before the captain.

"Can you smell it? It's out there, Steward," Eiriksson mumbled as he stared off into the darkening night. "We are going to get a wet ride tonight."

"I'll tell the passengers. No billiards or bowling or tennis. Fun and games will have to wait for tomorrow."

"Get the passengers stabilized and battened down for some weather. And wake up Bjarni. Have him make sure the deck cargo is double tied and well secured."

"What about our friends in steerage."

"What about them? They bought their ticket, now they get the ride of their lives."

"Shouldn't we be doing something for them?"

"Like what? Tell them a storm is coming, so they can work themselves into a fit of panic? Bring them up to our own staterooms? There are one hundred and twenty-six of them. Not room for even half. Should we tie them down in the hold, so they can't be panned about in their own vomit? Or the kids... Should we take them from their parents? Impossible."

"So we do nothing for them?"

"We tell them to douse their fires by 2200 hours. We tell them to secure their belongings. We tell them to pray, like the rest of us, to get through the night. That is all we can do..."

"I'll go down and stay with them."

"No, you won't. I need you up here."

"Why? You expect a big one?"

"How would I know? It's dark out there."

"I thought you always had a view of the bigger picture."

Eiriksson scanned the stars on the horizon through his Berlinerweise. "Sir Bernard Lovell said it pretty well," he smiled pensively. "'At the limit of present day observations, our information is a few billion years out of date...'"

"Then we just trust to our gut instincts?"

"Look out there. What can you see, after all these miles you've traveled? Can you tell what's up ahead? What's out there?"

"Darkness. Maybe storm. Certainly magic."

The Captain smiled, then looked up, through the open window, at the milky way. "At sea, time does not exist. Look up at those stars... We are just a speck in some unending cosmic dust storm..."

"But I thought you had a talk with the stars every so often?"

"Talk? Human voices drift out to nowhere. Are they heard? Probably not. Does anybody or anything out there really care? Probably not. But can we take the chance and not call out there?"

Eiriksson took a substantial swig from his goblet, and then roared out into the night through the open bridge window beside him. "Hey... You out there! What do you have in store for us? What's out there?"

"Careful... Someone may hear you."

Only Eiriksson and the steward remained on the bridge. The steward handled the wheel, as Ole the main helmsman had been given a break for a little sleep, in anticipation of needing him more later on.

Eiriksson stared out into the night, using his Berlinerweise as a mock telescope. He scanned the horizon, then shuddered slightly.

"Ahhhhh, fishshit. It is the great unknown out there... Alexis de Tocqueville put it about right. 'Here, man seems to enter life furtively. Everything enters into a silence so profound, a stillness so complete, that the soul feels penetrated by a sort of religious terror.'"

The steward put his hand on the engine telegraph. "But we are known... We are here and now. We exist..."

"Aahhhh..." my young Camus, "We are merely finite egos trying to establish our own reality in an eternal sea of the unknown..."

The steward lit up a Players, and blew smoke out his nostrils savoring the aromatics. "So what keeps you going to sea?... What keeps you coming back for another voyage?... Keeps you sailing onward into the night?... Your ego?"

"It's a job. I like the hours. I like the pay. I like the extras," Eiriksson scowled as he toasted himself and the ship and finished off the goblet.

"I think you like to try to see into the future... You think you can get a jump on everybody, by sailing Eastward..."

"Ah, yes... Eastward... The spin of the earth aids the process."

"Don't you look back, to see where we've been? Doesn't the past help to find your place in the future?"

"Fishshit. You and your dead reckoning... The past is but prologue, my young friend. What will be relies not on events past. We all sail on an inexorable current, a dynamic within the human kind that perpetuates all our stupid primitive passions, over and over again. We recreate our own destiny... over and over..."

"If what you're saying is that mankind will make the same mistakes again, I don't agree. We can change course, alter speed. I believe we have finally corked our passions with successful forms of civilized behavior."

"Civilized. Like Hiroshima. And Nanking. And Dachau. Those proud moments in human history that our nations justified so well as appropriate actions at the time... Wars and intolerance and bloodletting and exploitation are as rampant today as in any century before us. And so will they be for the next millennium. Don't you see it? We charge ourselves with the primacy of our own kind. We'll kill or humble anyone or anything that attempts to defy our aspirations or habits or ways of thinking. We want power, mastery, dominion. We convince ourselves we are demigods on earth. It's the thing that turns us on."

"But isn't there a blending of ideas and advances? As nations and cultures clash, don't they infuse and mold each other? Don't we all learn from the other guy and adjust our own ways of doing things? That's what our travel right here is all about, isn't it? Isn't that what history calls progress?"

"History? Your history is fantasy, my friend. You must discount history. Your history is a fragmented collection of myopic images and biased illusions, scribed down by sanctimonious egos whose imperfect views if not outright intentional distortions change the reality of things past. History is only the broken urn... shards of facts, imperfect pieces of the whole. History is most unreliable. We can only imagine, dream of the past. But what we do know... we know of human nature. We see its consequences. We see its primal passions still unchecked, still at work. You can find comfort by learning to read the sky, and human nature, Steward. But history? Alas, we know nothing of the real truth of the past, other than it existed..."

"But our own encounters... our own memories. They make history."

"Yes, we keep a log, Pilot. Even then, it is merely our edited impression of what is, our partial view, our snapshot illusion. We're but little boats, being tossed about and carried along on some grand undercurrent. Look out there. The fundamental truth of things is not on the surface of the sea. It is within."

The steward let this conversation vent for a moment, and took a drag on his cigarette. He looked up. The sky was black, no moon, stars had vanished, distance and time unfathomable.

Eiriksson lit up a Philip Morris, and pitched the match out over the side into the night. He again scanned the horizon through his goblet. "It's black as pitch tonight. I don't see anything out there. Do you?"

"Sort of like our view of the future?..." the steward replied.

After a moment of silence, he altered course slightly. "I've watched you, Captain. You can't stand it ashore. You can't wait to get out of port, to get underway again. And it's not the owners' timetable that drives you... You're driven to get back to the unknown out there."

"That's because everything I have seen in port is frivolous. What I look for, out here at sea, is profound.

"Profound." the steward nodded. "Pardon me for saying so, Sir, but what you're seeking is some kind of transcendence. But how you see, is through the bottom of a crystal goblet, quite out of focus. Most of the time I doubt you can tell the difference between nirvana and oblivion."

Eiriksson smiled, pulled hard on his cigarette, then blew smoke up into the air above him. "They are one in the same. As long as one transcends reality."

The steward patted his hand on top of the brass light hood of the compass pedestal. "Reality is here and now. We've got twelve passengers and a hold full of cargo and people that needs transporting from point A to point B. I like knowing where I am, and where I'm going. I'm here and now. So are you, right here on this ship. Sailing 015 magnetic, at fourteen knots. But you don't seem to care where we are. You just need to keep going, to keep searching..."

"Ahab said it better... 'All my means are sane, my motive and my object mad...'"

The wind picked up a few knots, causing the flag halyards to rattle against the bridge mast overhead. The darkness grew deeper. The barometer retreated perceptively. Waves changed direction coming now from the southeast, causing the Talabot to roll uncomfortably with each passing.

Eiriksson wet his finger and lofted it into the breeze as if to better sense the new reality coming upon them. "We're both trying to get to the same place in the end, Steward. You in your way... Me in mine. It's how we deal with chance and caprice and random circumstance, trying to grasp a touch of meaning out of life's absurdity... there's where you still could learn a few tricks in navigation."

"Is that why you talk to the stars at night?"

"Ah, Steward, the words of William Henley come to mind...

> *'Out of the night that covers me,*
> *Black as the pit from pole to pole,*

426

I thank whatever gods may be

For my unconquerable soul...'

The steward, not to be outdone, took the next stanza...

"'It matters not how strait the gate,

How charged with punishment the scroll,

I am the master of my fate,

I am the captain of my soul.'"

Eiriksson flipped his cigarette over the side in a long glowing arc like a miniature shooting star across the black sky.

"And so we sail on, my learned friend, into the portents of the fear-filled night... "

"In the end, do we both get there?"

Empty goblet in hand, the captain rose to leave the bridge. He put his hand on the steward's shoulder and looked him in the eyes with a mysterious grin. *"Faen i Helvete!"* Eiriksson laughed. "In the end, we are but fish bait, living only to become fishshit."

"Going up..."

"What?"

"It's elevator time," Eiriksson yawned. "Up and down. Three floors. Up and down, over and over again."

"That pretty well describes it... Burrrp," the steward nodded as he watched the horizon move up an down over the waves, feeling the blood in his head and the remainders of dinner in his stomach do a dead weight drag in opposition to each passing floor.

The weather had worsened significantly, but still the storm had not built into a rage. Rather, it merely caused the ocean to heave, up and down, over the approaching shallows of the Tsushima Strait. The wind never reached a howl nor did it bring torrents of rain. It did drizzle heavily and it did blow, and it did get threateningly dark. But somehow the Talabot was spared the brunt of a monster storm, as shifting fronts took its fury farther to the north, hitting the lower islands of Japan with full force.

"I think we will luck out on this one, Steward," the captain said as he lay back casually in his bridge chair. "The main front should have hit us hard by now."

"Hope so, Sir," the steward replied, hanging on to the hatchway. "It's still pretty rough, in vertical swells. I bet the passengers are selling Buicks by the boatload right about now..."

"Like this, we should be able to ride it out. This course is still good. I guess about eight hours to the lee islands off Kyushu."

The steward looked out at the ominous sky, jet black off to the southeast, and purple in the north. It stretched and pulled and vied for position against a dark shifting monster whose surface seemed only to seethe and froth, belying the powerful heaves of the underwaves that carried the Talabot from ladies lingerie up to kitchenware and back again. "Aren't we surly tonight?... Boil and bubble... Toil and trouble..."

"Herop."

"What?"

"*Arigato*. Tanku vully much fo herop."

"Oh, help. Yes, you're welcome."

The small man bowed frequently from the waist, making sure he had to look up to see the steward's eyes. This was no trouble, as the steward towered over him by some fifteen inches.

The scene had been one of tragedy mixed with comedy. In the after cargo hold one hundred twenty-six steerage class passengers lay strewn about, soaked, exhausted from vomiting, covered with their own filth and swimming amidst soggy belongings. To a body, they all seemed posed for one of the scenes so graphically depicted by Hieronymus Bosch.

The smell of vomit permeated everything. The air was almost unbreathable. Those present in the putrid pit became ill like dominos. It was all the steward could do in the confined space, even with his experience at sea, to control his own retching spasms. The seas had subsided somewhat, now that the Talabot had reached the lee, but the ship still moved up and down, but only one floor at a time now, from the bargain basement up to fine fragrances and back again. Going up? Going down?

The steward had left the bridge during the height of the weather after Ole had relieved him at the helm. He had not gone to his bunk, but rather staggered his way aft to the cargo hold, and peered over the hatchway. The Japanese may have a knack for doing things in lockstep, but this was absurd. With each heave of the seas, right at the crest, one hundred and twenty six persons would return the heave in unison.

Without asking permission, the steward had begun taking groups of four and five up to the main dining lounge. There, at least, some could find warmth and shelter from the rains, and fresh air and chairs and carpeted decks to lie on. He had brought up the mothers with children and the old persons first, plus a few more competent hands that seemed to be faring better than most. The vomiting did not cease, but it subsided substantially. Soon the majority were huddled in each others arms, rocking softly and dozing when possible as stomachs calmed down a bit.

The steward had not turned on the lights, but dealt with his charges in the glow of two night sconces on the bulkhead. Suddenly the overhead lights had come on, startling all in the room. Looking about, he had spotted Anthony Potter-Smythe standing in the hatchway, pipe in his teeth, feeling his pockets for matches. Without a word, the Englishman had frowned and left the room.

The steward had then returned to the aft hold, where the remaining sorry souls had been left in putrid purgatory, to fend for themselves.

The old man kept bowing. "Please stop." The steward put his hands on to his shoulders, and brought him upright. "It will be O.K. Weather calming now. You all be fine soon."

The old man knew little useable English, but seemed to understand. Then he pulled the steward over to show him a few of his fellow Boschians who appeared the worse off. After surmising the state of things, the steward selected three men of some resilience, and dragged them up the interior ladders and passageways to the crew's galley. He was surprised to see Erda standing there, so early in the morning, slowly stirring in some steaming huge pots that she had laced securely on top of her industrial range.

"I wondered when you would get here, Steward," she smiled. "Here. Things are just about ready." With that, she handed mugs of hot tea to the three Japanese and himself. "Drink this, then carry these pots down to your spaces for the others."

She lifted the lids, showing the bowing threesome the steaming oatmeal and rice within. Their eyes widened with relief. "It is all I could cook in this weather, my little friends," Erda said. "It will sustain you for the time being."

The men bowed rapidly, and sucked in their breath in loud surges. "If they spent more time doing and less time bowing, everyone will be better off, Steward. Please lead them down with the cereals and this large urn of tea. When they have emptied it, bring it back. I'll have more water boiling by then."

As the activities in the cargo hold seemed to be getting under control, the steward returned to the dining lounge, fearing a repeat of the worst. He stopped with a start in the hatchway.

Inside the lounge the lights had again been dimmed. A soft lullaby drifted in the air. In one corner, Fiona Landgrave sat on the deck, humming softly to a young child who huddled quietly in her arms while her exhausted mother lay alongside with her lidded eyes feigning sleep. Nearby, Shelley Boost knelt by another mother with three small children, holding a washbasin under them when necessary and wiping their chins with a bath towel. Across the lounge, Belle Brububber adjusted a blanket about an elderly woman who had been laid down next to the dining table. Pammy Sue sat across the room, talking softly to four sleepy children whom she held in her lap as their mothers dozed on the floor nearby. At the dining table, Ducky Potter-Smythe and her husband were passing out dampened hand towels from a pile, which they had dipped in a basin of fresh water. Tony had somehow found fresh matches, and his pipe smoke helped counter the smell of vomit.

The steward stared at the British couple, who nodded silently in reply.

"The other passengers?" the steward quietly asked Potter-Smythe. "They all right?"

"O'Rouark led the other men below deck, back to the after hold, to see what they could do to help..." he replied softly. "His wife followed with them."

The steward returned to the bridge. Eiriksson was not there, but Bjarni stood duty along with Ole the helmsman. After informing Bjarni of the state of things aft, he looked aft into Eiriksson's stateroom, and found it empty. On his way back to the bridge, he spied the captain standing at the very bow of the ship, hanging on to the gunwales and riding the waves like a schoolboy on a hydroplane, face into the wind and hair flying.

The steward worked his way up to the bow deck. He called out above the noisy air about him, "Captain? Are you all right?"

Eiriksson turned and grinned as the wind whipped by. "I've never been better!" he yelled.

The steward moved up within earshot. "Sir, I've taken the liberty of bringing some of the Japanese forward..."

"*Faen ta deg*! I know that. What took you so long doing it?"

"But I thought..."

"You must learn to make decisions on your own, Steward."

"Yes, Sir, but..."

"When things are obvious, act. Don't wait to be told," Eiriksson laughed.

"Yes, Sir."

"Feel the breeze, Steward? It's finally clearing. Your night of horror is over."

"It'll be over when I finish hosing down all the spaces, Sir. Maybe by next week..."

"Aaahh, the Japanese will do it. Willingly. Better than we ever could. It's their nature. They are clean freaks. They are quite embarrassed for making a mess. The are even more embarrassed by being in your debt."

They stood silently for a few moments, the wind in their faces. The specter of night changed perceptibly before them, from impenetrable darkness, to a first hint of dimension, to a potent pinkish gold aura breaking on the eastern horizon.

"See out there, Steward?" Eiriksson yelled over the wind. "Do you know what it is?"

Uncertain, the steward replied, "What, Sir? More trouble?"

It's the rising sun, Steward! A new day!"

—TOKYO—

"AAAAaiiiieeeehhiaaah!"

"That's pretty good. It took me months to learn Japanese."

"Aaaaahhh... OOAAAAHHHHH!"

"You're really becoming quite proficient at wind sucking. Excellent enunciation."

The steward slid finally beneath the searing waters, up to his chin. "AHHHHAAAAA! EEIIIEEE! Damn, that's hot!"

"They tell me it cooks your eggs in just three minutes. Saves a lot of women from unwanted pregnancies." Carty Thwaites lay almost submerged in the hot tub, arms resting on the edges, body splayed out under the waters. He lay with his head back on the tile rim, staring at the steamy ceiling above, waiting a tenacious condensation drop to do so.

The steward finally stopped breathing in short pants, and started to relax. He, too, found that no motion was the key. If one made waves, so to speak, the searing pain increased as new layers of scalding water brushed by the skin. "What is this, some kind of masochistic rite? Like skinning a tomato?"

"The Japs are clean freaks. Not because of soap. It's because they molt two layers of skin with each bath." Carter H. Thwaites was by now quite at home in Japan. He had been assigned to base

433

duty in Yokosuka for three years, and had enjoyed it so much he had requested to be discharged locally so he could stay on. He lived now in a tiny Japanese-style house in Kamakura, an hour south of Tokyo. He had had, surprisingly, no difficulty finding a job in Japan after his Navy service.

"So there I was, on the beach and starting to run out of cash in all the bars, so I knew I needed to get a job. I went to this local two man office of the American Chamber of Commerce, and they steered me to this guy, only about three years older then me, who had been sent over here by AMF to make a market survey for the potential for bowling machines. As soon as he got here, the Japs descended on him like flies, giving him orders. More orders than he could handle. Never did make his market survey. Seems like bowling was replacing Buddhism in its public appeal. I went right to work. All I do is write down where to ship the dumb machines, and take the letter of credit to a bank. I mean, these nuts are building bowling alleys like we plant beans. Not twelve or eighteen lanes, but eighty-four and ninety-six lanes at a crack. If all the bowling balls hit the backstops in one instant, Japan would have another earthquake, manmade... One thing you can still say about the Japanese... they're as fanatic as ever."

The steward shifted carefully under the human soup. "How'd you end up in this beautiful little house?"

"Mikki found it. She's pretty resourceful, actually. Three rooms, six *tatami*, one contemplation garden, a king-size *futon* and this blessed *o-furo*. She does everything. All kept neat as a pin. Does all the shopping. Meals. I'd be lost without her."

"Getting serious?"

"I doubt it will ever come to that," Carty sighed. "It's what's best described as a symbiotic relationship. We could each make it alone, but it works far better if we entangle our vines a bit."

"How'd you meet?"

"Mikki is your typical reconstruction *geisha*. Farm girl, poor but bright, no prospects at home, so like many she looks to the American military here for opportunity, knowing full well what currency she must pay in. At eighteen she ends up in a bar as a 'companion', keeping the boys happy and loaded with *sake* and beer. I met her in a dive near Yokosuka, and we hit it off. Our one night stand has lasted about two years now."

"You mean variety isn't the spice of life any more?"

"Ha! Guess I'm conforming. This is the land of conformity. They conform in their traditions, they conform in their food, they conform in their houses and furniture and in their art. They even conform in their new passion for social upheaval."

"Upheaval?"

"They can't put a name on it yet, but really what they are doing is dumping the past. The war certainly was a factor, but I think they see something else on the horizon. A new rising sun. Oh, they still love their temples and gardens and painted screens, but they are rushing madly into the modern age. Where one guy used to sit all day at a canvas waiting for just the right moment only to make one brush stroke and call it art, today everyone gets up at five in the morning and rushes to work, only to sit all day at a table soldering thousands of transistors into pocket radios. They conform to the norm of today. Now they have a passion for mass production. I mean these guys are really intense."

The steward looked about him, at the small room with the simplest of objects in it. A tile tub, big enough for two comfortably, three possibly, and four if you wanted lots of body contact. A simple wooden bucket and ladle. A small wooden stool. A scalding hot water faucet just daring one to open it some more. "Intense? This seems just the opposite. Serene."

"This is how they purge themselves at the end of the day. Steams out their passions. If you ever want to exert your superiority, do it just as somebody gets out of an *o-furo*. They're boiled lobsters, and quite docile."

"Hard to imagine anyone in a hot tub going to war."

"I call it hot tub imperialism. The little Emperor himself, Hirohito, back in the thirties, resold them the same old bowl of rice. He tells them they're the divinely chosen race. Reminds them he's descended from the Grand Dowager of the sky herself, the Sun Goddess, to lead them to rightful superiority over the barbarians. Says they should take over all the world's hot tubs by force, because only a divine race deserves to be lounging in a hot tub. Now that he's had his halo clipped, he sings another tune. As a mere mortal, he's telling them now they can take over by working their butts off building and selling the barbarians a better hot tub. Then all the Japs will get rich and buy anything they want. Know what? They bought it all over again. They're dumping the past that literally blew up in their faces, and madly charging into the future. These guys don't know moderation or compromise. It's all or nothing."

"Is it a passion for life, or for work?"

"To most of them, life is work, work, life. I know this *sushi* chef down in Kamakura center, all he does all day is make *sushi*. Fanatic little bastard. Stands there all day, along with some serious wind sucking, making *sushi*. Truly strives to be the best *sushi* chef in the world. Grab the rice, smear on the horseradish, pack in the tuna. Thousands he makes. But you know what? Each one, each crummy piece of seaweed is a joy to him, each slab of tuna a gift from the gods, each cut of the knife the signature of a samurai surgeon, each finished fishburger a magnificent work of art. He really takes pride in his work. Each one! It's truly amazing. That one could put such passion, such pride, such dedication into something so simple that in three hours will go into the *benjo* ditch. I still don't understand these people. Probably never will..."

"Sounds like he's a happy man, doing his own thing..."

"Not when he can't get prime quality tuna steak. He goes fucking wild. Knife flailing around the counter, voice screaming, jumping up and down, beating up on the dishwasher... This same quiet conformist, this master of the mustard, this artiste in glutinous rice, this dedicated traditionalist, this lord of the lumpfish, becomes a fucking madman. Can't stand things not going according to his standards. A real ego trip. He must have it his way, or gaboom! He thinks he's Supershogun. As imperialists go, I can see now why these guys were so hated. *Laissez faire* and democracy are concepts they can't even conceive, let alone pronounce. When other people won't or can't conform, they become wild beasts."

"Sounds like everybody needs a hot tub about then..."

"Keep 'em all in hot tubs, the world'd be a safer place..."

The rice paper *shoji* screen slid softly open, revealing a young woman in a lime cotton kimono kneeling at the doorway. She was looking down at her knees. "You and flend rike beeru, Cato?"

"Ah, Mikki my sweet. Your timing is perfection. Ambrosia to enhance our liquid paradise..." Carty sighed as he waved one of his wrists slowly above the water. "Now isn't she simply wonderful?"

The steward looked out at the smiling young woman, her eyes still downcast in respect, quietly accepting the approval of her master of the bath. She then slid a lacquered tray from behind the doorway, revealing two frosty bottles of Kirin and two mugs emblazoned with a decal of the U.S.S. Forrestal. She slid the tray into the room and up to the tub, then entered, still on her knees, to pour the brew into the mugs. Both men looked longingly at the cool amber liquid.

After handing a mug to each, she then pulled up her kimono sleeve and reached over to the hot water faucet and turned it on full blast, into the tub.

"AAAAAHHHHHRRRGGHHH! Enough! Please, Mikki! Stop! No more!"

She turned off the faucet and lowered her eyes, and still smiling, said, "Hot-to wata goodu fo whita skin. Make pink."

With that, she crawled back out the doorway and, once again in the same kneeling position, bowed slightly and quietly slid the paper screen back into place.

After their heart rates retreated, the steward asked, "She called you Cato. Mean something?"

"Means Mikki still can't pronounce my name. Seems they've conditioned all those face muscles to save face, and not into puckering up for l"s and r's. Carter becomes Cato. You should hear her mess up Thwaites."

"Seems she's learned enough to make your life pretty cushy."

"When the gods made woman, they should have wired them all like the Japanese model."

"What do you mean?"

"Perfect design. Works hard. Doesn't break down under stress, doesn't bitch when you go out at night..."

"They also serve, who lay and wait?..."

"They love to be faithful, even to a rat."

"I suspect Mikki has misjudged you?"

"You know what the Japanese women say about foreign guys?... 'It'su aru pink on outsido...'"

"They must have a different slant on things..."

"That all depends on how you look at it..."

"To pink. Our favorite color..."

"Cheers."

"*Banzai.*"

The ride from Kamakura was pure terror. Something out of a WWII movie, a Kafkaesque *kami-kazi* flight into madness or something. Carty had offered to take the steward up to Tokyo for dinner and a few drinks in a bar, before returning home to a typical business tomorrow. The steward had bid goodbye to Mikki standing in the raked sand 'garden' that was home to three pet stones, which graced their four foot by ten foot interior courtyard. She had bowed profusely and smiled graciously at their exit, and had then watched dispassionately as her cohabitant male headed off to the glamours of Tokyo nightlife while she dutifully stayed home and raked the sand. The steward felt as if she were blessing a flight of crazies take off from a flattop for a dangerous mission. She was not far from the truth. The road to Tokyo couldn't have been more dangerous if it had been mined.

There are many traditions that deserve maintaining within the Japanese culture. Some are beautiful, graceful, courteous, artistic, serene, tasteful, respectful, and the like. However, one... driving a car, is something alien wherein modern technology does not meld with the past. Probably a hangover from the mounted *samurai* days, when any body in the way got trampled or slashed into Rice Krispies. Put a Japanese in a car... and he thinks he's reincarnation of Minamoto Yoritomo himself, supreme *shogun*.

It would seem from the dazzling display of feudal jousting still played on the highway that Japanese rules of the road give the right of way clearly to the aggressor. If one driver decides to pass another, he speeds up and swerves right out into the oncoming traffic. The guy coming the other way either dives into the ditch, or dies head-on. The driver being passed retains the privilege of staying alive only by speeding up to not let the passer pass, because the passer, as soon as he gets his bumper ahead of the passee, has assumed the right to cut the passee off into a ditch. Amazing in all this, is the fact that the Japanese perform this madness with utmost formality and courtesy, all parties bowing and grinning and sucking wind until the moment of truth, a cut off or a head-on crash. Then, as the successful aggressor beams his buck ivories to an admiring world, the wretched passees are left in the dust to bow and scrape and hiss in, in abject embarrassment. Ah the power of it all...

The steward thought on power for a moment... "Mao declared that real power is in the barrel of a gun. Lenin preached that real power was in the hands of the proletariat. Mohammed found the power of the sword. Buddha believed that real power is getting so hungry that you reach the seventh level of bliss. The Catholics realized the power of fear of eternal damnation, the Protestants the power of industry. Thomas Paine taught us the power of the pen, Napoleon the power of a full stomach, the Greeks the power of the vote. Egyptians believed in the power of the flood, Romans the power of the phalanx, British the power of the fleet... The Japanese, it seems, have come up with a new one. Real power... is behind the steering wheel of a car."

"*Kami-kazi* Highway" Carty had called it. Truer words were never spoken. The steward had counted fourteen still smoking wrecks and disabled vehicles alongside the road as they zigged and dodged and raced their way North, driving on the flip side of the road, steering column on the right, knees pressed up in their chins in the cramped little four cylinder Honda, drawn with fanatic determination towards the big glow in the evening sky.

The steward was traveling light, with only a change of socks and skivvies and shirt and dope kit in a small softsack slung over his light jacket. He had again been given two days off after arriving in Yokohama. The passengers were out touring, first taking a bus to the shrine at Nikko, staying overnight in a country inn along the way, then coming back by way of the infamous Ginza for some serious shopping.

The steward had known Carty Thwaites from college and Navy days, and had heard he had stayed on in Japan after discharge. After a few dead-ended telephone conversations, he somehow, through the base operations at Yokosuka, had learned of Carty's new address in nearby Kamakura. Duffle sack in hand, he had set off, out of the sprawling grimy port of Yokohama, into a mysterious and bewildering land, to find his friend.

Carty had seemed more than happy to receive a surprise guest, particularly if it meant a night out on the town. Even with all the comforts of cohabitation, it would seem in Japan that certain predatory instincts die hard. If, during the daytime, the serene and stately Mount Fuji symbolizes the soul of the land of the rising sun, once that sun has set, it is an odd, pulsing prophetic glow in the sky above a small bay that epitomizes the true character of its peoples. Exotic, inscrutable, madcap, sinful, utterly dynamic... Tokyo.

Arriving in Shinjiku about dusk, Carty parked the Honda in a small building lot a block off the main drag in the Kabukicho quarter. They were famished by the time they stepped out into the crisp night air. Carty smiled mischievously. "Ready to live or die for food?"

"Yeah, I'm that hungry. What do you have in mind?"

"*Fugu.*"

Carty dragged the steward into a strange little restaurant with red lanterns hanging outside and in. Laid across the front window were a spectacular spread of many varieties of fresh fish over ice, squid, cuttlefish, tuna, flounder, salmon, shrimp and blowfish among the recognizable forms. After the obligatory bowing and scraping by the owner at the door, they were led by a kimono-clad hostess to a private cubby with a hole in the floor with a small clear lacquered table spread across it. Removing their shoes, the two large men struggled across the *tatami* mats into position, twisting their long legs into the hole.

A kneeling waitress appeared at the doorway, bowed very low. Then she crawled into the roomette, pulled back her kimono sleeve and placed placed a tiny tied-twig tray of steaming hot hand towels in front of each man.

"Wash up," Carty smiled. "For this might be your last meal."

The steward followed his lead, and washed his face and hands with the steamy towel, relishing in the refreshing afterglow it generated. The waitress collected the used towels with a low bow, and asked if they were ready to order.

Carty had become rather proficient in the local language, and rattled off a list of items, two of them striking a cord of recognition from the steward. Beeru, and hot sake. He smiled with salivary anticipation.

After but a few moments filled with idle musings, food and beverages started to arrive. Items were unrecognizable. Their display, however, was a work of art that even a smorgasbord chef had to admire.

"This is *hirezake*, an *aperitif* of *sake* scented with toasted *fugu* fins," Carty marveled as he saluted the steward and sipped the small glass. "Fishwine at its best."

The steward found it oddly to his liking.

"And this..." Carty beamed, "is *fugusashi*. Live dangerously, my friend. Life is sweet."

"What do you mean?" the steward asked, as he marveled at the *sashimi* sliced to a translucent thinness, spectacularly arranged like a chrysanthemum on a porcelain platter.

"Wait till you taste this sauce..." Carty mumbled on. "Horseradish, soy, bitter orange, minced scallions, and hot pepper. I got Mikki to try to duplicate it."

The steward took a bit of the raw fish before him. "Ummmmmm. Delicious. Delicate flavor. Almost crunchy texture..." He chewed for a moment, then swallowed. "Strange bite to the combination, though. My mouth seems numb. What's in it?"

Carty leaned back and grinned, wiping his mouth and taking a swill of *sake*. "Poison."

"What?" the steward swallowed hard.

"Poison... Neurotoxins," Carty replied matter of factly.

The steward went pale, wondering what kind of Machiavellian fiend sat across from him.

"Oh don't be worried. They leave just enough in it to tease your taste buds. If the fish killed you, they would loose their *fugu* license. That's much more important than one pair of blue eyes.

"*Fugu* license?" the steward struggled to drink a glass of beer.

"*Fugu* is a poisonous blowfish, you know, a puffer. Takes a special license to become a *fugu* chef. They go to school for months to learn how to remove the liver and reproductive organs. Must be tough to find the nuts on one of these little buggers, don't you think?" he pondered, poking about what might have been a tiny tail section remaining in the festive display.

"License to kill..." The steward looked strangely at his plate, and swallowed hesitatingly to himself.

"Really, it's safe. Eat up. This is top of the line dining for the Japs. Tempting fate. Seems the risk is worth the price."

Carty was wolfing down every morsel and droplet. The steward started poking about his plate again, sniffing and jabbing. Out of nowhere, the waitress appeared with more food, and began dispensing it. With a bow, she removed herself.

"This is *tetchiri*, chunks of *fugu* cooked with vegetables. Eat up. Later, she'll mix rice with the soup later to make *zosui*. They don't leave a part of this little guy uneaten. Guess they want the full thrill out of Japanese roulette."

"What's after the main course," the steward asked hesitatingly as he courageously put a fishy chunk into his tingling mouth. "Wait, don't tell me. It must be *fugu* ice cream..."

Happy to be still standing after so humbling a meal, the steward followed Carty out into the night air again. They strolled along the main drag, past *pachinko* parlors and bars and strip joints by the hundreds.

The steward marveled at the confused layout and heavy traffic and many pedestrians out on the street. "Is it always like this?"

"It's part of their grand plan. Keep everybody moving. There's 100 million Japs here, stuffed onto this tiny island. If they ever stopped to figure out things, they'd revolt."

"Like what?"

"Well, the smart guys stay on top by keeping everybody else baffled. Throughout their history... Illogical concepts like Fourth Street crossing Fifth Street... twice! Keep 'em baffled and you stay in power."

"Baffling..."

"That little street is called *Shomben-yokocho*," Carty pointed. "Means 'Piss Alley.' Pungent atmosphere, no?"

The steward marveled at the action of the evening... Drunken businessmen, students, couples running off arm in arm to some love hotel. "This town is sin central..." he muttered, as they passed by an obviously gay nightclub, with transvestite strippers visible from the street. "Is all of Japan like this?"

"Westerners may call it sin. They call it life. This isn't sin, it's a ritual, a celebration! They enjoy living. Or at least these people do. The mama-sans who stay home may not."

They walked on past pubs and bars and "No-pants Kissa" strip shows and massage parlors and Turkish baths. "That's one of the 'soaplands' places," Carty pointed out. "Get into a hot tub with one or two or more if you like. Started out that the girls were only to bring hot water. Seems like everybody wanted them to bring in hot lips instead. Now they're cat houses under water."

"What about all these tiny hotels? Seems they have a steady stream of couples going in and out."

"They rent rooms out by the hour. Literally. A quicky is good for the spirits. Particularly when mama-san at home is a hog."

"What do you mean?" the steward asked, as three dissimilar-aged couples ahead of them turned giggling into a hotel entrance.

"They still hang on to the old ways. Some thirty percent of marriages are still arranged. Families get married, not individuals. It's tough when you get someone with teeth like Eleanor."

"Escape on the town, eh."

"Escape from reality. The job is intense. Mama-san is boring or ugly or both. Kids are noisy. So every yellow blooded male reserves the right to go out on the town, for business meetings they tell everybody. Some business..."

"And I thought Japan was civilized..."

"That's just it. It is! Extremely civilized, on the surface. Bowing and scraping and honoring the departed grandparents and dressing up for all the ceremonies for the gods and respecting traditions and art and nature. All very respectful. Very civilized. They respect their emperor and their company and their asshole boss and their mother and even their wives if they keep quietly in their place. Only two things they missed, or they'd be perfectly civilized."

"What are they?"

"Having respect for anybody that's not Japanese, and respecting power a bit less," Carty grunted. "They are the most racially bigoted nation I have ever witnessed. Hitler was a pussycat compared to them. Down deep, these guys are still barbarians. They go fucking crazy. They are too inbred. Too homogeneous, too conformist, too insular, too fanatic. Look at their history. All that *bushido* bullshit. That 'Co-Prosperity Sphere' crap. Who're the kidding? They're power mad. It's all ahead full and fuck anybody in the way for them. It's in the blood."

The steward looked about him at the dozens of people on the street. Everyone was doing something to excess. Laughing too loudly, walking to intensely, talking too loudly, drinking to severely, pursuing the evening too passionately. But, on the surface, their actions looked like a good release from daily drudgery anywhere... It looked like a lot of fun.

Carty pulled him by the sleeve, and they entered a bar with the broken sound of jazz tinkling off some mismanaged ivories inside.

Carty brushed passed the main hostess, a tiny lady in a kimono at the door, with a big "Hi y'all t'night!" and headed into the main room, where he sat down at a table without being helped. Another hostess in kimono came over to the table and bowed. Carty ordered two large bottles of Yebisu beeru.

"There're places for Yanks and places for Japs. I always like to go to the Jap bars," Carty yelled above the honkytonk music. "Pisses the locals off, but you get lots better girls who are more than happy to see your dick get pink in a hot tub."

Before the beeru arrived, two smiling, giggling young women in pastel kimonos came over to the table and bowed. Carty gave them the once over, and pulled out two chairs for them. "See what I mean, mate? Prime pink puski!"

Drinks appeared before them, and after one long pull, it was as if they had been old friends for years, the girls chatting and pouring and mopping up spills and dabbing the foamy lips of the two fortunate Americans in a hidden Japanese valley of pleasure.

Their names were Kikko and Mitsi, shortened from Mitsuko in honor of a Hollywood starlet. Their ages were about twenty. Their education, from off the farm into the honors program at Nightlife University. Their profession... Grade A, government approved, state-of-the-art hostess.

The steward scanned the room, filled with smoking Japanese men and young raven-haired beauties in kimonos and overdone eye make-up who stroked their clients' upper arms and giggled a lot. The body language of a bargirl had seemed the same all over the world. Giggle and grin a lot, at anything the john says. Play coy, touch but don't grab, spice up the chase, enhance closeness with whispers, hint of imagined pleasures, and the price goes up. But here, it seemed to be different. The girls who hung on Carty's and the steward's arms didn't seem to be hooking for bed business, at least not overtly. They were doing their jobs. Making the customer feel at home, relaxed, happy. Talking on any subject he wished. Giggling. Smiling. Pouring drinks. Ah, yes. Pouring drinks by the score. Another? Why not. But surprisingly, the hostesses never touched a drop themselves. Here, in a Japanese saloon in Shinjiku, one of thousands that lined the streets, young women practiced an accepted age-old art perfected into its finest form. Here, hooker miraculously transformed into hostess. Here were *Naisu gyaru's*. Nice girls.

The piano shifted to softer recognizable melodies. *"Uroua..."* crooned the piano player, a skinny little man with glasses and long fingers and hair slicked back, *"And it was-sa Uroua..."*

"It's a great old tradition..." Carty barked over the music. "*Geisha*. It's still a respectable job. Pay is better than a factory or a farm. Clothes and fashions and food and nightlife fun all comes with the job. They use to have to dance and sing and play the *shamisen*. Today all they have to do is giggle and smile, and whisper sweet nothings into the ears of drunken boors."

More beeru appeared in quite the correct way, and went down the correct way. Followed by more beeru. Gradually, soft touching became more in exploratory, giggling more coy and seductive, the girls' secondary motives now betraying their earlier "I'm hard to get" pouts and bows and hidden eye looks.

"What do you think..." Carty yelled across the table as Mitsi massaged his thigh. "Interested in a little of Kikko-pu's joy juice?"

The steward looked about him, at all the smiling happy young faces of simple Japanese girls plying their art form on the customers.

Beautiful, graceful, delightful companionship... What more could a man want, other than a roll on the *futon*?

But the male customers had different expressions. Almost everyone else in the bar was Japanese. Businessmen, executives, managers, clerks, night out husbands, mostly white collar types, everyone smoking madly, all soaked to the bone on *sake* and whisky and beer. And all of them scowling at Carty and the steward, in spite of the fondling and fawning their own lovely companions were plying upon them. "We're sitting inside a powder keg..." the steward thought to himself.

Carty looked about the room as well. Suddenly a mischievous grin filled his face. "Let's have some fun. Watch this..." Carty laughed. He picked up his beer and went over to another table, to one of the drunken businessmen who rested on his elbows over his cups, one who had been scowling more intensely than the others, and put his arm around the man's hunched shoulders. Then he said something into his ear in Japanese, toasted him publicly by hoisting his beer to the air and then drinking it dry, and then he kissed the man on the cheek. The man turned deep shades of purple, and at the end of one massive sucking in of wind, froze in shock like a statue. His tablemates then followed suit, sucking the smoky air in past clenched teeth like industrial vacuum cleaners, then freezing in wide-eyed horror and dismay. Not a word was uttered from any.

A madly grinning Carty, after patting the man boldly on the shoulder and then bowing, swaggered back to the steward and the two ladies in waiting.

"What the hell did you say to him? He looks like he's in cardiac arrest."

Carty laughed heartily. "I got sick of this one guy's scowling at us, so I thought I'd teach him a lesson. I told him in Japanese that I thought his country was even more sophisticated than mine, and that he was obviously a gentleman of the finest order. Then I asked him if he had ever seen a pink prick before."

"I'd have clobbered you. Why didn't he?"

Carty howled. "These guys can only understand one thing at a time. They have to focus in, one task at a time. Otherwise they short circuit and fuse out completely. Must be their slit eyes, no lateral vision. Meiji-san there was still trying to figure out the gentleman bit. He really does think he's superior and more sophisticated than us, than any other race for that matter, even though we kicked their asses in the war. When I told him so directly, it blew his mind. How can he ever sock me if I just told him he was a gentleman and superior? It's a conundrum in logic he can't handle. Then I hit him with the kiss and pink prick line, and he fused out. His asshole buddies saw him get kissed, and not sock me, and they fused out as well. Hell, I could short circuit the whole fucking bar if I wanted to..."

The steward stared in disbelief. What a country. All the while their two young female companions were bowing and smiling and graciously pouring drinks, seemingly totally oblivious to the goings on, or to the fact that WWIII was at the cusp. "Remember Pearl Harbor, Mama-sama..." Carty toasted his companion, his big hug eliciting a sweet giggle from her tulip bud lips.

The piano player had shifted to butcher another familiar theme. *"You mus lememba this, a kisso stiru kisso, asahi jus asahi..."*

The steward looked about him through the smoke filled *nomi-ya* packed with eyeglasses and big teeth and loud, guttural sounds washing away the taste of daytime jobs. He smiled over at Dooley at the piano and said, "Lick's Prace... Pray it again, San."

The evening of laughing and giggling and drinking and scowling and fawning and wondering what the devil anything meant continued for about ten more minutes, during which more beeru arrived at the table without being ordered. Carty, full of life, lifted his new liter of Yebisu and started a long pull right out of the bottle. After a dozen good gusto swallows, his eyes started to blink, then glaze over. A strange smile appeared and froze on his face, as if he was trying to watch hummingbirds mate. Their two female companions cushioned the fall of Carty's head as it careened forward on to the table. Dumbfounded, the steward struggled with the comatose form before him, checking for pulse and breathing. After a few terrorizing seconds fending off fear from confusion, he realized that Carty had either passed out, or somebody had slipped him the old Micky Finn. Obviously time for a strategic exit.

Somehow amidst all the bowing and jabbering and wind sucking of the managers and bouncers, and the struggles to get Carty out the door and into a waiting taxi, the steward managed to pay the check. A hefty total of all of six dollars was required to cover the near half case of beer now sloshing around in Carty's gut.

The piano player recognized an opportunity, and bowed most gratuitously as they passed, hoping for a tip. The steward stuffed a dollar into a glass on top of the piano, hoping the gesture would buy a little extra exit insurance. As Carty was dragged by, Piano-san responded romantically, *"Goo nighta, Sreethot, tiru we mee tomollu... Goo nighta, Sreethot, poting such sreet sollu..."*

As the now quite alert steward climbed into the minitaxi on top of the sedated corpus of his friend, the manager smiled and bowed low from the glaring neon doorway and mumbled something in Japanese. Without recognizing a word, the steward fully understood his meaning. "Remember Hiroshima, pink plick."

Somehow the steward had communicated with the cabby, mainly by showing him the name and address of a small hotel in Shinjiku that Mikki had recommended. After an eight block ride past a noisy bars and strip joints and hundreds of *pachinko* parlors crammed with men of all ages mindlessly playing the Japanese version of pinball, the taxi pulled over and screeched to a halt.

"Heru *Cio Cio* Hoteru. One dorru." the driver called back.

The *Cio Cio* Hotel was a narrow, small six story building, squeezed in between two larger ones on a quieter side street right off the hot entertainment section. It was owned by one of Mikki's distant cousins, a strange little man called Goro-san, and his wife-san. Goro-san had provided overnight space before for Carty, both alone and with Mikki, on various occasions, and recognized the tall American slumbering in the back of the taxi. He shook his head softly up and down, while bowing low to the steward. "Flend hava goodu time?"

"Too goodu, thanks. You have rooms for us?"

The small man grinned widely, and clapped his hands. Three kimomo clad young girls came out to the curb giggling madly, long sleeves flapping in the breeze like wings, and with Goro-san and the steward, hoisted Carty out of the cab like happy butterflies trying to fly away with a roll of carpet.

The three fluttering Ariels pulled their load in through the doorway, and with great difficulty dragged Carty over a narrow three-foot bridge that arched a gurgling puddle near the concierge desk. Mama Goro-san rose from her bookkeeping and bowed profusely at the somnolent form as it passed. A more gracious welcome could not have been afforded a visiting head of state.

Given the weight of this snoring load, Goro-san assigned Carty a room on the second floor, reached only by stairs. It was a simple two-*tatami* rabbit hutch, maybe eight feet square, with sliding *shoji* door and one tiny rice paper window, one paper lantern lamp hanging on a cord, and a simple low two-drawer bureau. As soon as his shoes were removed, the body was plopped unceremoniously on the mats, and the bubbling butterfly girls unfolded and spread out a *futon*. Then, giggling and chattering madly, they stripped Carty's body of all clothing, folding each piece neatly and laying it over the bureau. A new wave of coy giggling accompanied the removal of his skivvies, revealing a rather dormant and not-so-pink appendage.

The steward stood by, out of the flurry of these professional bed makers, and watched them tuck his friend into Oriental dreamland. After much giggling, they determined that to put on the light cotton *yukata* sleeping kimono was imprudent considering the circumstances, so they just rolled him onto the soft mattress, lifted his head, and let it fall with a clunk on to something filled with rice husks oddly termed a pillow. "Well, Goro-san," he said, not caring if he understood or not, "I can see he's in the care of the angles now. Tomorrow, when he wakes, the head devils will take over."

Goro-san smiled knowingly. "We getta him up O.K. We giva hot-to *kohi*. Getta to work O.K. Do all time."

The steward bowed politely acknowledging the experience of the little hotelier, and thanked him for his help. Then he walked down the hall to the room that was to be his, following the bows and beckonings of the three timid Lepidopterae. It was a narrow hallway, with sliding rice paper doors every few feet. He heard laughs and giggles from behind most of them. Occasionally, a *shoji* would slide open, and a female head coyly would peer out, and then with a playful laugh vanish back inside the cubicle.

After the *futon* was spread, the flight of fluttering butterflies commenced an attack on his clothing. "Wait! I'm not staying right now. Dinner. Food. I'm going out. I want real food."

Blushing and giggling, the girls re-buttoned his shirt and fly, and bowing most graciously, led him amid a flurry of tee-hees back down to the small lobby with it's tiny arched bridge over crystal mini-puddle and its trickle of water re-circulating down a few water-worn rocks.

Standing at the desk were two miss-aged couples, the males obviously well sake'd up, laughing and cuddling as they signed in. Mama-san did the obligatory bowing and scraping once again, and then the three giggling butterflies towed them off to their appointed love nests.

"Everybody seems happy here..." he thought. "Right nice little place." He stepped over to Mama-san and asked directions to an inexpensive restaurant. Mama gave him sixteen bows in return, but no information. "Oops. No English."

Looking about for Goro-san, the steward started mumbling to himself in frustration. Then his eyes caught a glimpse of a female figure, in western clothes, seated over against a small bamboo bar, watching from the shadows. She spoke in his direction, "There are numerous good places to eat. Go left outside, and follow along that side street for two blocks."

The steward moved over into the shadows. There, seated on a bamboo bar stool, but not drinking, was a petite young Japanese girl, early twenties, dressed in black skirt and black sweater over a white blouse. She looked almost like a schoolgirl, almost in uniform, but something about her was different. She displayed a quiet poise, an individual assertiveness not easily noticed in most Japanese women.

She sat head high and strait-backed on the stool, with legs lightly crossed. She also wore a silky narrow white scarf, something like a banner with black characters on it, draped casually around her neck and shoulders like a shawl, and a red arm band on her left upper arm. Her hair was raven black, and pulled back severely into a bun, and she wore large round glasses which perched precariously at the end of her small nose. Unlike the kimono'd gaggle who had tended his *futon*, this girl's dark piercing eyes looked steadily into his, her glasses magnifying their size and directness. She did not smile, but continued with chin held high to quietly stare him out.

"Thank you, Miss. Long day. I was getting very hungry."

"You are not a tourist?" she asked with a level voice.

"Norwegian merchant marine," the steward answered.

Her expressionless face seemed to change, to soften, and she tilted her head with a hint of curiosity. "We are not honored with many of your pursuit," she said. "However, we do have an abundance of fair heads in our land today."

"I can assure you, mine is sun bleached. And I am fascinated by the more raven haired, like you."

She smiled and glanced back down into the open book before her. She spoke carefully,

> *"Let my heart be still a moment and this mystery explore...*
>
> *Tis the wind and nothing more!..."*

The steward nodded and returned the smile with proper refrain.

> *"Quoth the Raven, 'Nevermore'..."*

The steward was surprised. Here was a composed young woman, speaking fluent English. She had been reading from a collection of verse. "Your English is..."

"As is yours..." she softly cut him off. "It seems a necessary currency in today's world.

The conversation continued to the point where the steward asked the young woman to accompany him for a late meal. After looking curiously into his eyes for a few seconds, to his delight, she accepted. She had been waiting for over an hour for friends of hers to meet her at the hotel lobby, but they had never showed. Rather than sit the night away, she suggested they go instead to a local establishment that served light food and entertainment.

"Come," she took his hand and pulled him out into the night again. "I will show you a different side of Japanese society..."

She bolted sprightly out the door, as light on her feet as if she were stepping from cloud to cloud. Her personality lit up as she set her body in motion, her graceful movements and quick flashing eyes radiating hints of deeper talents within.

They walked for many blocks at a purposeful pace, not saying much of import but catching up on each other's past. The girl's name was O-Kuni. She was a drama student and modern dancer, of all things, who was studying *Kabuki* theatre and dance at the University of Tokyo. Her preference for things modern and Western had not provided her much comfort while studying the more traditional aspects of Japan's cultural past. She was very much of the new generation who looked to the West, particularly the United States, to reveal the directions of Japan's cultural future, but not necessarily its political one. While becoming well educated on the strengths and traditions of the past, O-Kuni was committed to the exciting, unknown future. For O-Kuni, the microphone was certain to be more powerful than the fan.

They walked and talked, passing through a veritable department store of Tokyo nightlife and noise called the Kabukicho quarter, passing pubs and bars and restaurants and huge advertisements and neon signs and strip shows and "soapland" exotic baths and massage parlors. Eventually the cityscape took on a different character, darkening into a maze of narrow alleys lined with sleazy, ramshackle pubs and teahouses, much like Greenwich Village drawing students and artists and intellectual types to its shadowy secrets.

They stopped in front of one doorway that cast a beam of light into the alley. "My friends may be here. A local favorite of students and intellectuals. The 'Quill and Brush'."

The steward followed after as the trim young girl took his hand and entered the half cellar of an old building. Odd noises were escaping out of the open industrial door. Not music, but strange screaming and shouting, pathetic pleas and dramatic wails and long syllables. His alert juices pumped forth, only to be embarrassed by a wave of soft clicking from within, which sounded like a thousand enthusiastic crickets.

Inside the smoky ex-factory workspace were crowded easily two hundred young Japanese, male and female, dressed in similar garb, basic black. Certainly not the kimono set, these young persons looked like students and intellectuals the world over - intense eyes, serious faces, eager movements, utter concentration on the performers, and beeru being guzzled from the bottle. In contrast to earlier pubs of the evening, this one housed a motivated crowd, cerebrally active, trying not to become the get blasted and drop out crowd. Judging by the level of public emoting and audience appreciation, these young persons were fired up about something in common. Anger and pain and concern burned in the voice of the bespectacled firebrand whispering so intensely into the microphone under the spotlight floor center. Slow wind sucking sounds encouraged him from all corners, punctuated by deep guttural groans and occasional sharp gasps. As the man with the mike struck the ultimate posture in his poetic outpouring, finger snapping applause burst forth from the crowd of crickets, tribute from this cadre of fledgling sons and daughters of Thespis eager too to reveal their deepest feelings to the crowd. The steward and his new friend had entered into a poetry reading nightspot.

"Quoth a few more ravens, more..." said the steward, surveying the students volunteering to assume the mic and spotlight.

O-Kuni led him by the hand through the crowded paths to some tables on the other side of the room. Many eyes looked up, startled at blond hair and blue eyes in their midst.

O-Kuni spoke back up into his ear as they walked. "We call ourselves *kawaramono*, or riverbed people, after those outcasts throughout our history who have been held down by tradition. Many of us are students. Many are artists and writers."

"Seems they all have the same tailor in common..." he replied.

O-Kuni gave him a serious look, then smiled at his sarcasm. "What we hold in common is our demand for change, for the rights and abilities of every person to be recognized."

"Sounds pink, inside and out..." the steward mused to himself.

The steward and O-Kuni sat down at a large community table, crowding themselves in amongst twenty or so students. Faces immediately turned to the steward, scrutinizing him severely. His friend said something, and everyone smiled and softened and bowed, and then returned to their private matters. Someone passed large bottles of beeru. Someone else passed down bowls of hard-boiled eggs, bundles of seaweed, short tubes of bland white fish sausage, and 'treasure bags' made from deep-fried *tofu* and filled with translucent noodles and other surprises. As late snacks went, considering all the beeru washed down earlier at Lick's Prace, the steward found everything to be very tasty and fulfilling, including the poetry.

After a few moments, the poets gave way to a small jazz combo who sat assembled with their instruments on a platform in the spotlight. The three young men somehow had mastered the most amazing feat of playing the monotonous sounds of Dave Brubeck backwards. One hammered a zither-like instrument called the *koto*, another tooted a flute, and the third tinkled on a guitar called the *samisen*. The steward watched and listened, amazed, as the three musicians seemed to be doing their own thing, individually setting off on solos, all at once. Cacophony? Or exquisite harmony?

O-Kuni saw his interest, and smiled. "This is a jazz group from our music department at the University. They are rather *avant-garde* in their compositions, combining traditional instruments and sounds with modern explorations and interpretations of Western artists. Our music is probably strange to your ears. Unlike your well-tempered twelve note keyboards, ours is pentatonic. Even more intricately, we will employ different modes. One for example, *ryo*, is male, another, *ritsu*, is female. More frequently, as now, even three modes are played simultaneously, in uneven phrase length. If you listen closely, there are intricacies and depths in our music that are very delicate and mysterious. One must listen past the obvious sound, to find the soul of the music itself.

"Bidurand West..." the steward mulled, as the three youths hunkered over their antique instruments, quietly and slowly hammering and strumming softly something which sounded like a modern jazz version of a day in the life of a guitar tuner, accompanied by his pet warbler. "A beer and a cigarette sure help..." he grinned.

She smiled and reached over and touched his hand. "Actually, I prefer Brubeck."

Above the music and the munching and swallowing and emoting and canting, the steward thought back on the information so forthcoming. Her name was O-Kuni. She was a student attending graduate studies at Tokyo University. She was twenty-two, emancipated and single by choice. Her passions seemed to be directed not to self-gratification or intellectual enrichment or artistic expression, but to some new cause not yet fully understood by the steward. O-Kuni had a beautiful face, but was trying seriously not to reveal it. She reminded him of an Oriental princess in common disguise, an Audrey Hepburn on holiday from more traditional courtly duties. It was obvious that she wished to be judged on some other standard than her femininity. She seemed pulled in different directions. On the surface she presented a controlled, serious facade. But behind her mask of intense focus and purpose were hints of feminine vulnerability and a passionate nature.

After twenty minutes or so, the jazz combo ended their gig. Wind sucking and finger snapping filled the smoky hall in earnest appreciation. The trio bowed just as earnestly, and with toothy smiles to the crowd, carted their instruments off.

Center stage, a young girl, rather chubby and wearing very thick glasses, now took the microphone. She posed in silence for the longest time, breathing ponderously, setting the new mood, then whispered quickly and dramatically in Japanese into the mic, emoting directly into the one harsh amber spotlight. When she had finished, and the soft snapping applause had subsided, O-Kuni leaned over and translated.

"So still.
And they sink into the rocks,
These voices of madmen.'

She's reciting her modern version of a classic *haiku* by the poet Basho."

"What does she mean?" the steward asked, bewildered.

"We are the future," she spoke into the steward's ear. "We must lay the foundations of a new Japan for generations to come. The old ways must go. They must die away. We are now part of the modern world. And women must take their full place in that world."

"All that in seventeen syllables?"

"What is on the surface, and seen by the eye, is never what is greeted by the heart."

"A rose isn't a rose isn't a rose?"

"Appearances are illusory. The true essence of being can only be intuited."

The steward looked at one of the treasure bags, and belched to himself, "There's more to it than meets the eye..."

A young man with a red armband took over the mic. He grimaced and groaned and grunted for a few seconds, then frowned deeply as he slowly sucked in enough wind for a most serious performance of a most profound two liner. Finger snapping again filled the hall.

O-Kuni translated:

"Snow is falling.
Meiji recedes into the distance."

"Meaning?"

She seemed particularly pleased with this innuendo. "Emperor Meiji is an era, the reign of the grandfather of Hirohito, whose reign is now called Emperor Showa. He is saying that the old way, an antiquated era, is fading away with the winter. A new Japan is emerging to take its place in the world. We, the young generation, are the fresh snowfall that will obscure its warrior heritage and mold its transformation."

"Obscure its warrior heritage?..." the steward thought to himself, eyeing the zealous, impassioned crowd.

Another young girl took her place at the microphone. Melodramatic posturing was an understatement, as the girl poured out her heart. Again, O-Kuni translated her updated version of a much-admired *sewamono*, a love-suicide play:

> *"Farwell to this world,*
>
> *And to the night, farewell.*
>
> *We who walk the way to death,*
>
> *To what shall we be likened?*
>
> *We who will not relive the heat...*
>
> *We who will not allow the blinding light...*
>
> *We who will not harm the butterfly,*
>
> *We will not suffer the starless night.*
>
> *To the frost on the road,*
>
> *To the graveyard,*
>
> *Vanishing with each step ahead:*
>
> *This dream of a dream*
>
> *So powerful."*

Avid clicking filled the hall, followed by a dull breathy roar of serious wind sucking and chattering and drinking. The steward scratched his head, trying to penetrate the veil of imagery presented before him.

O-Kuni touched his arm in sympathy. "To paraphrase our famous playwright Chikamatsu... In our art, our poetry, our theatre... things are unreal, yet not unreal, real, yet not real. Meaning lies between the two."

The steward nodded most seriously, and sucked in some wind.

After a few more brews and boiled eggs and seaweed bundles the steward found himself duly impressed with these Oriental clones of Tango singers. While performances were flawed and sophomoric, the sincerity of their deliveries was overriding, the intensity of their passion infectious. One after another, these young Japanese took the microphone and poured out their poetic souls to kindred spirits. Any stand-up would kill for such a supportive crowd. Yet it was more than just young persons connecting. Binding the various cantos and themes of their discontent... was pure and absolute conformity.

By this time everyone had consumed a lot of beer. Voices were becoming louder, laughter more energetic, wind sucks more violent. The mood of the crowd seemed to be changing. Brows revealed deeper more serious furrows.

The steward looked about him. These certainly were the chosen youth of Japan. The Crimson of Tokyo. Intellectual, intense, concerned about the future. Politically outspoken, they were making vocal waves, singing their hearts out on the hydrogen bomb and pollution of rivers and sky and the rights of women. For the most part they were the new elite, all attending local universities, and as such were assured of finding much opportunity in the new society. Japan's youth had in one decade become a powerful activist force, passionately political and brimming with principle... and extremely naive.

The steward listened with fascination to the translations of O-Kuni, watching this emotional pep rally unfolding before his eyes. He took note as one firebrand with a white headband tied about his brow, both fists shaking into the air, ranted and raged on some topic. He wore a red armband over his upper arm. The student became so emotional that he gagged on his own wind sucking, and dropped the mic with a loud CLANK.

"What's he all about?"

"*Zengakuren.* He implores everyone to attend the large demonstration tomorrow outside the Diet. He and his kind are trying to bring down the government."

"Why? I thought Kishi was well liked?"

"Buy the old, yes. The traditionalists. But not by the young. We Japanese have something we call *Zaibatsu*... Big business's undue influence on government. Kishi represents the interests of the industrialists, and those of the Americans."

"I thought Japan and the West had common interests, and common threats, namely the Russians and the Chinese."

"The West does not suffer our humiliation from the last war. Now we must seek peace, demand peace, fight if necessary for peace. Our Article Nine of the Constitution disavows war, and forbids our ever again having offensive armed forces."

"Your solution is to leave such ugliness to the Americans?"

"We students are against any and all military alliances, and particularly nuclear testing near our waters and our homeland. Japan must change. We look to the West for our future. But we cannot allow the domination of the Western powers to continue. We must free ourselves both from our past and from those who would be our masters."

The steward felt the deep pain in the girl's voice, and her firm commitment to a role in shaping the future. He reached over to touch her hand softly. Suddenly, abruptly, he was shoved from behind by one young buck who had had half a case of Asahi too many. The young man started in with loud rantings at O-Kuni, spewing forth a guttural invective berating her for being in the company of an American. At first, O-Kuni resisted standing up to him, but kept her gaze right into his rolling eyes. Then she stood, nose to nose with the heavily breathing youth, and in terse Japanese let him know something presumably like his conduct was shameful and it was none of his business who she was with and that her friend was from a Norwegian ship.

The student, emancipated in his views only to the degree that he was still not accustomed to being spoken to like that by a lowly woman, saw red. He slowly, dramatically raised a fist high over his head in a ritualistic move that was intended to intimidate his victim before pulverizing her. The steward, still seated next to O-Kuni in verbal oblivion but quite cognizant of body language, reached his foot out behind the student and hooked it and pulled. CRASH! The youth descended like a wooden statue of Buddha, fist still high in the air, falling strait down to a more befitting seated position on the floor, legs tangled under him.

Most neighboring students and tablemates laughed and pointed. The steward merely smiled and sat there with his arms folded on his chest, to all appearances having never moved. The drunken youth, face now quite lost amidst his immediate peers, sat sullenly in the crumbs and cigarette butts on the floor in dishonor, silently sucking wind in through teeth.

O-Kuni stood there frozen, looking down at the student.

"Come. Now." The steward quietly rose and took her arm. "It is time to go."

O-Kuni bowed eyes down to their tablemates and started out. The steward followed docilely, watching their backs while bowing and smiling to any who watched and wondered of his mission among them. But the drunken boy had been joined by others with angry faces who obviously shared his concern about the presence of spying blue eyes in their midst. Threatening stares began following them through the crowd. A toothy group of testy youths merged their valor and started after them.

The steward, trouble senses ringing alert, looked about him for another nearer exit. Seeing all egress blocked by staring eyes, he quickly snatched O-Kuni's book of verse, then stepped up into the spotlight and with a deep bow, took the microphone away from a startled poetess about to begin. He stared out into the narrow cone of brightness for a moment, striking a brooding pose. Then he opened the book to where her bookmark lay, and read aloud in a dramatic voice:

> *"'Prophet!' said I, 'thing of evil! -- prophet still, if bird or devil!*

Whether Tempter sent, or whether tempest tossed thee here ashore,

Desolate yet all undaunted, on this desert land enchanted–

On this home by Horror haunted – tell me truly, I implore–

Is there--IS there balm in Hiroshima?--tell me--tell me, I implore!'

Quoth the Raven, 'Nevermore.'"

Silence followed for an interminable time. The steward stood sweating in the glaring spotlight. Then like a huge vacuum cleaner starting up, wind started sucking in a long crescendo from the smoky room. AAAAAOOOOOOOOOOHHHH....

A solitary voice out in the darkness, finally comprehending something of the altered verse, said softly, "*Ah so... Ah so...* Bomb... Hiroshima... Nevamoru....."

Other voices took up the phrase, and heads started to nod as additional light bulbs of comprehension clicked on. "*Ah so!* Hiroshima... Qroth Ulaven...Nevamoru..."

As a wave of finger snapping surged over the crowd, the steward bowed low, then stepped down, took O-Kuni's hand, and led her through the swarming crowd and out of the smoke filled hall and out into the refreshing air and starlit night. Space... at last.

Once outside, O-Kuni stopped under a streetlight, looked out into the darkness and sighed out a long breath. Then she turned to the steward and said, eyes down, "Thank you. You prevented an unfortunate incident from becoming worse."

Her whole countenance looked different. Gone was her self-assurance, her feminist demeanor, her intellectual focus. She now looked soft and vulnerable, like a delicate flower in chilled air. O-Kuni held her arms about her breast and shivered ever so slightly. She bowed her head before him. "It was not all show. He would have struck me. Violence is in all their hearts."

"What do you mean?"

"Each rally becomes more confrontational. The riot police and the students will surely fight tomorrow."

"You will attend, won't you..."

"It is *giri*, my duty. I must not let my feelings dissuade me."

The steward took her by the shoulders, and slowly brought her to him, wrapping his arms around the shivering, delicate form that slowly, progressively, melted into his chest. He felt her heartbeat, fluttering against his.

"You are quite extraordinary..." he said softly. "You are full of principle. You are thoughtful. You have great courage." He held her close, and whispered to the top of her pulled back raven hair. "But I see you now in another way. Your feelings are deep. You are fragile, and sensitive. You are a beautiful woman, and you are also a beautiful child."

The night was clear. Golden stars lit up the heavens, even above the rosy glare that spilled into the sky around them. A strange silence somehow had overcome the bedlam of the nightspot and the adrenalin rush that hurried their exit. They started walking, slowly, down a quiet street, away from the glare and the noise, toward what appeared to be an expansive public park on a slight hill. He held his arm around her shoulders, comforting her. She gave no resistance, but fell willingly into the warm security of his side. The fragrance of autumn flowers filled their world with silent wonder.

They quietly strolled in through a high wooden gateway shaped like a giant upwardly arching 'T' on two legs. Flowers and trees and wandering paths and silent silver ponds and babbling streams soon created a dreamlike maze blocking the realities of the outside city from their thoughts. Deep shadows and intermittent moon glow and shifting weeping willows and delicately arched bridges over goldfish ponds and chirping crickets became their barrier to the past. Only the present seemed to hold meaning.

Other young couples stood or strolled here and there in the park, arm in arm, hand in hand. Some held each other closely. Some watched the stars silently. Some were kissing.

The steward whispered softly into her hair, "The night smiles on lovers... All the world is now silent..."

O-Kuni finally spoke. "Now and forever you'll mean to me more than the sun in heaven."

The steward, startled, somehow found it possible to take her comment in poetic perspective. He smiled down at her, as she hid her eyes from him.

O-Kuni continued, "And I admit that I liked you the moment when first I saw you... You are tall and manly, you smile is so charming and so easy. The things you say no one else ever told me. Now I am happy, I'm very happy..."

They paused near a feathery tree. He lifted up her chin with his hand, forcing her to look up into his eyes.

"Come..." he said tenderly. "Look at me..." He took her hands in his, and pressed them to his lips.

O-Kuni shivered. "Do love me just a little. We Japanese are used to things that are childlike... humble and pure and silent." She looked up into his eyes. "All our deepest feelings are tender yet eternal... like the sky, and the waves of the ocean..."

"Come with me... Come..."

She whispered shyly up to him, "Ah! Night for dreamers! Stars without number... All the world has gone to slumber..."

O-Kuni pointed out to the starry sky, and breathed in deeply of the clear night air, graced with fresh fragrances of the park. Then she put his hands to her cheek and held them there.

"The night is enchanted, every thing is breathing beauty... And the stars of love are blinking in the sky!"

"Come with me... Come..."

She stared into his eyes, expectantly, timidly, and shivered ever so faintly as he slowly bent to touch her open lips to his...

They did not talk during their walk back to the hotel. It seemed that nothing needed to be said. They quietly walked into the Cio Cio's lobby, slipped off their shoes, and crossed the small bridge over the puddle and past the bowing Mama-san and up the one flight of stairs and down the hall to his room. Once there, O-Kuni looked up into his eyes. As he drew breath to speak, she stopped him by putting her finger to his lips. Then with a slight bow, she bade him to wait as she slid the *shoji* screen after her. Within mere moments, the screen reopened. O-Kuni was kneeling at the side of the door, dressed in a flowing cotton kimono covered with a airy design of a thousand butterflies in plum and pink and white, fluttering about a blooming cherry branch. Her raven hair had been freed of its bonds, and now flowed across her shoulders and down her back to her waist. In her hand she held a small folded fan, which she deftly opened in a quivering inverse flight. Her eyes remained downcast as the steward hesitatingly, awkwardly, his shoes in his hand, entered the small space with the *futon* spread before him. Across the dimly lit room was a small doorway with hints of steam drifting skyward. On the lacquered bureau was a simple fragrant display of verbena and a soft, flickering candle in a paper lantern.

The steward entered bravely, knowing full well Pinkerton was about to be kissed and beaten into sublime ecstasy by the delicate wings of a thousand butterflies.

The steward awoke to giggles all about him. He looked up to see the laughing faces of the house butterfly squad of three, chatting in bubbly whispers. They pulled off the downy *futon* cover with a burst of glee, nearly revealing a point of interest that was quickly covered by a blue and brown cotton kimono that lay nearby. "Goro-san say up," they giggled, pointing appropriately. "You not up!" Then they left in a flutter of sleeves and a scurry of mincing feet into the hall.

"The attack of the human alarm clocks..." the steward muttered to himself. Then he recalled where he was. O-Kuni had vanished. The room was neat but empty, except for his own things. A piece of paper caught his eye, on top of the bureau. A note...

> *"Most wonderful when they scatter --*
>
> *The cherry blossoms.*
>
> *In this floating world does anything endure?"*

The steward shook his head at the poetic aphorism. "She could have said good-bye..." he muttered to himself.

Quickly he washed and shaved and dressed. As he walked out, he noticed that Carty's room was also empty, as were all the other rooms. "Didn't anyone stay the night?" he wondered.

At the concierge desk, he found Goro-san smiling and bowing. "*O-hiyo*. You flend go. See you in goodo hands, *Sayanora*."

With a little help from Goro-san, the steward found a small diner nearby, and ordered from a note given him by the little hotelier. He sat a small table with a hotplate built in, and watched as a waiter dumped cuttlefish and vegetables and other mysteries as well as egg on to the sizzling surface, to cook before him a novel omelet thing called an *okonomiyaki*. Served with a bowl of *gohan* and a steaming cup of *ochai*, the fare was fortifying indeed. Squid for breakfast didn't faze the steward at all, considering all his experience at the smorgasbord.

Following a simple map he had taken from the concierge desk at *Cio Cio* Hoteru, the steward made his way to the sprawling Shinjiku rail station. There, hoping he was headed the right direction, he joined with a multitude of Japanese waiting for the train or subway or whatever what was to stop at the platform marked Akasaka. Suddenly he felt a crush of bodies fill in behind him as the crowd started massing near the edge. Near panic confused his thoughts, and the squeezing increased to pain levels. He looked about for relief, seeking a pillar or post or something sturdy to hide behind. The crush moved him along the platform like a push broom.

Suddenly, from out of the *melange* of elbows and backs and grunting heads, a sleek yellow train whooshed to a stop and sliding doors popped opened in its numerous cars. The mob of travelers crushed and wriggled into the doorways like carp trying to swim upstream after a typhoon rain. For a society so courteous and serene one moment, bowing and smiling, it was curious that a buffalo herd mentality could reveal itself so abruptly. The doors stayed open 22 seconds. Exactly. During that time, literally hundreds of people entered and exited through the same portal, giving the term venturi a new meaning. The steward felt hands and knees and foreheads and briefcases and umbrellas pressing against his back, pressing severely, jabbing, shoving, pushing him forward into the car against a counterstream of inmates trying to escape into daylight. He craned his neck in attempts to see the most ardent perpetrator of pain behind him, wishing he could free his left arm so he could put an elbow earnestly into a mouth somewhere. SLAM! The door closed behind him crushing his duffle within its terrible rubber jaws. The steward turned to free it, only to see the smiling face of Attila the Pusher, proud in a freshly pressed blue uniform and cap, responding to his query by bowing and brushing his white gloves together in a movement which spoke out in universal language, "*So desu-ka*. 22 seconds. Job well done. Next?"

The ride was fast and smooth, a welcome trip out of the threshold of pain, into societal oblivion. The masses of Japanese commuters stood there, faces bland yet grimacing, heavy eye lids covering any sparkle of acknowledgement of others around, eyeballs never connecting, lungs sucking wind in through gritted teeth in obvious displeasure, yet mouths still too courteous to blow out their fishy smelling breath into faces which were mashed nose to nose with their own. Here was an Oriental standoff once again. A conundrum of codes of conduct that rendered them mute and incapacitated.

Somehow the steward spotted a sign for Akasaka flash by as they entered a new station, and he decided to jump in and go with the flow. Caught in a mass movement of feet, he was crushed into and then carried out the door and spewed out onto the platform, into relative freedom at last. As he brushed himself off, checking for wounds, he swore he would never serve sardines again.

Once somewhat apart from the crowd, he looked about. Off in the distance to the north, from his high view from the platform, he could see the large imposing buildings of what appeared to be federal architecture, highlighted by floodlights. But something else caught his eye. In front and around the buildings there was a strange blur, a shifting vibration about their bases that was strange indeed. Earthquake? He felt no shock waves but the imposing old buildings seemed to be trembling at their very foundation.

As he walked down the platform to the banks of escalators, he finally realized what he was seeing. Out before him were bodies, thousands of bodies, uniformly dressed in white shirts and black pants and carrying huge red flags and banners, locked arm and arm in lines of maybe sixty abreast, line after line following along in a huge human snake dance. The snake wrapped itself around the floodlit building complex on an outer ring road easily over a mile around. The steward had never seen such a mass of humanity in one place before. As he drew closer to the pulsing mass, he started to determine its nature. Here were wave after wave of passionate young people, students, workers, intellectuals, socialists, unionists, communists, joined elbow in elbow in identical dance, hundreds of red flags and banners flying above them, chanting and snaking about like a giant boa constrictor intent on gaining a monstrous strangle hold around the main building of government, the Japanese Diet.

The steward was pulled inexorably toward this jogging, chanting maelstrom to the north. He judged the experience not possible in his own land - total conformity and union of purpose - unless it was on a football weekend in Massillon, Ohio. Three hundred thousand individuals joined arm in arm in one singular act of defiance, chanting as one voice, dressed as one mass, dancing as one being, locked arm in arm and step in step, all to one end - the encirclement and disruption of existing authority and dogma.

"Dancing counter clockwise..." he mulled. "Must be leftists."

Fragments of student groups frequently came up to him and in broken English asked, some menacingly, some courteously, of his nationality and his purpose in being there. The steward had happened to have donned his jacket that morning leaving the hotel, the one supplied to him as ship's steward, which bore the name S.S. Talabot over a small Norwegian flag. That, when supplemented by his verbal reply that he was looking his girlfriend, seemed to placate the more probing inquiries. The fact that there were three hundred thousand young persons there, all looking and dressing alike, did not in anyone's mind seem to complex such a quest in any way.

The steward listened to the steady, throaty chant for a while, and then shook his head. "I can't get what they are saying..." he called over to a group of three students about to join the snake, punctuating his inquiry with body language.

"It is poritical statement," one called back. "Kirru Kishi!"

The steward pondered this political statement for a moment. Then, as he looked at all the intensity in the faces of the snake dancers, it became clear. "Kill Kishi. Democracy at work."

He tried to keep on the fringe of the massive snake. Most of the mob jogged along in perfect unison, both in footsteps and chanting, as the twenty yard wide snake unendingly wreathed and wriggled its way more tightly around the neck of government.

Across the surface of the moving tide of students and workers, a television news crew caught his eye. Edging his way nearer, the steward could see a news commentator standing on top of one of two vans, talking into a hand microphone to the camera mounted on top of the other van. In the background was the imposing Diet, awash in a surging sea of political surreality. The commentator was Western, as was the camera operator. After moments of talking to the lens, the commentator lowered his mic and with his free hand drew his finger across his neck. Cut and print.

The news commentator turned to survey the pulsing masses now dancing and chanting even more passionately as they passed his conspicuous van. He stood there in awe of the conformity, the commitment, the inner control of the huge crowd, and scratched his behind. Then he happened to look across the expanse of heads and red flags and banners and intense faces, to see one solitary blond head rising a foot higher than the pulsing jet-headed sea surrounding it. Without a word being spoken, the eyes of Walter Cronkite met the steward's, and held for a moment. If there is ESP, a mode of communication still unexplained, it happened then. The two looked about them, and then back. Their thoughts were loud and clear to each other... "What the hell are we, blue eyes, doing here, in this madness... It's going to explode."

Quietly, across from the snake lines, near one intersection, there appeared a small army of police. Police did not describe them accurately. An ancient Roman phalanx was closer to the truth. Nearly a thousand men were dressed in heavy boots and heavy uniforms and heavy *kabuto* style helmets with plastic or wire face guards, and holding before them heavy body-length shields with clear plastic strips near the top for vision. In their hands they held five foot long sticks about the thickness of one's wrist. They were joined together in a silent mass, moving forward like some huge menacing monolith of granite on rollers, toward the dancing snake. There was no sound from the granite. The snake, sensing its obvious adversary, let forth with a hiss of wind sucking that sounded like a giant cobra.

"Good time to exit," thought the steward, as he looked the other way for some side street. His heart sank as he faced a similar gray phalanx coming up the next street along the ring road.

He looked back a Walter, seeking some form of emotional support. Their eyes held for one last brief moment. Then with a muted salute of his hand, Walter bid the steward a poignant *adieu*, and turned back to the camera facing him. News time. Roll 'em.

To the steward's surprise, nobody seemed now to notice him. Their attention was, obviously, turned to the police phalanx still slowly marching their way toward the snake. The steward watched as well, seemingly transfixed with the strange ceremonial event about to unfold.

Out of nowhere, student minutemen conjured up and donned heavy helmets as well, some sports oriented, some traditional *kendo*, some makeshift wrappings of fabric. Flagstaffs and banner carriers became long wooden swords. Bunting and banners were wrapped about forearms and heads for padded protection. Would-be heroes osmosed through the masses to the foreground, terrified spectators and cowards sifted to the rear.

Rose Bowl Football in the U.S.A. could not hold a candle to the spectacle that unfolded. The massive police phalanx stopped and struck a pose, shields held high and wooden swords held higher. The students responded in kind, drawing a line in the dust with a long red banner. Cross this and die. Swords moved in slow positioning rituals eventually freezing in formal angles of attack or defense. Silence descended on the area, followed by the slow sucking in of a thousand lungs pulling one last gasp of oxygen. Someone whispered, "*Hajime.*"

A thousand throats, after sucking in all available air, answered as one, "BAANNNZZZAAAAAAAIIIIIIEEEEEEEEE!"

The roar propelled the two sides rapidly together like crashing waves, swords slashing and hacking and parrying and poking in a blur of wood and plastic and flesh. The acrid release of adrenalin glands pierced the air. Crowds of students and workers shifted toward and away from the fray, giving room or seeking shelter as warranted. Walter of the High Van was talking calmly into his mic, and pointing to key points of impact in a rather mellow body language that the steward found very reassuring. The cameraman kept his head buried in the eyepiece, tunnel vision adding some modicum of security to the exposure of his backside up on van two.

The ritualistic war lasted no more than fifteen minutes, shifting with individual prowess and fortitude, each side gaining then loosing ground. Wooden swords, while bruising, did little serious damage other than to ego, as the two sides slashed and hacked their way into exhaustion. Just as the students would look like they were gaining advantage, a fresh wave of police would descend with a new cry of "*Banzai*" into the battle, relieving their comrades. The students, while valiant in effort, slowly fell back into defensive clusters, exhausted. New police joined the ruckus. Those combatant students with enough brains or energy vanished into the crowd behind. Those felled on the field of honor were then whomped a few times more on the ground, then dragged off by police reserves to waiting paddy wagons.

"This is pure *bushido* ritual..." thought the steward. "Must be the inbreeding..."

He looked back over the flailing crowd seeking a comrade, only to lip read Walter's final statement into the camera, "And that's the way it was..." And with a terse cut of his finger across his throat, a now much less composed Walter and his cameraman quickly began wrapping up their gear and looking about for an avenue of strategic withdrawal. The steward felt the news commentator's experience at such times must be valid, and did likewise. He squiggled through the crowd like an eel, and finally found an alleyway that seemed open and leading to fairer pastures. He turned for one last look, only to see the police *en mass* push a group of students back, squashing them against a tall wrought iron fence that protected the buildings. Something pulled his eyes over the swarming, struggling crowd of students. He did a double take.

"Oh, my god..." he said out loud. "O-Kuni!"

Her face stood out, high above the crowd, chin held high, wide-eyed with excitement and intensity of purpose, oblivious to fear or survival instincts. She and her comrades were not retreating from their ground.

She was right in the midst of the group of a few hundred students, squashed up against the great iron fence. She stood steadily, seemingly unmoved by the crush, above the masses, holding a red banner high in the air above the crowd, poetically defying the advancing police cadre. Somehow she was raised above the heads of her peers, possibly by standing on a box or concrete ledge. She was shouting encouragement to those about her, banner raised in proud defense of her and their democratic rights. Her society, however, had not yet come to recognize such noble principles, and bore down with ancient wooden dogma onto newly enlightened views.

As the police hacked and pushed and beat the edge of the crowd in futile attempts to disperse it, their pressure only served to squash O-Kuni's group more unmercifully up against the fence. The crush increased. O-Kuni was carried from view. The pained cries of students filled the air. Bodies trampled bodies, arms and legs protruded from the imploding mass in awkward angles. Sections fell upon sections, bodies upon bodies. Hundreds of trampling feet pounded the interior. Finally a wave of heroic students with wooden swords made a final all out attack at the front line of police, hoping to free their comrades flattened against the fence. The strategy worked. A split in the police ranks allowed the trapped students to pour out into the open again.

Students ran every which way, dodging the slashing swords, fleeing the brutal power of law and order. O-Kuni had vanished.

The steward strained his neck to look about, but could not find her. Finally the last remaining students, stunned and mauled, staggered away from their terrifying confinement and into the steely clutches of the police.

The steward's heart sank.

Near the great iron fence lay a scattering of red banners and flags and pieces of clothing, and a crumpled black lump. It was the twisted body of a girl, dressed in black sweater and skirt, with a red armband, arms stretched out to the side. Partially wrapped about her, still in her fist, was a red banner.

A mass of crowd came towards him, struggling and running into the alleyway for escape. Try as he may, pushing and elbowing and fighting his way upstream, calling out to her above an impenetrable roar, the steward found himself carried backwards into the narrow bricked darkness by a human tidal wave. The last things he could see before submitting fully to the flowing wall were several police trucks blocking off the opening, sealing off this means of escape for any others.

By the time he had regained the ground lost, the rally was dispersed. Police lines cordoned off the streets and alleyways. Trucks blocked approaches. Uniformed soldiers formed lines to prevent closer approach. The Diet was again rendered impregnable and unapproachable. Once again the past had held on, firmly and successfully, against the insolent wave of the future.

The steward wandered around in a daze, watching the cleanup of rubble and political rowdies still courageous or foolish enough to linger in the area. The great masses of earlier in the day had vanished. The streets held a strange hollow calm, as persons went about their way with fleeting glances back toward the Diet compound. The steward was politely but firmly prevented at every turn, from approaching any nearer.

He sat down on the curb, bewildered, exhausted, frustrated.

Later that evening, the steward had managed to call Carty by phone, and had relayed his agonizing experience. Carty had already watched the evening television news, and knew even more about the encounter than did the steward. A girl had been trampled to death during the rally. He did not hear her name. The police were being blamed for excessive brutality, caused by their incessant advance on peaceful dancing demonstrators. One group of student demonstrators had inadvertently been cornered next to the great iron fence, leading to panic and trampling and ultimately to the girl's death. Initially the government was in disarray, quite embarrassed by the incident and the ensuing public outrage. The Communists and the Unionists were calling for the overthrow of Kishi and his cabinet. Anti-government sentiment surged throughout the country. The anti-nuclear activists were demanding that no U.S. atomic weapons ever be allowed on Japanese soil, not even temporarily inside Japanese harbours or naval bases. Anti-American sentiment had reached a new high. An upcoming visit by Ike was now seriously being reconsidered. The United States had been rendered hamstrung by an embarrassed Japanese government that seemingly had lost the support of its people.

It looked as if the demonstrators had succeeded most dramatically in their primary purpose, to depose a government and its traditions of privilege and power.

The steward felt hollow inside. He had only known her first name. He did not know where she had lived, or any of her friends. He did not know where to find, or view, or pay respects to her body. O-Kuni had existed for only a brief moment in his life, and in the next moment, she was gone. Like a softly glowing candle, snuffed out by some unexpected, unwanted wind.

But Carty had even more to add to his friend's frustration and pain. The young girl, it turned out after a hurried state autopsy, had not been killed by trampling, or by heart failure, or by any trauma brought on by confrontation with the riot police. The public's passionate outrage that the government had caused her death was now struck dumb with confusion. Television news now reported that the unfortunate incident seemed to have been orchestrated by someone else, by some individual or some group within the demonstrators, probably the Communists. The police were stating strongly that they were not to blame, citing that no shots were fired nor were other serious injuries incurred in the melee. All dispersal actions had been conducted according to legal means and procedures. All police samurai charges had been choreographed as in ages past, permitting passions to be unleashed in ritualistic combat, the result of which left the power clearly in the hands of the government. Malevolently, a spokesperson for the government had stated, someone had been made a martyr that day in front of the Diet. Regrettably, that young person had died. But it was determined to have been not of the government's doing.

The girl, found dead under the feet of the fleeing crowd, had been strangled.

—AT SEA—

0400. Night at sea...

Throughout a patchy mist, each swell haunts the darkness... slowly shifting and lifting and falling back again in perceptible unrest... betraying the stirrings of some profound unfathomable presence.

Above, casting a shivering mantle, dart airy nothings... mere wisps and illusions... charged into substance within luminescent spray... ghostly veils and beads of fire and pearls of light, simultaneously ephemeral and prominent, here yet there, borne about in capricious flight... skimming the crests of the swells... darting into shadow and back... And all the while... surreal wailings and whistlings energizing their dance...

Slowly the great blueblack awakens... stronger now, more alive... a power now apparent, its pulsing rich and deep... its movement outward and indomitable... its message reaching every corner and fold of the darkness... "I am... You cannot deny me."

Now a stealthy aura surprises the eastern sky, infuriating the night and sending the sprites and fire beads to race about madly, terrified for their very existence, screaming "Wait! Wait! It is not yet our time!"

Suddenly spears of fire pierce the darkness, exploding skyward, more, and more again, golden shafts and silvered rays in ever compounding brilliance, expanding everywhere, overwhelming the last vestiges of the night. Its dominion sure, the great blueblack heaves and fills and flexes. Above it, flailing about, desperately seeking sanctuary, some haven, some form of transcendence, screaming out to all ends of eternity, these last ghastly, tenacious spirits of the night flee into those few, final, narrowing voids – then only to vanish, without ever a ripple of their being, into the glaring shards and blinding mirrors and hungry shadows of the sea.

Again... As evermore... It is Dawn...

"Zero four hundred."

"Seems later."

"We're pushing into the edge of the time zone."

"Dawn gets pushed around, doesn't it?..."

"No. We do..."

The steward stood on the bridge wing, letting the fair night breezes hit him in the face over the steel spray shield. Eiriksson had startled him, coming up to the bridge, still a rare occasion so early in the morning. He seemed rather mellow, not clouded or energized with booze but awake and thoughtful and... well, mellow. He walked over to lean on the railing along side the steward, and lit up a Chesterfield. After exhaling and savoring a bit of the fresh tobacco smell, he offered his pack to the steward, who took one and lit up. The captain then spoke softly to the steward, his rich low voice cutting the headway breeze with surprising clarity.

"Want to talk about it?" he asked.

"Talk... What's talk going to do? Make everything better?" the steward replied.

"I meant the bigger picture... put it in perspective..."

The steward chuckled. "You and your bigger picture... I still can't even get a star fix in the charthouse, let alone in focus."

The two men stood there, looking out into the brightening east, watching a fat fiery orb slide up out of the black sea and into the sky, casting everyone and everything about with a red-orange glow.

The steward had managed to get himself back to Yokohama in time for the ship's departure. He had to pull himself away from the shore, away from the events that tumbled in on him, away from that crowded crazy island. It was as if someone had dropped a giant monolith on his head. His thoughts bounced around in his skull. He was stunned. He was stymied. He had no answers. He had so many questions. He had experienced tremendous frustrations. He didn't speak the language. He felt thwarted and restrained, forced outside of reality, outside of what actually happened, outside of the culture, outside of the intensity of the pursuits followed so passionately by the people he had just encountered, outside of the deepest feelings of one had barely begun to know.

"You were not meant to find out..." Eiriksson spoke at last. "It's the beach... It's always that way... on the beach..."

The steward forcefully blew smoke into the wind with frustration. "I don't understand anything anymore..."

Eiriksson pulled on his Chesterfield, and looked at its cherry glow in the breeze. "You think you're unique? We go on the beach, we're starving for life... We go kind of crazy, get drunk, get laid, we kick up our heels however we can... But we get only a taste of life ashore, only a taste... It's all too fast... We never become fully immersed in the people or the customs or the reality of it all... We are allowed to understand only a little..."

"It's like a crazy dream. Did it all ever happen? Was it only my imagination?"

"It's their world, not ours. We can only touch it, briefly, a mere *augenblick*. We share it, we share their time, just a piece of it... then we go back to sea again, on to another night, to another port, another adventure."

"You call it an adventure? That's all it is? An adventure?"

"That's all it ever is..."

"But what about what I feel, what I think? Why do I feel it so intensely? Why can't I just chalk this one up to adventure?"

"We get on the beach, somehow we assume some god-given right, or curse, to live it up to the fullest. All sailors are the same... It's our chance to live. Maybe it's because we know we'll only be there for a few hours, and then it's back to sea... Maybe it's because we have been looking at the horizon and the stars and the sky so much we're sick to fucking death of them, and we just have to go dive into drinking all the *akvavit* we can lay our hands on and loving all the women who'll have us and gorging on all the foods and wallowing around like drunken madmen in the mud. That's all it is... a short time on the beach... Thank *Gud* we are wise enough, or still animal enough, to live it up."

"I feel like I crammed a hundred days into a hundred hours..."

"And of those hours I bet you can remember each and every word, every look and emotion, as clear as a three-D picture..."

"Crystal clear! Plus smells and sounds and sensations and..."

"That's a night on the beach, *mon nautonnier*... It's concentrated, compressed... It's burned forever into your soul. Would you rather have it dull and boring? Would you rather not remember anything?"

"No..."

"Then savor the aftertaste, my boy. That's the dividend of being alive..."

They watched together as a huge seagull soared across their line of sight into the red sun, now a few degrees above the horizon, causing the tremendous glare to blink.

"I couldn't help her," the steward spoke softly. "I just stood there, and she got killed... And I didn't help her..."

"You're not back there, shipmate. That port is in the past. We're back at sea again."

"That's just it! I feel I'm more at fucking sea than I've ever been. And she's dead and I didn't do a thing to help her!"

The captain softly bit his lip, and resisted an impulse to speak sternly to the steward. He took a long pull on his cigarette, and exhaled out slowly. "You gave her joy. You were a part of her life, just for a moment in time, but you gave her joy. You are not the world's savior, my friend... Just a passing sailor on the beach, who gives a little, and takes a little."

"Joy! Who cares about joy. She's dead..."

"That was her destiny. Her time. She put herself in harm's way. Willingly. Passionately. She happened to die. She may be the pawn in some bigger strategy, but she's all the bigger herself for being there. She was part of her cause, whatever it was... Her heart was filled with principle, with passion. She believed in what she was doing, and in being there. Don't you see? That's why you found her attractive, that's why you two clicked. She was alive, and so were you. You encountered each other when she was alive with fire in her belly. That's what counts. She thrilled you. You saw deeper into her eyes than anybody else back there. You knew her, deep down into her soul... You knew a real person, not just a pretty face in a crowd of crazies."

"But she's gone..."

"So will we all be, some day. Fishshit. Who the fuck will care a hundred years from now? Today is what counts. Now. Live life now. It's our turn, now. Pack it fucking full, now. Not later. Not tomorrow. Because you can never be assured you're going to see tomorrow..."

The two men stared out into the distance. The huge fireball was now near ten degrees into the heavens. Strange clouds hung over the horizon, stringy in some places, puffy in others, stretching across the edge of the sea, now angry red in the morning glow.

"Occasion?"

"None."

"No occasion?"

"Who needs an occasion?"

"O.K., no occasion."

"That's the best kind of party, anyway."

"There's got to be an occasion."

"So what's the occasion?"

"Celebrating the Ginza binge. What else?"

The passengers had assembled in the lounge right on time, about 1900 hours. Some were already well into their cups from earlier cocktails, others had showered and freshened up.

They entered the large room in ones and twos, filing in like the Procession of the Magi. Everyone was dressed in their latest Oriental finery, with outfits making statements ranging somewhere from monk to *geisha*. Silky satins and elaborately colored *shibori* tie-dyes and starched cotton pin-stripes and intricate flowered *katazome* prints, fresh from the silvered stalls and pricey halls of Ginza, graced, or rather hid, their bodies. Costumes indeed unleashed repressed character. Women slinked their way about in silken kimonos, some with fans aflutter, batting their eyes demurely. Men strode briskly back and forth in starched cotton *yukatas* like bit part players from *The Seven Samurai*. Even Eiriksson stood proud and wide-legged like some Oriental Thor, bedecked in a great long cotton kimono of deep indigo, forcefully grasping an elaborate four foot sheathed samurai sword in his left hand like a thunderbolt. He took great pleasure standing at the head of the table, bowing slightly to all who entered, then in sucking in massive gulps of wind and grunting deeply, thereby regally emoting, with appropriate Japanese tonal inflection, his approval or condescension to everything that was said. There was no doubt who in the room was the dominant male personality, the most powerful arm, the wisest head at this place and time, the surrogate descendent of Emperor Jimmu and his Sun Goddess mom, the much admired shipboard Kuchio.

All willingly paid due homage to him, making certain they bowed more deeply than he did in return.

"*Ah so, desuka,*" he would comment in guttural tones as each came forward to bid him good evening and strike a pose. "You joina me foru dlink."

The merry troupe of passengers had thoroughly enjoyed their tour experience in Japan, with all the pampering service that went with meals, bathing, massages, and inn style living, leaving them with the assurance that Westerners were genetically superior and deserving of such treatment. Ginza, on the other hand, gladly relieved them of their remaining funds, particularly by proffering elaborately painted silk screens and ceramics, touted by some to be rare works by ancient masters, even if still damp.

Now they were all assembled once again, in Oriental drag, commencing their sixty-seventh dinner party of the cruise. This one, however, felt special, nearing the end of their journey, and spirits were high.

Against one bulkhead glistened one of the grandest smorgasbord spreads of the cruise so far, an all out artistic tribute to their nearing their final destination, Honolulu, and to the fact that the remaining finer delicacies deserved to be consumed before their disembarkation. The steward had rounded up the usual suspects in caviar, cold meats and sausages, cheeses, *gravlaks*, cold lobster and shrimp, salads and fresh fruits and vegetables and curried rice, but to that tonnage Erda had added her Norwegian form of raw salmon and tuna *sashimi*, and had elaborately prepared three varieties of steaming cooked salmon, tantalizingly bathed in sauces of mysterious composition.

The steward drifted innocuously about the room, serving the occasional cocktail or highball for those with a mean thirst. He himself was dressed in the long gray cotton kimono of a servant, one he had purchased for three dollars from a street stall in Shinjiku. Like everyone else's, his feet too were out of place. Feet of all shapes and sizes stuck out below flowing fabric, feet without socks, stuffed into one of a variety of pairs of sneakers and bathroom clogs and bedroom slippers and penny loafers and walking sandals. Yet all the passengers, flaunting their worldly experience, had truly found their sea legs, with feet now fitting firmly on merra-firma, regardless of the slow rolling of the ship. But alas, no woman passenger had had the whimsy or courage to buy, let alone hobble about in, the toe-strapped, raised clogs that would better compliment the graceful lines of the kimono worn above.

Eiriksson surveyed the assemblage, counting all noses present. Then he turned to the steward and said profoundly, "It's time for a Pimm's."

The steward went to work preparing a large silver chalice in public view, pouring in an array of devilish liquors and 100 proof grain spirits and sparkling champagnes and lemon juice with a flourish, frequently following Eiriksson's lip-smacking orders by adding "More!" The crowd watched in breathless anticipation as the bubbling, frothing brew reached the brim. Then, after wiping off the rim with a fresh hand towel, the steward, with great pomp and ceremony, set the heavy chalice in front of the captain. "Your boil and bubble, Sir."

The crowd cheered as Eiriksson blew off some of the greenish foam, then feigned removing some object from its surface, and casting it aside. "Next time, use only the freshest newts, Steward."

Eiriksson stood, cleared his throat, and panned his passengers eye to eyes. He slowly bowed low, rose again, and began speaking. "Dear guests, new found friends, faithful crewmembers, courageous travelers into the great unknown... We are nearing our journey's end. In two days we will dock at Honolulu, and you will depart from this old bucket, to go about your normal lives once again, back to your own countries and all their many bounties. I will miss you. We have become more than passenger and skipper in this voyage. We have become friends. We have encountered new ideas, and new cultures, new foods, and new experiences. Some have been exciting and wonderful. Others we may wish to forget (chuckle from the crowd). But please remember this... Together, we have made history. Oh, not anything formidable, but we have had our time together, our adventure, into strange lands and on the high seas together. It has become our piece of history. Just days from now, few others will even care about our travels, our antics and experiences, our seeing this crazy old world in a new perspective. But we will care. We will remember. Every bit of it. It has been our time, a wonderful time, a rich time, a time of privilege for us all. It has been our special time. My wish to you all for the future?... That you are able to use the knowledge you have gained from all the strange and wonderful cultures that so richly paint the surface of this lopsided orb. Cherish their diversity. Carry home the good ideas and customs and recipes with you. Build them into your own ways of living. Remember those peoples you have met and seen. And work to eliminate the inequities and injustices you have encountered along the track. Thank you for being voyagers in this great sea of time with us. And speaking of time, remember as we cross the International Date Line in a few hours, you will all be one day younger, a fact which should please the ladies in our midst immensely (more chuckles). Our best wishes to you all. From the Talabot, its officers and crew... *Skaal*"

The captain hoisted the silver chalice high by its two side handles, presented it forth, then took a long draught. "Aaahhh!" he exclaimed heartily, wiping off a green moustache on the back of his hand. "Here... Drink!.. Like tomorrow may never come! For today is the stuff of life." Then he passed the cup to the twelve voyagers assembled around the huge table, and cheered each of the twelve on to greater depths, and greater insights, here and now to be found in the bottom of a silver... Pimm's Cup.

The steward stood silently by, admiring the captain's mastery of crowd control, watching the mysterious green concoction being consumed with delight, speculating on the size of the run on APC's the following morning.

The seas had grown stronger during the night. The Talabot now rolled perceptively as it churned on through the darkness. The party had fallen into final disrepair about 0300, most of the passengers somehow making it back to their bunks without assistance. In all, it had been a good evening, no fistfights, no political scraps, no backbiting, no viperous gossip. Equals among friends the passengers had become, all their secular opinions and biases and protestations having long ago sputtered off into alcoholic oblivion. "The great equalizer, booze..." thought the steward as he stood again on the wing of the bridge, smoking a Players.

Ole was dozing at the helm again, but the swells still seemed stable and the ship was staying on course, so the steward let him have his catnap. The night was crisp but pitch black, no moon, no stars, no ships' lights on the horizon.

Eiriksson appeared out of nowhere, the great silver chalice still in his hands.

"Everything under control?" he asked with a big grin, nodding in the direction of Ole.

"Seas are building, but I don't see any weather out there. Black but lots of visibility. Nothing on the scope."

"Hello, night..." Eiriksson called out.

"Hello..." the silence of space answered back.

The ship lofted a few feet as it went over the crest of a large swell, then sunk down into the trough.

"This is what makes it all worth while," Eiriksson said, hoisting the great chalice in the air with one hand.

"It's what is going to kill you, Sir, if you keep it up like tonight."

"*Au contraire, mon Nautonnier,*" Eiriksson replied with a sly smile, gazing at the ornate silver side. "It is what keeps me going..."

"Herring keeps you going..."

"Ah, yes. I finally learned from Brububber how to spiral a herring... You have to lock your finger under the dorsal fin and..." he feigned a forward pass into the night.

"You and Brububber left a lot of chum back there, perfecting that pass... The sharks have had a field day..."

A strange gust of wind came right into their faces. It was damp and cold.

"Something's coming." The steward wet his finger and held it aloft. "Some kind of a blow, and wet weather..."

"Sea change is coming..." Eiriksson laughed.

"What do you mean?"

"We're coming out of the Current, crossing over into new waters. You're going to get buffeted around a bit."

"Want me to do anything?"

"Just face it... Head on."

The steward looked out into the night. He shivered as a chill now laced the air. The wind shifted to out of the Northeast.

Eiriksson stood leaning his back against the wing railing, face into the breeze. He had a serious look in his eyes, which was diffused by an enigmatic smile.

By the minute, the weather grew worse and worse, the wind now rushing in off the port bow, pushing the waves hard against the hull causing the little freighter to roll and pitch. Even Ole had sensed the change, and stood eyes alert now, both hands on the wheel.

The steward came back into the pilothouse and looked at the barometer. It had fallen significantly in the past hour. He glanced over the charts, made a few mental calculations of position and course and speed, and then walked over to Ole. "How're you holding?"

"Getting more difficult. The swells are off the bow."

"Keep it on this track as best you can. I'll see if the Captain wants to hold it."

The steward climbed out to the bridge wing. "Captain, the seas are giving Ole some problems holding course."

"And?"

"Request permission to alter course into the swells, Sir."

"That's your recommendation, Pilot?"

The steward nodded.

"You could turn tail and run with the sea..."

"This weather is moving in fast, Sir. Barometer's plummeted. It would only catch us. And we're so top heavy with cargo, I'd recommend we ride it out head on. Too easy to broach in trailing seas with this load."

"Where'd you gain all this nautical insight, Steward?"

"Erda, Sir," the steward smiled.

"So be it," he said with a sage nod. "Come into the swells."

The Talabot angled left into the waves, reducing the roll but increasing the extremes from rise to fall to rise again. The sky changed from merely ominous into an angry blackish purple. The seas started coming over the bow frequently, sending sheets of salt spray blasting against the bridge windows. The incessant pounding as the chubby freighter smashed down into each trough sent shudders throughout the ship.

For some twenty minutes, the weather built, and built. The small freighter chugged along, struggling to meet each rising swell, then riding down its backside with a crash.

Eiriksson remained out on the port wing, wind in his face, hair blowing across toward the pilot house, standing in his great indigo kimono whipping in the wind like some ancient lord, testing his metal against elements unknown. He had his Pimm's Cup in one hand and his great sword in the other. He was laughing out loud, calling out into the howling winds.

> *"Blow, Wind, and crack your cheeks!...*
>
> *Rage! Blow! You cataracts and hurricanoes, spout!..."*

Eiriksson took a long pull on the chalice. Mid-gulp, a brilliant flash of lightning lit up the sky, opening his eyes wide. With a roaring laugh he ranted on into the darkness.

> *"Singe my white head! You oak-cleaving thunderbolts...*
>
> *And thou, all-shaking thunder...*
>
> *Smite flat the thick rotundity o' the world!"*

"We understand now!! It is all vanity, and fishshit, and blowing in the wind!"

The steward hesitated, trying to figure out if the captain was just clowning around, or finally showing his evening fill. Just then, a large wave crashed up over the bow, drenching all the stacked crates of transistor TV's strapped down on the foredeck.

"*Faen ta deg!*" the captain called out, looking forward. "Don't try to soak my Sony's, you bastard sea!..."

Another wave ploughed over the bow rail, landing hard on the crates and knocking some of them loose from their strapping.

"Captain, we've got a problem forward..." the steward started.

"Ha! *Faen!*" Eiriksson roared back. That is no problem, *Nautonnier!* It is an opportunity!" He swung the silver chalice high over his head, toasting the foredeck.

"Ole," the steward turned to the wide-eyed helmsman in the pilot house, "You go and get Bjarni up here on the double. I'll take the wheel."

The young man left the bridge in a hurry, amidst a blast of wet water spray rising up from the port side.

Eiriksson still stood out in the howling winds, out on the port wing, looking out into the night. "See that, Steward? Isn't it magnificent? Look out there! The power! The glory!"

"Look down there, Captain!" he yelled back. "The cargo straps have failed. The crates are breaking up on the foredeck. We're going to be ass deep in TV sets with the next wave! "

"*Faen i Helvete!* The Devil take the fucking TV's!" he roared back. "Look out there... at the majesty of it all!"

The steward hung on to the wheel, fighting each quartering swell in attempts to keep the ship on course. "I'm looking at it, Sir! But I fail to see anything important right now except a hundred Sony's bouncing around the deck!"

"Damn it all to Hell, Steward! Don't you see it? Don't you see it? Look out there! It's just beautiful!"

The captain stood with one hand on the rail, spray and wind blasting his face. He was smiling. His head was held high, nodding slowly in silent acquiescence. He stood there for some minutes, laughing, staring out into the rage before him.

Another wave angled in and pounded the bow, further dumping TV's out of cargo crates. POW! POP! Picture tubes imploded in celebration as more and more TV sets bounced merrily about from port to starboard. POW!

Eiriksson still stood face into the elements, but now, his countenance slowly changed. Signs of mirth vanished. Now he stood calmly, solidly, chalice now hanging down at his side. Finally he smiled to himself, and exhaled, a sudden resolve coming over him amidst the howling elements. He careened over to the pilothouse hatchway and leaned in, silhouetted in the strange misty glow of the running lights on the sea spray, the roaring wind making wild patterns in the brightness behind him.

He spoke with a low, calm voice. "I'm going forward to toss those loose TV's over the side before they kick up more of a mess topside, Steward. You all right?"

"I'm fine, Sir. Bjarni and his guys are on their way. up Are you all right?"

Eiriksson looked him strait in the eyes, and held his stare. A soft smile crossed his lips. The wind howled behind him, lashing his great indigo kimono about like a cape.

"I've never been better, lad..." he laughed with a big grin, water pouring down his stringy white hair and beard. "This fresh night air sobers one up!"

"Why don't you wait for Bjarni, Sir? He's on his way..."

Eiriksson's gaze became filled with a strange power, sizzling in the steward's eyes for a second, then softened. "I still give the orders here, Steward."

"Yes, Sir."

"Keep it directly into the swells while I'm up there. Keep her at about five knots. Meet the sea head on."

"Yes, Sir."

"I am now leaving the bridge, Steward. You have the con."

"Aye Aye, Sir. I have the con."

Eiriksson gave him one last grin, a wide one, ear to ear. Then he laughed and turned into the howling winds and dropped down the ladder to the deck, out of sight.

The steward pulled at the wheel to dampen the yaw with each new wave, and looked out over the bow. The waves now seemed to break more evenly over the spray shield, as the ship met the pounding head on.

Eiriksson appeared into view, a great hulk staggering, leaning into the pounding roll, his kimono whipping in the wind and spray. He still had the silver chalice in one hand, and with the other, in between sips from the chalice, he lofted the damaged, loose cartons by their strapping, one at a time, and hurled them over the starboard side. He worked his way forward toward the crease, box by box, securing the cargo straps where he could, and slinging any damaged cartons and televisions out into the darkness.

Finally reaching the foremost point on the bow deck, he rose up from his labors, turned to the pounding seas before him, and held his Pimm's Cup high over his head. The wind buffeted him, the spray lashing and drenching him with each passing wave. Then he drank from the cup, heartily, tilting it back, draining every last drop. Finally, he held the cup high in his right hand and waved it vigorously into the howling winds and stinging seaspray.

Then, turning back to the bridge, his back to the darkness, he again waved the silver cup in the air, saluting the steward. A huge grin was on his face, laughter in his expression. Still careful to keep the bow headed into the seas, the steward saluted back exuberantly with a drawn out 'V' for victory blast on the ship's horn, *THUUUUT.. THUUUUT..THUUUUT.. THUUUUUUUUUUTTT!* that for an instant drowned out the howl of the storm with its deep throaty bellow. Eiriksson stood proudly confronting the sweet sound, his back full against the raging sea.

And then, in a second split from eternity, he was gone.

The steward had watched in disbelief, his heart screaming out, silently, "Watch out! Watch out behind you!"

Out of the depths of the blueblack monster, out of the howling gale and sheets of stinging spray, rose a rogue wave, up from the port side, up over the gunwale, up, up, a massive, towering, mountain of black water, not aligned with the swells, not in harmony with any of the elements, not expected, not sought, not to be believed.

Eiriksson, still grinning madly, had turned his head to see it coming. His mouth had seemed to open perceptively, not in horror, but in awe and recognition of the power about to overwhelm him. He had raised the silver cup even higher in hearty greeting as it crashed down on the bow deck, smashing down with a force so massive that it took all and anything before it, crossing over the bow, a tremendous blueblack mass, with ghostly white edges flailing like a tattered shawl across its shoulders, unstoppable power, seizing and carrying away anything in its way. The Talabot shuddered with the impact down to its very keel.

The steward was struck dumb. His eyes froze to the spot. Most of the bow deck had vanished. The coiled lines had vanished. The steel service boxes had vanished. The spray shields on the bow had vanished. The TV's and cargo crates had vanished. Eiriksson had vanished... Into the omnipotent sea...

The steward held on for all he was worth, holding back the panic, holding hard on the wheel, eyes straining over the starboard side, searching the blackness, probing the screaming seas, for any sign. He grabbed a life ring hanging on the bulkhead and hurled it out into the night. Then he pulled the ship's horn and screamed out in an irrepressible, agonized duet until his lungs could give no more..

THUUUUUUUUUUUUUUUUUUUUUUTTTTTTTTT!!!!!
THUUUUUUUUUUUUUUUUUUUUUUUUUUUUUUUUUUU
UUUUTTTTTTTT!!!!!

Bjarni suddenly appeared on the bridge, his face ashen. "I... saw..." he gasped for air, "I... saw... it..." He jumped back out on to the outer reaches of the starboard wing, leaned over and scanned out aft into the night. He grabbed another life ring hanging on the outer bulkhead, one with a small flash light attached, clicked it on, and threw it out into the blackness.

"I can't turn her, Bjarni!" The steward cried out into the wind. "I can't turn her! I can't stop her. I can't! She'll broach. She'll flip! She's top heavy!"

Bjanri finally fell back into the pilothouse, his agitation quenched by the spray and wind. He leaned back against the cold steel bulkhead, shaken, and looked the steward in the eyes. "She's in your hands, Pilot. Hold her into the seas. Strait into the swells."

"Bjarni..."

Bjarni stood upright again and put his hand out, on to the steward's shoulder. "He is home. The sea has him now..."

It had stilled the very being of the Talabot.

The day had brought varying levels of shock and pain to everyone. Hangovers were overwhelmed by shock, beaten down by heartache. Incredulity countered any desire to repair the deck area and clean up. Passengers and crew alike stumbled through the events of the day like zombies, seldom speaking and rising to task only because of necessity.

Daylight had brought with it better weather. The wind had died down. The little ship chugged on through calming seas, still on its intended course and speed. The sun had broken through the low, scattering cumulus clouds about 1100.

Bjarni had reached Honolulu by radio. Air searches were being dispatched, but without much hope of finding anything. The ship owners had been contacted, and they in turn were contacting the immediate family. A search message had been relayed to all ships in the area. The ship was to wait in Honolulu until its new captain was flown in from the West Coast, probably in three days. Bjarni had indicated to the owners that he did not wish to assume permanent command.

Somehow the word had been spread among the passengers and crew that, at 1830 hours, a memorial service would be held on the fantail. Until then, it was duty at sea, as usual.

The sun, now a deepening molten red as it reached for the horizon, painted the wake that churned behind the Talabot like lush velvet befitting a regal train.

The passengers and crew had assembled along the railing at the stern of the ship. Some smoked. Some sniffled. Occasionally someone sobbed. But each stared silently aft, transfixed by the setting sun, into a vermilion past. Each... transported back to another place and time....

After a few moments, Bjarni opened a King James Bible, one that had lain at the captain's headboard. Fumbling to a dog-eared page, he swallowed hard, and in a faltering voice began...

> *"O Lord, thou hast searched me, and known me.*
>
> *Thou knowest mine downsitting and mine uprising, thou understandest my thoughts from afar.*
>
> *Thou compassest my path and my lying down, and art acquainted with all my ways.*
>
> *There is not a word in my tongue, but, lo, O Lord, thou knowest it altogether. Thou hast laid thine hand upon me.*
>
> *Such knowledge is too wonderful for me; Wither shall I go from thy spirit? Wither shall I flee from thy presence?*
>
> *If I ascend up into heaven, thou art there; If I make my bed in hell, thou art there.*
>
> *If I take the wings of the morning, and dwell in the uttermost parts of the sea: Even there shall thy hand lead me, and thy right hand shall hold me.*
>
> *If I say, Surely the darkness shall cover me; even the night shall be light about me. Yea, darkness hideth not from thee; night shineth as the day: the darkness and the light are both alike to thee.*

I will praise thee; for I am fearfully and wonderfully made: Marvelous are thy works; and that my soul knowest well.

How precious are thy thoughts unto me, O God! How great is the sum of them! If I should count them, they are more in number than the sand: and when I awake, I am still with thee.

Search me, O God, and know my heart: Try me, know my thoughts. And lead me in the way everlasting."

Bjarni stood for a moment, in silence. Then he turned to the steward, and waited.

The steward's head throbbed. His mind raced with a thousand million thoughts, his heart pounded. He struggled wildly within himself. Finally, searching far back out over the calming wake and softening sky, smatterings of an ancient Gaelic blessing began welling up within him, to speak out, out over the trailing seas...

"May the deep peace of the running wave... and the flowing air... May the deep peace of the gentle night... and the quiet earth... May the deep peace of infinite heavens... be with him...'

He has found his truth, whatever that might be... He has joined his God, wherever that might be... He is as one now, with the eternal sea..."

As if choreographed, the passengers and crew then raised their assortment of glasses, bottles, tumblers, and stemware, and in one voice, as he had taught them, said simply... *"Skaal."*

After draining their drinks to the last, one by one they tossed their empty glasses out into the rose colored wake, out into the setting sun at its end, out into the final absolution of the sea.

On the bridge wing, Ole stood silently, watching. He pulled his last drop out of his Heinekin, and slung it over the side. Then he pulled down hard on the ship's horn, a final farewell that screamed out into the universe until the last gasps of steam strained out from the bowels of the boilers.

*THHHUUUUUUUUUUUUUUUUUUUUUUUUUUUUUUU
UUUUUUUUUUUUUUUUUUUUUUUTUUUUUUUUUUUUU
UUUUUUUUUUUUUUUUUUUUTTT!*

After a quiet few moments, the sun slipped itself slowly down into the horizon, dead center in the final traces of the ship's wake. All the others had left, to resume their duties, find another cocktail or wash up for dinner. Only the steward remained at the rail, looking aft.

Slowly, softly, the melancholy sounds of Mahler began drifting back from the galley area. After a while, Erda, came quietly up behind him, and spoke. "He thought the world of you..."

"And I of him..." he said without turning around.

"You know he knew... that this was his... final cruise..."

"Knew what?"

"That he was going to die. He was prepared."

"What do you mean?"

"Einar knew his insides were gone. He had maybe six months... He knew that he was finished at sea."

The steward stared as the last hint of cherry flame was quenched below the horizon. He nodded, somehow now understanding many things about this complex man.

After a moment, he asked softly, "Why did Bjarni not want command? He's qualified."

"You don't know, do you?"

"Now what?"

"Don't you remember Einar telling you to look past the surface of things?

"That appearances are illusory?"

Erda nodded. "You must learn to be more observant, Steward. You may have misjudged our Bjarni."

The steward turned to look at the pudgy little old woman. His mind began piecing the parts together. Bjarni never goes ashore. Bjarni always seems to be in a bunk somewhere. Bjarni is always hanging around the galley. He grinned. "It's you and Bjarni, isn't it?"

She smiled the knowing smile of a grandmadonna. "We've been married for fourteen years now. The crew only regards him as a timid, sex-starved old man, and me an easy old pincushion. It has been our special secret. It has made our life exciting, to steal secretly away from those around us. It is the life we have chosen. To be together. Here, at sea."

The steward eyed the little woman with even deeper respect. "And if he gets command, you may be separated, right?"

"Life has many surprises. Some of them one can preclude..."

"Some of them strike from out of the darkness..."

"Sometimes they do..."

The clear, crisp, darkening sky now beaconed forth with two, then three, then all of a sudden, immeasurable pinpoints of light. And high in the heavens appeared the affirmation of a new moon, a fine golden ring increasingly sure of itself against the changing aura of the night.

"Why do we do it?..." he asked eventually.

"Do what?"

"Live so madly..."

"I suppose each of us is trying to put our obvious fate to the test... believing that we alone hold the secret, that we alone are immortal..."

"Like bugs flying into an irresistible light..."

"Smart bugs fly wider and last longer than others..."

"Maybe they're trying to figure it all out..."

"Young man... We never figure it all out. And when we can't, we make up a name for our inability... We call it God."

The sky offered profound, silent response. The great reaches of the universe lay splayed overhead... a vast space, laced with substance, beaconing with infinite depth and mysteries.

"Why do we pursue it so?..."

"We are created with six senses. The five you know well... They are reality. They tell us we exist. They are today. But there is one more, the sixth, the most exciting one... It is the one which inflames our very soul, the one which drives us so passionately above and beyond the other five, beyond reality..."

"I think I know... it's our ability to wonder...to dream..."

Erda nodded at his perception. The breeze freshened in the clear night air. She looked out into the vastness of the heavens.

"Yes. It is our imagination... our ability to transcend here and now, to sense the fantastic, to journey out to that place beyond the ends of what is real, to what might be, what could be, what should be... our ability to dream beyond the present, even to probe into the grand design of everything. It is our imagination that likens us to your dancing bug. It is our imagination that excites us, and drives us even into lunacy, on to commit our most idiotic and basest deeds, on to build the impossible, on to reach the unreachable, and on to our highest ecstasies. Our actions give meaning to our lives. But our imagination... it is that wonderful fire that empowers life, that gives zest to life, yes even far beyond our wildest imagination..."

They stood silently for a while, watching a trillion stars light up the heavens.

"It's time, Steward. "

"Time? " He let out a soft sigh of air. "For what? "

"Time to set up for dinner..."

"So that's it? Onward we go?" He looked back at the trailing wake, now luminescent aquamarine under the brightening starglow.

"Yes. Isn't it wonderful?" She softly grabbed his arm, pulling him close, then with her other hand pointed out to the radiant sea and shimmering stars and deep blue heavens.

Out from the galley drifted glorious sound... the probing harmonics of Mahler's *Das Lied von der Erde*, carrying forth the rich assurances of Christa Ludwig... calling out... affirming to all the world....

> "*O Schonheit! Ewigen Liebens --*
>
> *Lebens -- trunk'ne Welt!*
>
> *Die liebe Erde alluberall Bluht auf im Lenz und grunt aufs neu!*
>
> *Alluberall und ewig blauen licht die Fernen!*
>
> *Ewig........*
>
> *Ewig........*
>
> *Ewig.........*"

As Erda walked back into the aft galley, the steward spied a bottle of Carlsberg remaining on the deck. He popped the cap, and took a long pull. Then he raised it up to the stars and, holding it by the neck in his hand, out past the stern flagstaff with its blue/white cross on red field rippling aft in the soft breeze, he released the bottle... and watched as it dropped... down into the peaceful, gilded wake that trailed back to the horizon...down into the great sea.

After what seemed like an eternity, the report finally reached his ears...

"Splat..."

16049559R00298

Made in the USA
Lexington, KY
01 July 2012